Brenn Owen, the new earl of Merton needed a wife

He didn't care what she looked like, as long as she was rich. But Tess Hamlin wasn't only wealthy . . . she stirred his blood as no other woman ever had before . . .

"Why do I have a feeling that Sir Charles was most anxious that you and I not have a moment's conversation alone?" Tess asked him.

"He's afraid I'll make a fool of myself and make an offer for you."

Her eyes brightened with interest. "Does he have a reason for fear?"

Brenn laughed. "That would be a fool's act, Miss Hamlin. I pray you don't think me a fool."

"And here I'd hoped you would be like the others and prone to wild declarations."

Brenn leaned forward, placing his hand near hers so their fingers almost brushed but didn't quite touch. "Do you wish a declaration?" he asked in a low, silky voice of a lover.

"I doubt if we are both talking about the same sort of declaration, my lord."

"I thought you meant marriage," he said with mock innocence.

Other Avon Books by
Cathy Maxwell

BECAUSE OF YOU
FALLING IN LOVE AGAIN
WHEN DREAMS COME TRUE
YOU AND NO OTHER

CATHY MAXWELL

Married in Haste

AVON BOOKS  NEW YORK

AVON BOOKS, INC.
1350 Avenue of the Americas
New York, New York 10019

To Erin and Brian McGlynn

May you be merry and lack nothing.
—SHAKESPEARE

Chapter One

London, 1814

*Tess Hamlin slammed open the door to the ladies' re-*tiring room. *"Where* is Leah Carrollton?"

The chatter of a half dozen young women dressed in their ball gowns of silks and Indian muslins came to an abrupt halt. The close air smelled of perfume, powder, and candle wax. All eyes turned to the doorway.

Tess smiled, pleased that she had their attention. She walked into the room.

Eyes widened and several pairs of lips formed silent O's but no one answered.

Anne Burnett, Tess's very best friend, gently touched Tess's arm, trying to pull her back. "Please, Tess. This isn't the time or the place. I shouldn't have said anything. Let us go back to the ballroom."

Tess shook Anne's hand away. "I am not going to let her get away with it. Not this time."

She confronted the young women. Many were new to this Season and, since Leah was one of them, her supporters. One or two others there

1

had weathered previous Seasons—although none, not even Anne, had seen as many as Tess.

Not that Tess couldn't have contracted for a husband any number of times over the last several years. Occasionally, a lord or two had made her pause and consider her obligations to marry, but she'd held off. She was an heiress and, without being vain about her looks, she knew men found her attractive. Why else would they have dubbed her "the Incomparable"?

But she wasn't ready to settle down. She enjoyed the stirring of male appreciation when she entered a room. It gave her a feeling of power, a power she'd lose once she was married. Yes, some women claimed marriage gave them new freedom, but Tess didn't agree. She'd watched too many women grow disillusioned and bored after the heady thrill of the wedding. Their lives were over. Even her brother Neil and his wife Stella went their separate ways.

To her, freedom had to mean something more than the liberty to come and go as she pleased without a chaperone or the opportunity to take on lovers once an heir was born. But she didn't know what the extra "something" was. Life *should* hold more than socializing and gossip, but what else was there? Until she knew the answer, she wasn't going to trap herself into marriage.

She brought herself back to the moment. The silly girls practically shook in their kid slippers at the thought of incurring her displeasure. She honed in on a tall blonde, Daphne, the oldest daughter of a duke.

"Daphne, do *you* know where Leah is?"

"N-no, I don't," Daphne squeaked out.

Anne shut the door behind her. "Tess, stop this. You are giving the poor girl a fright."

Good, sweet Anne. "If I don't crack the whip every once in a while then we'd all be run over by the likes of a Leah Carrollton."

"Did someone mention my name?" A young woman stepped out from behind a japanned privacy screen. She was a bold, voluptuous beauty with just the right touch of pout to her lower lip to make men dance in constant attendance.

Since the beginning of this year's Season, Tess and Leah had been cast in the roles of competitors, at first more for the contrast in their looks than any real disharmony between them. Tess was a proud red head who stood equal in height to most men. Poems had been written comparing her eyes to the light sparkling off the blue waters of the Mediterranean or the stained glass in Salisbury Cathedral.

Petite Leah's exotic dark eyes and coal-black hair seemed to have the power to mesmerize men. Even the Prince of Wales had succumbed to her charm.

In between these two rivals stood Anne with her soft, curling brown hair, heart-shaped face, and trusting eyes. Tess didn't understand why everyone didn't see what a noble, wonderful person Anne was. Anne preferred staying in the background and easily forgave slights from others. Why, she was so kind, she'd even forgiven that odious gossip Deland Godwin. Years ago when she was first presented to Society, he'd branded her a "toad eater," the term used to describe a woman without any means of support other than reliance upon the whims and good-will of her relatives.

Well, she'd not be ill-treated this time. She had Tess to champion her.

Leah made her way to a washstand to wash her hands. Her gaze met Tess's in the large mirror hanging on the wall. "Did you wish something, Miss Hamlin?"

"It's nothing—" Anne started but Tess cut her off.

"You know what you've done. The question is, do you dare own up to it in front of the others?"

Leah accepted a linen towel from the maid as she drawled lazily, "I haven't any idea what you are talking about." She moved away from the mirror toward the door. "Now, if you will excuse me, I am promised for the next dance."

Tess stepped right in her path. "*Mr. Hardiston.*" All her anger could be summed up in that one name.

Leah stopped. Her lips curved into a smile. "Archie?"

Tess almost growled with anger. "You know he was Anne's."

"I know no such thing. Had he made an offer?" Leah looked to Anne, whose face had gone pale.

Her expression gave Tess a stab of guilt but she forged ahead, speaking for Anne. "He was going to."

"But he hadn't, had he?" Leah said.

"His mother had talked to Anne's aunt."

"But *he* had yet to speak his thoughts," Leah reiterated, raising her voice so that all in the room could be privy to what was being said. "Had he?" she asked Anne directly.

Anne shifted and Tess knew she wished she were in a hundred different places than right here, right now. But Anne had to learn to defend herself. "Tell her, Anne."

"Please, Tess, let's leave before it's made worse."

"No, for once, I'm not worried about making a scene. You are my friend and I'm not going to let this little jade get away with disgraceful behavior." She turned to Leah. "He was about to, until you set your cap for him, something you did for no other reason than to strike out at me by hurting her."

"That's absurd!" Leah countered.

"Is it?" Tess demanded. "Mr. Hardiston has no grand fortune or connections. He is not what your grasping mother would consider an eligible party."

Anger flashed in Leah's eyes, but she didn't correct Tess's assessment of her mother. Instead, she said, "Archie's very dear. Character is worth more than money."

Tess doubted a Carrollton would recognized a decent, honorable character if it sat down to dinner with them, but she didn't put that sentiment into words. Instead, she called Leah's bluff. "So, we can all expect an announcement of your betrothal?"

"Of course not," Leah said quickly. "Mr. Hardiston and I didn't suit."

"Ummm hmmm," Tess said doubtfully. She lowered her voice. "I think your attraction to Mr. Hardiston had a great deal to do with the marquess of Redgrave offering for me two weeks ago. You and your mother had found a fine pigeon to pluck and then his attention turned in my direction and you couldn't compete."

Leah's chin came up. "Redgrave meant nothing to me."

"None of them mean anything to you," Tess replied. "You are going to the highest bidder."

For a second, it was if the air had been sucked from the room. Two bright spots of color appeared on Leah's cheeks. Anne gasped in surprise.

Then Leah struck back. "And they mean something to you?"

"Wooo," breathed their small audience at Leah's daring. No one had ever dared to challenge Tess. Even Anne's jaw had dropped.

Tess stepped back, reassessing her opinion of Leah. The chit had mettle. "At least I have a sense of honor."

"As do I."

"So you say," Tess returned without conviction. She addressed the others. "We must *respect* each other. Think how it would be if I set my cap for Daphne's beaux or yours, Amy," she said to another girl standing off to the left. "The Season would be chaos. We would be behaving little better than tribal women."

The comparison made several women frown in distaste.

"We have a code amongst ourselves. A sense of honor," Tess said. "Leah overstepped herself." Several of the debutantes murmured agreement.

"What nonsense!" Leah countered passionately. "I did nothing untoward to draw Mr. Hardiston's attention. He asked me to dance. I flirted. Where would any of us be if we couldn't flirt a little? Mr. Hardiston is free to go back to Miss Burnett anytime he wishes."

"I don't want him any longer," Anne hastened to interject.

Leah smiled in triumph. "See?" she said to Tess. "You blame me but Miss Burnett says she doesn't want him. I did her a favor by showing his true nature."

"Don't try and paint this white—" Tess started but Leah cut her off.

"You can't tell me what to do. You're not the queen, Miss Hamlin, but merely one of the players in the marriage game. A game you have been at for quite a few years. Oh, wait, I forgot. You enjoy being unattainable. You flaunt your looks and your precious inheritance. You accuse me of false affections, but in reality, *you* are the one who is guilty of the charge. You aren't really interested in marriage. You would have accepted Redgrave's offer if that was it. No, what you want is to be the center of attention, to be spoiled and made much of since you lack the *heart* to follow through."

"Why, you little—"

"Upstart? Yes, I am! I'm giving you competition, Miss Hamlin. You accuse me of not being honest? Why, you are the most dishonest of all. You are using Mr. Hardiston as a way to put me in my place, but you're not doing it for Miss Burnett. You're doing it for yourself."

Leah's words hit with sharp accuracy. Tess felt the color drain from her face.

Anne rose to her defense. "That's not true!

Tess has the greatest heart of anyone here."

Leah ignored Anne, focusing on Tess. "You've heard the name they've coined for you, haven't you?"

Tess narrowed her eyes. She doubted if Leah meant "the Incomparable." "Which name?"

"The Ice Maiden." Leah let her tongue roll over the words. "They swear you are the coldest of women, completely indifferent to anyone's heart but your own."

Leah's words were met with appalled silence. For a second, Tess stood stunned. She had heard the name whispered about but hadn't thought the sobriquet had applied to her. She looked around. The other girls had suddenly become interested in the ceiling or the pattern in the carpet. Anne was silent.

It took Tess a second to recover from her initial shock, but once she did, she found she did not dislike the title . . . and she liked Leah's bold frankness. Her earlier edgy restlessness vanished, replaced by the stirring of interest. The inkling of an idea tickled her brain.

Considering her rival with new respect, Tess said thoughtfully, "Perhaps we should settle this another way."

Leah raised a suspicious eyebrow.

Aware that everyone in the room strained to hear her quietest word, Tess said, "I want you to leave Mr. Hardiston alone. You, on the other hand, have stated in so many words that the two of us are equals."

"We are."

"*You* believe we are."

"Everyone says it," she shot back hotly.

"Would you be interested in *proving* that theory?"

That caught Leah up short. She frowned. "There is no way to prove such a thing."

"Yes, there is—in the way these things have always been proven."

"Which is?" Leah asked, her interest piqued.

"Marriage offers."

Leah sniffed. "Oh, well! You are the undisputed queen of that contest. Of course, you've been at this game longer than I have."

Her insult drew a chorus of "Oooo's" from the other girls, but Tess just laughed, enjoying herself immensely. "Not in the past, but the present, this evening."

Anne laid a hand on Tess's arm. "I've seen this look in your eyes before, Tess. Don't do whatever you are thinking."

"Oh, pish, what is life without a little risk?" Tess turned to Leah. "Plus the Garlands' ball needs a little enlivening. It's a complete bore. What do you say, Leah? Shall we make a wager?"

"I never gamble. It's a waste of money."

"Our wager isn't for money," Tess protested. "If I win, you will leave Mr. Hardiston alone—"

Anne groaned. "He means nothing to me. Not any longer!"

Tess held up her hand for quiet. Anne was being silly. Mr. Hardiston was her last chance for a decent match. Her aunt had threatened to hire her out as a companion if she didn't take this Season.

"And if you win, then I will—" Tess paused.

What did she have that Leah would consider to be a suitable prize? It had to be something she had that Leah didn't. *Connections.* "If you win, I will see that you receive an invitation to Mrs. Burrell's musicale one week from Wednesday."

Leah went very still. "*You* can do that?"

Tess smiled. "She is very fond of me. And who knows? If you impress her, you may receive the vouchers to Almack's that you have so far been denied. Then there will be no doors closed to you, Leah."

Leah wet her lips. "What are you proposing?"

"Nothing harmful. I'm willing to wager that I can receive a proposal of marriage before you can. This very night, in fact."

A gasp from around the room met her words.

"You're joking," Leah said.

"No, I'm very serious."

"Tess, that doesn't sound right," Anne protested.

Tess shrugged. "Is it right that they consider us little more than ornaments or bank accounts or brood mares?" She addressed the other women in the room. "In the last two hours, have any of you had an escort ask you about yourself? No, of course not. They rattle on and on about their interests and their pursuits but they don't care anything about us other than our appearances—and our dowries. Worse, most gentlemen believe you are fortunate they've even bothered to notice you. Of course, we can't help but notice them since most have sour breath or reek of Imperial water. I swear, the scent of cloves and frankincense at these events makes me nauseous."

Her observations were quickly seconded. Daphne added, "I danced with one gentleman who was so ugly I could barely look at him, but then he made a very unkind comment about the looks of another young woman. I wondered if he owned a mirror and could see himself! Worse, he trod on my feet. When I complained to Mama, she reprimanded me for speaking ill of him since he has an income of five thousand pounds."

Immediately, the other women erupted with testimonials of similar experiences.

Good, caring Anne tried to speak reason. "It's true some of us have been ill-used. I certainly want nothing to do with Mr. Hardiston after his perfidy—but it doesn't mean we should make a mockery of the sacrament of marriage. It's immoral to place a wager on something like an offer of marriage."

"Pooh!" Tess answered. "Men bet on this sort of thing all the time. Why, there isn't a men's club around St. James that doesn't have a betting book filled with the possible matches for the Season and wagers on each. I've been in that book dozens of times."

"I have too," Leah said. "Of course, the last time was when everyone thought Redgrave would come up to scratch. My father and brothers had placed bets—which they lost," she added with a bitter look at Tess.

Tess grinned, unrepentant. "Not bad for an aging debutante, hmmm?"

Leah's eyes darkened with anger, but then a smile came to her lips. "No, it isn't," she admitted.

"Whatever happened to Redgrave?" Tess

asked with idle curiosity. "Truly, all I did was smile at him. I was surprised when he abandoned his pursuit of you."

"Oh, he came back to me, but Mother has her eye on Tiebauld and told Father to refuse Redgrave's offer. I heard he's returned to his country estate whining that young women are fickle. I believe he should woo women closer to his age."

"Are there any that old?" Daphne asked with wide-eyed innocence and everyone laughed.

Except Tess. "What is this about Tiebauld?"

Leah shrugged, her lips closed. Everyone in the room quieted immediately. They knew about Tiebauld. Few people had seen him. He lived at the northernmost point of Scotland amidst thunder, lightning, and rain. The sun did not shine on Tiebauld. It was rumored he was mad. His sister who resided in London had been desperately searchng for a wife for him. The family wanted an heir to continue the line, but few young women wished to trade their souls to the devil. Dark stories surrounded Lord Tiebauld.

Tess reached out and gave Leah a hug. It was an impulsive, yet heartfelt gesture. "Life is changing too rapidly for all of us," she whispered. She turned to the others in the room. "Someday, we will be forced to marry, but until that happens, let's have some fun. *Everyone* take part in the wager—"

"Tess!" Anne warned.

"You too, Anne, *especially you*. For this night and this night alone, let's kick up our heels a bit. We can be as brash and judgmental as they are. Who knows, it may become the rage!"

Her suggestion was met with acclaim. Suddenly, the girls, who had seemed so dull and uninteresting when she'd first entered the room, sparkled with vitality. They compared quick notes on gentlemen of their acquaintance, and laughed with anticipation.

Leah held up her hand for their attention. Everyone quieted. "We must make one rule though. The marriage offer cannot come from a male who has previously made an offer."

"That's fair," Tess agreed, although she had been counting on winning the wager by flirting with Lord Hampson who declared marriage every time he saw her.

"Yes," Anne said. "And the wager is for tonight only. If no one receives an offer, the contest is a draw."

"But what if we receive an offer we don't want?" one of the younger debutantes asked. She was fresh from the schoolroom and disarmingly naïve.

"Then you simply refuse it," Tess said patiently.

"Oh, dear," the girl whispered.

Tess rolled her eyes impatiently. "There are a hundred different ways to regretfully refuse. Tell the gentleman he must petition your guardian and then have your guardian cry off for you."

"Is *that* what you do?" the girl asked breathlessly.

Leah covered her mouth over a startled laugh. She and Anne exchanged knowing glances.

Tess leveled the chit with a look. "With some I have. With others, I have done whatever is expedient. You must learn to handle men if you are going to be around them."

The door behind her opened. Their hostess,
Lady Garland, stuck her head into the room, the
peacock feathers in her headdress quivering with
indignation. "Here you all are! Come, come,
girls. The dancing is about to begin again and
you are wasting time primping. The young men
are anxious for new partners!"

"We'll be right there, Lady Garland," Tess replied, so dutifully that a few of the girls giggled.

"I'll expect you in *seconds*," Lady Garland declared. "And I will count." She closed the door.

Tess whirled on her fellow conspirators. "Be
careful; if she, your mothers, or any of the matrons catch wind of this, we shall be in trouble."

Heads nodded in agreement.

"Very well. Then let us go out and have a
good time . . . and may the best lady win!"

Her words were met with giddy laughter.
They pressed forward, anxious to charge out of
the retiring room.

Even Anne acted as if she was enjoying this
moment. She held her head high and she was
actually smiling. How different she seemed now
compared to when she had first arrived at the
party. Then, she had been completely depressed
by Mr. Hardiston's defection.

If nothing else, the confrontation with Leah
had achieved this, although Tess still worried for
her friend. Anne's aunt wasn't one to make idle
threats.

Tess had no fears of her own. Her brother Neil
was her guardian and so far she'd been able to
cajole her way with him, that is, if his wife Stella
wasn't present. Stella never approved of Tess.

The ballroom had been decorated to resemble

a rose bower. It was too early in the season for roses, but Lady Garland had purchased hundreds and thousands of hothouse roses to achieve her theme. The air was thick with their scent.

As the women entered the ballroom, the men hurried forward. Just as Lady Garland had said, the gentlemen were anxiously waiting to claim dances.

In a pleasant surprise, Anne was the first woman asked to dance. Granted, the gentleman who partnered her was half a head shorter and a good deal overweight, but he was just as capable of making an offer as any other man in the room. Wouldn't it be a coup if Anne won the wager?

Tess decided he must have noticed the extra color in Anne's cheeks and the sparkle in her eyes. She couldn't help laughing with joy when Anne dared to cast her a swift, triumphant glance. Her reaction made Tess feel good.

Then Tess noticed a dashing young officer staring in her direction. The candlelight reflected on the gold braid of his dress uniform and his thick blond hair. He was a handsome one all right. He was also the licentious rake Captain Draycutt.

No one of good breeding recognized him.

He set his punch cup on the tray of a passing servant and started purposely walking toward her. Tess sighed. It was too bad he was such a bounder. Everyone knew that military men were very susceptible to feminine charms. They often blurted out declarations within half an hour of being introduced to a young woman. Neil said war did that sort of thing to a man.

For a second, Tess considered encouraging him a bit. She wanted to win this wager. But she didn't want to damage her reputation.

Captain Draycutt stepped in front of Tess and Leah. He clicked his heels together and bowed. Tess was framing a suitable rejection in her mind when she heard him say, "Miss Carrollton, I believe this is my dance."

Through her shock and surprise, Tess heard Leah say, "Yes, Captain Draycutt, it is. Have you met Miss Hamlin?"

"Yes, Miss Hamlin and I have met." Captain Draycutt looked right through her. "I beg you to excuse us, Miss Hamlin." He threw the words over his shoulder as he led Tess's rival to the dance floor.

Tess watched with a touch of envy. The way he was looking at Leah, he'd probably make an offer before the end of the first set. Leah looked smitten, too. Had no one warned her about Draycutt's reputation—?

Suddenly, Tess realized she stood alone. All the other girls had been claimed for a dance, even Daphne.

But no one had asked her.

How unusual.

Her gaze skimmed the room. Card tables had been set up in a separate room and apparently many of the men were involved in there. The majority of the other men in the ballroom were those whose offers she had already rejected. They would refuse to dance with her out of spite, if nothing else.

Their sheer number made Tess pause. Had she *truly* rejected so many offers?

The thought made her uncomfortable. She took a step back, feeling too exposed. In the corner, away from the musicians, the matrons sat chatting. Most were older than herself, since the ones her age were usually breeding and not allowed out in Polite Society in such a delicate condition.

Tess looked away. Only that afternoon, Stella had announced she was with child. She couldn't picture Stella as a mother. Nor had she been prepared for the wash of jealousy she'd felt. Something strong and maternal had risen inside her, something she hadn't known existed within her until she'd heard Stella's announcement.

She'd also realized that a baby would make Neil and Stella a family. A family that would push Tess even further to the outside.

The pregnancy was to be kept a secret for as long as possible. Stella loved gaming parties and was not ready to "retire" from Society, something Tess hadn't understood. If she was pregnant, she'd gladly give up the dancing till dawn and the endless socializing—

Her thoughts broke off. The hair on her neck tingled and she sensed that she was being watched.

Tess turned and found herself staring directly into the dark eyes of a gentleman standing by the terrace door.

She didn't recognize him. She would remember him if they had met before. He was dressed all in black except for the snowy white of his shirt and neckcloth. The austerity of his dress made him

seem more masculine, more powerful than the
other men in the room. It made them look almost
like frivolous peacocks.

He was tall, very tall, with the broad shoulders
and lean hips that spoke of a man of action. Nor
was he classically handsome. He wore his hair
too long and his nose appeared to have been broken—at least once, perhaps twice. It marred the
symmetry of his face but enhanced his individ-
uality. As did the strong jaw, the wide mouth . . .
and the glittering eyes.

Tess smiled.

His generous mouth curved into an answering
smile.

For a second, Tess felt dizzy. Every fiber of her
being tightened and responded to his smile.

She'd never had that happen before.

The stranger was with Sir Charles Merriam
who had been an old friend of her father's. He
was talking to the stranger with animation, but
the gentleman ignored him. Instead, his razor-
sharp gaze rested on her.

Tess should have demurely blushed and
looked away. It was the way the flirting game
was played. But she couldn't avert her gaze. Not
this time. He held her spellbound.

"Ah, I see you have noticed our new arrival to
Town," a self-serving male voice said close to her
ear.

The spell was broken. Tess turned and gave a
cool greeting to Deland Godwin. This was the
man who had ruined Anne's chances years ago.
The publisher of a small weekly, he was a no-
torious hanger-on who adored gossip. His droll
manner laced with sly innuendo barely masked

a malicious mind. He never hesitated to print the *on-dits* he'd overheard whether there was truth to them or not. Everyone read his paper although few admitted it, and at least two men had taken their own lives over stories he'd printed. He wielded great power amongst the *ton*.

Normally Tess avoided him—unless she needed information he possessed . . . like now.

"Who is he?"

Godwin took a pinch of snuff with a dramatic flourish. "The earl of Merton. It's some obscure Welsh earldom." He sneezed and blew his nose with a creamy white kerchief. "He's come to Town in search of a wife. Former military man. Served on the Peninsula until he came into the title. I know very little beyond that, but I'm confident that in time I will know *everything*."

A wife? She glanced at the earl. He was talking to Sir Charles. She wondered if they discussed her.

Boldly, she said, "Have you been introduced to him, Mr. Godwin?"

Godwin looked down to where her fingers brushed the fine fabric of his coat and up at her again. "Of course."

"I wish to meet him."

Godwin's eyebrows almost rose to his hairline. "*You* are asking to be introduced to a gentleman? Don't say that the dashing Miss Hamlin is finally considering making a match?"

Tess shook her head. "Now, Mr. Godwin, if I told you, then you would know straight out and there is no fun in that, is there?"

"No, there isn't," he agreed, his interest definitely piqued. He raised her gloved hand to his lips. "But then, I have always been yours to command, my dear." Obviously smelling a story, he practically ran to perform his mission.

Tess watched him work his way toward Lady Garland. She turned back to the earl. He was watching her again.

Tess's heart started beating erratically. She looked away quickly. She knew it was only a matter of time before she met the earl of Merton and she didn't want to be thought forward.

From the opposite corner of the room Neil Hamlin studied his tall, beautiful sister. She held her head high looking as if she were the queen of the *ton*. No, he quickly amended his thought, she looked as if she were the reigning princess. She'd have to be *married* to be the queen.

He drained his punch cup in one gulp and reached for another of the brandy-based brew. What was he going to do? He was in a devil of a fix.

Their late father had trusted him to look after Tess's inheritance and Neil had tried to be wise with the money. But who knew that such a sizable fortune as Tess's could be wiped out so completely in such a short amount of time?

Of course, it would have helped if Tess had married years ago the way their father assumed she would. The fortune would have been removed from his responsibility, and then he wouldn't have these troubles.

Being the guardian of an heiress was hard work, especially when the heiress was Tess. She was too independent, and yet still naïve and in need of his protection.

When he'd first married Stella, she had urged him to arrange a husband for Tess and move her out of his house. He knew that Stella was jealous of Tess, but he'd hoped she would grow out of it over time. It hadn't happened. If possible, the situation had grown more touchy.

This afternoon, Stella had proudly informed him that she was with child—their first, finally!—and had decided that she wanted his sister out from under their roof.

Neil stared into the bottom of his now-empty punch glass. He'd be ruined if word of what he'd done to Tess's fortune leaked out. Worse, she'd never make a good match and he'd be stuck with two bickering women the rest of his life. There had to be a way to marry Tess off without the unlucky groom being the wiser.

But how?

Chapter Two

Brenn Owen desperately needed a wife. As the new, improvised earl of Merton, he didn't care if she was fat, ugly, or old, provided that she was rich.

He'd rather not marry for money, but he had no choice. Erwynn Keep, the estate he had inherited, was little more than an empty shell of a manor house surrounded by a village full of people who looked to him for their livelihood. The property wasn't entailed. He could have sold the lot and moved to London, but he wasn't the kind of man to shirk responsibility.

Besides, after years of war, he wanted peace. Often while facing battle, he'd dreamed of the life of a country gentleman. Now he had his chance to fulfill that dream, but he needed money for seed, equipment, livestock, and to rebuild the house.

Still, he couldn't prevent his gaze from drifting back to the flame-haired beauty who'd smiled at him from the doorway. Her smile could captivate a eunuch, and he certainly wasn't that.

"Merton! Are you paying attention to me?"

Brenn dragged his gaze away from the spar-

kling blue eyes and back to his host, Sir Charles
Merriam, a man some thirty years or more his
senior. They'd served together in Portugal. Back
then, Sir Charles had been Brenn's commanding
officer. Now, he was Brenn's guide on his wife
hunt.

"I'm sorry. My mind wandered. What were
you saying?"

The corners of Sir Charles's mouth turned
down. He had a balding pate and a strong
hooked nose. "It's hard enough to find a suitable
wife for you without you wool-gathering. If you
wish my help, you'll have to be more alert."

"Yes, sir," Brenn answered with almost military precision, although he couldn't help smiling.
He was very fond of old Sir Charles. The man
had been a damn fine military officer in his day.

"Good. I'm glad we have settled that matter,"
Sir Charles said with irascible agreement. "Now,
look over there across the room at that yellow-
haired chit."

Brenn stared in the direction he was pointing.
"I'm sorry, Sir Charles, but I see exactly four
yellow-haired chits between myself and that potted palm."

"Don't be impertinent. I'm talking about the
one with the row of diamonds around her neck.
The other three don't count. Not a jewel on
them."

Brenn now focused on the passably pretty
young woman whose gaudy necklace reflected
the candlelight. "The lady talking to the gentleman in the blue coat?"

"Yes, that's the one. Her father is related to
Marlborough. No title but she is worth two thou-

sand a year. What do you think? Handsome filly, what say?"

"Two thousand is considerable." But unexciting. Brenn shrugged, letting his gaze wander back to the redhead. She wore a dress of filmy white muslin with gold stars embroidered in the hem around the skirt and across the bodice. Her magnificent abundance of hair was artfully styled and held in place by jeweled stars.

Two foppish young men had gathered around her, each of them posturing and preening for her benefit. She appeared to be listening to them . . . then her alarmingly direct gaze moved past their padded shoulders and straight at him.

He smiled.

She smiled.

He had no doubt that she was as attracted to him as he was to her.

"I don't know what you want with a damn-fool wife anyway," Sir Charles grumbled. "They can be nuisances and dull bores. No amount of money is worth their nonsense . . . I've had two and I advise you to go back to Wales, live in your hut, and be happy. You always had skill with the ladies. Don't lash yourself to only one. Enjoy them *all!*"

"Who is the redhead?"

"Which redhead?" Sir Charles leaned around Brenn to see where he was looking. With an abrupt noise, he rocked back on his heels, his expression distressed. "Don't tell me *she's* caught your eye?"

"Who is she?"

"Tess Hamlin." He practically spat the words out.

"Is she married?"

"No! But you don't want *her*. In fact, you should pity the poor lads talking to her instead of sending murderous looks their way. She may be fair of face and rich as a Turkish sultan, but she has no heart."

"Rich?" The word whetted Brenn's hunting instincts.

"The richest. A fortune beyond compare."

"More than two thousand?"

"More like fifty."

Brenn's mind reeled at the number. "Then she's perfect! Exactly the woman I came to Town to meet."

Sir Charles snorted. "Hardly."

"What the devil is wrong with her?" Brenn demanded. "She looks perfect from here."

"Didn't you hear what I said past the word 'rich?' The woman is as deadly as a cobra. She mesmerizes men and then poisons them for life."

His words intrigued Brenn. He dropped his voice. "Is she wicked?" he asked with delicious anticipation.

"Think with your big head and not your small one," the older man said bluntly. "We are talking about a *wife* here. The gel's never been touched, but she's still not for you. Tess Hamlin was spoiled by her late father. He was a dear friend of mine but lacking sense when it came to his daughter. Both his children really. He has a son—silly lad . . . but not as selfish as his sister. The chit inherited money from her mother who passed away over a decade ago. *I'm* not surprised Miss Hamlin hasn't married. She thinks too highly of herself, too highly indeed."

Brenn couldn't help laughing. "Well, if I was rich, I'd be choosy too."

"It is more than being choosy. She toys with men as if all of this—" The wave of his hand encompassed the ballroom. "—was nothing more than a game." He pulled Brenn a step or two closer to the terrace door where they wouldn't be overheard. "She turned the marquess of Redgrave down last month. The man's a good friend of mine and he was besotted with her, had been for years. Recently, she had given him cause to hope. She'd smile at him—" He gritted his teeth in a poor imitation of a girlish "come hither" grin. "—and flash her pretty blue eyes." He batted his rheumy ones. "Why, Redgrave's head was spinning like a top, and he's almost as old as myself!"

"What happened?"

"He made an offer, fully believing that it would be accepted. Turns out the girl was just playing fast and loose. Oh, she begged off prettily enough, but the answer was still the same: no. Redgrave was devastated by her rejection. He left London immediately. Couldn't face all of us—and he is a man of the world like myself. Not some young buck like you who wears his heart on his sleeve."

Brenn, who was one and thirty, was amused by Sir Charles's verdict. "I think I can take care of myself."

Sir Charles stabbed a finger at him. "In combat you have no peer . . . but this is a different battlefield—and that girl is a crack marksman!"

Brenn almost roared with laughter.

"I'm not being funny," Sir Charles asserted.

"It didn't think you were. It's just that I had this image in my head of the girl in full military regalia taking aim at us poor men on the dance floor."

Sir Charles snapped his fingers. "Yes, that's just what it is like," he agreed without humor. "I wouldn't be surprised if she kept a tally of the hearts she has stolen."

"Now that's ridicu—"

"Lord Merton, Sir Charles," Lady Garland's trilling voice interrupted them. "I am so glad I found you."

"Didn't know we were lost," Sir Charles said grumpily.

Lady Garland laughed and swatted him on the arm with her ivory fan. "Such a dear you are. Cheeky, cheeky, cheeky. But I've actually come in search of our young earl. There is someone I especially wish to introduce to you, my lord."

She didn't wait for Brenn's answer but took his arm and started to steer him away. "Have a glass of punch, Sir Charles, and I'll return the earl in a thrice." She then gave him her back before Sir Charles could answer.

"I know you and he are close," she whispered to Brenn, "but I find him a bit trying."

Brenn merely smiled his answer. He placed Lady Garland's arm in the crook of his which made walking easier, especially with his limp. "Where are you taking me?"

"You'll see," she answered with a cryptic smile and directed him toward a group of men. She tapped the back of the nearest man with her fan. He shifted and Brenn found himself face-to-face with the lovely Miss Hamlin.

"Shoo! Shoo!" Lady Garland said, waving the other gentlemen away as if slapping flies. "I wish a moment alone with Miss Hamlin."

They had no choice but to gallantly step aside, although one mumbled something ungracious and received a rap of Lady Garland's fan for his temper. She released Brenn's arm and stepped forward. "Miss Hamlin, this is Brenn Owen, the new earl of Merton. It's in Wales." She made the country sound as foreign as Calcutta. "My lord, may I introduce Miss Tess Hamlin."

Brenn took the last step forward, conscious of his obvious limp, and yet Miss Hamlin seemed unaware of it. Instead, she met his eyes, her cool gaze as bold as any man's.

In that moment, he knew he liked her.

He bowed over her gloved hand. "Miss Hamlin."

"My lord." Her voice was warm, husky, and a far cry from the shyly sweet sopranos of the other debutantes he had met this evening. It made him feel as if he were the only man in the room.

"You don't dance, Lord Merton, but perhaps you can take Miss Hamlin on a turn around the terrace?" Lady Garland hinted.

He picked up on the cue. "That is an excellent suggestion. That is, if Miss Hamlin would enjoy a breath of fresh air."

"Yes, I would, my lord," the lady agreed.

"Then I'll leave the two of you to become acquainted," Lady Garland said, her eyes dancing with matchmaking possibilities. She then seized one of the disgruntled young gentlemen who had been wooing Miss Hamlin and hurried him off to dance with a shy, mousy girl who was a distant cousin of hers.

For a moment, Brenn wanted to pinch himself to see if he wasn't dreaming. There was no doubt in his mind that Miss Hamlin had been the one to request an introduction. He nodded toward the terrace door. "Shall we take a stroll?"

She smiled, a smile that made Brenn feel a touch light-headed. She was extraordinary. Her skin was like the smoothest cream, except for the smattering of light freckles across the bridge of her nose. He was glad they were there. They reminded him that she was human, although they didn't stop him from wanting to shout, *Marry me, Miss Hamlin. Let me make you happy in exchange for your prodigious fortune!* She was so delicious to look at, he'd been tempted to marry her even *without* money.

They had traveled halfway toward the door when Sir Charles stepped into her path. "Merton don't dance," he said bluntly. "And I have someone I want him to meet."

She didn't react to his rudeness. Instead, she held out her hand. "Sir Charles, you were one of my father's favorite friends. How good it is to see you again."

Brenn hid a small smile as his crusty old friend was forced out of his defensive stance to take her hand.

"Pleasure," Sir Charles said, his voice tight. "Hate to take Merton from you but I saw someone on the other side of the room that I particularly wanted Merton to meet. Come, lad, we shouldn't keep the fellow waiting."

He reached for Brenn's arm but Brenn eluded

him. "I am taking Miss Hamlin for a walk."

"But lad," Sir Charles pleaded. "This gentleman is very important."

"So is my turn around the terrace with Miss Hamlin," Brenn told him pointedly.

He took ahold of Miss Hamlin's arm at the point where her glove ended above the elbow and started to steer her around him but Sir Charles could not be dissuaded. If he could not deter them, he would join them. He fell into step beside Miss Hamlin. "You know Merton is a war hero," he told her.

"Sir Charles," Brenn said in warning. What was the man doing?

"A hero?" Miss Hamlin asked with interest.

"Aye," Sir Charles said. His eyes met Brenn's and he shook his head in answer to Brenn's silent, but no less clear command to leave it be.

Miss Hamlin caught the head shake. "Then you aren't a hero?" she asked, confused.

"He is!" Sir Charles quickly stated. Refusing to look at Brenn, he said, "He saved my life, almost lost his leg doing it."

"That's why you limp," she said with complete candor.

"From that and years of kicking Sir Charles, trying to get him to *keep quiet*," Brenn muttered.

But Sir Charles was determined to go where angels feared to tread. "If it hadn't been for Merton's quick thinking," he told Miss Hamlin, "I and a good score of men would have been French cannon fodder. He took out the cannon himself and then carried me across his shoulders back to camp. No one realized he was wounded until later."

Miss Hamlin tilted her head up at Brenn. "You are indeed a hero, my lord."

Brenn felt an unfamiliar heat steal up his neck. Why was Sir Charles doing this? He could handle Miss Hamlin himself without his war exploits being bandied about.

"A hero who blushes," she added softly. "I've never seen a man act embarrassed when being publicly praised. You are a novelty, my lord."

He was going to respond with some witty remark but at that moment, her attention strayed toward the dance floor. Her eyes narrowed.

Brenn glanced in the direction she looked while Sir Charles prattled on about the battle, oblivious to the fact he had lost his audience.

It appeared Miss Hamlin was frowning at Captain Draycutt, a pompous cavalry officer whom Brenn had dismissed earlier in the evening as more flash than substance. The man finished his dance with Miss Carrollton and led her over to a table for a glass of punch.

Brenn had met Miss Carrollton the evening before. The girl's family was practically bankrupt. All she had to offer a man were her looks and, though she was attractive, she didn't stir his blood the way Miss Hamlin did.

Few women had.

He wasn't going to lose this fabulous prize to a cavalry officer.

Reaching for the handle of the terrace door, he yanked it open and whisked Miss Hamlin outside. He took grim satisfaction in closing the door on Sir Charles's still talking face. The man frowned, shrugged, and then, with a roll of his eyes to wish Brenn well, wandered off to lose himself into the crowded ballroom.

Although it was late spring the temperature was chilly, so they were alone. The air smelled of rich earth and growing things.

Chinese paper lanterns strung from the corner of the house across to the trees in the garden cast yellow and red patterns on the ground around them. Their light reflected off the gold thread stars in the material of Miss Hamlin's dress. The stars mirrored the ones in the clear sky above them—and for a second, Brenn's imagination took over.

She looked like a goddess come to earth. No, not a goddess, a Titaness.

The minutes and seconds of his life seemed to have all led to this very moment. He wanted to capture it—to never forget the smell of wax candles burning in fresh air, the coolness of the night against his skin, the nuances in her expression and movement.

A shiver ran through her.

"Is it too cold?" he asked. "Shall we return inside?"

"No," she answered. "I'm a hearty English girl. The night air isn't bothering me." She ran her hand along the stone balustrade, walking its length away from the door and the sounds of music and laughter bleeding through from the other side.

Brenn followed her. She was a lure, drawing him toward the peaceful shadows of the terrace's far corner. A statue of Diana, the huntress, stood there.

Miss Hamlin lightly touched the shoulder of

the statue before facing him. "Why do I have the feeling that Sir Charles was most anxious that you and I not have a moment's conversation alone?"

"He's afraid I'll make a fool of myself and make an offer for you."

Her eyes brightened with interest. "Does he have a reason for fear?"

Brenn laughed. He sat on the edge of the balustrade, taking his weight off of his bad leg. "That would be a fool's act, Miss Hamlin. I pray you don't think me a fool."

Her lips made a small moue of disappointment. "And here I'd hoped you would be like the others and prone to wild declarations."

She was all but inviting him to make an offer. Poor Redgrave, Brenn thought. He'd been out of his league. But Brenn wasn't. He leaned forward, placing his hand on the statue so that his fingers almost brushed hers but didn't quite touch. "Do you wish a declaration?" he asked in the low, silky voice of a lover.

Her reaction was immediate. Her lips parted slightly in surprise. He could see the outline of her nipples tightening. She crossed her arms against her chest and stepped back. "I doubt if we both are taking about the same sort of declaration, my lord."

"I thought you meant marriage," he said with mock innocence.

"I doubt that, sir." She paused. "Perhaps I should return to the ballroom before my absence is noticed."

She started to leave but he reached out and caught her arm. "Don't go."

For the space of several heartbeats, they took each other's measure.

He released his hold. "What do you want of me, Miss Hamlin?"

She blinked, surprised. "Why do you believe I want anything?"

"Intuition. A man learns to rely on his gut instinct in battle."

"And are we at war?" she asked archly.

"The war between the sexes has gone on since time began."

She started to laugh, to hide behind practiced wiles, but then stopped. "You are like no other man I've ever met."

"In what way?"

She leaned against the balustrade. "Most men would be less forthright. More given to poetry and nonsense. They believe my head can be turned with a few choice compliments. And they would have taken my hint by now and promised eternal devotion."

"I'm not a poet. But if I was, I don't think I would wax on about the color of your eyes or the flame in your hair. I know I'd be ill-suited to describe the perfection of your figure, although I admit the freckles you attempt to hide with powder fascinate me."

Her hand come up to her nose. "Freckles aren't fashionable."

"They're adorable." He leaned back, crossing his arms. "No, if I could write a poem, I would dedicate it to your intelligence. To the proud way you hold your head and the sparkle of life I see in the depths of your eyes. I'd probably write about the way you laugh. I know that once I hear your laughter, I will never forget it."

Her eyes had widened with each statement. She moved closer to the statue and Brenn knew that he had made an impact on her. "You have a lurid reputation, Miss Hamlin."

She didn't pretend to mistake his meaning. "I've done nothing to encourage that reputation. Or discourage it. Men make fools of themselves with little assistance from me. But you are the first one to notice that I have wit as well as hair. Usually, they assume I'm brainless. They rarely even ask if I read."

"Do you read?"

"I read in three languages, my lord, and thank you for asking."

He grinned. "I'm surprised. Tess Hamlin, Society's darling, is a bluestocking."

Her eyes crinkled with laughter. She raised a finger to his lips to shush him. It was a spontaneous gesture and yet her touch sparked all sorts of indecent thoughts inside of him.

"Don't tell anyone," she begged laughingly. "I have a good ear for languages. My sister-in-law insists I keep it secret or I will be ruined. My brother is too self-involved to even care. But my governess was an enlightened woman. She taught me to love knowledge. She believed that women are capable of all the best qualities attributed to men, including honor. What do you think of that statement, sir?"

"I have known many honorable women."

"You have?" Miss Hamlin sat down on the balustrade beside him.

"I have even known women willing to fight and die for their country."

"I would. If England were threatened, I would do battle." She brushed her hand against Diana's stone bow before looking at him. "You don't laugh."

"I see nothing funny in the statement. I find it admirable," he said truthfully.

"Minnie was my governess's name. She passed away several years ago, shortly before my father died." Her voice softened. "I still miss her. She was the most honest, honorable woman I've ever known. She wanted me to learn to think for myself."

"And you have."

Miss Hamlin looked up at the stars. "I don't know."

The conversation had gone from lighthearted to heavy and Brenn wasn't sorry for it. He brushed a curl of her hair back behind her ear. "Life is too short to live it playing by others' rules."

"You speak from experience?"

"Years of it. Boarding schools, the military. Now, there are rules in Society. But shortly, I will be free to live my life under my own governance."

Her lips twisted ruefully. "I envy you. I will never be free. Someday I will have a husband and more rules."

"You have the wiles to set your own rules. You are not completely defenseless."

She shot him a sharp glance. "No, I play the game well, but—" She broke off.

"But what?" he prompted.

She stood, hooking her arm around the statue of Diana's shoulders before saying, "I envy Diana. I envy those who lived in a time of myth and magic. The games of the *ton* aren't really me."

"What is you?"

A wary look came into her eyes. "You don't want to know."

"Yes, I do." Brenn leaned forward. "After all, moments ago you were begging me to make a declaration."

"I never beg!" she informed him with mock seriousness and they both laughed. She released her hold on Diana and wandered a few steps away. He watched, waiting, as she held out her hand to see the play of the shadows under the lanterns' flickering light. And then she said softly, "Sometimes I wonder if there isn't something more to life. A reason for why I am here."

The statement caught his attention. "We all wonder that."

"Even war heroes?"

"There isn't one man who has ever faced battle without asking that question."

"And have you found any answers?"

Brenn didn't know how to respond. "Well, the clergy have their opinions," he said lamely.

"I know. I once asked Bishop Walters for guidance."

"What did he tell you?"

"That my purpose in life was to please my husband and have babies." She gave him a rueful smile. "But it doesn't seem enough, does it? I mean, all those stars in the sky, they have a reason for being, but me—?" She paused and then said with sudden fervency, "But it isn't enough to repeat prayers. I want to feel a sense of purpose, of being, here deep inside. Instead I feel . . ." She shrugged, her voice trailing off.

"As if you are only going through the motions?" he suggested quietly.

Light shone in her vivid eyes. "Yes! That's it." She took a step toward him. "Do you feel that way, too?"

"At one time I did. Especially after a battle, when men were dying all around me and yet I had escaped harm. I felt there had to be a reason why I was spared and they were taken."

She came closer. "Did you discover an answer?"

"I'm beginning to think that there is no answer to that question. Those men who died all loved life as dearly as I do. Some of them had responsibilities—wives, sweethearts, children. I think that perhaps we each have to find our own purpose. We can either continue to do what others expect of us, or we can search for meaning. My purpose in life is Erwynn Keep."

"What is that?"

"My estate in Wales. It's located in the heart of the Black Mountains. Beautiful country."

"But how can a mere piece of property give you purpose?"

"As a soldier, I've spent my life destroying things. Don't mistake my meaning, I've fought for good causes, but there is no joy in killing a man, whether justified or not. Now I want to *build* something, something that will outlast my lifetime. Something with meaning."

"I don't understand."

He took her hand and drew her down to sit beside him. "My father was estranged from his family. I didn't even know I had an uncle who was an earl until the day his solicitor tracked me down in France and told me I had inherited a title and a home. Erwynn Keep is like finding a lost piece of myself, something I hadn't even known I'd been missing. I'd never had a home in the sense of one place where I belonged. My father was a military man and my mother traveled with him. They either left me with cousins or sent me to boarding schools. Erwynn Keep is my birthright. It is where I belong."

"So you have found your purpose?"

"I think I have."

She studied the ground as if she could find answers in the terrace stone. "I used to have a home. But Mother passed away years ago when I was five. Then, Minnie died. She was the one person who cared about me. Father doted on me but it is hard for a man to be close to a daughter, don't you think?"

Brenn didn't know what to answer. Fortunately, she didn't expect one.

"Neil, my brother, and I were close until he married. His wife is completely selfish . . . and sometimes I'm scared because I fear I may be a bit like her—"

"You couldn't be," Brenn assured her, taking her hand.

"I don't know," she admitted with brutal honesty. "Life seems so empty. It's a bit frightening."

"Then find meaning," he told her with conviction. "Don't let yourself be like people you don't admire."

"It's hard." She looked down at their joined hands as if just realizing how close they sat to each other. A dark flush rose to her cheeks and she stood.

"I was right, you know," she said.

"About what?"

"About your being different. I can't imagine how we ever strayed to such—" She hesitated searching for the right word. "*Personal* subjects. Of course, you aren't one to toady up to people, are you?"

He stood, taking a step toward her and reaching for her arm so that she couldn't run away. "Toadying has never been my strong suit . . . although I would do many things for a beautiful woman." He touched her then, drawing a line down the velvet curve of her cheek.

Miss Hamlin caught his hand before it could stray further, her gaze holding his. "Most men don't go beyond the shell of the woman—or look past the fortune. Are you a fortune hunter, Lord Merton?"

Her directness, and its accuracy, caught him off guard. He recovered quickly. "If I was, would I admit it?"

"No."

"Then you shall have to form your own opinion."

It was a challenge and he knew she would respond to a challenge. She didn't disappoint. Her hand released his. "Tell me about Erwynn Keep."

"If you wish." He led her back to the balustrade, sitting her down beside him. "But first, you must close your eyes and imagine the land."

She shot him a suspicious look.

"What?" he asked. "Do you think I'm going

to trick you into a kiss? No, this is the only way you can truly picture Wales. Otherwise, you won't hear what I'm saying. Now close your eyes."

He didn't think she was going to do it, but then her lids fluttered closed. "What does the land look like?" she demanded.

He smiled. Her skepticism was charming.

He leaned close to her ear. "Wales," he said, making the single word a statement. "Picture a countryside that is not only rugged but magical. The mountains were formed when a great clan of wizards and magicians had an argument. In their anger, they kicked mounds of earth at each other until the mountains were formed and the valleys carved out. They threw off their capes and robes and those formed the green pastures. The hats they knocked off each other's heads became the forests."

Her lips curved into a smile. "I've never heard of such a thing."

"It's all true," Brenn assured her. Their lips were only inches from each other's. He ached to taste her.

"I . . . think you made the story up," she whispered. Her breath was hot and sweet against his skin.

"I wouldn't do that."

"Oh, I think you would." She opened her eyes. A flicker of surprise appeared in them when she realized how close they were to each other—but she didn't move back.

Brenn said, "I think I'm going to kiss you."

She blushed, the sudden high color charming.

"Don't tell me," he said. "Gentlemen rarely ask permission before they kiss."

"Oh, they always ask, but I've never let them."

"Then I won't ask." He lowered his lips to hers. Her eyelashes swept down as she closed her eyes. She was so beautiful in the moonlight. So innocently beautiful.

He tasted her, his lips just pressing against hers—

"Tess, are you here?" begged a female voice.

Miss Hamlin jerked away. The moment of the kiss was spoiled.

A young woman stepped out on the terrace, the light from the ballroom spilling over her.

Miss Hamlin cast an apologetic look to Brenn and rose to her feet. "I'm here, Anne." He came to his feet with her.

Anne rushed across the terrace. Miss Hamlin met her halfway.

"All is ruined, Tess. Deland Godwin learned about our wager and is telling everyone. The duchess of Westley ordered Daphne home before she went off into a swoon. The duchess has great power at Court and Lady Garland swears that you have ruined her rout!"

"I'd forgotten all about the wager. But calm down, Anne. It can't be as bad as all that. The duchess and Lady Garland are overreacting."

"No, Tess. It is worse than you can imagine. Every mother is dragging her daughter away from here. I had to dodge my aunt three times in my search for you. I fear what will happen once she finds me because the other girls are crying and telling everyone that you, I, and Leah were the ringleaders of the wager. Deland God-win is positively gleeful!"

Brenn took a step closer. "Perhaps I can help. After all, Miss Hamlin has been with me this whole time."

But before Miss Hamlin could answer him, her brother charged out onto the terrace. "Tess." He put a wealth of meaning in that one word, and none of it boded well for his sister. "This time you've gone too far!"

Chapter Three

Neil had never been more angry with his sister.

Inside the ballroom, matchmaking mothers, grande dames, and debutantes were in a madcap uproar and the blame rested on Tess's shoulders. He'd never get her married off—not after this scandal. He was ruined.

His mood wasn't helped when Tess replied, "Oh poo, Neil. It was only a game. A silly wager."

"A silly wager?" he repeated before words failed him, choked by incoherent anger.

Sensible Anne made a soft sound of alarm, but his impudent younger sister stood her ground. "We wanted to liven up the ball."

Neil practically roared his frustration. "You are too far out of the schoolroom to not know the implications of your prank! It's outrageous to think that young women of quality would be so bold—and callous enough—to wager on who could receive the first offer of marriage at a ball!"

Tess's eyes, so like his own, hardened. Her stubborn chin jutted out. "Men place bets on this sort of thing all the time."

"What men do and what women are *allowed* to do are very different subjects," he said forcibly.

"In some matters, yes," she dared to answer. "But this isn't one of them. I admit that perhaps we demonstrated a want of sensibility but nothing that can't be remedied."

"Can't be remedied?" he repeated incredulously. Jabbing a finger in the direction of the ballroom, he said, "Already a Mr. Breedlove is swearing injury because he had a secret agreement with the duke of Westley to marry the duke's oldest daughter. He's furious that she was encouraging other men."

"*Flirting*. She was flirting with other men—"

"Tell that to Mr. Breedlove. Apparently the man is monstrously insecure. Worse, the duke's daughter now knows about the agreement and she told Breedlove to his face that he was ugly and she was tired of him tromping on her toes when they danced."

Tess's eyes gleamed with elation. "She said that to him? Bully for her."

"Tess, stop talking like a stable lad." He took a step away and then turned, so angry he had to vent his rage or explode. "Marriage is a business arrangement! A contract binding two parties. Whether Breedlove stomps on the girl's toes or not, she should do as her father wishes. 'Course, *now* she won't and Westley will blame *me*. Everyone will blame me!

"Stella is right. You've grown too high in the instep. I should have married you off years ago. If I had, none of this would have happened! But now you will never find a husband. You've run

through all of your suitors. They're tired of flirting with you and they've had enough. And now!
Now it is *too late*—" He broke off, hearing the
desperation in his voice. Ah, yes, his sister had
destroyed him. Soon his folly would be discovered.

Tess placed her hand on his arm, pools of tears
forming in her eyes. "Neil, I'm sorry. I did not
expect matters to go in this direction. I will make
apologies. I'll talk to Lady Garland. Deland Godwin will spread gossip, but I will be so gracious
and pleasant, everyone will forgive me. Anne,"
she said, turning to her friend, "don't worry
about your aunt. I will tell her it was all my fault.
Nor will I let Leah or the others pay. I can do
this, Neil. You know I can."

He stared down into her shiny eyes and
wished that they could turn back time. He took
her hand in his own and remembered when, as
a baby, she would grasp his finger and never let
go. "Too late," he whispered hoarsely. "It's too
late for you, me, Stella."

"Neil, don't talk that way," Tess whispered.
"We'll see our way through. Don't you remember? Together."

Together. It was their family watchword and
had been for generations. Now it mocked Neil.

"Perhaps I can help," a deep male voice said.

Neil turned, and registered with surprise the
presence of another man. He'd been so angry
when he had come out on the terrace, he'd been
oblivious to everything but his sister.

The gentleman bowed. "Brenn Owen, earl of
Merton."

The title was vaguely familiar. Neil frowned

and then recollected. "Heard about you at my club. You've recently come into the title, is that not correct?"

"It is."

Neil took in the earl's appearance. He'd heard the earl of Merton was lame. The man in front of him appeared far from a cripple. In fact, his presence was so formidable, Neil didn't understand why he hadn't noticed him sooner. He shifted uncomfortably, afraid of what his temper might have allowed him to reveal in front of others.

"I thought the earldom of Merton was a Welsh title," he said cautiously.

"It is."

"You're rather tall for a Welshman, aren't you?"

The earl's teeth flashed white in the moonlight. "There's Viking blood in my ancestry. The earls of Merton are known for their height. And for their willingness to take a risk."

"A risk?"

"I'd like to make an offer for the hand of your sister."

"What!" The word burst out of Tess, but Neil was no less surprised.

"You're joking," Neil said bluntly. "Haven't you heard anything I've been saying? She's *ruined* and taken her family with her."

"All the more reason to marry her off," the earl said cheerfully. "It would save your family further scandal. I marry Miss Hamlin, whisk her off to Wales, and within a few months, no one will remember this evening—with the possible exception of your aunt," he said regretfully to Anne.

Neil's mind seized upon the idea. *This could be the answer to his prayers.*

"That's the most ridicu—" Tess started but Neil cut her off, almost pushing her aside.

"Yes, there are possibilities here. Wales is a good distance from London, isn't it?"

"A good ways," the earl answered dryly.

"Wait!" Tess shoved her way between the two men. "I'm not marrying anyone. Not now; not ever."

Neil felt as if his blood was boiling. How dare she contradict him in front of the earl! Did she believe she had no responsibilities to her family name?

He faced Merton. "My sister accepts your proposal, my lord. Call on me on the morrow and we shall discuss the settlements."

"Neil! No!" Tess stamped her foot. "I will not marry him!" She bit each word out.

And suddenly, Neil was tired, exhausted from juggling his obligations to his sister and his wife and his own wants. Here was a way out of danger. He and Stella had a baby on the way.

Tess's whims no longer mattered.

"She'll marry you within the week, my lord. See to a special license. I shall go in and announce the engagement." Without looking at his sister, he turned on his heel and walked back to the ballroom.

Tess stared after her brother, scarcely believing her ears. Anne placed her hand on her shoulder. "He's angry. He'll change his mind."

"He's drunk," Tess answered flatly. She immediately felt the sting of disloyalty. Neil *had* been drinking too much lately but he was still her brother.

She turned on the person solely responsible for this nonsense. She confronted Lord Merton. "How could you?"

"I merely offered a solution," he said with false modesty.

"I'd rather be sold into slavery."

He frowned. "Come now, marriage is much preferable to slavery."

"Marriage is little different," Tess countered. "Once a woman marries, she no longer has anything she can claim as hers. Even her identity belongs to her husband."

"I take it this is more enlightened thinking from your former governess."

Tess gave him a bitter smile. "Yes. Are you ready to cry off?"

His level gaze met hers. "No, Miss Hamlin. I'm ready to prove you wrong."

"You won't have the chance," she assured him proudly. With a swish of her skirts, she gave him her back and hurried to the ballroom to repair whatever damage she could. Anne followed close at her heels.

Inside, the chaos that Anne had described had subsided. But many of the girls who had made the initial wager were missing, as were their chaperones. Tess straightened her shoulders. As people became aware of her presence, all eyes turned to her. It was deadly quiet.

Neil stood in front of the musicians. "I've just announced your betrothal, sister dear." He raised his punch glass. "To my sister's happiness." The other guests joined him in the toast. Except for Lady Garland who sat sprawled in a chair by the door, fanning herself as if distressed beyond bearing.

"And to Lord Merton," Neil added.

Merton had come in from the terrace. He didn't stand by Tess but joined Neil and took a punch glass. "To the most beautiful woman in the room," he said, raising his glass in her direction. The toast was dutifully hailed.

Deland Godwin maneuvered himself close to Tess. "So the magnificent Miss Hamlin has been run to ground, the victim of her own cleverness," he said in her ear. "Of course, who would have thought a cripple would be the one to outfox you?"

Tess stiffened. Suddenly tired of playing polite games, she smiled. "Don't worry, Mr. Godwin. Even with his limp, he is more of a man than you will ever be."

Godwin jerked as if he'd been struck. The comment was overheard by several people. They laughed and repeated it to others.

Godwin's eyes snapped with anger. "Beware what enemies you make, Miss Hamlin. Your reign as queen of Society is about to be over. A married woman needs all the friends she can find, else she'll be forgotten." He turned and walked away.

Anne linked her arm in Tess's and watched him push his way through the lingering crowd. "What are you going to do, Tess?"

Tess swung her gaze to the tall, dark Welshman who fancied himself the man to claim her. "Fight back."

She went in search of a footman to take her home.

"You're a bloody fool!" Sir Charles declared the moment he had Brenn alone. They sat inside the close confines of a hired coach on their way home. It was almost dawn and at this early hour of the morning the streets were practically deserted. The only sounds to disturb their conversation were those of the horses' hooves and the wheels turning over the rough cobblestone streets.

"A bloody *rich* fool," Brenn corrected with a yawn. He'd drunk his health over and over this night. However, now, in the fresh air, the euphoria of good wine was wearing off. In its place loomed cold reality.

"You can marry money, lad, but you can't live with it."

"What does that mean?" Brenn asked. "I came to London to marry money." He ran a hand over his face, feeling the rough growth of whiskers. He needed sleep. What time had he told Hamlin he would present himself? He'd forgotten.

"I saw the look on Tess Hamlin's face. She doesn't want this marriage," Sir Charles reminded him.

"But her brother does. And frankly, she should be grateful I am saving her from scandal. By the way Lady Garland was behaving, Miss Hamlin will soon find herself snubbed by some of the best houses. She's better off in Wales."

"It just doesn't make sense," Sir Charles said,

half to himself. "Tess Hamlin has spurned a score of suitors and yet you walk into the room and she falls right in your arms. Not to say you aren't a catch, Merton, but you aren't—not to a diamond of the first water like Tess Hamlin. That silly wager story is all nonsense. Talk would have died down quick enough. And Hamlin's decision to marry her off in a week! Something is not right . . . not quite right at all."

Brenn leaned his head back against the hard leather seat. "Does it matter? His plans fit mine. The sooner I return to Wales, the sooner I can begin rebuilding the estate. Fifty thousand pounds! There isn't anything I can't do with that much money."

"This whole matter is too havey-cavey for my taste," Sir Charles warned him.

"It was the scandal," Brenn said dismissively, crossing his arms and closing his eyes. "Hamlin is a proud man. He wanted to save face. Plus, his sister is well past her prime. If she wasn't so attractive, people would have already considered her on the shelf." He smiled, picturing those spirited blue eyes, seeing her as she'd been this evening, passionately defending her views without the coquetry of other women. "As it is, she is just perfect for me. Just perfect," he repeated drowsily. "Do you believe Hamlin will transfer his sister's fortune to me upon signing the wedding contract?"

Sir Charles snorted. "Absolutely not. He'd be fool to turn over one shilling until the deed is right and properly done, after the wedding night. And you should insist on such terms too. You don't want this marriage annulled after you've invested so much into it. I've heard Hamlin doesn't have a good head for business. Or money. Spends it like he's swimming in it."

"Perhaps he is."

"Hmmm . . . one never knows."

Brenn opened one eye. "Why are you always so suspicious? Why can't you believe in good fortune? I was the man who was in the right place at the right time."

Sir Charles tapped his great hooked nose. "I get this itch on the left side of my nose whenever things aren't what they should be. It's saved my hide too many times over the years to ignore it now." He scratched his nose. On the left side. "The girl's money alone would have been enough to tide her over even the most outrageous scandal. No, something else is at work. Hamlin is hiding something."

Brenn shrugged. "And what if he is? I got what I came to London for, a rich wife. And one that isn't bad on the eyes either." He settled back in the seat with a grin.

"Yes, well, my nose has never let me down. It itches like a terrier right now. Before you think yourself too cocky, watch your back."

Brenn yawned and ignored him. But later, when he'd finally found his bed for the night, Sir Charles's words haunted his sleep.

Tess would not marry a stranger, no matter how mesmerizing he was.

She waited until well after noon and then hunted her brother down, finding him in his bedroom. He was still abed, nursing the very devil of a hangover.

Tess slammed the door shut.

Neil swore colorfully, grabbing his head with both hands.

"Did you celebrate too much last night, brother of mine? *At my expense?*"

"Please, Tess, I beg of you, walk more softly. I can hear your heels scrape the carpet!"

Before she could reply, the door banged open. Neil cried out in pain, even as his wife breezed into the room. A willowy blonde, Stella wore her favorite rose walking dress and a short Spencer jacket of cream kerseymere. The cherry ribbons on her straw bonnet bounced with her enthusiasm.

"Neil, Tess, I have heard the most infamous story about the Garlands' rout last night! Why didn't you tell me?"

Neil whimpered. "Please, my darling, speak softly. I beg you."

She ignored his request. Pulling off her gloves, she said, "I've just come from a lunch with Lady Ottley. She offered me congratulations on Tess's engagement. I didn't quite know what to say. I pretended I knew all about it when of course I didn't have an inkling. I *should* have gone with you to the Garland ball instead of the Watkins's card party. But how was I to know? So tell, tell me, is it true? Have you *finally* found a man willing to marry your headstrong sister?" She smiled at Tess as she added, "My heart goes out to him."

Tess resisted the urge to stick out her tongue.

Neil groaned. "I knew there was something I'd forgotten. You were betrothed last night."

"And it can stay forgotten," Tess jumped in.

"I have no intention of marrying Lord Merton. I don't know the man."

But Stella ignored her and squealed with delight, a reverberating sound that made her husband dive under the covers in agony. She pranced to the bed and threw her arms around him, hugging his head to her breasts. "I knew you would do it! I knew that once you heard about the baby you would not let me down. Oh, this is the happiest day of my life. Imagine, my sister-in-law will be out from under my roof. It will be my house. All mine. Neil, you are a wonderful man!" She kissed him noisily.

Neil was practically weeping in pain. "Stella, Stella, will you please not bounce so much," he begged. "And be good enough to hand me that cup of tea on the desk there."

"Tea? Neil, you never drink tea." She dutifully handed him the cup, perching herself on the edge of the bed and making irritating "goochy coo" noises. "Are you suffering from over-imbibing?"

He grunted his answer.

Stella "Ooooed" in sympathy—and Tess rolled her eyes, even as she felt a stab of jealousy. Watching the two of them sitting so close to each other, she realized again that her situation in the family was becoming increasingly tenuous.

And, deep down, she wished she was the one having a baby. Perhaps then her life wouldn't feel so empty. What would it be like to have a baby to love and to teach things the way Minnie had taught her?

Shoving the disquieting feelings aside, Tess

said, "Stella, Neil and I were having a *private* discussion. Please go to your room."

"Did you hear the way she spoke to me, Neil? She orders me around like she's the queen of Sheba."

"I want to talk to my brother, *without your interference*."

"There are no secrets between Neil and me," Stella shot back.

"Little do you know!" Tess retorted. Neil had a host of secrets, including a mistress in Chelsea, secrets Tess would guard out of loyalty to him. Although she couldn't resist a jab at Stella.

Stella stood, hands on hips. "I can't believe you talk to me that way—"

"Stella, Tess, please, my head aches—"

"He's my husband. *I'm* the one welcome in this room. Furthermore you have nothing to discuss with him, especially if you are going to attempt to cry off from this engagement."

"I must!" Tess said. "I did not agree to this marriage. No one asked me."

"No one *has* to ask you," Stella answered before Neil could open his mouth. "Neil is your guardian. He can arrange any marriage for you he wishes."

"That's barbaric!" Tess declared.

Stella smiled. "It is not barbaric. It's the way things are done, especially for a woman with an inheritance such as yours."

Tess turned to her brother. "I don't want to marry this man. I don't even *know* him."

"You don't have to know him," Stella singsonged. "It is up to your brother to decide what is best for you."

"He doesn't know him either, do you, Neil?"

Neil attempted speech. "I—"

His wife cut in. "Lady Ottley said your fiancé is a Welsh earl, a hero, very handsome in a rough sort of way and Sir Charles Merriam is sponsoring him. What more do you need to know?"

"What more?" Tess said incredulously. "Are you daft, Stella? There's so much more to be known before a person decides to marry a man."

Stella rolled her eyes dramatically. "Tess, you are impossible. And too picky. No wonder you aren't married!"

"Be honest, Stella. You just want the house all to yourself so you can bully the servants without my interference—"

"I do not bully the servants!"

"Last week, you had the upstairs maid in tears!" Tess accused.

"She broke my bottle of bath salts," Stella complained.

"You can replace bath salts—"

"Enough!" Neil's shout cut through the air. "Stella, take this cup. Tess, we will talk, but *lower your voice.*"

He motioned for Stella to pour him another cup of tea. "No, Tess, I will not let you cry off. Perhaps I don't *know* Merton well. I *may* have been a bit hasty. The announcement *might* have been rash. But the deed is *done.* I will not renege on my word whether it was given drunk or sober. You have six days in which to make his acquaintance . . . and after that a lifetime."

"Neil!" Tess said in outrage.

He put his feet over the side of the bed. "Stella will plan the wedding. We'll do it up right."

"A wedding! Finally!" Stella clapped her hands together and then, seeing her husband's wince, softly added, "I'm sorry."

Tess no longer cared about Neil's hangover. "I will not marry him," she said forcibly. "I will cry off myself if you will not do it."

"Oh, no, you won't, miss," Stella said, her fists doubling. "Not after that brazen little wager you placed with Leah Carrollton. Ha! You didn't know I knew, did you? Well, it's all over Town. Everyone can speak of nothing but your scandalous behavior. They blame you for everything and think it only right you marry Lord Merton."

Tess could have shot fire from her eyes. "It doesn't matter. I won't marry him."

Stella rounded on her husband. "Your sister is driving me to madness. Do something I beg you!"

"As my brother you should honor my wishes!"

Neil raked his fingers through his sleep mussed hair and walked the length of the room.

Neither Tess or Stella spoke. A gauntlet had been thrown down between them and they awaited Neil's decision.

He turned, his bloodshot eyes weary. "Stella, will you please give me a moment alone with my sister?"

Tess's heart gave a little leap. She stared at the floor so that Stella wouldn't see the gleam of triumph in her eyes. Another outburst might make Neil change his mind.

Of course, Stella did not obey immediately. "Why? Are you going to beat sense in her?"

"A few minutes, Stella, please," he repeated gravely.

Tess held her breath and then Stella said, "I'll wait outside the door."

She'll probably listen at it, Tess thought irreverently, but, for once, she kept her thoughts to herself.

"Thank you," Neil said, and he sounded like he meant it. He waited until the door closed before saying, "Sit down, Tess."

She remained standing, knowing that anytime he made her sit down, he was going to lecture her . . . which he'd been doing quite often' since the day he'd married Stella.

He sighed heavily and took his own seat behind the desk in front of the window. "Sit, Tess."

She had no choice then. She took the seat next to his desk, folding her hands demurely in her lap. "You don't seem at all yourself today."

"I don't feel like myself, Tess. My head aches from the inside out. And I don't want to have this conversation, but I must. I've put it off long enough."

He sat forward. "Tess, the time has come for you to marry. This Merton doesn't seem like such a bad sort. He might even make a good husband."

"I will marry, Neil. But not yet. Please, call on the earl and beg off for me. Tell him I'm ill or mad or *anything* just so that I don't have to marry him."

"Tess, what are you afraid of?"

"I'm not afraid, Neil. I just sense that there is something more to life."

"Other than marriage?"

"Yes."

He snorted. "Not for a woman. Tess, you've had your freedom. The time has come for responsibility. Besides, drunk or not, I gave the man my word."

"But *I* didn't. I wasn't even consulted. Please don't make me marry a man I don't even know. Father wouldn't have," she reminded him.

"Ah, Tess." He ran a hand over the shadow of his beard and stared out the window. When he turned back to her, there were tears in his eyes.

"Neil?" She reached out, but he pulled away. "Is something the matter?"

He nodded.

She reached again and this time he let her take his hand. "Tell me and we'll make it right. *Together.*"

He shook his head, gathering himself, and then said, "I remember when Mother was dying. You were no more than five and I was nine and the two us were both afraid. But I tried to be strong in front of you. Father said I had to take care of you and I feared I would break down and you'd see how frightened I was. Then Father would have been disappointed in me."

"But you were brave. Father said you were very strong. I remember that, Neil."

"You held my hand, Tess, just like you are now. And you asked me, 'Will Mother be all right?' and I said yes." He ran his thumb back and forth across her hand. "That memory haunts me. I lied to you. I lied."

He raised his gaze to meet hers and she could see in the depths of his eyes that he carried a terrible burden. "Neil, what is it?" she demanded, truly alarmed.

"I have something to tell you, something I regret." He paused. "I've lost your fortune, Tess. All of it."

She laughed, certain he had to be joking. But he didn't join in her laughter and suddenly, in the cold pit of her stomach, she knew he was telling her the truth.

She pulled her hand back. "I don't understand, Neil. How could you lose my fortune? It doesn't make sense."

He pushed up from the desk and began pacing nervously. "I made some unwise investments. I didn't do it on purpose. I thought I knew what I was doing."

"What investments?"

"A man came to me with an idea for some new mechanics." Neil sat on the edge of the bed. "A battery. It's a stack of copper and zinc plates. It gives off electrical current."

Now Tess knew her brother wasn't joking. He'd always been fascinated by mechanics.

"It was the most amazing experiment I had ever witnessed, Tess. Revolutionary even. He could make this dead chicken move with this battery. Imagine the possibilities, Tess! He could make dead material move. But he needed money to do more experiments. Of course, my money is entailed and Father's will makes it so that I must always turn to Mr. Christopher for permission. It's such a nuisance because Christopher is completely unyielding to my requests for more cash. Stella is expensive and Town living has its demands." He stopped his complaints and looked at her, his expression miserable. "I didn't expect to lose it all, Tess. I thought I was doing what was best for you."

Standing, she crossed over to him. "Where is this man, Neil? Perhaps we should talk to him."

"He's gone. I've looked for months now. He's disappeared with the money, probably back to Italy."

Slowly, the import of his words sank in. "I am not an heiress."

"No."

"Why didn't you tell me this sooner?"

"Because I'd hoped to work my way out of it. I believed that I would be able to cover the money I lost."

"But you couldn't."

He lowered his head. "I'd ask Christopher, if I thought he would advance the sum, but the amount I lost is so big and he'd refuse me, Tess, I know he would."

Tess slowly walked around his desk, tracing her path with the tips of her fingers on its polished surface. Only the ticking of the clock over the cold hearth broke the silence.

"Does Stella know?"

Neil shook his head. "I can't tell her, especially now that she is with child."

"Oh, Neil." She felt the hot sting of tears and choked them back.

Together. "What is the solution?"

He came to his feet. Reaching out, he touched her hair. "You are so pretty. Much like Mother, but prettier." He dropped his hand. "I can't let anyone know what I did. I have a reputation; I have connections. If this comes out, I will be ruined."

"What do you want me to do then?" She knew the answer before he'd even said the words.

"I want you to marry this Welsh earl. Leave London. Build a life with him and no one will be the wiser about my, ah, my mistake."

"But what about the money?"

"He has funds. I overheard at my club that his estate in Wales is quite ancient and very grand."

"Neil, is there no other way?"

"No."

"And if I don't?"

Neil shrugged and then spoke as if the words were hard to say. "We will see our good name ruined. And your chance to marry anyone will be gone."

For one horrifying second, Tess could imagine the laughter and snide comments of those who would take pleasure in her downfall. Like Neil, she didn't know if she could live with the public embarrassment. Fear rose up inside her, choking her. She swallowed it back, but still it lingered in her throat, making it ache. She whispered, barely able to talk, "Will you tell Merton the truth? You mustn't lie to him."

"I won't lie, but I don't have to tell him everything," her brother said quickly. "Or else he'll cry off. Then the rumors would fly."

Tess didn't like this. "But he will find out sooner or later."

"Yes, but by then you must make sure he is willing to forgive you."

"How?"

"*You* are asking me how? Women get men to

forgive their sins every day. Make him fall in love with you. Men in love will do anything."

At that moment, a knock sounded on the door. At Neil's call, Nestor, the butler, said, "Mr. Hamlin, the earl of Merton is here to see you. Are you at home?"

Neil turned to Tess. "Am I?"

She stood rooted to the floor, feeling as if her head had turned into one of those flying balloons while her body was a chunk of ice. Her brother waited. Finally, she nodded. "Yes, yes, you are at home."

"You'll marry him?"

Tess opened her mouth but it took a moment until she could say the words. "Yes. Yes, I will marry him."

Chapter Four

What the bloody hell had he done?

That thought had first struck Brenn as he'd stood shaving the razor to his throat. His predawn philosophizing had given way to stone cold reality after a good night's sleep.

Now, as he cooled his heels in the magnificent opulence of the Hamlin sitting room, he realized what Sir Charles had been trying to tell him—especially once he saw how wealthy Hamlin really was. Not only was the house located at London's most fashionable address, but the furnishings were fresh, new . . . expensive.

For the first time since Brenn had set off on his fortune-hunting trip to London, the future consequences of what he was attempting to do sank in. The bouquet of rose buttons and forget-me-nots he'd purchased from a street vendor began to wilt in his hand.

He walked across the thick carpet and studied the row of green antique vases trimmed in gold lining the mantel. A well-traveled man, he knew the cost of things, and he would wager just one of those vases had cost more than his officer's pay for the last year.

Last night, he'd seen the sparkle in Miss Hamlin's eyes and charged after her like a hungry trout striking bait. Now he was seeing the depth of her wealth. A woman raised in this luxury would expect to continue in this manner.

Brenn thought of Erwynn Keep as it presently was—the shell of a once-great house. Gaping holes marked where the doors and windows had been. Parts of the roof were missing. It was completely uninhabitable. Brenn lived, as his uncle had, in a small crofter's cottage within sight of the house.

Could a woman raised in this room, in this house, share his vision for rebuilding Erwynn Keep? Would she be happy living in a crofter's cottage until the house was finished?

He glanced around the sitting room.

The answer was no.

But he needed her money if he was to realize his dreams.

Sir Charles's warnings plagued him. Why was Hamlin pushing for the wedding to take place with all possible haste? Perhaps something truly was not right. Even *his* nose was beginning to itch.

His thoughts were interrupted by the sound of two maids whispering outside the half-closed door. Thinking that their presence heralded the approach of Miss Hamlin, Brenn moved toward the entrance.

"Who's in there?" he heard one ask the other.

"A gentleman caller for Miss Tess."

"Only one? Normally by this hour Miss Tess has a roomful of male callers."

The maid sucked in her breath. "You haven't heard then?"

"Heard what?"

"Why, Miss Tess has agreed to marry. That gentleman in there, in fact."

"Lor', no! And me not hearing a word! Tell all, Bonnie."

Their voices dropped even lower as they shared confidences. Brenn shifted from one foot to the other. He would give his sword to know what they were saying.

One of the maids giggled, the sound ever so slightly malicious.

Manners be damned. He moved toward the door just in time to hear the first maid cut short the idle talk. "I best get myself upstairs. She was sick again this morning."

"Oooo, three mornings in a row. I hear the doctor was in yesterday."

"Aye, it's true. Never any doubt in my mind, doctor or no—but don't breathe a word to anyone. She'd have my head if she thought I'd let it slip. It's a secret. You know the gentry. 'Course I know what she's hiding. When her belly pops out with that babe, they'll all know she was trotting around pretending nothing was wrong and all the gentry will be scandalized . . . or at least that is what the master's valet told me."

"He's been telling you a lot of things lately," the other maid said slyly. Her comment inspired a good bit of girlish laughter and then they were both gone—and Brenn had his answer.

Sir Charles had been right.

He stared down at the yellow centers of the rose buttons in the bouquet, wishing he hadn't heard the maids talking. For a long moment, his pride warred with his plans for Erwynn Keep.

He *was* being used. She was pregnant and needed a father for her child.

Of course, didn't he want to use Miss Hamlin for her money?

But could he accept another man's babe as his own?

At that moment, booted footsteps walked purposely across the marble floor toward the sitting room door. Brenn stepped back just as Neil Hamlin, followed by the butler, strode into the room.

"Ah, Lord Merton, what a pleasure to see you."

Brenn shook Hamlin's offered hand. The man sounded friendly enough but Brenn couldn't help noticing lines of strain around his mouth and that Hamlin's gaze didn't quite meet his own.

"My sister will be down shortly. Would you like Nestor to take those flowers from you?" He didn't wait for an answer but signaled for the butler to do so immediately.

Brenn pulled back. "That's fine. I'll give them to her." He wanted to use his small offering to see if her gaze shifted away from his own like her brother's had. The butler retreated, leaving a silent footman behind to see to their needs.

"Well," Hamlin said, clapping his hands together to fill the sudden void of conversation. "This is a momentous occasion. We need a glass of wine to celebrate." He moved toward a wine decanter and glasses on a nearby serving table.

Brenn watched him, the words *Is your sister carrying another man's child?* on the tip of his tongue. He'd always been one for plain speaking but then that had been before he was an earl ... before he'd wanted something as much as he did Erwynn Keep. The starched and carefully folded neckcloth around his throat seemed as tight and constricting as a noose.

And then he heard the rustle of skirts and smelled the scent of lilies. He turned ... and questions died in his throat.

Miss Hamlin stood in the doorway. Tess. Beautiful Tess. She appeared even more lovely in the light of day than she had in the garden last night, and he no longer questioned his judgment.

Her thick, red-gold hair was piled high on her head but without the fussy curls and jewels of the night before. Brenn imagined that if he pulled out a pin here and another there, it would tumble down to her waist.

Her dress, the shade of a robin's egg, brought out the vivid blue of her almond-shaped eyes. She raised those eyes to his and said, "How are you today, my lord?" in a honey-smooth voice.

It took him a moment to find his own voice. "These are for you." He shoved the bouquet forward, conscious that the flowers paled in comparison to her vibrant beauty.

She moved with a grace that made her seem to float across the floor. Her long, elegant fingertips brushed his as she reached for the bouquet. She didn't wear gloves and he felt the heat of her body all the way down to his toes.

What spell did this woman weave over him?

She lifted the flowers to her nose and he noticed her hands trembled, ever so slightly. "These are lovely," she murmured.

"So are you," he said. The words had come out unbidden; he couldn't have stopped them if he'd tried.

Her lips parted in surprise. Hamlin chuckled. "Merton, you will have to be less direct. You're not on a battlefield anymore but ready to join the ranks of married men. Mark my words, if you talk to my sister that way after the wedding, she'll walk all over you." He laughed at his own small joke.

But Tess didn't join him. Instead, two bright spots of color appeared on her cheeks and, for a moment, Brenn sensed the truth. It was there, plain to see. She was hiding something. Both of them were.

The heat of lust was tempered by a slap of cold reality.

His gaze dropped to her slim waist. No sign of breeding—yet.

A woman's trilling voice announced herself from the doorway. "My lord, pardon me for not joining you sooner." An attractive blonde swept into the room.

"Merton, this is my wife, Stella," Hamlin said, gesturing with his wineglass. He handed a glass to Brenn. "Stella, the earl of Merton."

Brenn bowed over the hand she offered. "Mrs. Hamlin."

"Stella, please," she corrected him enthusiastically. "After all, we are soon to be brother and sister in marriage, are we not? There is no purpose in standing on ceremony." She gave Tess's shoulders a sisterly hug that was not returned. "I am so excited that you are marrying our dear, dear Tess. And what a handsome couple you make. Brenn—I may call you Brenn, no?" She charged on, barely pausing for breath. "Neil tells me your family estate is in Wales."

"Yes, it is."

"And I imagine you wish to return as quickly as possible," Stella said almost gleefully. "Oooo, Neil, please pour a glass of wine for me."

"And you, Tess?" her brother asked. "Do you wish a small sherry?"

Tess didn't answer him. Instead, she said to Brenn, "Are you really expecting us to return to Wales?"

He answered her honestly. "Yes. Probably the day after the wedding."

Stella almost jigged for joy. "What an adventure for you, Tess. Imagine, the wilds of Wales. She's rarely been out of London," she confided to Brenn. "The change of scenery will be good for her. For *all* of us."

The woman Brenn had met last night on the terrace would have challenged Stella for making such a slur, but now, Tess murmured distractedly, "Yes, it will."

She took a small restless step and then, as if just remembering the flowers in her hand, said, "I should have these put in water." She would have made a quick exit except Neil stopped her.

"Not yet, Tess. We must toast your happiness. Give the flowers to the servants to arrange."

"Yes, a toast!" Stella echoed happily.

For the space of a heartbeat, Tess appeared

ready to toss the insipid bouquet in the air, lift
her skirts, and run. But she didn't. Instead, she
handed the flowers to one of the ever-present
footmen with the same resolve Brenn had used
himself to confront French cannons.

Her brother pushed a glass of wine in her
hand.

"To your happiness," he said.

"Hear, hear," Stella acknowledged, lifting her
own glass.

Brenn sipped, all too aware that his intended
had not moved since her brother had forced her
to take the glass. Instead, she ran her thumb back
and forth along the glass's crystal rim.

"Another drink!" Hamlin ordered, having
downed his own. He crossed to the wine cabinet
to refill it. "We must celebrate your future. By
the way, Merton, I will have my man of business
in on the morrow, say two o'clock? We'll discuss
the wedding contract at that time."

The wedding contract. *Fifty thousand pounds.
Swallow your pride.* Brenn glanced at Tess standing rigid and silent, her reluctance a dart aimed
at his deepest doubts. Would fifty thousand be
enough?

"I'd like a moment alone with your sister."
The words were out of Brenn's mouth before
he'd even realized his intent.

The request caught Hamlin off guard. Brother
and sister exchanged quick glances.

"A moment only," Brenn pressed, a hint of
steel in his voice.

"Of course you can," Stella said cheerily. "After all, I have a wedding to plan. Imagine, it must
be all done by next Wednesday! Neil, darling,

can we not hold it here instead of the church?"

"The church," he insisted curtly, still frowning at Brenn. He forced a smile. "But the wedding breakfast will be here." He paused. "I will not be far," he told his sister. With a stiff bow, he left the room, Stella traipsing at his heels and prattling on about wedding arrangements.

Tess looked as if she might follow them. Brenn dissuaded her by walking to the door and shutting it.

She flinched at the sound of the lock clicking in place. Her gaze flew up to meet his. There was definitely panic in her expressive eyes. She looked away, moving across the room to the front window overlooking the street.

"You don't want this marriage," he said without preamble. "Why?"

She turned, facing him, and he saw a flash of the spirit he'd seen in her last night. "My lord, I don't understand your question. Are you attempting to cry off?"

Brenn wasn't about to walk away from her now. He had given her his word. He crossed the carpet to her, stopping when they were less than a hand's distance apart. She observed his approach with the watchful caution of someone being stalked by a wolf.

He spoke. "We each have our own reasons for wanting this match. Let us clear the air and go on about it." Even as he said this, he wondered how much he was willing to reveal about his financial affairs. He didn't want her to bolt.

She started to speak. "I—" But then she stopped. Her chin came up to a stubborn angle and she glared at him almost defiantly. In a low, flat voice, she said, "I have nothing to confide. You are saving me from last night's scandal and I thank you."

Brenn felt the swift rise of anger. Why was she being so bloody difficult?

Why was he pressing the issue?

After all, what did it matter if she had been with another man or not? He was marrying her for her fortune. Then why did her refusal to be honest make him a little crazed?

Because it did, with a primitive anger at her stubbornness. And because it mattered, he resolved the issue with the same audacity he'd demonstrated on the battlefield.

He took her by both arms and kissed her.

At first she opposed him. She attempted to turn her head away, placing her hands on his chest. But something deep and primal that had been lurking within him from the moment she'd first walked into the room now urged him to press forward, to make her respond and bend to him.

It wasn't only lust. He liked the taste of her. Very much. More than he'd anticipated.

To his satisfaction, ever so slowly, she relented. He deepened the kiss. She responded, tentative at first and then with growing passion.

His tongue touched hers. She started to draw back but he wouldn't let her. His hand followed the curve of her spine, keeping her close to him.

Her nipples hardened. He could feel them even through the layers of clothes between them and he knew he could have her. Boldly, he pressed himself against her, wanting her to feel his desire.

She caught her breath, making a small sound of surprise. Brenn looped her arm over his shoulder while his other hand held her captive. Slowly, deliberately, he began making love to her with his tongue. He knew how to pleasure a woman. He'd learned the art of making love in eight countries.

And one of the things he'd learned was that not every partner sparked this sudden wild desire in him or responded with such innocent inhibition. Her body fit his. He rolled his hips against hers, aping the movements of his tongue. She moaned, both arms now around his neck, and he cupped her buttocks and lifted her slightly, the better to position himself close to her.

He grabbed hold of the material of her skirt, wanting to feel her, to see if she was hot, ready. He wanted the barriers removed between them—

A knock on the door was their only warning. They broke apart immediately and managed to place a small sofa between them just as Hamlin entered the room.

The smile on his face did little to mask the anxiousness in his eyes. "So, I hope the two of you have had a moment to get to know each other," he said with a false heartiness that made Brenn wonder what he had feared would happen when they were alone.

Her color high, Tess reassured him with a small laugh. "Lord Merton was telling me about Wales."

Brenn didn't like how easily the small falsehood had come to her lips. No, she was no virginal miss. No woman could respond with such wanton abandonment and still be untouched. Whether she carried another man's brat or not, he wanted her with a force that was startling. He wanted his seed inside her, to mark her and bind her to him.

"I am anxious to show Miss Hamlin Wales." He glanced at her lips. They were still rosy red and slightly swollen from their kiss. "Spring is always such a fertile time."

Her hand came up and she covered her mouth. Their gazes met, and she quickly glanced away. Brenn couldn't resist a grim smile of satisfaction. She'd known the direction of his thoughts.

He and Tess Hamlin would suit very well . . . and in spite of Sir Charles's warnings, and his own guarded instincts, he had to have her.

"I'll take you driving in the park this afternoon, Miss Hamlin," he said. "Sir Charles assures me that such an act is tantamount to an announcement in the papers."

"Quite right!" her brother cut in. "Although I will have the announcement posted in the morning papers. I want everything proper," he added with false cheeriness.

"Then if you will excuse me, I will return at five." Brenn crossed the room to her. "Miss Hamlin." He held out his hand.

Her reluctance was clear as she placed her fingers in his. What did she think he was going to do? Gobble her up?

The idea had merit.

Gallantly, he lifted her hand to his lips and kissed her fingertips. "Until five."

She nodded. He would have paid every coin in his pocket to know her thoughts.

"By the by," Hamlin said, oblivious to the tension in the room, "Stella tells me we are attending Lord and Lady Ottley's musicale this evening. It's an Italian soprano, nothing special. We wish you to join our party."

"Lord Ottley? Is he not the sponsor of that agricultural bill in Parliament?"

"I suppose so. I really don't know," Hamlin said. "I don't pay attention to politics myself."

Brenn thought a man who didn't pay attention to politics and the governing of his country was an idiot, but he kept that opinion to himself. "I would be honored to be your guest."

"Good. Come here at nine. We'll have a quiet supper and then go to the musicale together."

As Brenn took his leave he couldn't resist one backward glance at his bride-to-be. She stood perfectly still, her gaze fixated on a point outside the window.

He wondered again who the father of her baby was.

Leaving the house, he decided that always doing the honorable thing was damn hard business.

"It was . . ." Tess paused, at a loss for words. "It was *animal!*"

She and Anne sat in the privacy of Anne's small bedroom under the eaves of her aunt's house. It was a safe, familiar place. Tess had hurried there as soon as the door had closed behind Lord Merton.

"Animal?" Anne repeated. "A kiss?"

"Yes," Tess said desperately. "Worse, I can't believe I behaved so brazenly."

"I can't believe he just reached out and grabbed you!"

"Oh, he did," Tess swore fervently. "He acted like he was angry about something." For a moment, she was tempted to divulge her guilty secret concerning her loss of fortune, but then she thought differently. She couldn't stand the thought of anyone pitying her, even Anne.

Instead, she rolled off the bed and acted out the chain of events. "He took my arms with both hands and then, before I realized what was happening, he kissed me."

"Oh, dear," Anne said breathlessly.

"Yes," Tess agreed. "At first, I fought him. I thought I was going to be ravished, right there in my own home with my brother close at hand."

"And were you?"

"No." She dropped her arms to her side. "Instead, I kissed him back."

"You?"

Tess nodded.

"But you don't like to kiss."

That was true. "I've found it sloppy and degrading . . . but," she added in a whisper, "it wasn't disgusting when he kissed me."

"What was it like?" Anne asked, wide-eyed.

Tess searched her mind for the right word and settled on "Possessive."

"What did you do after that?"

"Nothing," Tess admitted helplessly. "My mind was so jumbled, I could barely string two thoughts together. And he kept watching me . . ."

She sat back on the bed, crushing a feather pillow tightly against her stomach. She was losing control. Whether she wished it or not, she was going to marry a man who had the power to make her feel excited and frightened and giddy all at one time. "Anne, what happens between a man and a woman once they marry?"

"What do you mean?"

"You know." Tess waved her hand in the air anxiously. "What happens on the wedding night."

Anne sank down on the bed. "I thought you knew."

"Knew *what?*"

Shaking her head, Anne confessed, "I don't know. Tess, living with my aunt, I might as well be in a nunnery. Whenever I've dared to ask a question, she's gotten all prune-faced and told me not to worry my head about that." She dropped her voice. "Once I even went to the lending library to search for a book that might tell me."

Tess sat bolt upright. "I did too. Did you find one?"

"No."

She shrank back down. "I didn't either. But I found some very interesting allusions in poetry. The poets make it sound like something earthy and enjoyable."

Anne leaned forward. "Why don't you ask Stella?"

"I can't do that! We detest each other." For a moment, Tess curled her tongue, remembering those motions that the earl had made with his hips and how she'd felt them, deep down in a place below her stomach. She hadn't known she could feel anything down there. Just remembering that kiss seemed to churn a host of confused, dizzying emotions she'd never known before.

"I know who we could ask," Anne said, "but I don't know how you feel about her."

"Who?"

"Leah Carrollton. I saw her today when I was at Parisham's with my aunt. She told me to thank you for taking the blame last night. She truly appreciates it. I've heard her mother is very strict about public behavior." She paused a moment and added, "I appreciate it too. I had to listen to my aunt lecture me about *your* outrageous behavior but at least she didn't imprison me up here on bread and water, her favorite punishment. Was it too bad for you?"

"No, apparently all is forgiven provided I marry and leave London. Stella says that even Lady Garland is willing to forgive the whole incident."

"Leave London? Tess, you didn't tell me that!"

"No," she admitted in a small voice. "My earl is a Welshman and he wants to return home."

"Tell him you won't go. I can't imagine being here without you."

"I don't have a choice, Anne." Tess set the pillow aside and rose from the bed. She paced the length of the room before saying, "Do you really think Leah would know?"

"Leah's mother is strict in some matters but not so much in others. I overheard my aunt gossiping that Leah's mother encourages her to throw herself at every titled peer who has a bit of cash to his name. I've heard whispers of her kissing in the garden." She lowered her voice. "Captain Draycutt was at Parisham's. My aunt was skeptical of his motives for lurking among the dry goods especially after Leah arrived. Of course, the two of them acted surprised to see each other. My aunt says that if Leah isn't careful, a man like Draycutt will have her ruined in no time. And I think Leah wants that to happen."

"But Draycutt has such a terrible reputation."

"She had stars in her eyes, Tess."

Leah. "Do you really think she would know?"

"We can find out. We should see her tonight at Lady Ottley's musicale."

A musicale would be the perfect opportunity to ask such a personal question. Anne and Tess had learned long ago that some of the most public places were also the most private, since their chaperones were usually too involved with their own affairs to pay close attention.

"Yes, we should ask her tonight," she agreed.

Two hours later, Tess found herself sitting beside Lord Merton, trotting around Hyde Park in an elegant carriage. It was obviously a hired equipage but Lord Merton had a good hand with the horses.

The day was overcast but there were still many people out taking a ride in the park. Tess knew the announcement of her engagement would be old news by the time it appeared in the papers. She said as much to Lord Merton. It was really the only intelligent thing she *did* say.

They sat side-by-side while Lord Merton kept a steady monologue going on about the joys of Wales. She, who was usually so glib, felt tongue-tied and nervous. She hadn't acted this way since she'd been seventeen and presented at Court.

She was terribly aware of him. If she looked at him, she'd catch herself staring at his lips and remembering how they felt upon hers. And she couldn't help but notice how his breeches outlined muscular thighs. Even watching him drive offered no peace. His light touch on the reins reminded her of the way he'd guided and pressed her to his will.

As he turned the horses toward home, she felt a wild impulse to confess the truth. To let him know she wasn't a grand heiress, that she was a fraud. Yet the words could not leave her throat because such a confession would destroy the brother she loved.

At last, he escorted her to her doorstep. She faced him. "Thank you for the ride, my lord."

He pulled off one leather driving glove. "Do you not think it is time to call me by my given name?"

"I—ah—"

"Brenn."

"What?"

He smiled, his teeth even and white. "*Brenn.* That's my name."

She nodded, dutifully repeating, "Brenn."

He backed down the steps. "I'll see you this evening. Lady Ottley sent me an invitation to her musicale. My social standing is rising."

"You may not thank me after you hear one of her sopranos."

He laughed, the sound easy, and she felt a bit more at ease. "I will see you later, Tess."

She liked the sound of her name on his lips. It

almost sounded different than she'd ever heard it before.

Behind her, Nestor held open the door, but she waited, watching Brenn's tall figure walk toward his stamping horses. *I'll make a good wife to you*, she promised him silently.

As if he'd heard, he turned before climbing up into the carriage and saluted her with one finger to the brim of his hat. With a snap of the reins, he was off.

Turning, Tess hurried inside, anxious to dress for the musicale. She had to talk to Leah.

Chapter Five

"*Men have sticks,*" Leah imported to them in a low voice that no one could have overheard above the warbling of Signora Luiguisi, Lady Ottley's Italian soprano.

The three young women sat on the far left side of the assembled guests, close to a bank of potted palm trees. Everyone else in the crowded room appeared entranced by the singer's vocal gymnastics—and to the casual observer Tess and the others gave the impression of attentiveness. They had all perfected the art of appearing to listen without actually doing so.

However, this piece of intelligence was too shocking.

"Sticks?" Tess exclaimed, just as the signora paused for breath. In spite of her having whispered, the word seemed to reverberate with a life of its own.

Heads turned in her direction. Lady Ottley half-stood, searching for the source of the interruption. Tess pretended to be looking for the nuisance too, although she did shoot a glance over her shoulder at Lord Merton—no, Brenn, she mentally corrected herself—to see if he had noticed.

He stood in the back of the room and if he'd heard her interruption, he gave no indication but appeared to be listening intently to the aria.

Anne jostled Tess with her elbow in a silent warning to keep her wits about her. Leah leaned closer. "Does it bother you that he is lame?"

"I rarely notice," Tess said from the side of her mouth, a fact which was startling, but true. The only time she'd been aware that he'd limped had been their initial meeting. On the terrace last night or even this afternoon, she hadn't given it a thought.

"It would bother me," Leah said with a slight shiver. "I don't know if I would want to see him with his clothes off."

Her words made Tess's stomach do a little flip. Over dinner, with Brenn sitting across from her, she'd had just the opposite thought.

Interesting that out of all the men of her acquaintance, he was the first one to make her wonder about taking off clothes. "Tell me more about the stick."

A young matron behind them rapped Tess's shoulder with her fan and gave them a "shush."

"Afterward, in the retiring room," Leah whispered.

Anne gave Tess an impatient nudge. "What did she say?"

"Later. In the retiring room."

Anne nodded.

Once Signora Luiguisi took her bow, the three young women didn't hesitate to excuse themselves immediately to the retiring room, only to find that it was too crowded. Instead, they slipped into Lord Ottley's library.

"Now what is this about sticks?" Tess demanded. She and Anne both sat on the leather couch.

Leah stood in front of the hearth. "Men are built differently than we are," she lectured matter-of-factly.

"I know that," Tess said. "I'm not a complete goose."

"Then why are you asking me questions?" Leah said. "A man's stick is here." With a semi-comical gesture, she showed where the "stick" was located. The three giggled with forbidden knowledge.

Tess shook her head. "It doesn't make sense."

"I'm just telling you what the upstairs maid told me."

"You mean your mother didn't say this?" Anne asked.

Leah pulled back. "Mother would never talk of such an improper thing."

"Did you ever ask?" Tess said, curious.

"Once. She boxed my ears and informed me my husband would tell me everything I needed to know." Leah slid a glance at Tess. "Did you ever ask your sister-in-law?"

"Would I be talking to you now if I had?" Tess countered tartly.

Leah warned, "You both must swear to secrecy. Mother would give the maid the boot if she'd known she'd talked about this. But the maid said, and I agree with her, that it's wrong to keep silent and then expect a girl to know what to do on her wedding night. Or why gentlemen want to get us off alone in a dark corner and fidget around."

"Yes, that's what we want to know," Anne said. "What is it that they try to do and why shouldn't we let them? It must be something more than a kiss."

Tess was still puzzled about the previous point. "I can't imagine any man having a stick in his breeches. Wouldn't it show? Or be uncomfortable?"

Leah made an impatient sound. "It isn't a stick all the time. It grows."

Anne scrunched up her nose. "Grows?"

"Yes."

"Then what is it *most* of the time?" Tess asked with a touch of exasperation.

"A pillow."

Stunned, Tess and Anne glanced at each other and then burst out into laughter.

Leah stood before them, her hands on hips. "If you are going to laugh, I won't go on."

"We can't help it—" Tess protested.

"Please go on!" Anne begged. "But the image is so odd. You are telling me that men have sticks that are really pillows and these are in their breeches. How do they sit? And why is it all such a mystery?"

"Would you want someone to know you had a pillow in your breeches?" Tess couldn't resist, before hooting in the most unladylike manner possible.

"It's *not* a pillow when it's important," Leah said. "And if you are going to mock me, I'm not going to tell you more."

She made as if to leave the room but Tess

quickly ran after her and pulled her back. She sat Leah on the couch between herself and Anne. "All right. Tell us all and I promise I won't make light of the matter."

Leah frowned. "I doubt if you can keep that promise. You'd laugh at anything, Tess Hamlin. But before I tell you any more, you must pledge to do a small favor for me."

"What is it?" Tess asked.

"Never mind. Just agree or else I'll leave."

"All right, I will do a favor for you," Tess said simply, "that is, if it is within my power."

"It is," Leah assured her. "Very well now." She motioned them closer. "The pillow becomes a stick when a man touches you. That's why men like to touch us so much and our mothers warn us not to let them. Or encourage us to, *if* the man is rich enough," she added bitterly.

"Then what happens?" Anne demanded. "Certainly there is more."

"Once a man has formed his stick, he sleeps with a woman and she has a baby," Leah finished in a no-nonsense tone.

Tess digested all of this in skeptical silence. Neil and Stella had separate rooms but she knew that from time to time they slept together. And now Stella was going to have a baby.

"Is that it, then?" Anne asked. "There must be more! What do they do with the stick?"

Leah pulled a face. "I'm not certain. But the maid said that sometimes, it is the most terrible thing that can happen to a woman. And other times, if it is with the *right* man, his touch will make you go warm with pleasure."

Go warm with pleasure. Yes, that was how Tess

would describe being kissed by the earl.

"And they like to touch your breasts," Leah informed them.

Anne sat back. "Breasts? With their sticks?"

"Don't you know anything?" Leah said. "With their hands."

"What?" Anne said, offended. "Do they just slap their hands on them?" She looked down at her own small breasts.

"Some do," Leah admitted, and then colored prettily at what she'd revealed. "Mother tells me there is no harm to it. She even says I must encourage them a bit." She glanced over at Tess.

But Tess's mind was working on other things. "It's called 'copulation.'"

"What is?" Leah asked.

"What happens when you sleep with a man," Tess answered. "My governess Minnie left a copybook. It's like a journal where she wrote down poems and snippets of thought. I didn't understand most of it at first. Some of it is very radical. She had ideas that Father and Neil would never have agreed with."

"What does it say about this copulation?" Anne asked.

Tess searched her memory for the words. *"Sweet, sweet copulation, I take my lover in to me."*

"That doesn't make any sense," Anne said.

"Poetry never does," Leah admitted candidly, "unless some man is writing about your smile."

"What does 'copulation' mean?" Anne demanded.

At that moment, the door to the library opened and four gentlemen started into the room, one of them Lord Ottley. The presence of the young women caught them up short. "Why, Miss Hamlin, I hope we aren't disturbing you and your friends?" His curiosity at their presence in his library was obvious.

Tess mumbled some excuse about needing a moment of solitude after the signora's brilliant performance as the three women slipped out the door.

"Do you think he overheard us?" Anne asked anxiously.

"I doubt it," Tess assured her.

They were about join the other guests when Leah reached out and pulled Tess back. "You go on, Anne. Tess and I will be with you in a few moments."

Anne shot Tess an uncertain look but had no choice other than to leave them alone. Leah drew her back a few steps from the salon doorway. "Take this," she said, pulling a small, folded piece of paper from inside the palm of her glove.

"What is it?" Tess said.

"Never mind what it is," Leah answered. "Just see that it is delivered for me. You promised me a favor if I told you what I know about men and this is what you must do in return. This note must be sent to Captain Draycutt as soon as possible. He has quarters in Taverick Lane. And whatever you do, *don't let anyone know I gave it to you.*"

Tess slipped the folded paper under her glove. "I'll have one of my footmen deliver it, but before I do, you must tell me what it says."

Leah's chin came up at an obstinate angle. "Better you don't know. But it must reach him tonight. Do you understand? Tonight."

"Leah, is this wise?"

The younger girl's gaze drifted to a point past Tess's shoulders for a long moment. "Lord Tiebauld's sister talked to my father this afternoon," she answered, her voice carefully devoid of expression. "They argued over the marriage settlements. Father wants more. She will give it to him. It is only a matter of time before I, too, shall be a bride."

"Oh, Leah," Tess said in a horrified whisper. She placed her hands on Leah's shoulders. "He is such a terrible man."

"Is he, Tess?" Her brown eyes met Tess's and Tess couldn't lie to her, not when she asked with such honest emotion.

"I've only heard whispers," she admitted.

"What do they say?"

Tess didn't know if it wouldn't be kinder to keep silent.

"Please," Leah asked. "My mother tells me nothing and when Lord Tiebauld's sister calls she is unusually quiet."

"It's nothing really, only something I overheard Stella say." She looked over her shoulder to be sure that no one was listening. "It is whispered that he is little more than a heathen."

A shiver went through Leah. "Are you superstitious, Tess?"

"I try not to be. Minnie always said superstition was a sign of ignorance."

"Then I shall not be superstitious. But I don't want to leave my fate up to my parents." She grasped Tess's hand. "Deliver the note for me. I beg you."

"It shall be done."

"Thank you." With those words, Leah turned and walked into the salon.

Tess thought her incredibly brave. The folded note felt strange in the palm of her hand. She would see it delivered immediately, but first she should go into the salon and make an appearance else Neil or Stella thought something was amiss.

She walked toward the salon but caught sight of Brenn talking to a group of three men just inside the doorway. She stopped and, for a moment, studied him.

His broad-shouldered figure stood out from the other men and she couldn't help but think him the most handsome of the group. She let her gaze drop. Each of the men wore satin dress breeches. The material left very little to the imagination and Tess noticed that Brenn's pillow—because it certainly must be a pillow right now and not a stick—was larger than the other men's.

Much larger.

The thought brought a frown to her forehead as she contemplated the possible significance of this discovery.

It was then she realized that the gentlemen had noticed her staring. They all turned to see where she was looking and ended up staring at Brenn's breeches.

There was a general discreet coughing and a row of hidden smiles.

Tess suddenly realized how brazen she must appear. She ducked her head and hurried off in the opposite direction.

* * *

Brenn didn't have any idea what Tess was up to, but he was certain something was working in that redheaded mind of hers.

"I say, Merton, was that Miss Hamlin ogling you gentlemen only a moment ago?" Deland Godwin asked. The man had played a hand in Brenn's introduction to Tess, but Brenn did not trust him. He'd read the paper Godwin published, and was not impressed.

The newly knighted scientist who had been boring Brenn and the others with a discussion of his latest theory answered Godwin with a slightly embarrassed laugh. "She must have been searching for Lord Merton. He's engaged to her, you know."

"Yes, I do know," Godwin said. "I am the one who arranged an introduction. I did not realize at the time that my simple request would turn out as fortuitous for you as it did, my lord. Please accept my congratulations." He held out his hand.

Brenn shook Godwin's hand. It was damp and lily-white. He forced a smile. "Yes, I am fortunate."

"I take it you and Hamlin have discussed the marriage settlements?" Godwin drawled. "The financial amounts?"

If Godwin thought Brenn was going to let him pry into his business, he was wrong. Brenn smiled, the expression pleasant but firm. "I am well pleased. Now, if you will excuse me?"

He turned on his heel and would have walked off except for Godwin's saying, "I wasn't finished speaking, my lord."

Brenn took the full measure of the man and

didn't like what he saw. He'd put up with enough pompous asses in the military. He didn't have to any longer.

"I am," he responded and left the group. If Deland Godwin was the only enemy he'd made here in London, he could sleep at night.

Some of the guests had left but the salon was crowded. He scanned the gathered assembly, searching for Tess's flaming hair. She wasn't to be found. Not with the group gathered around the Italian warbler and not around the refreshment table.

Brenn wandered out of the salon. A long hallway ran toward the main hall. It was quiet compared to the noise he'd just left. Then he heard her voice. It came from one of the side rooms.

He started walking toward it, but stopped when he heard her say, "Harve, you must deliver this and not a word to anyone. Not even Mr. Hamlin."

Brenn took a cautious step forward until he could see around the corner. Tess stood with her back to him. She was addressing a servant wearing the Hamlin livery.

The servant pushed a note back toward his mistress. "Miss Tess, I don't know."

"Please," she entreated, in a voice that would make a man do anything.

It worked on Harve. He held out his gloved hand. "I don't feel right about it."

"It's nothing terrible," she promised. "And remember, not a word to anyone. I can trust you on that, can't I, Harve?" She placed a gloved hand on his arm.

His Adam's apple bobbed up and down a moment before he whispered, "Yes, miss."

"Good," Tess cooed and then jolted Brenn by giving the footman Captain Draycutt's name and address.

Fearing discovery, and having heard enough, Brenn turned and quickly walked back to the salon before she caught him spying. A few minutes later, she, too, joined the rest of the company.

Brenn watched her move easily around the room. She was so poised. So beautiful. She would be an excellent countess.

And a faithless one.

Tess was with child and she was sending notes to Captain Draycutt. A bloody cavalry officer with a reputation for seduction.

You're a hypocrite, some inner voice told him. *Don't you have secrets?*

Yes, but could he put up with infidelity?

Could you give up your dreams? that wicked voice countered.

Abruptly, Brenn turned and went in search of Hamlin to take his leave. After paying his addresses to Lady Ottley, he left without saying one word to his betrothed. He wasn't feeling particularly charitable toward her.

Finding Draycutt wasn't difficult. The man habituated all the haunts patronized by cavalrymen. Brenn found him at his club, just as he'd finished rising from a losing game of cards.

"May I have a word with you?" Brenn said pleasantly.

"Of course," Draycutt answered. "Merton, no? Artilleryman. Congratulations. I hear you've landed Tess Hamlin."

It took all of Brenn's willpower not to wrap

his fingers around Draycutt's neck. Instead, he slapped his leather gloves against the palm of his other hand and motioned the cavalryman toward a private corner of the room. Once there, he said almost pleasantly, "Don't ever let Miss Hamlin's name cross your lips again."

Draycutt pulled back in surprise. "I beg your pardon?"

Brenn continued, his voice level, "Because if it does, I shall call you out."

The younger man stared at him. "You're serious?"

"Deadly serious."

Draycutt blew the air out between his cheeks. He signaled for a drink from a passing waiter. "I hear that in spite of your leg, you are a noted swordsman."

"And a crack shot, but then my leg has never interfered with my aim."

Draycutt took a sip of brandy before shrugging. "Very well. I shall never say her name again." He even smiled. "My word of honor."

For a second, Brenn was tempted to call the man a liar. His promise had been too easily given. Either that, or else he didn't give a tinker's damn about Tess or the baby.

To Brenn, a man who didn't honor his obligations was beneath contempt. He left the club without looking back.

Tess was his. He'd claimed her the moment he'd kissed her. He'd protect her and her reputation with his life. The day after the wedding, he'd whisk her off to Wales, away from the wagging tongues and the perfidious rabble known as the *ton*.

* * *

That night, Tess had trouble sleeping.

Brenn had left the Ottleys' without wishing her a good evening. What manner of man was he? Stiff, formal, correct—and then suddenly, without provocation, he'd kissed her as if he could drain her soul from her very body then charged off without a word to her. Of course, her staring at a line of men's private parts might have warned him off.

At last, tired of tossing and turning, she put her feet over the side of the bed and, with a heavy sigh, lit a candle. Her uneasy mind was not going to let her sleep.

She padded across the carpet to a leather-bound trunk filled with personal objects. Out of it, she pulled Minnie's copybook.

Sitting cross-legged on the floor, the candle beside her, Tess flipped through the pages. This journal was all she had of the woman who had been so influential in her thinking. The rest of Minnie's meager possessions had been sent to her brother in Surrey.

The first time Tess had read this journal, she'd been fourteen. Minnie had just passed on and there were tearstains on the pages where Tess had mourned. She'd not understood much of what she'd read, but she'd cherished the copybook.

Now Tess studied the poems Minnie had written. She ran her finger across the pages. She knew this handwriting as well as she knew her own.

Many of Minnie's poems were about love. And kisses. And loss.

This one spoke of something more:

Sweet, sweet copulation,
I take my lover in to me,
I shield him with my heart
Offering what is only mine to give.

The poem was dated 1794. For the first time, Tess read it with a woman's heart . . . and understood.

Minnie had had a lover. She'd been an attractive woman. Perhaps there had been a scandal, something that would drive a Surrey vicar's daughter to London and the penurious life of a governess. Minnie had always been firm in her admonitions to Tess to be a model of propriety.

"I wish you were here now to answer my questions." Tess sighed.

Then she blew out the candle and, rising, went back to bed. She tucked the book beneath her pillow. In a week's time, she would offer Brenn what was only hers to give. She thought of him not as the aloof man he'd been this evening but as the man she had laughed with on the Garlands' terrace. The man who had kissed her. The man she and Neil were deceiving.

She shivered and placed her hand upon the book. In this position she fell into a sound sleep to dream of sticks that turned into pillows and pots of gold that disappeared when she reached out to touch them.

The next week was the most hectic, unsettling one of Tess's life. It was as if her world had been turned upside down.

Stella was in her zenith. Everyone in their social circle vied for invitations to the wedding.

Consequently, Stella wanted only the best for the celebration and was willing to pay lavish amounts for it.

Neil behaved as if he had no money worries. When Tess confided her very firm feelings that he should talk to Stella about scaling back the guest list to the wedding breakfast, he'd laughed. He'd said that nothing was too good for his little sister.

"But what of money, Neil?" she'd pleaded.

"Tess, my fortune's intact. Stella and I are paying for this." He then gave her his back as he helped himself to a freshly opened bottle of port.

"Then why don't you reimburse me for the money you lost?"

Neil over-poured his glass. He wiped up the spilled wine before saying, "I can't do that, Tess. You know I can't."

"I don't understand why you don't. It's the only honorable thing to do." She crossed her arms. "I overheard you talking to him about the marriage settlements. I think we should either tell him the truth or you should share some of the money Father settled on you."

"Tess, that is such a radical idea. And it won't fly. It won't fly at all. Why, Christopher would never authorize such an expense. He is always going on about how extravagant Stella and I are." Neil gulped down his wine.

"Talk to him, Neil. Explain."

Her brother set the glass down with force. "I can't! Don't you understand? If Christopher finds out, I'll never gain control over my own fortune. Father's will was deucedly unfair. I can't live this way. Not much longer!" He stormed out of the room before Tess could say more.

That afternoon, Brenn brought over pen and ink drawings he'd done of Erwynn Keep. He had talent as an artist.

Tess studied the pictures of the stately brick mansion sitting on a crag of land that jutted out over a lake. Rosebushes and ivy covered its walls. Mountains framed the background.

She pointed to them. "Is this where the wizards kicked their feet?"

Brenn smiled at her reference to his story. "One of them. This is where the herb garden will be." He pointed to a location in back of the house. "Off the kitchen."

She nodded, not really interested in herbs at this moment. Since the Ottley musicale, Brenn had been cordial, but distant. She was tempted to ask him if anything was wrong but feared the answer.

She studied the drawings. "It looks peaceful."

"It is," he assured her. "The mountains keep the world at bay. No war, no hunger, no bloody death . . ." He murmured the last words, as if speaking to himself.

"I thought soldiers lived for war," she said.

"Only those who have never seen it." He spoke without thought because the moment the words had left his lips, he acted as if he wished he could call them back. "Not *noble* of me, I know, but I've had my fill," he explained curtly and started to roll up the drawings, handling them as if they were the most precious objects on earth.

Tess stopped him. "Wait. Tell me about the weathervane." She pointed to the cupola on the roof of the house and its fanciful dragon weathervane. "I've never seen one quite like it before."

"No, and you won't. I designed it." A frown appeared on his forehead. He cleared his throat. "I, uh, had a fit of whimsy. It isn't crafted yet and I may not use it."

She looked at the coiling body of the dragon. The fire coming from his mouth pointed in the direction of the wind. "I like it."

"You do?"

She nodded. "I enjoy whimsy."

For the first time in days, he smiled at her. His grin was slightly lopsided. She liked it.

"Well, I'll have Cedric Pughe fashion it then." He began re-rolling the drawings.

"Who is Cedric Pughe?"

"The blacksmith. There's a village within a mile of the house. About twenty families live there. Their livelihood depends upon the earl of Merton."

Tess sensed that something was bothering him, but she didn't feel comfortable prying. "I'll be able to hire help then for the house, although I'm sure you already have some servants on retainer."

"Retainer?" He said the word as if he'd never heard of such a concept.

"Yes. Certainly you have servants who have been with the family?"

Brenn went still. "Well, no. My uncle was rather . . . eccentric."

At that moment, Neil came in and dragged Brenn off to have a drink at his club. Tess watched them go. Twenty families. And she would be the lady of the manor. She had never considered that role before. She knew very little about country life.

Then, the Monday evening before Tess's wedding, Leah pulled her aside. They were at a small soirée featuring country dances. The crowd was young, and the atmosphere lighthearted.

Brenn stood to one side discussing farming methods with their host. Such a discussion would usually have caused Tess to roll her eyes with boredom. Now, she wondered how to encourage him to discuss such things with her. She even turned down offers to dance, hoping to capture his attention. If Brenn noticed she was available, he gave no indication.

Leah swept up behind Tess and linked an arm in hers. "It's like churning butter," she whispered in Tess's ear.

"What is?"

"Copulation." She purred the last syllable of the word. "Oh, Tess, I'm in love and it is the most wondrous thing."

"With Tiebauld—?" Rumor said her engagement to the Scot lord was almost finalized, although that hadn't stopped Leah from contacting Tess twice more with messages for Captain Draycutt.

"To the devil with Tiebauld! I won't marry him, Tess. No matter what anyone says. I can't! My heart belongs to another."

"Draycutt?" This was even more alarming information. "Leah, he's a ne'er-do-well. Everyone knows he doesn't have a feather to fly with. Besides, you've just met him—"

"You don't know him. Not like I do!" She

drew Tess closer. "I've given my heart. I've given him *everything*."

"Oh, Leah." The words came out almost as a prayer for protection. "Be careful. Please, be careful."

Leah gave her a swift hug. "How far we've come! Only last week, we were bitter enemies."

"Not enemies. Rivals."

"Oh, Tess, love is *sweet, sweet*," she said, repeating the lines of the poem. "I feel invincible. As long as I love, nothing can harm me." She danced off before Tess could ask more. She *should* have asked more.

In spite of the fact that Leah was playing a destructive game, Tess envied her. Leah *knew*.

Suddenly, the hairs along Tess's neck tingled. She turned. Brenn watched her. Boldly, she stared back. His lips lifted into a rueful smile. His gaze lowered and she felt it against her breasts as surely as if he touched her with his hand.

For a moment, she lost her breath. Her nipples tightened and she could swear that he knew his effect upon her.

Then the moment was broken when the duke of Westley's son, a lad two years her junior, asked her to dance. She had no choice but to agree. When she glanced back at Brenn, he was engaged in conversation with their host again.

Stella opened the bedroom door. It was the night before Tess's wedding.

"Not sleeping, are you?" Stella asked. She was still wearing the dress and jewelry she'd worn for the dinner she'd hosted for the wedding party earlier that evening.

Tess sat up in bed, so full of anxiety she was happy to see anyone, even Stella. "No."

Stella carried a candle to the bedside. "No one ever sleeps the night before her wedding." She sat on the edge of the bed. "Neil has been encouraging me for days to have a little talk with you . . . but—" She shrugged. "Silly me, I put it off."

"Talk about what?" Tess asked cautiously.

"About the wedding bed."

Tess pulled the covers up to her neck. "Oh."

"Well, I suppose no one has told you?" Stella hinted.

"I've heard things." She paused. "Stella, do you love Neil?"

Stella's eyes blinked wide open at the suggestion. "What sort of question is that?"

"An honest one." She thought back to the sparkle in Leah's eyes. "Do you love him?" she reiterated.

"We get along passably well."

"Did you love him when you married him?"

Stella stood. "What is all this about? Why are you asking these questions?"

"I want to know."

"Well, you'd be wiser to concentrate on your obligations and stop talking nonsense. Tomorrow night, I've prepared our best guest room for the two of you."

"What is wrong with this room?"

"This is the room of your childhood. Besides, the other room is further down the hall and you won't disturb anyone if there are problems."

"Problems?"

Stella smiled complacently. "Don't worry, Tess dear. I realize how difficult this might be for a woman as proud as yourself. A couple of glasses of wine should dull the pain. Drink heavily."

Leah hadn't mentioned anything about pain . . . but then, she was in love. Tess felt her stomach tie up in a knot of foreboding.

"When the time comes for you to share your husband's bed," Stella was saying, "do as he tells you. Don't fight. It never helps to fight."

"Why would I fight?"

"Fear." Stella seemed to enjoy saying the word. "But if you behave—something that has never been your strong suit—then the *ordeal* will be over before you realize it." She walked to the door.

"Ordeal? Stella, what are you talking about?"

"Good night, Tess," her spiteful sister-in-law whispered, and left the room without looking back.

Tess stared at the ceiling. Obviously, copulation wasn't pleasant for everyone. Only for those like Minnie and Leah who were in love.

It was a long time before she fell asleep.

Chapter Six

Brenn had never been so nervous as he was on his wedding day.

Waiting at the front of the church, with Bishop Walters on one side of him and Sir Charles on the other, he was conscious that all eyes watched his every move. And why not? The bride was late.

Guests were packed into the pews. Everyone of importance attended this wedding. In fact, no less a personage than the Prince Regent himself, fondly known as Prinny, sat in the second row.

Brenn watched Prinny's expression change from one of supreme boredom to surprised interest as people started checking fob watches. The minute hand moved slowly toward half past the hour.

Where was Tess?

Sir Charles leaned close. "Your bride may have bolted."

"Not Tess." Even as he said the words, Brenn prayed they were true. Last night, for the price of a guinea, Harve, the Hamlin footman, had conveyed the information that Tess had sent two more messages to Draycutt over the past week. Draycutt had been wise enough not to answer them.

Brenn had sought out the footman after meeting Deland Godwin in his club. The publisher had whispered in his ear that all might not be as it should be with Tess.

"I'm passing on that tidbit for your own good," Godwin had told him with sanctimonious sincerity.

Brenn had been tempted to ignore him. Who in his right mind would trust a journalist? But he also feared Godwin might have found out about Tess's baby. Tess had seemed unusually preoccupied over the last few days, as if something weighed heavily on her mind. The thought of her pining for her cavalry officer made him almost dizzy with jealousy. Not to mention the public humiliation she might be handing him. What if Godwin printed what he suspected?

And yet, running away seemed out of character for her . . . So did having an illicit affair.

Fears, hopes, and dreams for their future together sparred with self-doubt. He wished now he had honestly confessed how desperately he needed her money.

Or had she already found out and that was why she was missing?

Sir Charles's voice brought him back to the present. "She isn't coming, Merton. We can't keep standing here—"

"She'll be here."

At that moment, there was a stir at the door of the church. Heads turned. Watches checked. Eyebrows raised. And Brenn released his breath.

Tess had arrived.

The wedding began without further delay. The first person up the aisle was Stella. Sophisticated, elegant, so obviously pleased that she was the center of attention, she took her time walking to her place in the first pew.

Then came Anne Burnett. Tess had chosen the sweet, unassuming girl to be her single attendant. She wore a dress of gold and sea-foam-green muslin. Spring flowers peeked out from the curls of her hair.

A murmur from the guests drew his attention to the back of the church. He turned to see Tess standing there, escorted by her brother.

Dressed in lavender satin trimmed in lace, she had never looked more stunning. His doubts evaporated.

From a hidden alcove, Lady Ottley's Italian soprano began singing a lilting aria of love blessed. Tess glided up the aisle. Her dressed shimmered with her every movement. The noonday sun coming in through the church's antique stained-glass windows played on the fiery highlights of her hair.

Brenn felt his chest swell with pride.

And then she was beside him. Her brother placed her gloved hand on Brenn's arm and stepped back.

She was trembling. Brenn tried to give her a reassuring smile but she wouldn't raise her gaze to meet his. He moved his arm so that he could clasp her hand. Her fingers were stiff and awkward.

Emerald pins held her hair in place and a necklace of blood-red ruby flowers chained together by emerald leaves circled her neck. They reminded Brenn of how much she was bringing to the marriage and how little he had to offer.

The moonstone wedding ring in his pocket dimmed in comparison to the precious gems she already wore.

He should stop the ceremony. Tell the truth. That there was no castle at Erwynn Keep except in his imagination.

But he wouldn't do that.

He wanted her. The future would take care of itself. Right now there was only this moment.

Bishop Walters began the ceremony. He'd earlier told Brenn that he had baptized Tess when she was a wee babe. Listening to their vows were men and women of wealth and means, the very ruling class of England . . . and they accepted Brenn as one of them because of his title and his association with this woman.

Brenn repeated his vows to "comfort her, honor, and keep her in sickness and in health" but then quietly broke tradition. Lacing her fingers with his, he said in a voice low enough for the two of them alone, "You will never regret this marriage."

Her lashes swept up and for the first time she looked at him. Her clear blue eyes were a mirror of her soul—but instead of appreciation, acknowledgment, or even that most feminine of all emotions, love, he read panic.

For one insane moment, he had the impression that she was ready to cry off, that she wished to turn on her heel and run for the door of the church.

He tightened his hold on her hand. She gulped for breath.

Bishop Walters frowned. "Is it possible for us to continue with this service?" he asked pointedly in an undervoice.

Tess nodded. The bishop began saying her vows. She repeated them in a faint, solemn voice.

Listening to her, Brenn couldn't help wondering sourly if she thought of Draycutt. He'd make her forget that rogue if he had to lock her in the bedroom and make passionate love to her every hour of the day . . . an idea that didn't sound at all distasteful. No, not at all—

"My lord?" the bishop's voice interrupted Brenn's thoughts. "Do you have the ring?"

"The ring?" Brenn repeated blankly.

"It's time for the ring," the clergyman whispered with a touch of exasperation.

"Yes, the ring," Brenn answered. He pulled the moonstone from his pocket.

Tess removed her gloves. Her hands were like blocks of ice.

He slipped the moonstone on her finger. It wouldn't go beyond her knuckle. He pressed harder, fighting off a sick sense of dread. He'd designed this ring himself. He'd had it sized especially for her. Paid the jeweler extra to rush its fabrication. It had to fit.

"Don't force it," Bishop Walters warned through a frozen smile. "Sometimes this happens when the bride is very nervous. Her fingers have swollen."

"Oh," Tess said, embarrassed. She closed her fist so that she could keep the ring in place. Tears welled in her eyes and she gave him an uncertain smile. "It's lovely."

Brenn covered her hand with his warm one, fighting off a sense that this marriage was going to be a disaster. Together, they would build a life for themselves. "Together," he repeated.

Tess gave a small start. The tears vanished as if by magic. "Yes, *together*," she echoed. Her smile was like a ray of light on an overclouded day.

Brenn couldn't help but return her smile, his doubts evaporating even as the bishop's voice filled the corners of the church. "I pronounce they are man and wife."

The deed was done.

Brenn placed Tess's hand on his arm and turned to face the congregation. He walked down the aisle, proud of the woman by his side. Faces he hardly recognized beamed approving smiles at them. Tess's brother seemed inordinately pleased. Stella was sobbing softly for effect, huge tears rolling down her cheeks from remarkably clear eyes.

They paused at the door to sign the register as man and wife. Then Brenn escorted her out of the church. The day was fresh and sunny with a fair breeze. Lazy clouds drifted across a blue sky. The perfect day for a wedding.

A shiny green barouche with brass trimmings and a high-stepping set of matched grays waited for them at the front step. Brenn had hired the conveyance to drive them back to Hamlin's house where the wedding breakfast would be held. Surrounding it was a group of idlers and gawkers, members of the populace who wanted to see the fancy people or catch a glimpse of Prinny. The Hamlin footmen attempted to wave them away.

"We want to see the bride!" one impudent voice shouted out. The demand was quickly echoed by the others.

"Come," Brenn said to Tess. "Let's give them what they want. Let them see the most beautiful bride in the world."

Tess colored prettily. She waved to the crowd and they "ah'ed" their approval.

"Kiss her!" a chimney sweep's lad shouted. He'd pushed his way to the front. A footman tried to push him back, but the lad ducked and repeated his demand.

Brenn didn't know what was considered proper—behind him, Stella complained about the "dirty rabble outside"—but a kiss sounded like an excellent idea.

The last time he'd kissed her, he'd been demanding, wanting to know the truth of his suspicions. Now, under the blue sky and in front of the world, he approached this kiss with reverence. This was his wife. His helpmate. The one for whom he had forsaken all others.

As his lips came down on hers, her lips parted and then sweetly fit against his.

Kissing Tess could be habit-forming. The world around them faded and there was only this delicious woman in his arms.

The crowd roaring with approval brought him back to his senses. He broke off the kiss. Her face was red but her eyes sparkled with laughter. He didn't think she'd ever looked more beautiful.

He helped Tess into the carriage and with a

snap of the whip, the coachman drove them on their way. Children ran at its wheels while the adults shouted good wishes.

Tess leaned out the window and waved until they'd gone around the corner. She sat back on the velvet seat, her color still high.

"Look," she said proudly and held up her left hand for him to admire. The moonstone ring was in its proper place. "I was so nervous," she admitted. Then she looked away before adding softly, "I still am."

"I am too."

Her eyes flashed up to him. "You?"

He nodded.

She pressed her lips together, her gaze dropping as if she didn't know what to do with the information. "The ring is lovely."

"It's a moonstone." He could have added that it was the only thing of value besides his dreams that he owned.

She turned her hand this way and that to catch the gem's pearly light.

He said, "It's a dull stone when compared to emeralds and rubies, but in India it is considered sacred." The words came out a touch bitter. He was all too aware of how little he had to offer her. And she was bringing so much into the marriage.

She self-consciously touched the rubies around her throat. "Together," she whispered.

"What?"

"You said it in the ceremony. You said, 'Together.' That word is a motto of sorts in my family."

"I didn't know."

She smiled. "Then perhaps it is an omen." Her expression turned pensive. "Perhaps this was meant to be."

Brenn reached for her hand. "I purchased the stone from an old beggar man. He promised me good fortune if I paid his price." He traced the swirl of gold around the stone. "The stone reminds me of the night we first met. The moon was full."

Her lips curved into a shy smile. "It was. A full, silver moon." She paused. "Did you pay his price?"

"What? Oh. No. You haggle. It's expected."

"Even when something is sacred?" she asked softly.

He gave her a sharp look. His wife was beautiful, but he hadn't really thought her insightful. He ran his thumb back and forth across the back of her hand. "The moonstone is also said to arouse the passion of lovers."

"Really?" Her voice had gone breathless. Her cheeks turned bright pink, a maidenly blush that made him think of taking her to bed.

Suddenly, Draycutt and the baby no longer mattered. He wanted this woman. Passionately.

He eased his arm around her shoulders and pulled her close. "I know your secret, Tess."

She jerked away. "My secret?" she repeated, horrified.

Brenn took her hand again. "It doesn't matter. All I ask is that you be a good wife to me. That you honor the vows we made this day."

A small frown formed between her eyebrows. "*You know* and you married me anyway?"

Feeling noble, Brenn nodded.

But her reaction was not what he had anticipated. The color drained from her face. "Who
else knows?"

He wasn't going to tell her about Godwin. "No
one."

Even then, the information did not relax her.
He didn't get a chance to say more because at
that moment they drew up at the Hamlins' front
door. Almost before the wheels had stopped
turning, his bride opened the door and jumped
down to the ground. She hurried back to the
coach following them, waiting impatiently for
her brother to climb down.

Puzzled, Brenn watched brother and sister
have a hurried consultation. Hamlin hadn't been
interested in what she had to say, until she apparently repeated herself. He then quickly hurried her inside.

"What the devil?" Brenn asked himself, and
then realized he'd been left behind by the rest of
the wedding party. He followed the celebrating
guests at his leisure, mulling over his wife's state
of panic.

Guests were arriving from all directions. They
swept Brenn inside the door on a tide of good
wishes. Inside, glasses of champagne were
poured and downed with only the briefest of ceremonies. The *haut ton*, the elite of London, was
a group of people who knew only excess. They
now celebrated Brenn's wedding with bottle after bottle of the finest vintage. Nor did they notice when Brenn set his glass aside.

He wasn't a heavy drinker. There had been a
time, when he'd first seen battle, that he had
turned to the bottle, but he had quickly learned

there was no solace to be found there. He preferred a more prudent and sober course now.

Suddenly, Hamlin was at Brenn's elbow. His manner was one of supreme agitation. He pushed him toward the relative privacy of his study. "How did you find out?"

Brenn shook his head. He wasn't going to admit to eavesdropping on the servants. "It doesn't matter. I've taken her to wife."

"But it matters to me! Who else knows?"

"No one, and no one ever will," Brenn promised. "After all, what good would it serve me? It is between Tess and me."

Hamlin stared into his face as if searching for an ulterior motive. At last, he eased his guarded stance. "You have relieved me of a terrible burden. You're a good man, Merton." A group of gentlemen spied them in the doorway and called Hamlin's name.

He turned to them. "Gentlemen, let us drink to the good health of my new brother-in-law!"

Such a suggestion didn't need to be seconded.

They toasted the wedding soberly at first, their enthusiasm building with each subsequent toast. Hamlin, of course, egged on his fellow drinkers.

There wasn't a man there that didn't claim to envy Brenn. He'd married the prize, the most sought-after heiress of the Season, the beautiful princess. However, when they started toasting Tess's fingernails, Brenn decided the time had come to leave. He wandered away, going from room to room searching for his bride and meeting relatives.

Suddenly Tess appeared by his side. She held an empty wineglass and her expressive eyes brimmed with happiness.

"Uncle Isaac!" she cried, throwing her arms around the old man's neck in a gesture of genuine affection.

"My favorite niece," Uncle Isaac responded and started talking about the day he'd first held her in his arms when she was a tiny babe but Tess interrupted him.

"This is my wonderful, wonderful husband," she declared, linking her arm in Brenn's. "You'll excuse us, won't you, dear uncle?" She didn't wait for an answer but skillfully guided Brenn away.

"He is so long-winded," she whispered.

Brenn took the empty glass from her and handed it to a servant. "Do you drink much?" he asked in a less than casual voice.

"Oh . . . no, not often." She swallowed. "I have had a glass or two to relax me a bit. For tonight."

Tonight. Yes, he wanted her relaxed for tonight. Desire raced through his veins.

Then, in a voice that made him feel like Sir Galahad and Saint George the Dragon Slayer combined, she said, "I can't tell you what your acceptance of the situation means to me. You have saved my family."

He pulled her aside to a small corner of the hallway where they could have some measure of privacy. "Tess, I want to always protect you."

She smiled, her eyes shiny. Reaching out, she smoothed his shoulder with the palm of her hand. A wifely gesture.

Brenn took that same hand and pressed a kiss in the palm before promising, "I shall claim the baby as my own. You need never fear on that account."

The smile froze on her face. "The what?"

He looked over his shoulder both ways to prevent anyone from overhearing. "Your baby," he whispered. "I accept it."

"*My* baby?" she squeaked out. She looked around as if searching for someone and then turned back to Brenn. "You think I'm having a baby?" She started to draw her hand away but he held it fast.

"Isn't that the secret you've been hiding? I overheard the maids talking. That's how I knew."

"You think that's my secret?" she repeated blankly.

"Well, isn't it?"

Tess blinked and then seemed come to her senses and said, "Yes! Yes, that's it!" She took a worried step away from him and then muttered, "I need a glass of wine. Oh, my Lord, I need a glass of wine."

She grabbed a glass off the tray of a passing footman and to Brenn's surprise downed it.

He took her by the arms. "Are you all right?"

She smiled up at him. "I'm fine." She held her empty glass out to be filled to the brim by a passing servant carrying champagne. She raised her glass.

Brenn intercepted the glass before it met her lips, lifting it right out of her fingers. "Tess, is it wise to drink this much?"

"I daresay, not. It's just that—oh, Brenn, oh Brenn." She paused and then said half to herself, "The moonstone is beautiful and everything will be fine. Just fine. I must find my brother; you'll excuse me?"

"Wait, I'll go with you," he said, setting the glass on a hallway table. When he came back around, she was gone.

He would have gone in search of her, but Uncle Isaac caught up with him and proceeded to hold forth, reminiscing about Tess's father. Brenn listened with half an ear, expecting the old codger to confide that drunkenness ran in the family. On the other side of the hall, he saw Neil Hamlin chirp his way merrily from one room to another, a glass of wine in each hand.

Finally Stella had the butler announce that breakfast was served. In actuality the wedding breakfast was a full, heavy meal of ham, leg of lamb, and a good side of sirloin. Rounding out the meal were fish courses, soup, Turkish figs, and lemon ices.

And to Brenn's chagrin, a new wine was served with each course. It took all of his ingenuity to save his wife, now seated by his side, from drinking herself under the table. She completely ignored him, keeping her back to him as if pretending that if she didn't see him, he wasn't there.

What the devil had come over her?

After her third glass of wine, he waved the wine steward away—only to watch her attempt to drink from a neighbor's glass. He ended up draining one glass when she wasn't looking and then boldly knocked over another.

No one noticed his antics. They were all too busy doing the same thing! The whole affair was in danger of turning into a drunken orgy. Prinny was burbling in his champagne glass, the hairstyles and ostrich feathers of usually dignified women were listing at odd angles, and even the discreet Anne Burnett giggled with unusual brightness.

Worse, Hamlin kept leaning across his sister and drunkenly carrying on about what a "rum fellow" Brenn was.

"But you must treat her right," Hamlin repeated over and over. "She's worth more than diamonds."

After nearly two hours Brenn had had enough. When Uncle Isaac rose to propose another bloody toast, Brenn "accidentally" knocked Tess's elbow as she lifted her glass, spilling her wine on her lovely dress. Her soft cry of dismay alerted Stella, who seemed to be the only person besides Brenn left sober. She smoothly announced that it was time the ladies left the table to freshen up for the dancing scheduled to follow dinner.

Brenn sat back, exhausted. His brother-in-law was busy overindulging in port with the other male guests but Brenn didn't care. His one thought was of Tess. It was half past three and already a long day.

"Not much longer, eh?" Deland Godwin moved to take Tess's vacant seat.

"Longer for what?" Brenn asked curtly.

"Until you claim the prize." He winked as he said those words.

"I don't understand your meaning," Brenn said stonily, his coldness a warning. He had little patience left.

Godwin pursed his fat lips. "So many of us have watched Tess tease and promise over the years." He lifted his brandy glass. "We are just wondering if she is going to be worth the ride."

Brenn acted on instinct. He would not have his wife's name bandied about by the likes of Godwin. He grabbed the man by his starched neckcloth. The brandy glass tumbled out of Godwin's hand onto the white linen tablecloth while his face turned a shade of beet-red.

"You listen, and you listen well," Brenn said in a silky voice. "I will not have you or any man speculate about my lady wife. Do I make myself clear?"

The room had gone quiet. Godwin made a choking sound but Brenn didn't release his hold. He might have been overreacting but Tess was his and he would let no man denigrate her.

The silence was suddenly broken by the sound of Prinny laughing. "Great God, it is about time someone grabbed Godwin by the throat." He stood. "Merton, I salute you!"

A chorus of "Aye's!" supported his declaration. The other men stood and raised their glasses to Brenn. *Anything for another drink*, Brenn thought, completely jaded.

He released his hold on Godwin who fell back into the chair, his legs too weak to support him. He reached for his neck. "You have made an enemy, Merton," he croaked out.

"I can sleep with that fact," Brenn answered. "I've offended better men than you."

Hot color flooded Godwin's face, causing Hamlin and the others to drunkenly laugh out loud. Godwin stared at them with burning eyes, but the revelers showed no fear.

He staggered to his feet. "I will make you pay, Merton." With those words, he turned, pushing the man standing next to him aside, and stormed out of the room.

"Very good, Merton," Hamlin said happily. "I've been waiting for that man to receive his comeuppance for years. You did it handily." He hiccuped on the last word.

The hiccup reminded Brenn that he had another concern. Tess. "Shouldn't we be joining the ladies?"

"Oh, yes, yes!" Hamlin said, and motioned everyone toward the door.

Outside the dining room the house was more crowded than ever. Apparently, a good number of guests who had not been invited to the breakfast had now arrived for the dancing. Brenn made his way through their company, searching for Tess. The dancing started, only adding to the confusion. The noise rose as guests spoke louder to be heard above the music.

Every few feet or so, he was frustrated in his quest by people stopping him and wishing him well. *Where the devil was Tess?*

At last he caught sight of his wife's red hair in what Hamlin called the Garden Room. Here the music wasn't so loud and groups had gathered to converse. He breathed a sigh of relief, until he realized she was still wearing her wedding dress. She gestured to whomever she spoke with an empty wineglass.

Brenn shook his head and started toward her but stopped in mid-stride when the gentleman Tess was talking to raised his head. He found himself looking into the laughing eyes of Captain Draycutt.

At that moment, someone laid a hand on his

arm. Brenn turned, still stunned by the blasted man's presence at his wedding party, and found himself staring at Stella.

She smiled up at him. "I want you to meet my Aunt Sally. Auntie, this is my new brother-in-law, Brenn Owen, earl of Merton."

Ancient Aunt Sally held out a shaking hand. "A pleasure, my lord." But Brenn didn't take it.

Instead, he demanded, "What is that rake Draycutt doing here?"

Stella blinked at his vehemence. "Tess invited him. I know he is a bit—" She hesitated, as if not knowing the right word.

"Unsavory?" Brenn supplied for her.

"Well, um, he is very amusing."

As if to punctuate her words, Tess laughed at something Draycutt said to her.

Brenn couldn't ever recall her laughing at anything he'd ever said, at least not in the way she was over Draycutt's words. And then Draycutt lifted a hand and brushed a stray strand of Tess's hair back from her face.

It was a small gesture, almost offhand . . . and it sent anger roaring through Brenn.

He charged forward.

Tess must have sensed him coming. Weaving slightly, she turned and greeted him. "Brenn, have you met Captain Draycutt?"

That stopped him dead in his tracks. He couldn't believe his wife would dare to introduce him to her lover.

He glared at Draycutt who straightened and took a cautious step back. "Her name hasn't crossed my lips," Draycutt assured him.

Brenn could have cheerfully murdered the man on the spot.

Suddenly, he'd had enough of ceremonies, drunken relatives, nosy gossips, and cavalry officers. He wanted Tess to understand that she belonged to him now. She was his. And no one poached on his territory.

Acting with the swift decisiveness of a man long accustomed to command, he took his wife's wrist and started for the door.

He'd moved so quickly that she didn't have time to dig in her heels until they were out in the hallway. "Where are you taking me?" she demanded.

"To bed," he replied.

Chapter Seven

Tess attempted to shake away his hand. "You're mad!"

Brenn agreed with her. He was feeling very insane at the moment, insanely *jealous*. He would not be cuckolded at his own wedding.

When her declaration didn't stop him, she pretended to walk at his side. "We can't leave yet," she said with touch of desperation. "The dancing has started. Everyone expects us to be here. Brenn, please, it's too early."

He came to an abrupt halt, his hand gripping her wrist. "Madame, for what I have in mind, there is no set time of the day *as you well know*."

She sputtered an unintelligible response but he had already started his relentless march to the stairs. She grabbed ahold of a chair to keep from following him. He pulled her along with the chair until she let go of it.

By now, the wedding guests were starting to notice something peculiar was going on. They moved to line the hall, drawn out of curiosity. Stella motioned for a maid to pick up the chair.

Hamlin stood by the front stairs talking to his cronies. As Brenn approached, he hailed him, his eyes bleary from drinking. "Claiming her now, Merton?"

"Aye."

"Jolly good."

"Neil!" Tess cried in exasperation. "Stop him!"

"Oh, no, can't do that, sister dear. Never get in the way of a man on his wedding night."

"It's not night!"

Hamlin laughed. "Night is when your husband says it is. Better work on subservience, Tess!"

His words were met with guffaws and shouts of "Good luck" from the guests. Even some of the women laughed. Tess practically spat with outrage.

She grabbed the newel post with her free hand, refusing to climb the stairs with him. Brenn resolved the issue by sweeping her up into his arms so quickly she lost her hold. He proceeded up the steps, his limp barely bothering him.

The guests started to follow, laughing and calling out. But halfway up, he turned to them. "I'll handle this alone," he said in a voice no one dared disobey. The beribboned and befeathered guests suddenly sobered . . . until he climbed a few more steps. Then they continued their good-natured, bawdy comments.

At the top step, he set Tess on her feet. "Which room?"

With an unsteady weave, she hiccuped. "I'm not going to tell you."

"Then I'll choose one." He took her arm.

"Have you no shame?" She tried to twist out

of his grip. "Everyone is downstairs. They'll know what you are doing."

"Everyone expects *us* to do it sooner or later."

At that moment, a maid exited one of the bedrooms. "Which is my lady's chamber?" he barked.

Taken aback by his gruff manner, the maid dropped the linen towels she carried and pointed to the door she had just exited. "This is the one we set up for the wedding night, my lord."

"Good. We'll use it now." He stomped past her, dragging a reluctant Tess behind him.

"May, tell Willa I need her—" Tess started.

But Brenn interrupted. "She needs *no one*." He slammed the door in the maid's face and released his wife.

Tess scrambled back from him, rubbing her wrist. Her eyes sparkled with rage. "I have never been so humiliated in all my life!"

"You are foxed," he said, shrugging off his finely tailored jacket.

"I am not a fox," she shot back crossly. "Here now, stop getting undressed. We are going back down. We've got to dance."

She started for the door but he blocked her way with his arm. "I don't dance, Tess. And I'm tired of smiling and pretending. The time has come for you to set aside any thoughts of Draycutt."

That stopped her cold. Her brows came together in confusion. "Draycutt? What does he have to do with any of this?" She raised her hand to unsuccessfully stifle another hiccup.

He lowered his arm and jerked his shirt hem out from his breeches. "My hat is off to you, madame. You could earn a living as an actress with the skills you have demonstrated. But it is too late. I know your secret, Tess."

She frowned boozily and sat down on the bed with a small bounce. "No, you *don't* know the secret. If you did, you would be furious with me."

Brenn walked over to the side of the bed. "More furious than I am that Draycutt is your lover?"

She looked up at him, her expression one of misery. "Yes." She slurred the word from a high pitch to a low.

"Ah, Tess." She looked so miserable he couldn't help but feel a bit sorry for her.

He sat down on the bed beside her, intending to reassure her. She smelled of champagne and woman . . . and his anger was replaced by a very real desire for her. "You are my responsibility now. I am your protector."

"I don't deserve that."

"You deserve it and so much more." Then he did what he'd ached to do from the first moment he'd seen her. He pulled one of the emerald-tipped pins from her hair, and then another, and another. Her hair tumbled down past her shoulders, just as he had dreamed it would.

He ran her hair through his fingers. "Your hair is like fire," he whispered reverently. She was his. This beautiful, vibrant woman was his.

She watched him, her expression guarded.

He tipped up her chin. "You have no need to fear me, Tess. Your secret will remain between us. For better or worse," he reminded her gently.

He then brought his lips down on top of hers, catching her in mid-hiccup.

He couldn't help but laugh. This was a far cry from how he had imagined his wedding night.

She pulled back with surprise and then ever so slowly, her lips curved into a smile. "You are the most amazing man."

"And you are an amazing woman," he answered. Damn, but he wanted her and, at this moment, he didn't care how many men she'd slept with or for what reasons.

He kissed her again, only this time with more passion. Her lips parted. An invitation. She started to hiccup again but it turned into a low moan.

Brenn bent her back toward the bed, deepening the kiss. He stroked her with his tongue. Once, twice, and then felt her tentative response. She copied his motions.

Oh, sweet, sweet Tess!

He was already hard for her. He pressed her back against the mattress, taking the kiss deeper, letting it become more demanding.

Following the line of her body, he cupped her breast, feeling her nipple hard and tight against his palm. With his other hand, he began searching for the laces of her dress.

Tess broke the kiss. "I'm dizzy." Her eyes were heavy-lidded and drowsy from kissing.

"The world will right in a moment," he promised and kissed the sensitive skin where her collarbone met her neck.

She gasped. He soothed the spot with his tongue and then kissed lower.

Her hand came up to stop him but he nudged

it aside. At last his searching fingers found the laces and he began untying them.

Tess started to rise. "I don't know—"

He interrupted her with a kiss and gently forced her back down, resting his leg over hers. He kissed her again and again and again while edging her dress down over one shoulder.

"Dear God, I want you," he whispered against her skin.

She shivered, goose bumps forming along her arm. "Please, Brenn, I'm afraid. I'm not certain what to do."

"Trust me."

"But your stick? Will that hurt? It can, can't it?"

"Stick?" Brenn frowned. He rose up on one elbow. "Someone has used a stick on you?"

"No!" she said swiftly. "Not yet but—"

"I've never taken a stick to a woman and I never will. If Draycutt treated you in that manner, I will put a hole in his black heart."

"Why do you keep talking about Draycutt?" she demanded, struggling to sit up.

He gently pushed her back down. "Because I detest men like him who use a woman without teaching her about pleasure." Now was his chance to distinguish himself from the selfish cavalry officer. Before this night was out, he'd make his wife forget she'd ever known Draycutt.

"Marriage is union, Tess. It's two people working together to build a life together. Do you understand?"

She nodded her head in solemn silence and then used her palm to rub her nose. It was an unaffected gesture, a far cry from the sophisticated woman who'd reigned over Society, and it softened his heart. Sober, she was a rare beauty; tipsy, she was adorable.

"I can make you very happy, Tess. I *want* to make you happy."

She nodded, her expression as trusting as a child's.

He rolled on his stomach. "Ah, Tess . . . we are going to wake up each morning in each other's arms. We're going to build a life for ourselves and raise a family. I can picture them now. We'll have little girls with your clear blue eyes and red-gold hair. The boys will probably look like me. Well," he conceded, "they might have your eyes instead of my dark Welsh ones . . . but they'll be tall and bold and strong. I can even hear their laughter. Someday they will be grown and leave to seek their fortune but they'll always come back because Erwynn Keep will be home. It will be a haven, a place of peace."

"I don't want you to worry about that wee babe you are carrying. Of course, if it is a lad, he won't be able to inherit the title, but that will be the only difference between him and his brothers."

He wasn't accustomed to such long speech and was almost afraid to look at her. Instead, he waited, expecting her to express gratitude. When she didn't speak, he reiterated, "Do you understand what I'm saying, Tess? I accept this child as my own."

Still she didn't respond. He was pouring his soul out to her, agreeing to concessions beyond the rationale of any sane man . . . and she had no comment?

Brenn shoved aside his flash of irritation and

rolled over to face her. "Tess, have you *nothing* to say?"

Her hair covered her face. But her mouth was open and from it came a soft snore.

Brenn stared at her, unable to believe that she had passed out on him. He shook her. "Tess?"

She didn't wake.

She wouldn't wake, either. He knew the drowsiness of too much champagne. She'd sleep like the dead for hours.

What a bloody fool he was! He sat up, wondering if his dreams for Erwynn Keep were worth shackling himself to her. He had no desire to be one more man ruined by the antics of a fickle woman.

And if she thought she'd escape consummating this marriage, she was mistaken.

Tess woke in stages. There was light. At first she thought it was morning, and then realized it was the flame of four candles burning brightly on the table in the corner of the room. Squinting, she looked away.

Her mouth felt like she'd been chewing her shoes. She wanted a drink of clear, fresh water. Anything to erase the taste.

What time was it?

She began to remember. The wedding. *Her* wedding. She'd been nervous. They'd married and then come to the house. She had visions of herself sipping champagne. She'd never had a head for wine. No wonder she felt so miserable.

She was still wearing her dress . . . but the laces were undone. It was night. She knew that now—

"Good evening," Brenn's low, gravelly voice came from across the room.

She turned her head. He sat in the circle of light dressed in his fancy dress breeches and white lawn shirt. He'd removed his neckcloth.

Tess looked down and was almost embar-rassed to see that he wore no shoes. The sight of his toes though the white silk stockings was disturbingly intimate. She'd never been in the presence of a man so casually dressed.

With almost meticulous precision, he refilled his brandy glass from the bottle on the table beside him.

She hesitated a moment before asking, "Did we marry or did I dream it?"

"We married." He drained the brandy glass.

"Oh." Tess watched him warily. She wanted to ask if the marriage had already been consummated. However, taking a quick mental inventory of things, she decided they had not. Certainly she didn't feel any differently than she had earlier, other than having a wine headache.

He answered the question for her. "We haven't done it yet."

She didn't need to ask to know what "it" he meant. And they still had yet to do "it."

Anxiety caused her stomach to knot. "Excuse me," she murmured, fearing she would be sick. Practically crawling off the bed, she stood. The world spun and then settled. She hurried to disappear behind the small privacy screen modestly set up in the corner of the room. Over the top of it hung a nightdress of the finest white lawn and lace. She was to have worn it to her marriage bed.

It was embarrassing to see to her needs with him sitting on the other side of the screen, listen-

ing to her every move. She used tooth powder
and then wiped her mouth with a fresh linen
towel. Her hair was a tangled mess. She used her
fingers to comb it since her silver brush set was
on the vanity across the room.

Tess pinched her cheeks for color. She was
sure she looked as haggard as she felt. Worse,
she'd muddled everything and probably made a
fool of herself. If only she could remember!

At last, she could postpone facing him no
longer. She stepped out from behind the screen.

He still sat in the chair where she'd left him.
His features in the flickering light could have
been carved from stone. She squared her shoulders bravely, wondering what to say.

No sound marred the silence between them,
not even the ticking of a clock.

She was the first to break the silence. "The
wedding party is over." The words sounded stupid.

"It ended several hours ago," he replied without emotion.

"The guests left early?"

"It's two or three hours before dawn. The
party lasted a good long while."

She didn't remember when she'd fallen asleep,
but it had still been daylight. "Have you been
sitting in that chair for hours?" Her voice
squeaked on the last word, betraying her fear.
She cleared her throat and continued, "No wonder you don't seem pleased with me. You could
have used one of the other bedrooms—"

"Tess, come here."

The quiet command almost made her heart
stop. She eyed the brandy decanter. It appeared

half-empty. Neil grew boisterous when he drank. Obviously, Brenn didn't. In fact, he seemed almost deadly calm.

"Come here, Tess," he repeated in a deep, silky voice.

She took a first hesitant step in his direction. Her feet felt like iron weights. One step. Two steps.

She stopped.

He set the brandy snifter on the table. "Not there, Tess. I want you here, in front of me."

She licked suddenly dry lips. He seemed a far cry from the man she'd married.

"Here, Tess." He pointed to a space on the carpet before him.

She moved forward. He leaned back in the chair, watching her, waiting. She stopped where he'd indicated. Her toes were no less than six inches from the edge of his chair, his legs on either side of her.

"Undress."

She gasped, not certain she'd heard him correctly.

"Undress," he repeated calmly and then added with a slight twist to his lips, "Tess."

"You can't be serious?"

"I am."

"But . . . I—I . . ." She paused, at a loss for words.

"I'm your husband. Undress."

She considered defying him. Considered stamping her foot in childish rebellion or bolting from the room.

And yet, there was something deliciously sinful in his command, too.

Nor was she one to cry coward.

She tossed back her hair. Then, her movements unsteady, she reached behind her and started to finish unlacing her dress. He didn't offer to help. Instead, he watched, his face expressionless.

Her fingers shook as she drew out the last of the laces. The bodice of her dress loosened.

Their gazes met.

She knew what he wanted.

Almost defiantly, she shrugged and let the bodice slip down over her breasts. He didn't move. She drew a deep breath, and the lavender satin fell to the floor, pooling around her feet.

No man had ever seen her thus. A part of her felt shame, while another part, deep inside, experienced a surge of pride. She was a beautiful woman. Poems had been written about her. Men had scurried to do her bidding. Women were jealous.

But Brenn Owen, the earl of Merton, *her husband*, didn't blink.

Worse, her nipples tightened and pressed against the thin material of her chemise. She wore little else but her petticoat and stockings. Her face burned with the heat of a blush, but she refused to cover herself. It was a war of wills now, a test.

And she was winning.

Where before there had been blankness in his eyes, there was now hunger—and the watchful wariness of a wolf at bay.

Conscious that he followed her every move, she brought her hair forward to cover her breasts. She then slid her hand under the strap of her low-cut chemise and pushed down first one, then the other. It took courage—and a sense that her time had come, that she was now on a path that every woman had to travel to pass from girlhood to womanhood—for her to pull the material down to her waist. Behind the curtain of her hair, her nipples tightened so hard they hurt.

Brenn did not move. "Go on."

"You want to see me completely humbled, don't you?" she snapped waspishly. It wasn't right that her body shivered with anticipation, with excitement, and he could be so calm.

Almost angrily, she pulled at the ribbon tapes fastening her petticoat to her chemise. First one, then another and another until she'd come to the last. With a dramatic gesture she untied it and her petticoat and chemise dropped to the floor over her dress.

She stood before him naked, save for her white silk hose tied at the knee.

She felt ridiculous. It took all her courage to not cover the most intimate part of her body with her hands, to not run and hide.

The silence between them was unbearable. It taunted both of them.

She lifted her chin, refusing to be a coward. "Are you happy now?" she goaded him. "Have you looked your fill? Here." She flipped her hair back, exposing her breasts. "Now you see all of me."

His answer was a low, deep growl. He shot up out of the chair, the movement so swift, she didn't have time to react. His arms wrapped around her. The buttons and seams of his clothes scratched her skin. His lips covered hers.

She had thought his previous kisses passionate but this one was carnal, devouring, hungry . . . and she kissed him back, unsure of what else to do in the sensual onslaught. He tasted of brandy and yet there was the hint of something, something unique to him alone. She opened herself to him, wanting more.

His tongue teased hers. With a happy sigh, she received the intimacy. His hands cupped her buttocks and pressed her to him even as he lifted her and began walking toward the bed. He broke the kiss.

She shook her head in an attempt to clear her befuddled senses. But before she could, he laid her on the bed. The cotton bedclothes felt smooth against her skin. And then he covered one nipple with his mouth.

"Brenn!" The word burst out of her in surprise. The heat of his mouth against her flesh made her skin tingle all the way to the woman's part of her.

Who could have imagined this? He licked and gently pulled and she felt his touch down in the deepest, most secret parts. Yet when he started to draw back, she buried her fingers in his thick, dark hair and brought him back.

His rough, masculine hands traced the line of her body, down the curve of her waist, over her hipbone. Her legs had turned to jelly. Instinctively, she parted them and felt his hand boldly cover her. His fingers caressed her intimately.

Dear Lord, she would die from the pleasure of it! She gasped. She moaned. She feared it; she craved it. His lips sought her mouth again, smothering the small sounds she was making.

This is too much! she thought. She shouldn't—he must stop—she never wanted him to stop!

Her body trembled beneath his touch. She hugged him close, afraid that she would fly straight up through to the ceiling if she ever let go of him.

Him. The world had ceased to exist and there was only him. If he had been a demon prince, he could have possessed her soul at that moment and she would have done naught to stop him.

Abruptly, he slipped from her arms. She cried out and opened her eyes.

"Shhh," he whispered and pulled his shirt over his head. He threw it aside. The planes of his hard chest were beautiful in the candlelight. He was her prince. Beautiful, bold, masculine.

His fingers unbuttoned his breeches and then he pushed them down and Tess had her first glimpse of a fully aroused male. She quickly averted her eyes, embarrassed. Her hands moved to modestly cover her body.

He captured her hands and held them down by either side of her head. "Tess, look at me."

Her body still humming from the impact of his touch, she could not refuse anything he said. She opened her eyes.

His expression fierce, he commanded softly, "Don't hide yourself from me. I am your husband. I and no other."

Wide-eyed, Tess nodded.

"Touch me." He said the command in the barest whisper.

Almost mesmerized, she reached out to brush her hand against what was most surely the stick Leah had described. But it didn't look like any stick. It didn't feel like one either. It was hard, and yet softer than baby's skin.

When she started to pull away, he captured her hand and brought it back. He curled her fingers around him. "Hold me, Tess."

She couldn't let go.

He leaned forward and kissed her breast, her collarbone, the corner of her mouth. Nuzzling her ear, he said, "Stroke me."

She didn't know what he wanted! She felt a second's panic and then his hand covered hers. He began teaching her a movement, a way he liked to be touched.

"That's the way, Tess. Gentle, lass. But firm." His voice hummed through her body, only heightening her awareness.

When he felt she had it right, his hand left hers. It slid down her stomach. His fingers touched her and began moving to the same rhythm.

At his first touch, a quiver of sensation shot through Tess and then it continued, wave after wave. She caught herself pressing against his hand, her body arching up to meet him.

His lips came down on her breast and she thought she would die from ecstasy. Nothing had prepared her for this. *Sweet, sweet copulation!*

"Tess." Her name on his lips sounded like a benediction.

He moved, rising up over her. She let go of him. He shifted and settled himself between her legs. They fit very well together that way, her breasts against his chest, her legs around his hips. It wasn't uncomfortable at all.

But she missed his touch. Deep inside of her, she ached for something she didn't know. But he knew. He knew.

He kissed the lobe of her ear. "After tonight, Tess, there will be no others. Just the two of us." He kissed the sensitive skin under her jawline. His lips nibbled their way down the curve of her neck.

She whispered his name.

He smiled against her skin. She could feel the movement. She laughed at the feel of his rough whiskers.

"Tickle?" he asked.

"Yes."

His tongue circled her nipple. She laughed, instinctively drawing her legs up. The action positioned him even more intimately against her. He rubbed her with his length.

Passion burned in her blood. She began moving, stroking herself against his body.

"Ah, Tess," he whispered. "You are so perfect."

"Yes, perfect," she repeated dreamily. This was all so wondrously perfect.

"I can't wait to be in you." His voice sound hoarse with a pent-up need that mirrored her own.

Sweet, sweet copulation. I take my lover in to me.

His hands slipped under her hips. He lifted her up. In one smooth, fluid movement, he plunged himself deep into her body!

Pain stabbed her.

But worse was the shock. She cried out, digging her heels into the mattress, trying to move away from him.

His weight came down on her, pinning her in place, his eyes bright with surprise. "You're a virgin."

Chapter Eight

"Of course," Tess answered. "What had you expected?"

"I thought you and Draycutt had—" Brenn broke off.

"You thought Captain Draycutt and I had what?" she prodded. He was still inside her but the pain had passed. It almost felt . . . comfortable. Her heartbeat steadied.

Brenn opened his mouth. Words didn't come out. A lock of his hair had fallen over one eye. He pushed it back, shifting his weight, and she could feel the movement of his body deep within her.

It tickled; it did more than tickle. She moved, uncertain.

His reaction was instantaneous. "Tess, hold still," he warned, "or we shall be over before we've begun."

"We aren't finished yet?" She panicked. She wanted to toss him over the side of the bed and run.

He must have sensed the direction of her thoughts. Capturing her hands, he pressed her back on the bed. "No, we aren't finished. The best is yet to come."

She didn't know if she believed him. Her muscles around him involuntarily tightened.

His breath caught in his throat. "Ah, Tess, you are incredible." He began moving, slowly, carefully. "Relax. Open to me, love," he commanded softly.

Love.

There was that word.

He kissed the crook of her neck, the curve of her ear, whispering words of love to her. She felt herself respond. The hot, swirling sensations he'd inspired began to build again inside her.

He pushed himself in deeper.

His voice rumbled through her, telling her how beautiful she was, how much he wanted her, how he had to have her. She could hear her own heart beating in her ears and the next time he thrust, she raised her hips to meet him.

"You're mine," he whispered. "Mine."

Yes, his, her body echoed. *His, his, his.* His to do as he wished; his to guide and direct; his to command. She responded to him. Only to him.

He repeated her name over and over as if just as lost in the heady whirl of passion as herself. Tess clung to him, having no choice but to trust that he knew what she needed, what she wanted, better than herself.

The movements of his body became more demanding. And inside her she felt a peak building. She strained to reach it, feeling him push her higher and higher and higher—

Suddenly she was there! A shooting star. Chinese fireworks. A blaze of light.

He buried himself deep within her, crying out as if caught by surprise. His seed spilled into her; her senses were full of him.

And then she felt herself fall to the earth.

He collapsed, drained. His heart pounded against her chest. "It was good. So damn good," he whispered to himself.

Yes, it had been good.

He rolled onto his back, carrying her with him in his arms. He kissed her forehead. "My proud—" He kissed her eyes. "—beautiful—" He kissed her nose. "—Tess." He kissed her lips. "I couldn't move if I wanted to." He sank into the feather mattress, snuggling her to him. Closing his eyes, his cupped her breast, his thumb flicking the nipple that was still red and extended from his lovemaking.

Her head resting on his chest, Tess listened to his heart slowly steadying. Her own was beating at a much faster pace. Her reactions to him had stunned her. How could she have lost control that way? It was as if he had practiced sorcery over her.

Especially as reality reared its ugly head—

"You thought I'd given myself to someone else?" Her voice reverberated in the stillness of the room.

He opened one eye. "I—um." He paused.

It was confession enough. In one graceful movement, she slipped out of his arms and rolled off the bed.

He came up on one hand. "Tess?"

She hurried to the sanctuary of the privacy screen. Practically ripping the nightdress down from where it hung, she threw it over her head.

He'd thought she was the sort of woman who would have consorted with lovers? But instead of confronting him directly, she announced, "That was *nothing* like churning butter!"

"Butter?"

Tess popped her head out the side of the privacy screen. He sat on the bed, just as she'd left him. "I don't ever want to do anything like that again," she vowed, but he didn't respond.

Instead, he stared at the sheets.

Curiosity drew Tess closer. What was the matter? He shifted to look at her and the candlelight fell on the stain covering the sheets. *Blood.*

"I'm an idiot," he confessed. He swung his feet over the edge of the bed. Naked, he looked even more powerful than he did clothed. His eyes burned with self-loathing. "I didn't hurt you, did I?"

His concern embarrassed her. She retreated to the shelter of the privacy screen.

Sinking her hands into the lukewarm water, she heard him moving on the other side. He was dressing.

A second later, he spoke from a point just at the edge of the screen. "Tess, I know you weren't expecting what happened between us."

That was an understatement!

"You caught me off guard, too," he continued. "I didn't expect a virgin."

"Why not?" The sharp words hung in the air. It was hard for her to comprehend his logic. "I would never have disgraced my family by—" She searched for the right word. "By doing what you have accused me of."

"Tess—wait, I can't talk to you with this

screen in the way." Before she realized his intent, he stepped behind the screen with her. He wore only his breeches. He'd put them on hastily and not all the buttons were fastened. A light smattering of hair covered his chest and she remembered how its silky texture felt against her bare skin.

His presence in the small space was intimidating. Especially after their having been so intimate. Even now, her treacherous body responded to him. She took a step back, confused by the sudden welling of desire.

He misinterpreted her action. "I did hurt you." Another step forward. "I didn't mean to." He reached for her.

She ducked under his arm, escaping to the bedroom. She hid unsettling emotions behind her anger. "I'm fine, but insulted. What made you think I was the sort of woman who would have—" Words failed her. She waved angrily at the bed.

He raked his hair with an impatient hand. "I'm sorry," he said. "I thought you and Draycutt—" He hesitated, frowning.

"You thought Captain Draycutt and I had done *that*? Is that why you made a spectacle of me earlier?"

Brenn looked heavenward, praying for a deliverance that wasn't going to come.

"Well?" she prodded impatiently.

"I know you arranged to have notes delivered to him. I thought he was your lover."

Her eyes almost crossed with disbelief, and guilt. She should never have helped Leah.

Brenn continued. "What was I supposed to believe? This marriage came about in such a hasty manner. I couldn't understand why you would marry me out of all the men in London. I suspected you were carrying Draycutt's child and wanted to pass the child off as mine—"

Completely shocked, she held up a hand and cut him off. *"You thought I was carrying Captain Draycutt's child as well as being his lover?"*

"Tess, you have to make love to have a child," he said matter-of-factly.

"I know that," she bristled. "But why did you think I was pregnant?"

"I overheard the servants talking about you," he mumbled.

"Me?" How could that be? "No, they were talking about Stella."

"Stella?"

She crossed her arms. "Well, why not? She and Neil have been married for a number of years. But Stella wants to keep her condition a secret. Once it becomes common knowledge she will have to stop going out in Society. Stella loves gambling. The thought of giving up her pleasure for a long confinement upsets her."

"Stella! Of course. Tess, I am sorry. But what about the notes I caught you passing to Captain Draycutt?"

"I didn't write them. Leah Carrollton asked me to deliver them to him for her." She frowned uncomfortably before confessing, "She has been seeing him in ways she shouldn't. But I understand why. I would feel the same if I were to be betrothed to Lord Tiebauld."

"Tiebauld?" Brenn's lips curled in disgust. "I've heard of him."

"Everyone has. He is dangerously mad, but his sister is desperate to find a wife for him so that he can breed an heir and carry on the family line. But what woman wants a madman for a husband? Even a rich man? And what would her child be like?" Tess shook her head. "I didn't have the heart to say no when Leah asked me. Plus, I owed her a favor."

"A favor for what?"

Suddenly, Tess realized her mistake. She wasn't about to confess to Brenn what she and Leah had discussed. How stupid and naïve she'd been to believe that pillow and stick nonsense.

"Never mind." She moved toward the bed.

He followed. "Tess, when I said earlier that I knew about your secret, you and your brother both made much over it. Your brother even thanked me. If Draycutt wasn't what you were talking about, what was?"

The guilt at how she and Neil were deceiving him returned. Her husband was no one's fool and would doubly resent being tricked. He would be completely within his rights to publicly denounce her. She'd be ruined. All doors would be closed to her. No one would want her.

And yet telling him the truth was the only honorable thing to do.

The dilemma made her head spin.

"You misunderstood us," she said stiffly.

"No, I didn't."

She frowned at him. He'd never rest until he discovered the truth, but lies didn't come easily for her. Not like they did for Neil.

A secret, a secret, a secret!

"My age. Neil feared you wouldn't want me if you knew how old I was."

"How old are you?"

"Twenty-three, but people think I am twenty-two. I spent a year in mourning when my father died and Neil thought it best if we pretended I was a year younger."

He stared at her as if doubting her sanity. "What difference would it make?"

"Well, none perhaps to you. But there are men who only want a young wife. Now, if you'll excuse me, I'm very tired." She lifted the covers, climbed into bed, and pulled the blankets over her head. Tomorrow. She would consider the matter in the morning when maybe her mind wouldn't be such a jumble.

He slid into bed beside her and curved his large, solid body around hers. "I don't care how old you are." He spoke right next to her ear. His hand rested on her waist, easing its way up to her breast.

"Some would," she mumbled, closing her eyes and pretending to fall sleep. "You do not know what it is like." She protected her breast from his marauding hand.

His deep voice held a hint of mischief as he said, "The marriage hasn't been fully consummated—not until we've made love several times." He snuggled himself against her. His pillow wasn't a pillow anymore.

Oh, dear, Tess thought, feeling her traitorous body start to melt against him. "I'm tired."

"Ah, Tess. I've apologized. I just want to make it right for you without surprising you like I did the first time." His voice turned husky. "It gets better the more we practice." He moved against her.

Her blood started to heat. He nibbled her ear. Her toes curled.

"Don't be in such a pet," he whispered. "My only sin is in wondering why a woman such as yourself would want to marry a Welshman of a little-known earldom. Is that wrong?"

His question was like being doused with a bucket of cold water. *What was she doing?*

Guilt, honor, and pride drove her out of the bed. She couldn't let him make love to her. She couldn't confess the truth. "I think I will sleep in the chair."

"Tess," he protested.

"You thought I had made love to another man," she said, desperately hiding behind the first excuse she could think of.

He sat up, his dark eyebrows coming together in anger. "Tess, as I told you, none of it made sense to me. Why you, a beautiful, vibrant, wealthy woman, would chose me—a man with a limp," he said candidly. "You could have married any man in London in spite of that silly wager at Garland's party. If the circumstances were reversed, wouldn't you wonder?"

"I don't know."

"Of course you would. Everyone in the city is! Half of them think we are both madly in love with each other. The other half swear you're in some sort of trouble and are marrying to escape it."

She felt the color drain from her face.

"You are hiding something," he said. "If not a lover or a baby—then what?" He leaned forward. "Tess, if you are in some difficulty, tell me about it. We are husband and wife now. I meant the vows I took today. From this day forward, our fates are intertwined."

She wet her lips, pacing anxiously away from him. She couldn't tell him. She wanted to, but therein lay madness. No man could forgive learning his wife was penniless. Especially if she and her brother had deceived him. She sat down in the chair.

"Tess, why are you over there?"

"I think I'll spend the night here."

"What?" He stood, stark naked and completely oblivious to it. "Come to bed. I'm not going to attack you. I'm tired. You have worn me out. And not in the way I had anticipated."

She tucked her bare feet under the edge of her gown, crossing her arms. "I want to stay here."

Brenn studied her a moment. "I don't understand. You are a woman of contradictions. You kiss like the most hot-blooded of courtesans and yet you're a virgin. You insist on this marriage but show up late at the church—"

"That wasn't me, that was Stella. The baby makes her nauseous sometimes."

"Ummm hmmm," he said, unconvinced. "You grab my arm in front of Uncle Isaac, then drink yourself under the table to avoid me."

This time she didn't counter him.

He shook his head. "Is it all a game? Is there nothing real to you?"

"I'm not playing a game," she averred softly.

"Then why do I feel like I'm being teased?" He let his words sink in before continuing, "I want to build a life with you. I have dreams,

Tess, big dreams. But what we make of this marriage is going to depend on your meeting me halfway.''

She studied him a moment. Her confession was on the tip of her tongue . . . but her courage failed her. She turned her head and stared into the flickering flames of the candles.

He watched her, waiting.

Why was he so persistent? Why couldn't he leave her alone?

She faced him. ''What we did earlier—that is, in bed,'' she added, so there could be no mistake. ''It is supposed to be wonderful if you are in love.''

His expression grew guarded. ''That's what the poets tell us.''

''It's what Leah Carrollton says, too.'' She met his gaze. ''You had done it before, haven't you?''

''Make love? A time or two,'' he admitted dryly.

She wished he would cover himself. He was as bold as a buccaneer and twice as deadly to her peace of mind. ''Was it wonderful that time or two?''

''Why do I feel I am stepping onto very thin ice?'' When she didn't reply, he said, ''I found pleasure in it.''

''But was it *wonderful*?''

''As wonderful as can be expected,'' he snapped out. ''Tess, come to bed. We'll hash this out in the morning.''

She sat back in the chair, drawing her knees protectively in front of her. ''I think I will stay here.''

He glared at her. ''I'm tempted to argue with

you. To march over there, pick you up, and toss you onto the bed where you belong—"

His words challenged her. She was ready to deliver a scathing retort when he finished, "But I won't. Because it might be a battle I'd lose," he continued in answer to her unspoken question. "And I always like to win, Tess Owen. Always. So you can sleep in the chair if you wish."

He lay down then, finally covering his glorious body with the bedclothes. Giving her his back, he rolled over.

Tess sat vigilant in her chair, expecting him to jump up at any moment. Her muscles started to cramp, but she kept still—until she realized he had fallen asleep! Just like that.

She blew out the candles, but not without taking one long look at this man who was her husband. He looked so big in the bed. His broad shoulders seemed to take up almost a full three quarters of it.

In an instant, she could recall the feeling of his body joined with hers. A shiver of foreboding ran through her. "He wouldn't have wanted to hear the truth," she told herself. She could still hear the echo of his words: ". . . a beautiful, vibrant, *wealthy* woman . . ."

What was she going to do when he found out the truth?

But when she did fall asleep, it wasn't her fears that haunted her but the echo of Leah's voice whispering how wonderful it was to be in love.

The next morning, Tess woke to find herself in bed, the covers pulled up to her neck. She knew she hadn't gotten there herself. She rolled over, expecting to see Brenn grinning at her, but he wasn't there.

She listened, hearing no sound other than her own breathing. Slowly, she sat up and searched the room. She was alone.

But he had been here. The edge of a copper bathing tub could be seen from behind the screen and the air smelled of his shaving soap. He didn't use the perfumed bars so many men favored. Instead, his soap reminded her of warm cinnamon and other spices of the Indies.

A knock sounded on the door. At her call, her lady's maid, Willa, entered carrying a tray of chocolate and rolls. "Good morning, my lady," she said cheerily. She set the tray down on the table and crossed to open the curtains. "We've about got your things packed for the trip, but it is best you be up and not lazing about." Bright sunlight filled the room. "Just imagine, you are a countess now!"

Tess rose from the bed. "What time is it?"

"Half past nine. Lord Merton said he wants to be on the road well before noon." She stopped, her eyebrows coming up in surprise at the haphazard order of the blankets. "My, it looks like the two of you did a bit of wrestling last night."

Tess felt herself blush from her head to her toes. She hurried behind the screen, hiding her embarrassment behind her role of mistress. "I need a bath. See to fresh water, please."

"Yes, my lady." The maid left.

A heartbeat later, there was another knock. The door opened without her answering.

Tess stuck her head around the screen, fearing it was Brenn. She wasn't ready to see him just yet. To her relief, it was her brother. His eyes were bloodshot and his hair mussed. She wondered if he'd made it to his bed at all, or had he once again passed out from drink in the library?

He gave her a crooked smile. "Good morning, Tess."

"Neil."

"Sorry to disturb you but, ah, it is my duty, you know."

"What is your duty?"

He made a face. "To ensure the marriage has been consummated. Christopher will ask," he explained, referring to the man of business who had almost absolute control over their lives according to their father's will.

No, not enough control, Tess amended to herself. If Mr. Christopher had been the overseer of her inheritance, she would never have been forced to marry.

Neil threw back the sheets. "Ah, the marriage was consummated."

"Neil, this is so medieval," she protested in a faint voice.

"Medieval or not, it is how things are done," her brother said briskly. "I don't want Merton claiming the marriage was not legitimate when he discovers the truth about your fortune."

"Are you going to tell him this morning?"

Neil drew back, horrified by the thought. "Absolutely not. We don't want him to know until the very last possible moment. Besides, you need time for him to get to know you better. You don't want him to set you aside once he finds out he's been duped."

Duped. She hated the word.

"Oh, don't prune up," her brother said. "After a few weeks with you, he'll be so daffy in love, money won't matter."

Tess doubted Neil's optimism. "But the two of you are signing papers and Mr. Christopher will be here. Certainly Mr. Christopher will want to see that my financial affairs are in order? He'll know."

"He won't." Neil frowned. "I told him I've taken care of it. Tess, you must stop putting a dark cloud over everything. It will all work out—if your manner doesn't betray us."

"Please, tell him."

"If you want him told, you do it. Of course, don't come crying to me if he leaves you. Then everyone will know. You will be the laughing-stock of the *ton*. Will that please you?"

Tess could not imagine a worse fate. Her courage faltered. "What shall I do?"

Her brother smiled. "It's simple. You are the man's wife. Go with him to Wales. Please him. You know how to control men. Soon, he won't care about your fortune." He kissed her on the forehead before adding, "Besides, Merton isn't without resources of his own. Sir Charles said he owns a good portion of Wales. He's probably so wealthy your lack of funds won't matter."

Knowing what little she did of Brenn, and men, Tess didn't believe that statement for a moment. She also knew her brother didn't believe it either—but arguing would be fruitless.

Neil tilted her chin up. "You'd best get dressed. Merton wants to leave as soon as the papers are signed." A second later, he left the room.

Tess sat down in the chair, her legs feeling as if they'd turned to jelly. She took a sip of the chocolate. The sweetbitter taste calmed her frazzled nerves until she realized just how quickly her life was changing. In hours, she would be gone from London, her family, and her friends. Few people would think it the least bit sad. Neil and Stella were actually happy to see her go, relieved even.

The only person in the world who seemed to want her was an all-too-perceptive Welshman. And she was deceiving him.

Worse, there was something disturbing about a man who had the ability to slip past her carefully erected defenses. Something unsettling.

Brenn Owen was the one man who could break her. She sensed that on a deep, almost primitive level. He'd already thwarted her at every turn.

She could not let him closer.

Tess had not felt so alone since her father's death. This time when the tears threatened, she did not fight them. Minnie had always said that a good cry was balm for the soul.

But, Tess discovered, they couldn't cleanse a troubled spirit.

Outside the bedroom door, Brenn raised his hand, ready to knock. He'd met Hamlin in the hallway. His new brother-in-law had briskly informed him that he had inspected the wedding sheets. The marriage had been "well and truly consummated" and he would meet with Brenn in his study fifteen minutes from now to finalize the transfer of Tess's money over to her husband.

Brenn had been shocked at the man's callous attitude toward his sister. Inspecting the sheets! It was completely ridiculous—and just the sort of thing to bring out Tess's temper.

He'd rushed to Tess as quickly as he could, but now he paused. Through the thickness of the door, he heard crying. He leaned against it, listening intently.

It had to be Tess. His strong, independent Tess. She cried as if her heart was breaking.

Flattening his hand against the door, he wished she trusted him enough to let him comfort her. But she would not appreciate his presence and he knew without asking that she would deny that anything was wrong.

Perhaps he should have been more open with her last night. He could have confessed that the fine manor house of Erwynn Keep existed only in his mind, that it would take years of work before the estate matched the image he'd drawn on paper. That it was nothing but a shell of a house now, though he would restore it to its proper glory. But he feared giving her more reason to armor herself against him.

No, he would earn her trust . . . and maybe, someday, he would earn her love.

Love? The thought had come from nowhere, completely unbidden.

Brenn had grown up knowing love. His mother and father had been more than just man and wife; they had been lovers in the truest sense of the word. He'd realized the difference between them and other couples at an early age. He was a product of their love—and loved by each of them—but their first love was saved for each other.

Because she loved her husband, Lydia Owen had followed the army, a hard life for any woman, even an officer's wife. Because he loved his wife, Geoffrey Owen had renounced his birthright. And when Lydia had died of pneumonia, her husband had drank himself to ill-health and then embraced death.

The way his father had grieved after his mother's death had embarrassed Brenn. It had angered him and irritated him . . . and saddened him. Once again, he'd been left out.

When his father had died, Brenn had driven the corpse back to the small church in Portugal where his mother had been buried. There, he had ordered the priest to bury his father in the same grave as his mother.

Now, he stood silent outside his wife's door, listening to her tears and contemplating the sort of love that made a man follow a woman to the grave . . . and knew that he did not love Tess in that way.

It is supposed to be wonderful if you are in love. Her words of the night before reverberated in his brain—and gave him an idea: if Tess loved him, she would forgive his small deceit about Erwynn Keep. Love did that to women. Look at what hardships his mother had put up with over the years because she had loved his father.

Brenn backed away from the door, knowing he had stumbled upon a solution.

He would make Tess fall in love with him. Oh, perhaps it wouldn't be a love like his parents had . . . but then he and Tess didn't know each other very well. Certainly, she didn't trust him or else she wouldn't have spent a portion of the night in a chair. Or have told him that silly story about her age being a secret.

But he'd remedy that on the trip to Wales ... and then maybe, just maybe, she wouldn't cry anymore.

Chapter Nine

A few minutes later, Brenn *sat in* Hamlin's *study and* watched his new brother-in-law make himself a stiff drink with trembling hands. There wasn't much to admire in Neil Hamlin. He was soft— as were so many of the young men of wealth and privilege Brenn had met in London. Hard to believe Hamlin was related to Tess. She had far more fire and pride than her brother did.

"Perhaps you should try a glass of water," he suggested mildly.

"Can't. Devil of a headache. Cheers." Hamlin sucked the glass dry.

Brenn stretched out his leg. It was bothering him. He thought of Tess crying up in their room. He was anxious to leave. "When is Mr. Christopher arriving?"

As if on cue, a knock sounded on the paneled door. The butler announced, "Mr. Christopher."

Mr. Christopher, a short, balding man wearing gold wire spectacles, entered the room. For all his lack of physical stature, he was one of the most respected men of business in London. His presence reassured Brenn. Neil Hamlin might be a bit of a loose fish, but not when it came to money.

Without fanfare, Mr. Christopher quickly drew out the marriage contracts. "I believe everything is in order as we discussed, my lord," he said to Brenn.

Brenn reviewed the documents, aware that Christopher had pointedly ignored Hamlin. Hamlin seemed unaware of the snub.

Everything appeared to be as agreed to in the contracts—although no mention was made of an exact monetary accounting of the marriage settlements. Brenn tapped the document thoughtfully with his finger, debating whether or not to push the issue.

He decided to push.

"I notice there is no mention of the marriage settlements." He looked expectantly to Mr. Christopher.

Mr. Christopher met his gaze with a level one of his own. "Mr. Hamlin personally oversees his sister's affairs."

Brenn sensed that Mr. Christopher was discreetly telling him something. He turned. Hamlin still stood next to the liquor cabinet, one hand wrapped around the neck of a decanter as if holding it for support.

Realizing he must give an answer, Hamlin shrugged. "Let us finish the contracts and then I'll discuss Tess's affairs afterward. I'm willing to answer all of your questions."

"But shouldn't a monetary figure be stated in the contract?" Brenn asked.

Hamlin dismissed the question with a wave of his hand. "You receive it all. Of course, it's invested. Finish with Christopher and then we'll go over it."

Brenn glanced at Mr. Christopher but no opinion showed on the man's carefully schooled features. Looking down at the cramped writing covering the contract, Brenn decided his reservations were groundless. After all, it was common knowledge that Tess was an heiress.

Dipping the pen in ink, he scratched his name at the bottom of all four copies. Two were for himself, one for Hamlin, one for Mr. Christopher as the Hamlin family executor.

Hamlin wobbled forward and signed his name. Mr. Christopher served as witness. With the fastidiousness inherent to his business, Mr. Christopher then sanded the signatures and rolled the documents into scrolls. "Do you wish to take your copies of the document with you, my lord?"

"I'll take one. Have the other delivered to Rupert Goining on Beckon Road," Brenn said. "He's my man."

"Ah, I think well of Mr. Goining," Mr. Christopher said.

"He speaks highly of you also."

"I shall see it delivered to him. Now, if our business is concluded, I shall take my leave."

"Yes, yes," Hamlin quickly interjected. "You are free to go, Christopher. I'll be round to see you next Tuesday as usual."

"Yes, sir." Christopher paused by the door. "May I again offer my congratulations, Lord Merton? Your wife is a singularly lovely and gracious woman."

Obviously the man had never been on the

sharp end of Tess's tongue. Brenn smiled with genuine amusement. "Thank you, Mr. Christopher."

The accountant hesitated as if he had something else he wished to say.

"Yes?" Brenn prompted. The man was a financial genius. Brenn wanted to hear his opinions.

Mr. Christopher glanced at Hamlin. A small crease of disapproval appeared on his forehead, but when he shifted his gaze back to Brenn, his decision to leave well enough alone was plainly written on his face. "I wish you all the best, my lord." Mr. Christopher left the room.

Brenn had the premonition that Mr. Christopher had wanted to warn him about something. He stared at the door the accountant had just used.

"That man's a cold fish," Hamlin declared. "Drink to your health, Merton? And to a safe journey?"

Brenn rose and removed the glass from his brother-in-law's hand, setting it on the table. "I want to talk about the marriage settlements."

"Oh." Hamlin smiled at him.

Brenn smiled back, a small smile, one without amusement. "The settlements."

Hamlin walked around his desk. "Well." He "ahemed," and then reached into a drawer, pulling out a stack of papers. "I'm never certain how much it is at any one time. But it is considerable," he added quickly.

"Certainly you have a general idea of the figure?"

Hamlin shuddered as if such crass accounting

was beyond good taste. "I never keep that sort of thing in my head. Too dangerous."

Such a verdict didn't surprise Brenn. "Well, do you have it written down somewhere?" he persisted.

Hamlin clapped his hands together. "Yes, I do. It's all here." He slapped the stack of papers.

Brenn leaned across the desk, spreading the papers out to read. He frowned. "These are in Italian."

Hamlin nodded as if it were the most commonplace thing in the world. "I placed Tess's money in a very sound business."

"An *Italian* business?"

Hamlin sat back in the chair and smiled. "They should be worth quite a bit. And I'm sure you can now see why I don't have an exact accounting."

No, Brenn didn't. He squinted down at the top paper, attempting to decipher the minuscule writing. It all looked like gibberish. Nor was there any monetary value, in lira or pounds mentioned in the document. "Is all of her inheritance in these investments?"

"Yes."

Brenn wondered what to do. He needed money. His fortune-hunting trip had cost him more than he'd planned. Plus, he'd purchased farming equipment for Erwynn Keep. He had less than thirty pounds in his pocket at this moment.

Hamlin rose. "Wait, one more thing." He crossed over to a small leather chest sitting on a side table and carried it back over to the desk. "This is a wedding gift from Stella and myself."

Brenn opened the chest, and then smiled with relief.

"Three hundred pounds," Hamlin said proudly.

"This is so generous—"

"Think nothing of it." Hamlin poured himself another drink. "Tess means the world to me. I expect you to treat her right," he added seriously. "*Cherish* her, *love* her, *honor* her."

Brenn looked up into Hamlin's blue eyes that were so much like Tess's and struggled with a pang of conscience. "I will," he said solemnly, but he felt a fraud.

But Hamlin wasn't able to read minds. Instead of denouncing Brenn, he grinned. "Capital! Now, let's a have a drink to seal our pact." While Hamlin drank, Brenn wrote a note to Mr. Going instructing him to convert these investments to pounds sterling with all possible haste. Ironically, it was Harve, the footman, who answered his ring and set off to deliver the note and papers to his man of business.

Out in the grand foyer, the house was in an uproar. Huge trunks and hatboxes were piled everywhere. They had not been there when Brenn had entered Hamlin's study.

"What is this?" he asked, shifting the weight of the money chest from one arm to the other.

Hamlin snorted, a bit unsteady on his feet. "Tess's trunks." He turned to the butler. "Nestor, is there a problem? Why aren't these loaded?"

"The first coach has arrived, sir, but we are waiting for the luggage coach."

"The luggage coach?" Brenn frowned. He'd hired a coach to take them to Wales—at the tune of one shilling, six pence per mile—which sat outside, waiting. He'd not considered the need for a separate luggage coach.

Stella came down the stairs. "Neil! I am developing one of my headaches! I can't abide seeing the front hall in this state. When will the second coach appear?"

"I don't know, my dear," her husband answered cheerily. "Merton, when will the second coach toddle along?"

Before he could answer, Stella interrupted, "You have been drinking again." She released her breath in a huff. "Just once when there is something to be done, I wish you would stay sober enough to see it through."

Hamlin rocked back on his heels, apparently unperturbed to be upbraided by his wife in front of the servants. "How right you are, darling. I say, you won't mind if I take a bit of a nap, do you?" He didn't wait for her answer but started toward the stairs. "Good-bye and good luck to you, Merton. Give my sister my best."

He didn't even look back.

Stella turned on Brenn, the cold look in her eye anything but friendly.

"I didn't hire a second coach," he told her.

"Didn't hire one?" Stella repeated, as if he'd announced that he wanted to chop off his foot. Even the servants gaped in surprise.

"You *must* have a luggage coach," she declared. "How else is Tess going to take all her dresses with her?"

Now it was Brenn's turn to be shocked. "These are just dresses?"

"For this Season," Stella answered. "Her winter wardrobe and the household items are to be sent by wagon. You *did* commission that, didn't you?"

"I hadn't even considered it," he replied honestly. "What household items?"

"Tess's furniture, the things that belonged to her mother. I had to have the whole house redone when I married Neil. I shudder to remember what it looked like before my advent. I was going to throw the old furnishings out, but Tess wouldn't hear of it. She is very attached to all of it. It's been in storage. Neil was supposed to have discussed its removal with you."

"He never mentioned it."

Stella heaved a world-weary sigh of exasperation. "Well, you must arrange for its removal. Of course, the silverplate will travel with you."

"Silverplate? Yes, of course; it could probably come with us."

"The chest is over there."

Brenn looked in the direction that Stella nodded and found himself staring at a chest the size of a trunk. He raked a hand through his hair. How would it fit in the hired coach?

He couldn't let the silverplate travel unattended. There would be a danger of it disappearing. Plus, he did need household furnishings. The crofter's cottage he'd been living in had a small bed, a chair, and a table. Fine enough for a former soldier, but not the sort of style that a wealthy young wife would expect. "I can have her household goods shipped with the seed and farm tools I purchased. It should be leaving London in two weeks."

"Perfect!" Stella said. "Write down your instructions and Nestor will see they are carried out. I'm certain two wagons will be enough for Tess's goods."

"Two wagons—?"

"Meanwhile, you must make arrangements for a luggage coach."

"Can't we leave most of it here and have it go with the wagons? I am anxious to be on the road."

"You can't mean for Tess to walk around naked," she complained, and then gave a high, horsy trill of laughter. "Or perhaps you do!"

When she noticed that he wasn't laughing, she cleared her throat. "Actually, you don't need to worry about leaving before the luggage coach arrives. Willa can see to the arrangements."

"Willa?"

"Yes, Tess's maid. You couldn't have thought she'd travel without her maid?"

Brenn stared with amazement at the piles of luggage. "This is incredible."

"What's incredible?" Stella asked.

"I came to London with little more than my saddlebags. I now have one wife, two coaches, two wagons, a household of furniture, and a lady's maid. The whole situation is overwhelming."

Stella gave him a patronizing smile. "My dear man, did no one tell you that wives were expensive?"

At that moment, he heard a sound from the

staircase. He looked up . . . and his breath caught in his throat.

Tess stood there wearing a lovely peacock-blue dress and matching hat. The vivid blue brought out her coloring . . . but her eyes looked tired and there were signs of strain around her mouth.

"Good morning, Tess," he said.

She nodded and came down the stairs, her head high, her back straight. The nod was her only concession to his presence. "Is Neil here?"

Stella snorted. "He's gone off for a nap."

Tess's lips curved into a silent O. "I thought he would see us off."

Stella didn't answer, and Tess didn't appear to expect her to. She turned to the butler. "Aren't we ready to go?" she asked, pulling on her gloves. "Why is all of this still unpacked?"

"Because the luggage coach hasn't arrived," Brenn answered. Was she *trying* to ignore him? "Your maid will bring the luggage coach later."

Tess nodded as if not really hearing his explanation. She turned to the butler. "Nestor, take care of yourself, especially when you get the croup."

The man's eyes softened. "Yes, my lady. May I add, you make a lovely countess."

She smiled, brushed his arm lightly with her gloved hand, and murmured, "Thank you."

Slowly, she made her way around the room, wishing the servants farewell, speaking to each by name. They came from the other sections of the house as well: the cooks, the upstairs maids. Several cried quietly.

"She has her following," Stella observed sardonically. "But notice none of her friends among the *ton* are here."

Tess didn't even miss a beat. "That's because they weren't ever true friends, Stella. You'd be wise to remember that," she added.

Stella sniffed her disdain. "I thought at least mousy Miss Burnett would say her good-byes. Or that common Miss Carrollton whom you decided to take up with over the past week."

For a second, Tess's composure wavered. Brenn stepped to her side, placing his hand at her elbow. "It is time for us to leave." He turned his wife toward the door, adding in a low voice, "Don't give the cat the satisfaction."

In answer, Tess's chin came up at a defiant angle. "Farewell, Stella."

"Good-bye, Tess."

Brenn took his hat from Nestor, his other arm still carrying the money chest. "It may rain later," he observed.

She nodded, seeming to concentrate on the stairs she was walking down. Her bottom lip had a suspicious quiver.

He pulled his handkerchief from his pocket and offered it to her.

"I don't need it," she said tightly. "I shall be all right."

Brenn turned her to face him. "You are not alone. Not any longer. I'm here."

For the first time since she'd come downstairs, she looked at him, truly looked at him. She had not forgiven him for last night. He could feel her resistance in the tension of her body.

He lightly touched the bonnet ribbon beneath

her chin. "If you fall, I will pick you up. If you fear, I will protect you."

The independence deep-seated inside her reared in response. "I don't ask it of you."

"That's the way it is," he said simply. "To-gether."

She pulled back as if he'd said the wrong word.

"What's the matter?" he asked, alarmed.

"Nothing. It's nothing," she repeated and climbed into the coach.

The coach he'd hired was a drab, serviceable conveyance, especially when compared to the green brass-trimmed barouche that had carried them from the church the day before. He'd put his money into the horses, a set of bays driven by a postboy who claimed to know the roads between London and Wales. Brenn's own horse, Ace, the surly dark bay that he'd ridden to London, was tied to the back of the coach.

Inside, the coach was a cozy affair, especially since the silver chest had been set on the floor toward the far door. Approximately three feet high, its cherry-wood top was slightly higher than the seat.

Brenn took a moment to hide the money chest under the seat. Then Nestor claimed his attention with a question concerning the luggage wagon. By the time he'd returned, Tess had moved the silver chest so that it sat directly in the center of the small confines of the coach. She sat on one side, and apparently planned for him to sit on the other.

So, she thought she could erect a fence be-tween them. She was wrong, but he didn't say anything. Instead, he removed his beaver hat and placed it on top of the chest like a signal flag recognizing the barrier between them.

Tess appeared not to notice. She stared out the window, her chin in her hand.

He'd just closed the door when he heard someone call Tess's name. Anne Burnett and Leah Carrollton came running toward the coach with unladylike haste.

"Anne!" Tess lowered her window and stuck out her arm.

"Oh, Tess, I'm glad I made it in time!" Anne shouted, breathing heavily. "My aunt refused to let me go out but I slipped out the servants' entrance. I had to say good-bye to you. I ran into Leah on the street. She had to come too."

"You are both not alone, are you?"

"No," Leah assured her. "My maid is following us but she couldn't keep up."

"Oh, Anne, Leah," Tess said happily. The girls clasped hands.

"Be safe, Tess," Leah said.

"You too! Don't do anything foolish!"

Leah laughed. "There's no need to worry about me." She lowered her voice. "Was it what you expected?"

Tess shot a cautious look toward Brenn. "Different."

Brenn frowned, wondering what she referred to . . . and having a suspicion.

"And you, Anne," Tess said. "Send me a letter. I must know how you are."

"I will, I will! But what is the address?"

Tess looked to Brenn. "What is the address?"

He'd wondered when she was going to finally

acknowledge his existence—when she needed something! "Erwynn Keep, Gwynfa." He spelled the word for her.

She repeated the address to her friends.

"Are you ready to go, my lord?" the posting boy asked from the other side of the coach.

"Yes," Brenn said curtly.

Anne and Leah's eyes filled with tears. "May God go with you," Anne said.

"And may He watch over both of you," Tess replied, struggling with tears herself.

Brenn sat grumpily in his corner, feeling like a perfect dog for parting the three friends. Moments later, the posting boy shouted at the horses and they were off.

Tess leaned her head out the window and waved to her friends until they'd gone around a corner and were out of sight. She sat back in the seat. A sniffle escaped.

He pulled out his handkerchief a second time and offered it. She took it without comment.

He sat in silence, giving her time to compose herself. At last, she had a rein on her emotions. Other women would be boo-hooing all the way to Wales, but not Tess. She had bottom.

He thought about telling her that, too, but she spoke first. Without looking at him, she said, "I know we are married and you have the right to my bed. But I've been thinking, and I believe it best if we remain cordial and not do what we did again last night too often."

Brenn stared at her, uncertain that he'd heard her correctly.

She didn't elaborate further but pulled out a

book from a satchel the servants had loaded earlier and proceeded to start reading.

He frowned. "Wait a moment, Tess. I don't
feel cordial at all. Cordial is a damn cold emotion. You're my wife. And I expect you to be
such in every sense of the word."

"I don't admire swearing." She turned a page
of the book.

A flash of temper shot through him. He reined
it under control. Temper was not the way to woo
a woman. "You're right." Those words were
hard to say! "I admit I can on occasion be a bit,
um, salty. I will watch my language."

She continued reading her book.

He was apologizing and she had nothing to
say? What did she think he was? Some schoolboy
she had put in his place? "Tess, don't ignore
me."

She ignored him. Her finger ran down the
printed page. When she came to the bottom, she
flipped the page over and started again.

Her actions, even the prim tilt of her nose, in-
furiated him—until he thought of last night.
He'd been ham-handed. A sheepherder would
have shown more finesse. And now, he was re-
moving her from the only home she'd known.

But he couldn't undo the damage unless she
paid attention to him. Nor did he think her fit of
airs had to do with last night.

As the wheels of the coach turned, he brooded.
The brooding turned to plotting. The plotting to
action.

Brenn stretched out his bad leg, resting his calf
on top of the silver chest. His booted foot hung

in front of her book. She couldn't ignore him now.

She shot an annoyed glance over her shoulder. He pretended not to notice. After all, he could be as good an actor as she was an actress.

"Do you mind?" she demanded.

Brenn feigned surprise. "Oh, so you are going to admit I exist?"

She frowned at his jibe. "Your foot is on my book."

"No, it isn't. It isn't even touching your book."

"I can't read around it."

"Do you wish me to read to you?" He snatched the book out of her hand before she could keep it from him.

"*Belinda*," he read from the title page of the book. "Ah, one of Miss Edgeworth's romances."

"What do you know of Maria Edgeworth?" Tess said waspishly.

Brenn thumbed the pages of the book. "I know she is very popular with the ladies. Perhaps I should read this. Mayhap I will learn something about the female mind. Mayhap I will understand my wife."

If a look could boil a man in oil, the one Tess was sending him would have served him for dinner in less than two snaps of her fingers. He braced himself, ready for her to wish him to the devil and beyond.

Instead, she said succinctly, "I wish to be left alone."

He closed the book with a resounding clap. "That's the rub of it, Tess. You are no longer alone. We are man and wife. We *must* deal with each other."

His words caught her off guard. She stared at him, her brows coming together not in anger but in bewilderment. He could actually see her pulse beat with distress against the white skin of her throat above her collar.

Stop fighting it, Tess.

In answer to his silent plea, her chin lifted. "I'm going to sleep," she announced tightly. To his consternation, she gave him her back and did exactly that.

Brenn was left with Maria Edgeworth. He turned the book over and over in his hands. Perhaps he really should read it! He sat back in his corner of the coach, swearing silently that he'd never met such a stubborn woman as his wife.

But if Tess thought she could rule the game, she was wrong.

When he'd embarked on his wife-hunting venture, he'd been convinced that he didn't need anything from his wife but her money. He was discovering he'd been wrong. He wanted Tess to desire him . . . and he wanted to sleep with her without a fight.

Of course, now that he'd decided he wanted their marriage to be something more than in name only, how was he going to persuade his wife?

Brenn smiled. He had his ways—and he wasn't ashamed to use them.

Full of confidence, he opened Maria Edgeworth's book and passed the time until they arrived at their inn for the night thoroughly entertained by her story of matchmaking and love.

And he did gain an idea or two.

Chapter Ten

Tess slept for several hours and when she woke she had one thought. *Keep up the silent treatment.* She didn't know what else to do. His presence was far too disturbing in the close confines of the coach . . . especially as the hour when he would expect her to share his bed again drew ever-closer.

Her sense of what was right and honest battled with her fear of discovery. She wanted to confess; she feared confessing.

Over the years, she'd flirted and teased with a number of men without any pangs of conscience. But Brenn was different. The circumstances were different. They'd exchanged vows before God . . . and she'd already broken hers by withholding the truth.

In her confused, guilty frame of mind, she felt her only recourse was to protect herself as much as possible by keeping a distance from him. Of course, it was hard to ignore his presence, when his broad shoulders and long legs took up almost three quarters of the coach. And when he showed nothing but concern for her well-being.

"Did you sleep well?" he asked in that deep rumbly voice.

She shrugged, staring out into the gloom of the fading day.

"We'll be stopping soon," he said.

Silence.

"We'll spend the night at the King's Crown. Your brother recommended it."

Night. An hour looming too close for comfort. Her heart started racing with an unsteady beat.

She could feel him watching. Why was she so aware of him? She'd known many men but none had had this effect on her.

Suddenly, a book dropped into her lap. She looked down. *Belinda.*

"I enjoyed the book," he said.

Tess unbent enough to hum a response. She loved talking about books. They were her passion. But she had vowed herself to silence.

"I didn't always agree with the authoress. I found her point of view on matters concerning men and women decidedly different from my own."

What a provocative statement. Tess wanted to ask him what he meant. *Belinda* was the first book of Maria Edgeworth's that she'd read and since the first reading, she'd reread it several times. It never failed to capture her imagination.

"You could have written that book," he said. "And probably done a better job."

Tess whipped her head around to face him, startled by such a conclusion.

He accepted her action as a response. "You could have," he assured her.

"But you've never seen anything I've written!"

The words burst out of her, breaking her vow of silence.

"Tess, you are a woman of intelligence," he replied smoothly. "Why would you not be able to write a book?"

She sat back in her corner of the coach, totally astonished by his statement. And yet, it was not so farfetched.

Running her thumb along the spine of *Belinda*, she admitted, "I have thought of a story or two from time to time. But," she added with a shake of her head, "I couldn't write a book."

"Of course you could. Maria Edgeworth did it. Poets do it all the time and make a great deal less sense than this lady did."

"But how?" Tess said, speaking her thoughts aloud.

"How what?"

"How does one write a book?"

"I imagine one sits in a chair and starts writing." He lifted his bad leg up and rested it again on the silver chest, his lips curving into an apologetic grin.

This time, she did not mind his leg in front of her. Her concern was on other matters. "That's absurd—!" she started and then stopped. It really wasn't such an absurd statement. For a crystal moment, she considered it, but the idea was too revolutionary. She rejected it. "No. An author is someone with a gift for writing. Ordinary people are not writers, especially women."

Brenn leaned over to massage the muscles of his leg along the outside thigh. "I suppose you are right." He pondered it a moment longer and then added, "However, it is a very good thing no one said as much to Maria Edgeworth."

"Said what?" Tess asked suspiciously.

"That women were not writers. She might not have written her book if they had."

Their gazes met and held. She wondered if he was teasing her, but he seemed completely serious. "It's an outlandish idea," she murmured.

With a lift of his shoulders, he let her know that it made no matter to him either way. Still, the idea, the thought that *she* could write a book, lingered at the edge of her mind.

Minnie had often told Tess she was a good writer. But to write a whole book! And what would she write about? Why, at this moment, she couldn't think of one coherent idea.

The coach pulled into the yard of the King's Crown, an inn that catered to the trade and whims of the gentry. Tess had stayed there years ago when she had traveled with her father. Neil and Stella used it whenever they ventured in this direction.

Stable lads charged out to greet their coach. The innkeeper personally welcomed them.

After helping Tess down from the coach, Brenn saw to their horses and their luggage. The innkeeper escorted Tess to her room.

Tess's mind still buzzed with the possibility of writing a book. The second the door closed behind the innkeeper, she pulled Minnie's copybook from her satchel. Thoughtfully, she turned the pages. *This is a book,* she realized in wonder. All Minnie had done was diary her thoughts and experiences and yet, taken as a whole, it was very readable.

The door opened. Tess closed the copybook

and hid it behind her skirts as Brenn walked into the room, his limp more pronounced than usual.

He pulled off his riding gloves. "The inn-keeper says that our supper is waiting for us in the downstairs private room—" He paused, one eyebrow rising. "What are you hiding, Tess?"

Heat stole up to her cheeks. She didn't know why she had kept the copybook from him. She felt silly now. "It's nothing." She pulled the book out. "Just a copybook my governess used for recording her thoughts and snippets of things." She changed the subject. "You move as if your leg is giving you pain."

He tossed his leather gloves on the bed with his hat and shook his head. "It's stiff. It doesn't like resting in one place too long. If I move it, the muscle will loosen. Come, I'm hungry." He held the door open for her.

"Sir Charles said you injured you leg rescuing him and the others. How did it happen?" she asked.

They walked down the hall to the stairs, his hand on the small of her back. The inn was quite busy although Tess didn't recognize anyone of her acquaintance. They started down the stairs.

"A French sniper shot hit the bone," he said. "It never quite healed."

"But certainly a physician could have set it right?"

He laughed, the sound without mirth. "There was none on the battlefield that I would have asked for doctoring. They would have taken my leg." He prodded her into the room he'd re-served for them. Dinner waited, the serving girl having just removed the last cover. She curtseyed and left them in privacy.

"And there was nothing that could be done?" Tess persisted.

Brenn held a chair out for her and then, with easy negligence, dropped into the one across the small round table from her. "Look, rack of lamb, my favorite. Do you care for some?"

Tess stared at him. "You don't want to talk about this, do you? You didn't even like it when Sir Charles bragged about your heroism."

"There are no heroes in war." He placed a slice of lamb on Tess's plate before helping himself to a generous serving. He was about to take the first bite when he noticed she hadn't moved. "What?"

"You're not bitter either. I've never heard you complain."

"Why should I? I'm alive and I have my health. I also have plans. I'm going to build the sort of life I'd only dreamed of. As you know, the *only* thing my leg stops me from doing is dancing," he said pointedly.

"I don't—dance—much either." Flustered, she picked up her fork and knife.

He smiled at her, filling her glass with red wine. "Laughing lasses should always dance."

"I don't have the rhythm for it. I trip over my own two feet."

He laughed with genuine amusement. "At last, a chink in the perfection of Tess Owen."

The sound of her married name made her hesitate. Tess Owen. It reminded her of their sharing a bed, something that she'd tried not to think about.

Her appetite left her.

"What is the matter? What did I say?" he asked.

She looked up at him, surprised that he had noticed her change of mood. "Nothing, nothing," she averred quickly. She forced herself to take a bite of meat. It was tasteless. She swallowed it down and took a sip of wine before saying, "Neil said that you haven't had the title long."

Brenn nodded, tearing off a piece of bread. "I didn't even know I had an uncle who was an earl."

"How is that?" Tess asked, genuinely curious.

"No one told me," he answered simply. "My father was estranged from his family. He'd sinned in the eyes of his family by falling in love with an English girl."

"Why was that a sin?" She took another bite of lamb.

Finished with his meal, Brenn set his napkin aside. "The Welsh are proud people and probably the most independent in all the world. My father's family had sent him to Chester to sell horses. Instead, he met my mother. She was the local horse dealer's daughter and it was love at first sight. She said he proposed on the spot. Worse, Father was so distracted, he practically gave the horses away to her father. His family was not amused to receive such a poor price and an English daughter-in-law."

Tess laughed, completely charmed by the story. "Do you believe in such a thing? Love at first sight, I mean? It has always sounded so fantastical." She speared several peas in her mouth.

He played with the stem of his wineglass, a small smile hovering around his lips, before shrugging. "I don't know. But I have learned over the years to never disregard anything. The most incredible bit of nonsense can turn out to be true. And it is true that my father renounced everything for his English bride."

"The family didn't like her just because she was English?" She lathered a healthy bit of butter on her bread and took a bite.

"Worse than not like. They informed him he could have had his choice of half a dozen Welsh beauties and a Saxon wench was not what they had in mind."

"A Saxon wench?"

"The Welsh still call the English Saxons. Old habits die hard there."

"What happened when he refused to give her up?" Tess prompted.

"They showed him the door."

"How cruel!"

"How like my father's family is more like it. The truth is," Brenn said, leaning both elbows on the table, "Father's family was more than a bit eccentric. Father claimed he had never fit in with them and said he was happy to leave. He bought his commission and joined the army."

"But what of your mother?" Tess asked. "How terrible for her to have left behind the life she knew only to be rejected by your father's family."

"What an imagination you have," he said with a laugh. "I don't think she ever regretted her decision to marry him. She loved him. Wherever he was sent in the army, she traveled by his side."

He added almost as an afterthought, "She was a brave woman."

"Yes," Tess agreed thoughtfully. She'd cleaned her plate. She set her knife and fork aside and asked, "What happened after that?"

"Happened? Not much. I was born three years later."

Tess glanced down at her wedding ring. "Yes. You said you had been in India."

Brenn poured them each another glass of wine. "I served in India," he corrected. "I was sent there right after I purchased my commission, but Mother never let me live there with them."

"Why not?" she asked, sipping her wine.

"She feared fever. I grew up here, living with relatives or a family my parents hired to take care of me. I rarely lived with my mother and father."

Tess frowned. "That must have been lonely."

"It wasn't. The family had six boys. I didn't have a moment alone until I went off to school."

"Yes, but didn't you want someplace that was your own?"

He sat back. "That is exactly how I felt," he admitted softly. "Amazing that you who have always had everything could understand that."

Tess pulled a face. "Since Neil married Stella, I have felt as if my home wasn't my own anymore. As if I no longer belonged there."

Brenn nodded. "I felt that way until I saw Erwynn Keep. I promise you, Tess, Erwynn Keep is the most beautiful place on earth. The lake, the sky, the mountains . . . it's the first true home I've ever had."

"But what of your family?"

"There is no one of my father's family left, except for the villagers who live within a mile of the great house."

"What did they say when your father's half-English son inherited? What *will* they say when you bring home a Saxon bride?"

His eyes gleamed with amusement. "This is the best part of the story. My uncle, the earl, who never married one of those half a dozen fine Welsh lasses, was apparently a very strange character given to bad moods and spouting off nonsense. After his parents died, his behavior was so exceedingly odd, the Welsh would have welcomed anyone in his stead, including me. I am now considered their only hope to return Erwynn Keep to its former glory."

"Returning it to its glory? What is the matter with the estate? It looked perfect lovely in the picture."

He seemed to falter a bit. "It is," he quickly said. "Very lovely." But his reassuring smile didn't quite go past his cheekbones . . . and then he admitted, "But it does need work. My uncle was not a good businessman."

"Oh, I can understand that a bachelor residence would need work. I shall look forward to the challenge."

"Ummm," he said, noncommittally. "But what of you? We married so quickly there are many things I don't know about you."

Tess was not accustomed to taking about herself. "There isn't much to say."

"Tell me about your parents." He again filled their wineglasses, finishing the bottle.

Tess crossed her arms. "My mother died when I was five."

"So you don't remember much about her."

Tess nodded, unwilling to talk. Funny that he should hone in on what distressed her most. She couldn't remember what her mother looked like. She remembered her smile, but not her eyes. She could recall her touch, but not the texture of her hair. "I remember how she smelled. She'd designed her own fragrance and was known for it. It was a combination of lily, rose, and a hint of lemon verbena."

"Your fragrance."

Her gaze met his. "Yes," she confessed with a touch of surprise. "That is my scent. You noticed?"

"I notice everything about you, Tess."

His words started that dizzy little awareness of him.

"So." His hand came across the table and rested a mere inch from her own. "Were your parents a love match?"

She almost laughed. "No. Papa always said that heiresses like Mama and myself are too valuable to be turned loose to their own inclinations. Their marriage was arranged." Heiresses! She'd forgotten.

Tess closed her eyes, wishing her papa was alive. Wishing everything was different. "I miss him."

Brenn's hand covered hers. Where his fingers touched, her skin tingled. She opened her eyes, staring at where their hands rested together. What would happen if she confessed the truth? Right now, this minute?

"Tess?"

She started. "Yes?"

"You seemed miles away. Is something the matter?"

She pulled her hand out from underneath his. "I was just remembering."

He nodded as if she had confirmed his suspicions and then pushed his chair back from the table. "Are you ready to turn in for the night or would you enjoy a walk around the stables?"

"A walk, please," Tess answered. Fresh air would help clear her mind of this terrible guilt that weighed heavy with her. She wasn't anxious for the day that would inevitably come when he'd learn the truth.

Nor was she anxious to "turn in for the night."

Outside, mists of fog rose from the ground. There was rain in the air. Inside the stables the smell of it mingled with that of hay and horses, a not unpleasant smell. Brenn's horse, Ace, nickered a greeting. Tess stepped over the fresh straw and ran her hand along his coat. She'd not worn her gloves and the animal's skin felt warm against her palm.

"He's not a beautiful beast," Brenn observed. "But he's rugged and he has great heart. Don't you, boy."

Ace bumped Tess's hand with his nose, begging for another pet. "I think he is very handsome."

"I value him more for the fact that he succeeds at whatever he sets his mind to—much like his owner."

Tess didn't think those words were mere lighthearted banter. She glanced around them. The stable lads and posting boys were busy swapping tales at the other end of the barn. "What are you trying to tell me?" she asked Brenn carefully.

His hand came down to her waist. He turned her to face him, her back to the horse. "Last night was awkward for you. But tonight will be different."

It was what she'd feared. "Are you offering to forgo your husbandly rights?" she queried tartly, attempting to take a step away from him.

His arm came out to block her escape. He leaned forward. His lips brushed her ear. "I want you, Tess, but I'll not take you against your will."

I want you, Tess. Those words stirred already unsettled emotions within her. Lustful . . . needy . . . apprehensive emotions.

He kissed her, right on the lobe of her ear, and then placed another kiss an inch down on the ticklish spot where her neck and jawline met.

Tess tilted her head. He stood so close, her breasts brushed his chest as she arched her back.

"Don't harden your heart to me." His low voice hummed through her. "Let me have a chance. Let *us* have a chance."

His lips moved to meet hers.

Brenn was going to kiss her. He was going to kiss her like he'd never kissed a woman before and then he was going to take her to bed and make love to her all night.

Closing his eyes, he brought his lips down and placed a big wet smack on Ace's side.

He opened his eyes. Tess was gone. She'd ducked and slipped out from under his arm.

That was the second time she'd done that to him. She now stood several feet away from him, her hands behind her back.

What was bloody wrong with her!

"What?" he demanded irritably. "All I was going to do was kiss you."

She sent a meaningful glance toward the stable lads, a silent instruction to keep his voice down. Well, he didn't feel like keeping his voice down!

He wanted a kiss. A plain, simple kiss. He'd set up for it, he was hungry for it, and he wanted it! "Come here, Tess."

She shook her head no.

It was a game then. All right, he would play. He took a step toward her.

She stepped back.

His sense of humor slowly started to return. He took three quick little steps.

She blinked, staring at him as if he'd gone mad. Her aristocratic nose lifted up in the air. "I'm going to bed."

"Excellent idea. I'll go with you."

She didn't like that at all. She stopped, her skirts swirling around her ankles. "On second thought, I'll wait. The luggage coach hasn't arrived and I need Willa to undress me."

Brenn fell into step alongside her. "There's no need to wait for Willa. I can play lady's maid."

"It wouldn't be proper."

"I don't care about what is proper."

"Will you keep your voice down?" she said between clenched teeth. "There are people watching."

Brenn made a big show of exaggeratedly noticing the stable lads had stopped talking and were listening to their argument with avid curiosity. He shrugged them off. "I don't care if the king is watching, Tess. I want a kiss."

A loud guffaw escaped from the cluster of stable hands. Even in the dark Brenn could see Tess coloring a pretty shade of berry-red. "Why are you doing this?" she whispered.

Because I can, he wanted to flash back. *Because I'm your husband and will not be treated like a lackey*. He would not be one of those men whose wives controlled them.

Theirs was a battle of wills, one Brenn was determined to win, although he was genuinely puzzled. He'd never had difficulty with women before. They loved to kiss him. They hoped to jump in his bed—every woman, that is, but his wife.

"You found some pleasure in last night. You can't deny it."

Still he was put off balance when she suddenly agreed, "All right. One kiss."

Brenn closed his mouth which had dropped open. Now that he'd won, he didn't want to kiss her in front of stable lads and in the middle of the bustle of a busy inn yard any more than she did . . . but he couldn't say that now. The lads were cheering for him!

He bent to receive his bounty. She came up on her toes. Her hands rested lightly on his shoulders. Sweet Tess.

Their lips met even as he felt her weight shift and her knee lift. Warning signals flashed in his brain. He leaned back. But her knee wasn't the weapon. He should have known that Tess was still too naïve about men to know how to vitally hurt them. No, his bride put her weight and energy into stomping the heel of her shoe on his foot.

He thought she had crushed his big toe! With a grunt of pain, he lifted the foot and almost toppled to the ground. She used those moments to daintily lift her skirts and sail away toward the inn.

The stable lads hooted. Even the horses seemed to laugh. His wife had bested him and they all knew it.

With an élan he was far from feeling, Brenn made a rackety bow in their direction before hobbling off after his wife.

Tess's heart pounded in her ears so loudly she barely heard the door open. She was in bed, the covers pulled up over her ears, pretending to be asleep. Of course, she would be more convincing if she could stop shaking.

His heavy footsteps crossed the wooden floor. His limp was more pronounced.

She squeezed her eyes shut, knowing there was no way she was going to fall asleep.

A sound. Holding her breath, she listened. It was the soft whisk of material against material. She could hear him remove his jacket and toss it over a chair.

Why didn't he say something? Why didn't he rant or rave? Even she was startled by her boldness—but his insistence that she kiss him in front of stable lads had angered her. She wasn't a common trollop or the sort of woman who jumped at any man's bidding!

He sat on the edge of the bed. Without ceremony, he removed first one boot and then the other.

Tess tensed, not knowing what to expect next. Silence.

What was he going to do?

The ropes of the bed sprang back into shape as he stood. She strained her ears.

Nothing! No sound at all.

Where was he? She couldn't handle the suspense any longer. A peek wouldn't hurt. She pretended to sleepily turn toward his side of the bed. Ever so carefully, she pulled down an edge of the covers, just enough for her to see out of one eye. It took a moment for her eye to adjust to the light—when it did, when she saw what he'd done, she screeched, "You're naked!"

He stood by the bed, as bare-bottomed as the day he was born. Throwing his folded breeches onto the same chair holding his shirt and jacket, he answered, "Yes."

Tess yanked the covers up before she had a full frontal view of her husband. "Why are you naked?"

"I always sleep this way." He snuffed out the candle and, to her horror, lifted the covers and climbed into the bed beside her.

"Why, Tess," he said pleasantly, "you are still fully dressed."

She rolled out of the other side of the bed. "You can't sleep like that. It's indecent."

In answer, he feigned a snore.

She placed her hands on her hips. "I won't sleep in the same bed with you!"

He snuggled deeper under the covers. "Enjoy

the chair then." Before her eyes, he fell well and truly asleep.

Tess felt strangely deflated. "What is the matter with you?" she said in frustration. "Less than fifteen minutes ago, you'd been willing to make love to me in front of strangers, and now you completely ignore me."

She expected him to answer. To laugh and tease her. But he slept on.

And it hurt her vanity. Men had done many things around her, but they'd never ignored her.

She threw herself down into a chair, crossing her arms, watching him . . . but it didn't take her long to tire of such a boring vigil. Or for her eyelids to grow heavy.

The hard wooden chair with its straight back was far from comfortable, especially after riding in the coach all afternoon. The bed beckoned.

She could lie down on top of the covers. That would be proper.

She tried it, at first fully dressed, but the light boning of her stays cut into her skin. "You are being ridiculous," she told herself. Brenn was sleeping so soundly, he didn't even know she was in the room. Undressing, she put on her nightgown and then climbed back onto the bed, on top of the covers.

A chill ran through her from the early summer air and she wished she'd asked for a fire to be laid in the hearth. Of course, the temperature would be fine if she had the covers over her.

She glanced at her husband. Brenn was apparently dead to the world. She doubted if he would notice if she slipped between the sheets. Another shiver convinced her this was not only wise but prudent. It wouldn't do if she were to catch a cold.

In a few seconds' time, she had the covers up around her neck and, hugging the far edge of the bed, instantly fell asleep.

Chapter Eleven

Tess woke in stages, all cuddly warm under the covers.
The cotton sheets felt good against her skin. The
damp morning air tickled her nose. Snuggling
with her pillow, she stretched—and found herself pressed against something hard and unre-
lenting. Her husband!

Her *aroused* husband!

His arms cradled her close. His manhood
pressed against her bottom. A large, callused
hand cupped each breast. "Morning, love," his
husky voice whispered in her ear.

She started to jerk away, but Brenn's arms
around her held her close.

"Ah, Tess, I don't want to fight." His breath
prickled her skin. "Not this morning. Never in
the mornings. Especially when you smell so
good." He drew out the syllables of the last
words. His hands cupping her breasts caressed
them.

She liked the feel of his hands on her this way.

His lips lowered and nibbled the sensitive skin
of her neck.

It did feel good. Yes, very good. Slowly, ever so slowly, she relaxed against him.

She could almost imagine that the two of them were in a world of their own. His legs intermingled with hers. He tickled the bottom of her foot with his toe.

A giggle escaped. She started to rise.

"No, stay here," he commanded sleepily and traced the line of her ear with his tongue.

Warm and drowsy, Tess whimpered and felt his lips curve into a smile. He bit her shoulder, a little nip, and then soothed the spot with his tongue.

She turned her head and found her lips captured by his. The doubts and questions of last night evaporated. His tongue teased hers, opening her to him. Almost timidly, she answered, copying his motion.

His response was immediate. With a low, satisfied growl, he leaned over her, the better to claim her mouth.

Once again, Tess found herself devoured by his kiss. And she was kissing him back.

The palm of his right hand ran down along the line of her abdomen. His fingers circled her belly button. It was a playful gesture and she started to laugh and he used that moment when she let her guard down to drive the kiss deeper.

Tess could kiss him like this all day and never let up. When his hand dipped lower and his fingers stroked the most intimate part of her, she parted her legs for him.

He pulled her back against his chest. "Yes, Tess, this is the way it should be. Don't fight it, sweetling. Let me in." He slid one finger into her body.

She gasped at the pressure. His thumb began drawing small circles even as his finger moved in and out in a steady rhythm.

"Brenn!"

"Yes," he purred in a satisfied voice. "Let me show you how it can be."

He touched her in places she hadn't known existed. Tess feared she might die from the sheer pleasure of it. She tried to close her legs, afraid of feeling so vulnerable and open to him.

His lips brushed her neck. "My love, my dear, dear love," he cooed. "Take that fierce pride of yours, Tess. Turn it to passion."

She was slick and hot. A yearning for something *more* built inside of her. She struggled with this terrible wanting even as her body began pushing against his hand, urging him on.

Brenn took the nipple of her right breast in his mouth. She cried out. He licked it, matching the strokes to the movement of his hand. The warmth of his mouth went straight to her soul.

She no longer fought him. She couldn't. Her whole world centered on him. This was good. So, so good. She closed her eyes, letting him have his way with her.

And then he shifted. His hand left her.

She made a soft moue, disappointed, but then, her buttocks against him, he slid himself deep inside her. This time, there was no pain. No shock.

In fact, this was much better than his hand.

He filled her. Her body stretched to accommodate him.

Brenn was whispering love words in her ear. His large hands began touching, caressing. Slowly, surely, he pulled himself back and then thrust again, going even deeper. She could feel his body reaching into hers.

The next time he did it, she moved instinctively to meet him—and he was the one to gasp in astonishment.

The sound made her feel powerful. Something feline unfurled inside of her, something that delighted in this newly discovered power.

They moved together now. He cradled her with his big body, his hands on her breasts. His voice had gone husky with desire. He whispered that she was lovely, that she felt good, that this was what she was meant for. She couldn't speak. She was too involved in sensation.

He rested one hand against her mound, his fingers stroking with each thrust, and it was her undoing.

One second, she was searching, aching with need—and in the next, it was as if one of those Chinese fireworks had gone off inside of her. She felt it through her whole being. Hot, tingly, sparkling, shattering. It radiated through her in ever-increasing rings of passion.

Brenn must have felt it too. His arms came around her. He held her tight as he made one last deep thrust. He called her name and then released himself inside her.

They collapsed together on the bed. Neither could move. Her heart raced and the blood pounded through her veins.

"Can we die from such a thing?" she managed to ask.

His answer was a feeble laugh. Kissing the back of her neck, he said, "I could." He kissed her again.

Tess covered his hands, still around her, with her own. "It was incredible."

"But was it wonderful?"

Wonderful.

The word hung in the air between them.

"Almost," she answered.

He grunted his dissatisfaction. "I shall have to try harder."

"Oh, I hope you might." With a sigh of contentment, she closed her eyes.

A few hours later, Tess woke to find herself alone. She reached over to Brenn's side of the bed. The sheets still smelled of him.

She heard the splash of water and looked up to see her husband standing in the golden sunlight of the room's single window. He was dressed, with the exception of his dark blue jacket which was on the chair where he'd tossed it the night before. His broad shoulders stretched out the confines of the shirt and his buff leather breeches did nothing to hide the manly shape of his legs.

She'd married well.

Brenn glanced over at her as if he'd read her thoughts and grinned. "Good morning." He cleaned the razor off in the basin and wiped the soap off his face. In two steps he was by her side on the bed. He propped his head on his hand. "Why are you smiling?"

Heat rushed up to her cheeks.

He laughed, lightly touching her nose. She

liked the clean, bold scent of his soap. Then his expression turned serious. He was staring at her lips. "Do you remember earlier?"

She didn't have to ask what he meant. Hooking her legs together at the ankle, her hands behind her head, she pretended to consider his question.

Brenn gave a sharp bark of laughter. "You're not that good of an actress, Tess Owen." He nuzzled her with his razor-smooth cheek. His lips brushed her ear. "Now what do you say?"

His voice vibrated through her. "I won't ever forget it," she whispered, wanting him to say the same.

But he didn't, although his dark eyes flashed with pride. His lips found hers. She brought her hands up around his neck. This time when his tongue teased her, she fearlessly touched him back. She wanted him. Already her body tightened in anticipation, so she was surprised when he was the first to break off the kiss.

He stood. "We leave in an hour. You need to be up and dressed."

Tess let her irritation show. She wouldn't have minded a repeat of their lovemaking. "I can't get dressed without my maid."

He raised an eyebrow.

"I assure you, I've never dressed myself in my life. Last night was the first time I'd undressed alone."

"Ah, Tess, you have a lot to learn."

"Are you going to teach me?" She didn't know where such cheeky words had come from. They'd just popped out of her mouth.

And she was glad she'd said them when he

answered, "There are many things I want to teach you." He kissed her again. This kiss went all the way to her toes.

Tess could barely breathe when he was finished with it.

"I'll send your maid in," he promised and left the room.

Tess dropped back on the bed, praying her thumping heart wouldn't fail her. How silly of her to have avoided marriage all these years ... but then she must have been waiting for Brenn.

She only wished that she had a fortune to give to him. The thought wiped the smile from her face. Neil had promised that her lack of fortune would not be a problem if she gave Brenn what he wanted.

She'd certainly done that this morning!

But was it enough?

Tess understood with a woman's instinct that whereas she had been completely lost to passion, Brenn had maintained control. He'd enjoyed himself, but he hadn't lost control.

That thought was sobering.

She told herself not to be a goose. In neither word nor deed had Brenn ever acted like a fortune hunter. Besides, with a magnificent house like Erwynn Keep, he couldn't lack for money.

But still, how could such an honest, forthright man forgive Tess for such a deception?

The question didn't have an answer.

A moment later, Willa entered the room and Tess pushed her doubts aside. Still, last night had changed her. Brenn had changed her.

"Willa, do I have any copybooks packed in my luggage?"

The maid looked up from refilling the wash-basin she'd just emptied out the window. "I don't know, my lady. I could check."

"Please do." Tess slipped the nightdress over her head and tossed it on the bed. "I believe I am going to become a writer."

Willa gasped. "You, my lady?"

"Yes, me." She reached for a dress of periwinkle-blue kerseymere. White lace accented the low neckline and the sleeves.

"What are you going to write?" Willa asked, her expression saying much more than mere words could that such an idea was completely preposterous.

Tess fingered the lace on the dress, considering her question, and then she smiled. "I think I shall write a romance. One of those like Maria Edge-worth's. Except this one will be *my* story," she added softly.

Downstairs, in the public room, Brenn settled his bill with the innkeeper. The price of the room and the change of horses was exorbitant. He was fortunate to have Hamlin's three hundred pounds.

He deliberated over writing another letter to Mr. Going, urging him to swift action in getting the cash out of Tess's investments, but discarded the idea. He didn't want to look too anxious, even if he was, but how long would it take to receive funds from Italy?

He hated thinking about it.

A few minutes later, Tess came down the stairs to join him for breakfast. He liked her in blue.

The color brought out the red in her hair and the blue of her eyes.

As she walked across the room, every full-blooded male turned and stared. But they'd noticed more than just her beauty. There was something special about her this morning. She was in love. She literally glowed with it.

Brenn recognized the signs. He could read it in her smile when she first caught sight of him and the way her expression softened into dewy-eyed hero worship.

He crossed to meet her, taking her arm and leading her to their private dining room, another expense he hadn't anticipated.

"Good morning," he said.

"Good morning," she replied and then blushed with perfect maidenly modesty.

"I took the liberty of ordering breakfast for both of us."

"Oh," she said, "I rarely eat breakfast."

Brenn wished he'd known that. The meals in the King's Crown were three times the price they should be—but he didn't say anything. Instead, he enjoyed a hearty breakfast of eggs and sausages and sent Tess's meal out to the posting boys.

She watched him eat, blushing whenever he looked at her. They sat so close together, his thigh brushed hers. The thought crossed his mind that now would be a good time to tell Tess the truth . . . but he didn't.

He told himself it was because Tess wasn't like most women. Her mind was keener. She would see right though his tactics.

No, it was best to let these newfound emotions season a bit. He promised himself he would confess the truth before they reached Erwynn Keep, but he wouldn't do it any sooner than he had to . . . in case she didn't take it well.

Within half an hour, they were back on the road. This time the silver chest was not between them.

"How long will it take us to arrive at Erwynn Keep?" Tess asked.

"We should be close to the border of Wales by late today. We won't actually arrive on my land until the day after tomorrow."

Tess nestled beside him. "That's a long time to be cooped up in this coach."

The heat of desire flared up in Brenn. He brought his arms around her. "I know of ways to make the time go faster."

"How?" she asked. She was still so sweetly innocent.

He bent his head and placed a kiss on the warm skin above her collar. "You smell good." He kissed the underside of her chin.

"My mother's fragrance—"

He interrupted her with a kiss. She responded.

Pulling her skirt up one thigh, he slipped his hand under the petticoats and rubbed the warm, tender skin of her thigh. She sighed against his mouth, and he discovered she was already wet and ready for him.

Who would have thought that Tess Hamlin, the Ice Maiden, would be such a sensual creature? Her arms curved around his neck, the movement thrusting her breasts against his chest, and the next hour, aided by the rocking of the poorly sprung coach, passed very quickly and pleasurably indeed.

Later, sated and drowsy, his half-dressed wife

in his arms, Brenn finally conceded that marriage wasn't such a bad thing after all.

They stopped for lunch at a picturesque inn located beside a small stream. The food was delicious. They then continued their trip without taking time for rest. After another hour of travel, they turned off the main road to continue their journey to Wales. The poor condition of these roads would slow their journey. The luggage coach followed at an even slower pace.

Tess didn't mind. She was completely lost in a world of passion. She had discovered the elixir, the meaning of life. Men and women should always make love, she decided. She could become addicted to it.

Tess, the Debutante, had vanished and in her place was a woman who was just now beginning to understand what life had to offer.

Her stocking feet in Brenn's lap, she said, "I don't want this trip to end. Not ever."

He stopped massaging her foot. "It has to end if we are to reach Erwynn's Keep."

Tess stretched with the satisfaction of a cat, enjoying the way his eyes followed the movement of her breasts. Her husband was a passionate man. They were well-suited.

"I don't need Erwynn's Keep," she said. "I have everything I want right here." To emphasize her meaning, she lightly rubbed her foot against the masculine bulge in his breeches and almost purred when she felt him respond.

He laughed, his hand pushing her skirt up her leg. "Don't tell me you are bored."

"I could be amused." She slid him a sly smile.

His fingers untied the garter of one stocking. "I think I can imagine a game or two we can play."

Tess giggled. "You're tickling."

"Really? Right here?" His fingers found a new spot. A place that made her gasp.

But before she could answer, a pistol shot rang out.

The horses screamed in fear. The coach halted with a mighty jerk, throwing Tess to the floor. The postboy shouted as he tried to control the animals.

And then a strong male voice shouted, "Stand and deliver!"

"Highwaymen?" Tess said. She'd never imagined herself involved in anything so dangerous.

"Damn," Brenn said succinctly. He lifted her back up on the seat, pulling her skirt down as he did so. "Tess, put on your shoes. We are going to have company."

"But what will they do to us?"

"Nothing, as long as we do what they say."

She'd just slipped on her slippers when the coach door was yanked open. A bedraggled man in a burlap sack mask, with two holes cut out for eyes, ordered them to get out. "You first," he ordered, pointing at Brenn with a huge, ominous-looking pistol.

Brenn held up his hands to show he had no weapon. "Easy with your weapon, mate. There is no need for bloodshed."

The highwayman didn't answer but stood back. Tess could see that as her husband unfolded himself out of the coach, his size and breadth made the highwayman nervous. Brenn started to help her down but a gruff command for him to move back from the coach door forced him to step back by the wheel.

Too frightened to speak, Tess climbed down. Her one stocking was still free of its garter and it hung loose around her ankle. Her hair was mussed. She refused to show fear.

The coach had been stopped where the quiet country road took a little dip into a gully. The area was framed by oak trees and overgrown hawthorn bushes. The luggage coach must have been at least a mile or more behind them.

The highwayman was not alone. His accomplice wore a similar mask and sat on a horse a few yards away, the rifle in his arms aimed straight at Brenn. The postboy, who in actuality was a man in his late twenties, stood with his hand on the horses' reins so they wouldn't bolt.

Tess choked back the desire to whimper and eased a step or two toward Brenn. She'd heard that people were robbed all the time, but this couldn't be happening to her.

One of her trunks suddenly fell on the ground. She looked up. A third robber stood on top of the coach, ransacking her trunks.

She cried in outrage, and took a step toward the thrown trunk. The lid had come open and her delicate petticoats, scarves, and other intimate apparel were scattered all over the ground.

Brenn took her arm, silently warning her not to move. Of course, any movement from him was considered threatening.

The highwayman who had ordered them from the coach waved his pistol menacingly. "If you know wot's good for you, you'll step back and away." He had a trace of the Irish in his muffled voice. "Or you could make it easy and just tell us where the money is."

Brenn took two steps away from Tess. She started to follow him, but he gave an almost imperceptible shake of his head—no.

The Irishman nodded. "That's right, guvner. Let the lady stay here." He placed a hand on her arm and pulled her close. Tess glanced at Brenn, uncertain what to do. Then the Irishman pointed the pistol at her head. "Where is the money?"

Tess wished she were the type of woman who swooned. She would have liked very much to close her eyes and black out, but it wasn't to be.

Suddenly, the man on top of the coach said, "This isn't what I was brought in for. I don't want any killing."

"Shut your mouth and keep looking," the Irishman ordered.

"The money chest is in the coach," Brenn said.

"Well then, fetch it," the Irishman commanded.

"Release her first," Brenn countered. Tess could not believe how calm he was. She was ready to swallow her heart whole, and he acted completely undisturbed by the presence of weapons.

She stood so close to the Irishman, she could see his glittering eyes through the face mask. He exchanged a glance at the man on the horse. A silent communication seemed to fly between them before he roughly shoved her in the horseman's direction.

The Irishman waved his pistol at Brenn. "Fetch the money."

"Fetch it yourself," Brenn said calmly. "It's under the seat in the coach."

The Irishman did not like his response at all, but he didn't quibble. Instead, he stuck his pistol in the waistband of his pants. "Watch him close," he ordered the rifleman and started to search inside the coach.

In a matter of seconds, the Irishman found what he was looking for. He straightened. In his gloved hands was the small money chest Brenn had been carrying around with him. "This is what we've been looking for! Let's go, lads."

Suddenly, Brenn moved, pushing Tess away as he reached in his pocket.

What happened next occurred quickly. A shot was fired. One moment the man sat on the horse, the next he had toppled over backward. The animal reared, its hooves too close to Tess for safety. She fell to the ground, covering her head with her arms.

The man on top of the coach jumped down, landing heavily. The Irishman shouted someone's name. The coach horses whinnied wildly, thrashing in their harnesses. Heavy footsteps ran past her.

And then another shot was fired.

A heartbeat later, all was quiet.

Chapter Twelve

Tess opened her eyes in the silence. The rifleman lay less than five feet from herself. She saw his fingers make a crawling movement against the ground. Then his hand went slack and his eyes took on the cold-eyed stare of death.

Tess rolled over, ready to scream, but Brenn was by her side. He lifted her into his arms. "Are you all right?"

She nodded mutely, still too shattered to speak.

He hugged her close. "It's over, Tess. You don't need to be afraid. It's over."

The postboy spoke. "The horses don't like the smell of death."

"I'll take care of it in a moment," Brenn said impatiently.

"That other one ran into the woods," the postboy informed him.

"And he won't stop running until he reaches the sea," Brenn answered. "Come, Tess, do you think you can stand now?"

She nodded. How could he be so calm? It was

almost as if the taking of human life meant little to him.

On wobbly legs, she managed to regain her balance and let him lead her back to the coach. She sat on the step and then gasped when she noticed the Irishman's body sprawled by the wheel. "Is he—?"

"Yes," came Brenn's grim reply.

"You should have seen Lord Merton, my lady," the postboy said. "I've never seen a man move so fast. He killed that one on the ground by the wheel with the man's own gun."

"What happened?" she asked Brenn.

"I moved faster than they did," he answered.

"His lordship had a pistol," the postboy said. "And good aim. Knocked the one right off his horse."

"See to the horses," Brenn ordered, his voice curt. He reached in the coach for the hamper of food he'd ordered earlier at the inn. There was a bottle of wine in it and he poured Tess a generous glass. "Drink this."

"Is it true? Did you have a pistol?"

"Drink."

She did as he asked and he pulled out of his coat pocket a pistol no larger than the palm of his hand.

"When did you put that there?" she asked.

"I always carry it."

"I hadn't noticed."

Brenn shrugged. "There is no reason that you should."

"I've never been more frightened," she confessed. Her gaze strayed to the bodies stretched out on the quiet road.

"Don't think about it."

"It was so sudden."

"They made their choices, Tess."

"But it could have been you lying there."

He frowned his answer. He obviously didn't want to discuss it. Instead, he lifted the money chest from the ground. It had fallen open and a handful of gold coins spilled out.

"How much is in there?"

"A little less than two hundred and fifty pounds."

"Two hundred and fifty pounds!" The words exploded out of her. "Why, that is an insignificant sum for which to risk your life!"

"Two hundred and fifty pounds is far from being insignificant," he argued.

Tess shook her head. "Brenn, the petticoat for my presentation at Court cost more than that."

He stared hard at her in disbelief. "You're joking."

"No," she said with a shake of her head. "It is made of laces fashioned from silver and weighs almost more than the dress I wore, which is made of the finest brocade."

He frowned at the petticoats and scarves scattered across the ground. "Is it one of those?"

"No, it's on the luggage wagon."

"Thank the Lord," he said under his breath and bent down, favoring his bad leg, to pick up the coins off the ground.

At that moment, the luggage coach rolled around the bend with Ace tied to the rear. The postboy driving shouted for the horses to stop. He jumped down and came running to Brenn.

Willa's head popped out of the coach window.

A second later, she threw open the door. "What has happened, my lady?" she cried.

"We were almost robbed," Tess said, surprised that her voice sounded so steady. "Come and help clean up the mess."

Willa hurried to do as she was bid, making clucking noises of concern. When she saw the two men lying on the ground, she paused dramatically, clutching her heart. "Lady Merton—!"

"They are dead, Willa. They cannot bother us now." She said the words calmly. In truth, she still hadn't come to terms with what had happened. "Come and help repair these trunks."

The other postboy looked around, taking in the petticoats and scarves strewn across the ground and the bodies of the dead men. "Blimey," he said, one word and it seemed to sum it all up.

"You should have been here, Clarence," their postboy told him. "Lord Merton took them both. I could barely believe my bleedin' eyes."

Brenn placed the money chest in the coach and then walked to the boot of the coach, pulling on his leather driving gloves. Tess followed. "What are you going to do now?"

He removed a small spade from a wooden box in the boot. "Bury the bodies." His tone was grim.

"Why you? It isn't your job. Have the postboys do it."

"I killed them, Tess."

His words startled her. "They would have killed us."

"Aye, but once you kill a man, the least you

can do is bury him." He motioned to their post-boy. "What is your name?"

"Tim, my lord."

"Help me drag the bodies off the road, Tim. In fact, you help too, Clarence. Then I want the two of you to reload the luggage."

They did as he said.

Tess and Willa were left alone. Willa kicked dirt over the bloodstains in the road. "It's a pity when decent people can't go where they wish without being set upon by murderers and vagabonds."

Murderers. Tess pushed the thought out of her mind. It could have been Brenn or herself lying there.

A few minutes later, the postboys returned. One trunk was hopelessly damaged from being tossed to the ground. Willa carried on about the damage and made Clarence and Tim unload both coaches so that she could repack, something both men did reluctantly.

Over an hour had passed and Brenn hadn't come back. How long did it take to dig a man's grave?

After another thirty minutes in which Willa, Clarence, and Tim bickered incessantly, Tess decided to go look for him. "I'm going to find my husband."

"He's in a clearing down by the stream over yonder," Clarence told her while Willa continued to tell Tim what a stupid knave he was.

Tess walked into the forest in the direction she'd seen the postboys return. In a few minutes, the coach was out of sight.

She stopped and listened. She didn't hear digging but she could hear the sound of a stream making its way through the forest. She walked toward it and came into the clearing, just as Clarence had said.

Two fresh graves now rested beneath the shade of a spreading oak. There were no markers. Brenn's jacket and shirt lay on the ground beside the graves.

She frowned, and then found him. The clearing sloped down to the stream that ran by the spot. Brenn knelt on the bank washing his face and hands.

Tess watched him a moment. Something warned her that this was not the time to disturb him.

He sat back on his heels, looking out over the swiftly moving water. His dropped his head forward and covered it with his arms, the position one of grief.

Tess stood in indecision, afraid to move because if she did, he would know that she had intruded on his privacy. And yet, she could not leave him, not now.

Taking one careful step forward and then another, Tess approached him. He didn't seem aware of her presence.

"Brenn?"

He whirled on her. Even when he saw it was her, he didn't relax.

She reached out and placed her hand on his warm skin. "Are you all right?"

He stared at her, almost as if he didn't understand her words. Then he covered her hand on his shoulder with his own. "Tess." He kissed the inside of her wrist. "Tess." Her name sounded like a prayer on his lips. Another kiss, and another.

"I was worried."

He nodded, his expression still distant. His head lowered and he buried it in the crook of her neck. "Tess."

She didn't know what to do. Gingerly, she laid her hand against his back, feeling the strength in his muscles. *Dear Lord, she was so glad to be alive.*

He gently sucked the sensitive skin of her neck.

"Brenn—" she started but got no further. His mouth covered hers and he kissed her urgently. Using his weight, he pressed her back on the long, green grass along the bank. His hand pulled her skirt up.

She was aware of the dampness of the earth beneath her and the blue sky crisscrossed by tree limbs overhead. Birds sang and from some place overhead, a squirrel chattered.

He entered her without warning, without preamble. And she accepted him.

The force of his need caught her off guard. This was nothing like their earlier lovemaking. Before he'd been attentive, playful. Now he sought release.

Tess stared up at the sky and held him. An intuition as old as time told her that this was right. He needed her woman's body to cast out his own demons . . . and when at last he came, it was with a great shuddering release.

His body fell heavily down on hers. He was spent.

Tears filled her eyes. She blinked them away, flattening her palms against his back. His heart beat as if he'd just finished running a race. The air around them smelled of green grass and sex.

"Brenn?"

He raised his head and looked around as if just now realizing where they were and what they were about. "Oh, God, Tess." He started to lift himself off of her but she held tight.

Laying her hand against the side of his face, she gently forced him to look at her. She found what she expected to see. There, in the inside corner of his eye, was a tear. She brushed it with the pad of her thumb.

"Why?"

He didn't want to talk about it. His reluctance was plain to see. A dull stain edged up his face.

"Why?" she repeated.

"Because I'm an animal—"

"No! I don't mind this," she said slowly, realizing the words were true. Her body still cradled his. His weight felt good. "Just explain to me."

"I'm tired of death." The bleak expression on his face caught at her heart.

A lock of his hair hung down over one eye. She brushed it back. "You had no choice."

"I reacted, Tess. I reacted like a soldier."

"You may have saved our lives."

"I took theirs." He released a deep breath and gathered her in his arms, squeezing her close. "I don't want to kill anymore," he whispered. "I'm tired of fighting."

Tess tilted his head to look in his eyes. "You don't have to fight anymore," she promised. "We have each other. Remember? *Together*. Your life now is with me."

Her words echoed those he'd spoken to her at the church. Pressing the tips of her fingers against the lines on his forehead, she realized that in some way, they had crossed a threshold. "No more war. We'll find peace at Erwynn Keep."

"Yes. Peace." He hugged her tight. "I don't deserve you." The conviction in his words made her nervous—especially because she knew what he didn't. She wasn't everything he thought she was. She should tell him her secrets right now.

But she didn't. Instead, she kissed him, thankful for the warmth of his lips and the strength in his arms. He'd saved them today. She prayed he'd forgive her when the truth was finally known.

He smiled and, for the first time since she'd found him by the stream, seemed to relax.

His weight shifted. "Come. They'll wonder where we are." In one graceful movement, he came to his feet. He rebuttoned himself and then reached for her.

She used both hands to take ahold of his. He easily set her on her feet. Bending, he brushed the grass from her skirt. "I've made a mess of your hair."

"I don't care."

He shook his head as if to say she were hopeless, and maybe she was. Something had happened between them, something more than the mere act of coupling while he put on his shirt and jacket.

She pulled the pins from her hair and quickly braided it. As they walked back to where the coach waited, their steps matched each other's. Perfectly.

Brenn had tucked her hand in the crook of his arm, and again she marveled at his quiet strength. This afternoon, she'd learned the sort of thing only a woman married to a man could ever know. She took this piece of knowledge and pondered it, close in her heart.

They pulled into the yard of a farmhouse shortly before dusk. Dogs barked, heralding their arrival.

Tess looked out the window. "Where are we?"

Brenn spoke. "Duck Pond Inn. I hope you don't mind. It is out of the way, but clean. I stay here every chance I can."

She stretched. "Why is that?"

"Because there are some lasses here I can't resist." Brenn opened the coach door.

Tess froze. "Lasses?"

He laughed and jumped to the ground. "You must meet them," he told her.

At that moment, high-pitched voices shouted joyfully, "He's here! He's here! You're back!"

Tess poked her head out of the coach and the swift jab of jealousy vanished. Two precious little girls charged across the yard from the front door of the yellow brick farmhouse. They couldn't have been more than eight and six. They were followed by a third curly-haired lass whose short legs couldn't keep up with her older sisters.

All three girls hugged Brenn around the waist with unabashed adoration. The youngest one raised her hands and he swung her up into his arms.

"Marigold," he said. "You have straw in your hair." He pulled a strand from her dark curls.

A dimple appeared in the corner of her mouth. "Sukey has had puppies. Do you want to see them? We've just come from there."

"In a moment I will," he said. "But first I want the three of you to meet someone special." He led them over to the coach. "This is my wife, Lady Merton."

"Oooo, she's lovely," Marigold said. The older two hung back, too shy to speak. They watched Tess with wide brown eyes.

Tess stepped down to the ground, thoroughly entranced. These three little girls in their home-spun dresses and pinafores were darling.

Brenn introduced them, laying his hand on the oldest's head first. "Tess, this is Amanda, and here's her sister, Lucy, and, of course, Marigold Faraway. And this," he said, moving toward the doorway where a woman stood, "is Sarah Faraway, the mother of this brood."

Sarah turned out to be a lovely woman with snapping brown eyes, a cupid's mouth the same as her daughters', and a belly pregnant with another child. A sandy-haired man wearing an innkeeper's apron come up behind her, resting his hand on her shoulder.

"Brenn," the man said good-naturedly. "You didn't spend long in London. You must have . . ." His voice trailed off into a low whistle as his gaze lit upon Tess.

"Darryl, this is my wife, Tess. Tess, Darryl is a gentleman who fancies himself an innkeeper," Brenn said with genuine affection.

"We're doing a fine business, thank you very much," Darryl boasted.

Tess heard the conversation over her head as

she knelt in front of the older girls. She held out her gloved hand. "I'm pleased to meet you," she said to Amanda.

Amanda shyly took her hand, wiping hers off on her pinafore apron first.

Lucy, however, was braver. She dared to speak. "Are you the wife Uncle Brenn promised to fetch from London?"

Startled, Tess flashed a look up at her husband. *Uncle* Brenn?

He wasn't paying attention. He talked to Sarah while bouncing Marigold on his arm.

She said to Lucy, "Did he tell you he was going to fetch a wife?"

"Oh, yes," both girls assured her.

Brenn suddenly claimed Tess's attention. "Lucy will give away the family secrets if we let her."

"Is there a touch of nervousness in your voice, *Uncle* Brenn?" Tess asked archly.

He just laughed.

"I thought you said you didn't have family."

"Darryl is one of the sons of the family that took me in," Brenn answered. "And he continues to take me in."

Sarah said, "Come, you both must be tired from traveling."

At that moment, the heavier luggage coach pulled up. Amidst the confusion and the dogs barking, Willa climbed out. "Merciful heavens, this can't be where we are going to stay? This isn't a decent inn. My lady doesn't stay in hovels, especially after a day like today. Isn't there something better?"

"Willa," Tess warned. "Mr. and Mrs. Faraway are relations."

Willa covered her mouth with her hand as if she could call back the words. Whirling around, she directed her sharp tongue at supervising the unloading of the coaches.

Tess turned to Sarah and Darryl. "I'm sorry. Willa doesn't always know her place."

Her apology was immediately accepted by the easygoing Darryl but not by Sarah—or by Willa, who huffed a response under her breath.

Marigold interrupted then, begging Brenn to go out to the barn and look at the puppies. Tess was aware that Sarah was taking in every detail of her appearance. She also sensed she was *not* meeting with Sarah's approval.

"Let me show you to your room," Sarah said, adding stiffly, "my lady."

"Please call me Tess," she said, anxious to be included. "After all, we are like family."

"Yes," Sarah agreed, but there was no acceptance in the word. She showed Tess to an ample room in the back of the rambling house. A few minutes later, Willa led Tim, who was carrying in the luggage for the night, into the room and Sarah excused herself.

Willa started to say something about the furnishings in the room, but Tess quickly warned her, "Not one word."

The dresser sniffed her opinion then, muttering something about doubting if they had decent accommodations for herself. Tess ignored her.

Instead, she removed her hat and gloves and went in search of Brenn. Outside, a line of baby ducks following their mother marched across her path. Surprisingly, the dogs—a yellow hound and a small terrier, both of doubtful lineage—let them pass. Tess watched them waddling, then heard the sound of laughter. She followed it and found Brenn standing by the side of a good-sized pond, throwing rocks to the delight of the girls.

Lucy noticed her first. "Come join us, Lady Tess," she shouted with excitement. "We are having a contest to see who can skip a rock the most times."

"Skip a rock?" Tess smiled. "Whatever is that?"

"You've never skipped a rock?" Lucy demanded.

"We can show you how," Amanda offered.

"Like this!" Marigold exclaimed and heaved a rock into the pond where it landed with a plop.

"No," Amanda corrected her. She started telling Tess how to skip a rock and in minutes they had Tess included in the game. She'd never done anything like this in her life and her rocks sank, but she had a good time laughing at her own mistakes.

She also found she enjoyed being in the presence of children. At first, she was a bit stiff. Children had never been a part of her circle. But these girls were delightful and she became more at ease with them.

And she liked watching Brenn handle them. He listened to what each girl told him, helping Marigold when she needed it, answering Lucy's endless questions, and drawing Amanda into the conversation. This was how her father had been with her. No matter what he was doing, he always had time for her.

Too soon, Sarah called them to supper. Picking his jacket up off the ground, Brenn took Tess's hand. The girls ran ahead of them.

"Darryl and Sarah want to make this house into a successful inn," he said.

"Have they been innkeepers long?"

"A year or two."

Inside, the Duck Pond Inn had a small common room that was empty at present.

"Don't have trade until later in the evening," Darryl told them.

"But it is coming along?" Brenn asked.

"Aye, slow but steady," Sarah answered for her husband. "We will make a success of it."

The word "we" was not lost on Tess.

"I have your dinner set up in here," Sarah said, directing them to a room off the main hall.

Brenn stopped. "What is wrong with the family's quarters? That's where I've always eaten before."

"I thought it would be best to be more formal. You're a lord now." Sarah didn't look at Tess but Tess knew she was the reason behind this change of tradition.

"Don't be a goose, Sarah," Brenn said. "I was a lord three weeks ago, too, and you fed me in the kitchen. Besides, Tess wants to eat with the family too. Don't you, Tess?"

"Of course," she agreed quickly.

The expression on Sarah's face said that she didn't believe her, but Sarah did as Brenn directed. She carried their plates back into the kitchen, where she practically threw them onto the table already set for the rest of the family.

Brenn and Darryl exchanged glances. Darryl

shrugged. "She's pregnant," he whispered.

"It may be me," Tess said in a low undervoice to her husband.

Brenn rested his hand against the small of her back. "Or me. Since Sarah married Darryl, she treats me like a brother. Which means she can get as angry as if I were her brother too. This won't be the first time I've upset Sarah's plans."

"You should have invited all of them to the wedding."

He shrugged. "Since I've come into the title, she's been somewhat distant."

"Willa's comment didn't help."

"Don't let it bother you," he advised her.

But it did. Brenn's affection for the whole family was plain and Tess understood why. The girls were charming and Darryl's teasing made her feel at ease.

Tess had never eaten in a kitchen before. But surrounded by the Faraways' three daughters, with the smell of freshly baked bread and cooked meats in the air, she decided she rather liked it. It became important to her to earn Sarah's goodwill.

For that reason, when they had finished eating and Sarah and the older girls got up from the table to clear the dishes, Tess rose with them. She picked up a plate.

"You don't have to do that," Sarah said. "You're a guest."

"I'm family," Tess gently reiterated.

For a second, Sarah studied her skeptically. Then she said, "I'd wager you've never cleaned a table before."

"Can it be that hard?" Tess countered.

Sarah's mouth twitched into what could almost have been a smile. "Suit yourself. Come, girls." Even Marigold did her share.

Doing dishes wasn't difficult, and it was pleasant to be included. The girls chattered happily and the chore was done in little time. When Sarah disappeared, Tess caught sight of her in an alcove off the kitchen talking to her husband. He was kneading her back.

She paused, watching. Neil and Stella rarely touched in affection, nor did most of the couples Tess had known. As Darryl finished easing the tension in his wife's neck, his hand followed the line of her arm. Their fingers brushed, then hooked, and a slight squeeze passed between them.

That was it, a little squeeze, and yet Tess had never witnessed such an honest display of affection.

She wondered if Sarah had brought a dowry to her marriage. Or did Darryl love her just for who she was?

Tess had known women far more lovely and certainly richer, but in that moment, she envied Sarah Faraway.

The family quarters were comprised of two bedrooms and a sitting room and were located just beyond the kitchen. Sarah led them to the sitting room. "Darryl has gone to work in the taproom," she told Tess. "We have a good spot of business late in the evening."

Brenn sat in a winged back chair of front of the cold hearth. Marigold climbed into his lap. "Now you tell a story," she demanded of him. "You promised."

"Yes, a story," Lucy said. Even, Amanda hurried to Brenn's side.

Sarah offered Tess the chair next to his, which was obviously hers but Tess waved for her to sit in it. She was comfortable on a footstool and Sarah looked like she needed a moment or two off her feet. After lighting a candle, Sarah reached for a basket of sewing.

"What is this about a story?" Tess asked.

Sarah smiled. "You didn't know that Brenn is the finest storyteller for five parishes around?"

Tess shook her head, smiling.

"It's the Welsh in his blood," Sarah confided. "Means he's full of Celtic nonsense."

Brenn made wounded noises but Tess laughed, happy to be included.

"What story are you going to tell?" Amanda asked.

Lucy and Marigold started to suggest old favorites, but Brenn said, "How about a new one that I've learned?"

"What is the story?" Lucy asked eagerly.

"It's about a young sheepherder who lived by the most beautiful lake in the world."

He had Tess's attention. "Like that beside Erwynn Keep?" she asked.

"Perhaps," he answered, a smile on his lips. He started the story. "One night the moon was so round and full, the shepherd couldn't sleep. He lay awake by the side of that lake, watching his sheep, when suddenly a beautiful young girl rose up out of the lake."

Marigold gave a great gasp of surprise. "What was she doing in the lake?" she whispered.

"She was magic," Brenn answered.

Amanda and Lucy grinned at each other. Tess wondered if any young girl could resist such a story. It was the stuff dreams were made of.

Brenn continued. "The shepherd fell instantly in love with her. He didn't waste a moment but fell to his knees right there on the side of the lake and asked—no, begged for her hand in marriage."

"Like you did with Tess?" Amanda surprised them all by asking.

"Amanda, such a fanciful notion," her mother scolded but Brenn nodded.

"That's right," he said. His gaze met Tess's as he continued, "And the lady said yes to the marriage because the shepherd was a very *handsome* lad."

Tess rolled her eyes and the girls giggled.

"But," Brenn said, "the lady told him she would only marry him if he agreed to one condition. If he struck her three times without cause, however lightly, she would be forced to return immediately to the lake."

"But he wouldn't strike her, would he?" Lucy said.

"Of course not," Brenn assured her. "Or at least, that is what he thought. The two of them were wed. They had several sons and were very happy . . . except that over the years the shepherd tapped his beautiful wife once or twice. He did it without much thought and unfortunately, he did it a third time. Within the blink of an eye she vanished into the lake. Overcome by grief, her husband jumped in after her."

"What happened then?" Amanda asked.

"He drowned, more like," Sarah said, tying a knot in her needlework.

"No!" Lucy cried out. "He couldn't. He was so in love."

"He may have," Brenn said sadly. "No one ever saw them again. But their sons lived on and to this day the Black Mountains are populated with the offspring of that shepherd and his magical lady."

"That's where you live, isn't it, Uncle Brenn?" Amanda asked. "The Black Mountains in Wales."

"That's right, poppet," he told her. "And that is how I know the story to be true." He shifted Marigold. She had fallen asleep in his lap.

"Here, let me put her to bed," Sarah said, starting to put aside her sewing, but Tess stood up quickly.

"I'll take her. You relax." Before Sarah could comment, Tess scooped the toddler up in her arms. At that moment, Darryl appeared in the doorway, asking for Sarah's help with customers.

"We'll put the children to bed," Brenn told them.

"Thank you," Sarah said and then hurried to join her husband and see to her duties as the innkeeper's wife.

Rising from the chair, Brenn said, "I'll take her if she is too heavy for you."

Tess shook her head. "I've ached to hold her from the moment she fell asleep during your story." Marigold's weight in her arms felt good. The slight jealousy she'd felt when Stella had announced she was pregnant came back full bore.

Burying her nose in Marigold's dark curls, Tess felt an overwhelming desire to have a child of her own. No, not just any child. She wanted to carry Brenn's baby.

Lucy and Amanda had quickly claimed his attention. He laughed at something one of them said, his near-black eyes gleaming with laughter—and in that moment, Tess fell in love.

It was the most incredible sensation.

One moment, she was alone and separate; in the next, she'd been forever changed.

She stared at Brenn. He was still who he was, still had the broken nose, still the ready smile. Still the warrior who yearned for peace. But her perception of him had changed.

He was finer, better, braver, stronger, smarter . . . *nobler* than she'd ever imagined. He was worthy of her love.

Her vision blurred even as her heart swelled with pride.

She was in love.

She wandered after him as he saw the older girls tucked into their beds, watching him with a sense of wonder. Together they both lay Marigold down. The child's hands were doubled in loose fists.

Reading her mind, Brenn ran his finger lightly over that little fist. "She's an angel, isn't she?"

Tess could only nod, so much in love she feared to speak lest she burst out in happy tears.

They went to their room after that. Tess felt as if she'd lived five lifetimes in this one day—and yet, she wasn't tired. Instead, her newfound love made her feel as magical as that lady in the lake.

He reached for her when they were both in

bed. They made love. They took their time about it. There was much laughing and teasing about shepherds and maidens with magic powers.

And it was wonderful.

Chapter Thirteen

The next morning, Brenn left Tess with a kiss and went to find Sarah, who was preparing breakfast. He leaned against the door for a moment, watching her efficient movements.

"Does carrying the baby when it sticks out like that bother you?" he asked.

She turned in surprise at the sound of his voice and then laughed. "No, I've become so used to being pregnant I can do almost anything in spite of it. I do grow tired though." She forked some sausages on a plate. "Where is your bride?"

"With her maid."

Sarah said, "Ahhh," in understanding, but Brenn also heard a hint of criticism in that one sound.

"She's not what you think," he said, coming into the kitchen. He gave her a light kiss on the cheek.

"Is she rich? Did you find what you were looking for?"

"She could buy out the treasury," he bragged. "I'll be able to help you and Darryl out a bit now."

"We're doing fine on our own," Sarah said briskly, wiping her hands on her apron. "We have enough time for managing the inn and for the children, which is exactly how we want our life. *You*, on the hand, had better do a bit of thinking."

Straddling a chair, Brenn asked, "What sort of thinking?"

Sarah considered him a moment. He'd known her since he was little older than Marigold. She had always been with Darryl, and Brenn valued her good common sense and her friendship.

But she surprised him by saying, "When you set off on your errand to find a wife, I'd hoped you wouldn't succeed."

"Why not? I needed the money."

"Brenn, marriage is more than just having silver in your pocket. Darryl and I often worry where the money will come from, but we wouldn't trade what we have found with each other for any fortune. I can't imagine my life without him. Can you say the same about Tess?"

Brenn thought back to the warm, willing woman he'd just left in bed. They'd made love for hours last night. He'd rarely had such a responsive lover. Just thinking about her made him hungry for more. And then yesterday, when he'd lost himself . . .

The directions of his thoughts must have showed in his face because Sarah gave him a playful slap. "Men! You are all beasts!"

"Even Darryl?"

"Him especially! Why do you think I waddle around here pregnant almost every change of the season?" But there was no anger in her words.

She placed her hands on his arms and looked into his eyes. "Brenn, be serious now. Tess is a lovely girl. And, since you are the type of man who achieves whatever he sets his mind to, very rich. But I worry."

"About what? I'll treat her well."

"Women are not like men. At some point she is going to want more from you than 'good treatment.' "

"What more is there?"

She shook her head sadly. "If I have to tell you, then it isn't worth the saying."

He frowned. "I'm not good with riddles, Sarah. Not first thing in the morning."

"Does your marriage mean nothing to you?"

"It means a great deal. With her money, I'm going to build the finest house in all Wales."

"Have you told her the truth about Erwynn Keep?"

"What? Do you think I'm daft?" Sarah had a way of going straight at a problem.

"You must. It will only be harder on you the longer you put it off."

"I'll do it in my own time, in my own way."

She "tisked" softly before saying, "My handsome friend, marriage must be something more than a business arrangement."

"The *ton* arranges marriages all the time. Tess's own father even said that an heiress should never be allowed to choose for herself."

"And would he have chosen you?"

She had him there. "He would have seen my potential."

Sarah sat down at the table across from him. "Potential doesn't strike me as a good quality in

a husband. Worse, you have captured a hothouse
flower. I doubt if she will enjoy living in the
wilds of Wales."

Brenn sat back. "You're wrong," he said confidently. "Tess is made of sterner stuff."

Sarah looked at him doubtfully. "Last night
was the first time she'd ever picked up a dish
from her own table in her life."

"But she did it."

"Aye, that she did."

"Besides, she'll have servants to do her work
at Erwynn Keep," he said, dismissing Sarah's
concern with a shrug. And then, because he valued their friendship, he stood and gave her a kiss
on the forehead. "You worry too much, Sarah.
Tess and I will be fine."

"Why does she worry about us?" came Tess's
voice from the doorway.

Brenn and Sarah turned with a start.

"Good morning," he said quickly, wondering
how much she had overheard.

"Good morning," she answered, walking into
the room. Her dress was cut in the latest fashion
. . . and she looked sorely out of place in Sarah's
kitchen.

"You are wearing blue again today," he observed.

"Yes, you said you like that color," Tess answered. "I shall wear it every day if you wish."

Her avowal underscored Sarah's concerns and
he felt a flash of guilt.

"Good morning, Sarah," Tess said.

"Good morning," Sarah answered. She shot a
glance at Brenn. She'd known what he was
thinking.

Brenn shook his head. Sarah was wrong. He and Tess would deal famously together. Last night in bed had more than proven that fact.

Now it was his wife's turn to read his mind. She colored prettily and suddenly became interested in the pattern of the floorboards. Against the tight bodice of her dress, her nipples hardened.

Dear Lord, he had the urge to sweep her off her feet and return to bed with her. He forced his insatiable lust into some semblance of control and invited Tess to sit down for breakfast.

She sipped a cup of tea while he did justice to Sarah's breakfast. When Sarah was called away by one of the girls, Tess leaned across the table. "I've started writing a book, just as you suggested."

He didn't remember the suggestion.

"The day we left London," she prompted. "Don't you remember?"

"Maria Edgeworth."

"Yes," she said.

He'd talked about Mrs. Edgeworth to needle her, but if writing made her this happy, she could write Bibles for all he cared. "Are you going to write about matchmaking and husband hunting?"

Tess laughed. "I could." She sobered. "I started writing about our journey. Actually, it is more of a journal, a bit like Minnie's was."

Brenn felt a touch of guilt.

Within the hour, they pulled away from the Duck Pond Inn's yard. The three little girls and Darryl waved farewell enthusiastically amid calls to come back. Sarah was more reserved. But then, even weeks ago, before he'd set off for London, he'd known she didn't like his plan.

Women's heads were full of romantic nonsense.

"I don't think she liked me," Tess said, once they were out of sight of the inn.

"Sarah does like you. She's just always been too serious."

"Well, I can understand some of her worry."

"You can?"

Tess nodded. "She is obviously concerned about the type of wife you've married. I mean, we really haven't known each other long." She hesitated and then asked in a soft, worried voice, "Brenn, why did you marry me? Was it only to save me from scandal?"

"What do you mean?" he asked cautiously. Tess was too perceptive.

"When you were telling that story last night, the girls wanted to believe it was about us. Amanda and Lucy both asked me about it this morning."

Brenn felt a rush of relief. She didn't suspect a thing. His smile was genuine as he said, "Well, they have vivid imaginations. They place themselves in every story I tell."

Her hand came down close to his which was resting on the seat. "Did you know I'd begged an introduction to you the night of the Garlands' ball? I knew you were searching for a wife, but there was more."

"What more?"

"I saw you staring at me and, well, I don't know . . . it just seemed as if something *special* passed between us." She fixed a hopeful blue gaze on him. "Did you not feel the same?"

Brenn remembered the moment clearly. He'd

wanted her. It had been lust, guilt-free, undeniable.

But he couldn't tell her that.

And yet, Sarah had goaded his conscience. He had to be honest with Tess. So he admitted, "From the moment I saw you, I wanted you."

He was glad he had told the truth, because she was in his lap in a heartbeat, raining kisses on his face. "I knew it!" she said. "This morning, before I came down to join you, I wrote the shepherd's story in my copybook. It is the first thing I wanted to write because I never want to forget it."

Pleased with himself, Brenn shifted her weight in his lap and put his arm tightly around her waist. His mind pictured other ways she could show her appreciation but at that moment the coach stopped. He pulled down the window and shouted for Tim. The postboy jumped down from his horse.

"I beg pardon, my lord," Tim said. "But you wanted to stop when we reached the Welsh border."

Tess opened the coach door and was out in an instant. Brenn followed her. The coach rested on a small knoll. The sky was a vivid blue with huge puffs of clouds floating across it. The sun caught and gleamed off a stream that wound its way across the landscape. Along the steam, sheep dotted the fields like miniature versions of the clouds in the sky.

A gentle breeze captured a few stray strands of hair, blowing them into her face. She pushed them back. "It looks like England," she said with a touch of disappointment.

"England?" The word burst out of Brenn. How could she not see the difference? Even the earth smelled differently to him. It made his senses feel alive, and had from the first time he'd crossed this border.

It was his home.

With a jolt, he realized that Tess didn't feel his kinship with the land. He started to understand what Sarah had been trying to tell him.

And he began to worry.

What was Tess going to say when she beheld Erwynn Keep?

As they traveled into Wales, Tess noticed that Brenn had become very quiet. She shouldn't have blurted out that she couldn't see a difference between Wales and England. She'd immediately sensed the change in his attitude as soon as the words left her lips.

So because she wanted to please him, she talked about how much she was looking forward to arriving at Erwynn Keep. "Do you have your drawings close at hand?" she asked. "I'd like to look at them again."

"I'm not certain where they are," he answered, his voice sounding strained.

"You aren't coming down ill, are you?"

"No. Why?"

"You don't sound like yourself."

"Nothing is the matter," he said and, to prove it true, he started talking about the farm equipment he had ordered for Erwynn Keep's fields.

Tess didn't think any conversation could be more boring than one about the different shape of plows.

*   *   *

Around one o'clock, they pulled into a village off the main road. Tess was famished; they hadn't come to a town for hours. Brenn assured her Wales was more populated by the coast.

It was too bad they hadn't been traveling along the coast when she'd grown hungry.

Tim drove the coach to an inn whose door sat invitingly open. It was located at the end of a row of houses lining either side of the road.

The luggage coach pulled up behind them. Willa hopped out, needing relief. She ran to the back of the inn, muttering about never finding a place to stop in this uncivilized land.

"Willa exaggerates," Tess told Brenn, before following Willa.

"I am not exaggerating," Willa defended herself when Tess came around the corner. "I feel we are driving into a heathen nation with accommodations to match!"

"Don't be silly."

"Clarence was telling me stories. These people don't think like us."

"They don't know us."

"Not *us*—the English."

Tess shook her head with a laugh.

"It's true," Willa stressed. "They call us Saxons."

"So? It's just an antiquated way of saying the English. They may be a bit backward here, but they are good people," she declared with confidence.

A few minutes later, she questioned her opinion.

The inn was so small, it was obvious that there

would be no private room. The main room was busy, but all talk came to a halt when their party walked in.

Tess leaned back toward Brenn. She covered her mouth with one gloved hand before saying, "I have been known to cause a stir when I entered a room, but I've never struck anyone speechless."

He chuckled. "Come sit over here." He directed her to a trestle table in a far corner.

A man who had the bearing of an innkeeper approached. He spoke to Brenn in gibberish.

Now it was Tess's turn to stare.

Brenn spoke gibberish back. It surprised Tess to see that the innkeeper understood what he'd said and answered Brenn in English.

"We've got rabbit today. A good cheese and ale."

"That will be fine," Brenn told him.

Tess sat at the table, feeling very much the center of speculation. The table was not the cleanest. Willa's eyebrows came up to say, *I told you so.* Tess frowned at her to sit down.

As the innkeeper turned to fetch their luncheon, the other customers decided to go back to their business. The air filled with the sound of a foreign tongue.

"What language are they speaking?" Tess whispered to Brenn.

"Welsh."

"Welsh? Why don't they speak English?"

Brenn laughed. "Because the Welsh are cursedly independent."

"Do you speak their language?"

"Just enough to say I don't speak Welsh."

Tess frowned at him, irritated.

"What?" he said, responding to her unspoken criticism.

"Why didn't you tell me this before?"

"Tell you what?"

How could he be so thickheaded? "That this isn't England."

"It *is* England. They just speak a different language. And there are always people who speak English."

Tess sat back, listening to the voices around her. "Not many."

Brenn flicked a bit of caked food off the table. "Not in the country," he conceded. "Along the coast, a good number of the Welsh speak English."

"What about at Erwynn Keep?"

"Oh, well." He took a moment before saying, "One or two speak English."

Willa made a humming sound. Her back was ramrod-straight.

Tess glanced around the room. Everyone looked respectable enough. But she couldn't help saying under her breath, "This is a long way from London."

At that moment, the innkeeper arrived with their food. To Tess's surprise, the meal was delicious. She even liked the ale. It was sweeter than any she'd had before, with a bit of a bite.

She was just about to say as much to Brenn, when a young man dressed little better than a sheepherder stepped in from outside. Everyone greeted him. "Daniel!"

But instead of answering them, Daniel began reciting.

"What's he saying?" Tess asked Brenn.

"Poetry."

Tess looked over the man's rough costume. "Poetry."

"They all do it here, Tess. The Welsh have a love for rhyme and song. They can go like this all day."

To add truth to Brenn's words, once Daniel had finished, another man stood up and began reciting. And then another who appeared little better than a chimney sweep. They were cheered on by the innkeeper and his patrons.

She finished her meal, thinking this was all a bit upside down. "Would you mind if I took a walk before we set off again?"

Brenn started to rise. "I'll go with you."

"No, you continue eating. Willa can come."

The maid was only too happy to oblige. She'd barely touched her food.

Outside, Tess tied the ribbons of her bonnet into a bow as she drew a deep breath. "Let's go this way," she said, pointing to her left.

Willa immediately started voicing her complaints, starting with all the posturing and carrying on in the inn. Tess listened to her with half an ear. She had her own sense of disquiet to deal with. This was her new home . . . and she was a stranger in her own country! Perhaps after a short visit to Erwynn Keep, Brenn could be convinced to live in London. She longed for what was familiar.

They'd crossed the road and started their way back toward the coaches when a group of boys jumped out from between two houses, shouting and yelling.

"Merciful Lord, they're attacking!" Willa shouted. She would have started running except that Tess grabed her arm.

"Don't be ridiculous," Tess said sensibly. "They are boys . . . shouting at a bush." Which was the truth. The lads gathered around a scraggly bush, shouting in Welsh at it.

"No, they are heathens worshipping!" Willa cried.

One of the boys threw a rock into the bush. At that moment, a scrawny black cat crawled out from beneath the bottom leaves and streaked through the lads' legs, running for its life. The boys gave chase.

"It's a cat!" Tess cried. "A poor little cat!"

She started after them, alarmed that anyone could mistreat an animal in such a manner.

The cat ran, its head low, its ears back. The screaming boys followed, and Tess followed the boys. Her straw bonnet came flying off to bounce against her back, held on by only the ribbons around her neck. Behind her Willa called for help and deliverance.

Unfortunately, the cat's path was blocked by the stamping coach horses. Unnerved, the animal swerved and then started to dash for the only safety it could see—the door to the inn.

Just as the cat would have run inside, Brenn stepped outside. The little cat smashed headfirst into his boots. Its paws scrambling, it started to run away but Brenn caught the animal in his gloved hands, lifting it up by the scruff of the neck.

"What have we here?" he said.

The boys skidded to a halt, their eyes widening at the sight of the tall stranger. Almost as one, they turned and scattered off into different directions.

Tess came charging up. "They were chasing this poor cat," she said, trying to catch her breath. "You may have saved its life."

The innkeeper and patrons crowded into the doorway behind Brenn, their eyes agog at the sudden commotion.

Brenn brought the cat up to eye level. It hissed and spat, trying to break free. There wasn't much to him. Sores and bald patches marred his coat. One ear looked as if it had been torn. He was so thin, Tess could see his bones. Her heart went out to him.

The innkeeper stepped forward. "Here, let me take him from you, my lord. That there is the vicar's cat. He's nothing but a nuisance."

"The vicar's cat!" Tess said with indignation. "Why does he not take better care of his pet than this?" She reached for the cat before the innkeeper could have it.

The poor kitty recognized a safe haven. It dug its claws into Tess's bodice and watched the innkeeper and the others with round yellow-green eyes.

"Why, the vicar's dead," the innkeeper said. "He passed on almost a year ago."

"Then why doesn't someone take care of this cat?" Tess asked. "Look at the poor thing. It's starving!"

To give truth to her words, the animal let out a pitiful "meow" that was met without a blink of sympathy from any of the patrons of the inn.

"Everyone has enough cats of their own," the

innkeeper said. "Besides, those lads—" He shrugged. "They are the sons of Dissenters. We've a good number of them around and there's not a person that wants some Church of England cat."

Tess wasn't certain she had heard him correctly. "Are you saying that people in this village will not take in this cat for no other reason than because it was owned by a clergyman with the Church of England?"

"Yes, my lady," the innkeeper said without an ounce of hesitation. "The Dissenters are a strong-minded lot. They have conviction."

"Then I'll take the cat" she snapped. "He'll make his home with me!"

"Tess," Brenn started to protest.

"I'm keeping the cat, Brenn."

He looked from the mangy animal and back to her. "Very well. If my wife wants a cat, she shall have a cat. Innkeeper, do you have a hamper for this cat to travel in? And we'll need an assortment of your best table scraps."

"That's one lucky kitty," the innkeeper said.

While the innkeeper did Brenn's bidding, Tess petted the poor cat, saying calming words to it.

"I was afraid you were going to be murdered, taking out after those boys," Willa said dramatically.

"Well, I wasn't and I have this fine kitty for my troubles," Tess answered.

Brenn reached out but instead of petting the cat as she'd thought he was going to, he rubbed the back of his gloved fingers against her cheek. "You were brave, Tess. Foolish but brave."

Brave. No one had ever said that about her. In

that moment, Tess could have fallen in love with him all over again.

A minute later, the innkeeper returned with choice table scraps and a hamper with a lid.

Brenn helped Tess and her new friend up into the coach. He knocked on the side, and they were off. "Look," he said to Tess.

She leaned across his lap to look out the window back the way they'd come. The innkeeper and his patrons still stood on the road, watching the coaches drive off in profound silence.

"Do you think they'll write a poem to us?" she asked archly.

Brenn laughed, the hearty sound filling the coach and frightening the little cat.

He calmed it by scratching under its chin. "What are you going to name him?"

Tess considered a moment. "Miles."

"Why Miles?"

"I like the name."

For his part, Miles growled deep in his throat at Brenn, apparently not ready to forgive his capture.

"Quiet," she told him. "If it wasn't for him, those boys would have gotten you."

To her delight, Miles stopped his growling, although he did keep a cautious eye on Brenn.

Miles was grateful for the food. Tess tore the pieces of meat into smaller morsels. Brenn warned her not to give Miles too much or he'd get sick.

She put a shawl in the bottom of the hamper and Miles curled up into an exhausted ball and went to sleep.

"What a sweet cat," Tess said. "I can't imagine

anyone mistreating him. Especially over religion. I thought all of that was settled centuries ago."

"It's never settled as long as men have differing opinions."

"But I thought there was only one church in England."

"Tess, there are almost as many different faiths as trees in England. Perhaps in your circle most people are of the same religion but it is different out here in the country. Do you not have any friends who are Catholic?"

"No. I met a Catholic woman once . . . and I've seen Jews but I've never associated with them."

"You did live a sheltered life."

The criticism stung a bit. She crossed her arms and asked the question uppermost on her mind. "Will Erwynn Keep be like that village?"

"My uncle was a staunch Church of England man. However, don't let different opinions stop you from exploring new ideas. The world is full of good people who share different beliefs."

"Then you think those boys were justified in throwing rocks at poor Miles."

"No, they weren't. And that's not what I said."

"Then I hate that religion. I think Parliament should pass a law and make it a crime to practice something so horrid."

Brenn took her hand. "Parliament did do that years ago and it threw us into civil war. Tess, don't hate the religion. It's intolerance that makes people do evil."

"Is that what the village boys were? Intolerant?"

"Absolutely, but don't stop with religion. Intolerance is everywhere. Why, in my few weeks in London, I witnessed members of the *ton* socially ostracize those who didn't follow social protocol to the letter. It was ridiculous. Look at men like Deland Godwin. With his paper, he attempts to destroy anything that doesn't fit his particular ideas—and for what reason except to puff up his own consequence?"

"Oh, yes, Godwin." She frowned. "He is the reason Anne can't find a husband. When she was first presented, he made terrible fun of her for no other reason than because he likes to choose one debutante to ridicule. It has been very hard for her ever since. I call her a friend, although some girls were afraid to."

"I didn't like him."

"He's very powerful though."

"People like him exist because the rest of us are either followers or refuse to stand up to them. You are neither of those things, Tess. You befriended Anne and you chased off those boys. You were a fine sight." He smiled as he said those last words, but there was pride in his voice.

Tess slid closer to him. She slipped her hand in his. "I don't think I've ever talked to someone in such a straightforward manner as I do with you. And in my first three days of marriage, I've had more new experiences and been introduced to more new ideas than in all the years since Minnie died."

"At Erwynn Keep," he said, "we will create the type of world we wish it to be. No war. No hunger. No selfish men wishing to rule the world with their own petty ideas."

"No intolerance."

"Yes."

"But isn't it already like that?"

Her question caught him off guard. He hesitated, his brows coming together in a frown.

"I mean, the pictures you drew," she said lamely. "It looks so lovely and peaceful."

"Yes." His voice sounded distant. She looked up and discovered that he watched her intently.

"What is it?" she asked.

His fingers tightened around hers momentarily and then he released her hand completely. "It's nothing. I'm just anxious to return home."

That night, they stayed at an inn that was not as cozy as the Faraways' or as ostentatious as the King's Crown. Miles delighted her by wanting to sleep on her pillow.

Later, while she and Brenn made love, Tess whispered the words she'd discovered in her heart. She told him she loved him.

He didn't answer, but held her close and she fell asleep at peace with the world.

Brenn couldn't sleep.

She'd told him she loved him. She'd spoken the words as he had released his seed inside her.

He stared up at the ceiling, not knowing what to say to her. Her words should have made him happy and yet he felt guilty. On the morrow, they would reach Erwynn Keep and the truth would be out.

The wealthy debutante he'd married was changing. She was giving far more to this marriage and to him than he'd ever imagined.

He could only pray that once she laid eyes on Erwynn Keep, she would forgive him.

Chapter Fourteen

Miles woke them both the next morning, anxious to go out. It was just as well; Tess was anxious to make an early start and to see her new home.

"When shall we reach Erwynn Keep?" she asked.

"By midday." Brenn stood shaving in front of a square mirror. He was dressed except for his shirt. He rinsed his razor off in the basin and scraped a few more whiskers off. He wasn't moving very quickly.

"Are you feeling well?" she asked.

"What?" He acted as if her question didn't register a moment and then said, "Oh, yes, I'm fine. Just preoccupied."

She crossed over to him. "You act tired. Did you not sleep well?" She was teasing him but he answered her seriously.

"I slept fine."

Still wearing her nightdress, Tess put her arms around his waist and rubbed his back with her breasts. "I slept *wonderfully*," she whispered.

He froze, and then lowered the razor and turned to her. Half of his face still had the shaving soap on it. "Tess—" He lifted a hand to her face. His thumb brushed her lips. She parted them and touched his thumb with her tongue.

His arm pulled her close. "It's hard to believe you were once called the Ice Maiden."

"That was before you." She pressed her lips to the warm skin of his chest. "Before I fell in love."

Brenn sucked in a breath. She snuggled closer, her voice humming with desire as she said, "Are my hands cold? Do you want to warm them?"

Placing his hands on hers, he moved them from around his waist. "I'm trying to shave." He reached for a towel and dried his face. "You could cause a man to slit his own throat coming up like that." He wadded the towel and set it beside the bowl before noticing the expression on her face. "What have I done?"

"Nothing." She wasn't going to tell him either but then the words slipped out. "You're so distant."

He raked his hair back with his fingers. "I'm sorry, Tess. I'm just ready to go home."

Home. The word sounded solid. "Of course you are," she agreed, anxious for any plausible explanation for his distant behavior.

Later, over breakfast, Tess watched him eat. Perhaps he'd learned her secret. Could she, at some time during the night, have whispered the truth about her fortune? She had always had vivid dreams and could talk in her sleep—

She set her teacup in the saucer, scarcely able to breathe.

Now it was his turn to be concerned. "Tess, what is the matter? You've gone pale."

For a second, her mind spun with fear. She

forced herself to look at him. "Is everything fine?" It took all her courage to ask those few words.

"Yes!" He slid around the table to her side. "I just have something on my mind. But are you all right? You look ready to swoon."

She grabbed hold of his hand as if it were a lifeline. "If you had something to say, you would say it, wouldn't you?"

He smiled. It didn't quite reach his eyes but that was fine once he said what she wanted to hear. "Yes, of course I would."

Her heart resumed its normal beat. Colors, shapes, objects returned to what they should be. He didn't know.

But she could tell him.

Tess grasped his hand tightly. She looked up at him. "Brenn—"

At that moment the postboys tramped into the common room and gave Brenn the sign that the coaches were ready. "Tess, the time has come."

She pushed aside the confession she'd just been about to make. Later, she would tell him— but not now. She wouldn't spoil his homecoming for him.

Willa was already settled in the luggage coach. Brenn handed Tess up into their coach, passing to her the hamper with Miles inside. Clarence and Tim hopped on their horses and without flourish they were off.

The day was overcast. Rain threatened but did not come. Occasionally they passed a farmer's wagon or someone walking on foot but otherwise they saw no one on the road.

Tess asked to see the drawings in Brenn's portfolio. She spread the pen and ink drawings out between them, running a finger over the proud dragon weathervane sitting on top of the cupola. "This house looks amazingly modern for its age. The windows are a nice size."

"Hmmm, yes," Brenn agreed noncommittally.

She glanced at him. He was staring out the window, lost in thought. Outside the coach, the terrain was changing from rolling hills to the steeper landscape of the Black Mountains. The curves in the road became sharper; the lack of decent springs in the coach more noticeable.

"What of the servants?" Tess asked. "I imagine many have been in the service of the earl of Merton for generations."

That question roused Brenn out of his contemplation. "There aren't any."

"No servants?" Tess glanced at the large house in the drawing. "I would think an estate of this size would have a host of servants running it."

"My uncle was eccentric. He didn't like people around." He stretched out his long legs before admitting, "The house is the worse for his pigheadedness. It needs quite a bit of work. I, ah, took a bit of license with the drawings."

"Oh." Tess wondered what he meant by that. "Well," she said with determination, "we'll set it all to rights. I'll hire servants from the village."

That caught Brenn's interest. She could almost see him relax, as if he'd feared her questions. He laced his fingers with hers. "Yes, together we'll set it all back to rights, won't we?"

"*Together*," she promised. "Tell me about the village."

"It's called Erwynn Keep, after the house. The

site of the house and the village both date to before the Middle Ages."

"What is the history?"

"Nothing dramatic. This part of Wales is secluded, almost a world of its own. The events of history bypassed Erwynn Keep. The main house was built close to six hundred years ago as a nunnery," he added with a smile. "It was confiscated during the Reformation and that is when the first earl took control in the name of Henry the Eighth. For two hundred years, an earl resided there until the family decided it preferred London. My father's father was the first to move back."

He took the drawings and paged through them until he found one of the landscape. It showed a wooden bridge over a bubbling spring and the rooftops of a village built into the sheltering haven of a mountain. The paper, a smaller rectangle than the others, was curled and yellow.

"I didn't draw this picture," he said.

"Who did?"

"My father hung it on the wall of every house he lived in. Looking at it is what made me decide to try my hand at drawing."

"And you found you had talent."

He shook his head. "Not my father's talent. I used to study this picture and wish I could put myself in it. This is the village from the vantage point of Erwynn Keep." Leaning toward her, he gestured to the bottom of the picture. "You walk over the bridge and around a bend and there is a long drive off the road. Huge pines with their boughs dripping needles line the drive like sentinels. Father said that in the autumn, you can walk knee-deep in those needles as if they were snow.

"You'll walk a fair distance and then you will start to see a flash of the lake between the trees. The drive curves around and there you are with the whole valley laid before you and in its heart is *Llyn Mynydd.*"

"*Llyn Mynydd?*"

"Mountain Lake."

"And the house?"

He shuffled through the drawings, pulling out the one of the front of the house. "It sits atop a crag of land jutting out into the lake. The house sits on top. On a clear day, the image of the house is reflected on the water." He edged closer. "Tess, there is no water clearer than that of *Llyn Mynydd*. You can see straight to the bottom, and the fish—!" He measured a span of air with his hands.

He lowered his voice. "When I first rode to Erwynn Keep, I got off my horse and walked the distance from the bridge to the house. It all seemed so familiar . . . and then I realized it was because all the stories my father had told me as a child had originated in this house."

"Even the one about the lady in the lake?"

He smiled. "Especially that one. Another story Father told me was of the *Tylwyth Tegs* who danced every night on a bridge; the movement of their tiny feet is what creates the bubbling of the stream."

"*Tylwyth Tegs?*"

"Fairy people." He tapped the drawing of the bridge with one finger. "This is the bridge he spoke of. I knew it the moment I stood upon it and heard the sound of the stream over the rocks. Later, I asked one of the shepherds if he had heard of the *Tylwyth Tegs*. He told me he'd even seen them dance." Brenn's eyes twinkled with laughter. "It was like coming home, Tess, to a place where I knew I belonged."

She took his arm. "Let us walk the distance, too. I want to see Erwynn Keep as you first saw it."

She expected him to be pleased. Instead, for a moment, he seemed ready to deny her request and then he kissed her, once on the forehead, the second time on the lips.

Passion rose up inside of her, just as it did every time he was near. She realized with a shaky start that he was her home. Wherever he was, was where she was meant to be.

"I love you," she whispered.

"I know you do, Tess, and a lucky man I am."

But he didn't tell her he loved her.

Brenn didn't know if walking the path leading to Erwynn Keep was a good idea. He needed her to be in the best mood possible before finally confronting her with the truth.

However, she was adamant especially after her first glimpse of the picturesque village.

Erwynn Keep's village seemed to have been frozen in time. Roses in full bloom climbed the stone fences and up the gray stone walls of the cottages with their slate roofs. A person could easily imagine knights in shining armor and fine ladies riding through its narrow street.

Tess breathed out a sigh of satisfaction.

Cedric Pughe, the blacksmith, was not at his

forge but his wife stood alongside the road talking to a neighbor. Her children played with several others. They all stopped and stared as the coaches drove past, scattering a group of chickens who had ventured out onto the road.

Word of Brenn's return would spread through the village in no time.

At the bridge, Brenn signaled Tim to halt the horses and climbed down from the coach before helping Tess down.

"What is it, my lord?" Tim asked.

"Take the coaches on," Brenn ordered and gave him directions.

The expression on Tim's face let it be known that he thought they were a bit daft to be wishing to walk the last mile, but Tess laughed adventurously. She'd let Miles out of his basket and he followed them.

She stepped onto the wooden planks of the bridge with anticipation in her eyes. "This is the bridge where fairies dance."

She untied her bonnet and removed it before tilting her head and listening. Water burbled over the rocks beneath the bridge as the stream made its way to *Llyn Mynydd.* "I can hear them," she whispered.

A quacking started and she bent over the stone wall railing to watch baby ducks swim around their mother. Laughing, she turned to him. "This is really a lovely place. I was so afraid that it would be like that other village, but it's not. It's not like any other place I've ever been."

She leaned back against the railing. "What we need is a swan swimming with the ducks. Would that not be the loveliest thing, Brenn?"

For a moment, Brenn couldn't speak. In the soft light of a dreary, overcast day, she was like a ray of sunshine shooting through the clouds. The children had stopped their playing and craned their necks to look at her. He could see their mouths turning to round O's of admiration.

At this moment, Tess was like a child herself, full of enthusiasm and the joy of life. "Come," she demanded, already starting up the road. "Show me everything."

He followed with less eagerness.

Wildflowers budded in the grass along the side of the road. She paused to pick some and giggled when Miles decided to chase a butterfly.

Her shoes weren't the best for walking but she didn't seem to mind. She took his arm and the two of them strolled as if they were in Hyde Park and not the heart of Wales.

He remembered walking this distance the first time; then, he had been a battle-weary soldier. As if in sympathy, a pain shot through his leg.

"Are you all right?" Tess asked.

"Fine."

"But your leg?"

"Is fine."

She obviously didn't believe him but didn't press the issue. In reality, it was nice to have someone fuss a bit about him. It was—he searched his mind for the right word—it was *domestic*.

They turned onto the drive leading to the house. Tess stared up into the pine boughs. "I didn't realize it was like a canopy over your head."

And she shouted with delight at her first

glimpse of the lake through the trees.

Brenn steeled himself for the moment of truth. It was taking more courage for him to make this little walk with his wife than it had to face a company of French dragoons.

They passed his uncle's cottage. It was a rambling affair built into the hillside. Across the way from the cottage, a distance off the road, was a huge barn. Several paddocks were built around it and there was a small pond. A cow lowed in the distance as if welcoming them. Tim and Clarence waited by the coaches there.

Over on the far hillside was a flock of sheep. "Those are mine," he told her.

Tess nodded, uninterested in sheep. "Where's the house?"

Then they turned onto the piece of road leading toward the lake.

Tess stopped. Her gaze searched the skies and the mountain. The lake reflected the heavy gray of leaden clouds. The Black Mountains loomed around them.

Brenn waited, wishing it could have been a brighter day.

She spoke. "Why, it is almost pagan." She looked at him. "Do you understand my meaning? It's bold here and uncompromising."

Yes, he understood. He'd felt the same sense of awe in the face of this majestic, seemingly uncivilized country.

But his grin faded as he realized he must now tell her the truth. He held out his hand, hoping for the best. "Come."

They only needed to walk a hundred feet further for her to see the crag of land jutting out of

Llyn Mynydd. On its summit was the skeleton of a house, two stories high. It had walls a foot thick but no door, no windows, no roof.

Willa came down from the barn with questions but Brenn waved her off. This was his moment with his wife.

He waited. She didn't say anything. Taking her hand, he guided Tess to the lichen-covered granite steps leading up to where the front door used to be. Miles climbed along with them until he saw something move in the grass and he hied off in pursuit of it.

Tess grinned. "I think he likes it here."

Brenn didn't answer. Instead, he stopped on the top step and turned her so that she could have the full impact of the view overlooking the lake.

"It's breathtaking," she said, before innocently looking up at him and asking, "But where is the house?"

"Here, Tess."

"Where?"

Brenn gently turned her by the shoulders in the direction of the ruins. "This is it, Tess," he said in her ear. "You have to use your imagination. It doesn't look like much now but come a year's time, there will be no finer house in Wales. I promise you that."

"A year's time?" she repeated blankly. She glanced around her, her gaze following the walls and taking in the stone stairs leading to the second floor. And then understanding came upon her swift and sure. "*This* is Erwynn Keep?"

"Yes."

Tess rocked back against him. "But the drawings . . . I thought it was a full house with doors and windows."

"It has doors and windows," Brenn said. "They just aren't filled in yet."

She shot him a look that said his wit wasn't appreciated. She placed her gloved hand on the pitted red limestone of the doorway.

"The rock is from a quarry around here," he hurried to say. "We can get the slate tiles for the roof from the same quarry, too."

She didn't utter a word in reply. Her footsteps echoed on the slab floor. The earth beneath the slabs had shifted, and now grass and weeds grew here and there. Then she pointed to the staircase. "Is it safe to walk up there?"

"Yes. The foundation is solid . . . although the floor must be redone. We will lay a new stone floor and then overlay it with wood mosaic. I saw it done that way in a French chateau."

When she didn't comment, he added, "They haven't built houses like this in years."

"For a reason," she noted dryly. "I imagine all of this stone is cold in the winter. It makes me wonder how the nuns kept warm."

Brenn interpreted her small jest as a good sign. She was growing accustomed to the idea. He relaxed a bit.

She started up the stairs. "I take it the dragon weathervane doesn't exist either?"

He followed her up the stairs. "Cedric Pughe, the local blacksmith, says it can be done. He has my design."

Tess poked her head into one room and then another. The back wall of the third had caved in and the room had a clear view of the stream winding its way to the lake.

She started down the back stairs. "How many years has this house sat abandoned?"

"Two hundred," he answered.

She turned. "But I thought you said your grandfather moved back here. And your uncle lived here."

"I didn't say my uncle lived here." He pointed to the floor. There was no longer any purpose in evading the truth. "The family lived in London until two generations ago. Unfortunately, my grandfather was a gambler—a terrible one. He was caught cheating at cards and lost almost everything when his markers were called in as a result. For that reason, the family was forced to leave London."

"And they moved here."

"Yes, and built that barn you saw on the way in."

"Ummm hummm."

"But they didn't have the money to rebuild the house."

"So where did they live? Where will *we* live?" Tess asked.

"The little cottage."

She took a step away. "Well, I wasn't expecting that, but if you are going to rebuild the house . . . ?"

"I am." Brenn straightened, feeling hopeful. She was taking this very well. He had expected her to demand to be returned to London immediately.

He took her hand. "Tess, this house has wonderful possibilities. Plus, we can correct the mistakes that were made years ago."

"What mistakes?"

"Like the location of the kitchen." With renewed enthusiasm, he pulled her to the back of the house. "The kitchen was located in an outbuilding because of the heat of the fire, but of course we will modernize." He kicked a stone, which skittered across the floor. "I propose that we put the kitchen on this floor where the dining room and breakfast room will be. Right between them."

"Between them?" Tess frowned. "In London, the kitchens are below stairs."

"Yes, but the food is never hot. If we place the kitchen between the two rooms that use it—"

"Then you will find the smells of roasting things will completely overwhelm the house." Tess walked through the rooms to be used as dining room and breakfast room. She turned. "Could this wall come down?"

Brenn walked over. "Of course. We can make any changes we like. Expanding the house is a definite possibility."

"What if we built a cooking wing off of these rooms?"

He considered her suggestion. "It could be done."

"If we do that, we move the kitchen out of the path of guests and the family but we'll also have the convenience of it on this level."

"You're right!" He grinned. She was as challenged by the project as he was. "Do we want to build up another story above the kitchen? Maybe a workroom of sorts?"

"No," Tess said. "I've heard the newest kitchens are being designed with the ceiling built with glass so that light comes through."

"Then that is what we'll do," he agreed. "I'll take some measurements and do some sketches. You can pick out the kitchen you like best."

Tess bit her bottom lip. "I don't know that much about kitchens."

He placed his hands on either side of her face and looked into her eyes. "It doesn't matter, Tess. This is *our* house. We can do whatever we wish."

The worst was over. He'd confessed the truth—and she had accepted it.

With adorable shyness, she looked around the dining room. "My mother's dining set will look good here."

"Come look at the sitting room." She had to skip to keep up with him. "What do you think of in here?"

Tess walked into the middle of the room. "The view is beautiful. It would be nice to have large windows to take advantage of it."

"We can do that. We can put in window doors. All I need to do is knock down more of the wall. I thought a terrace like Lady Garland's would be nice here, too, so we can sit and enjoy the lake. I might even be able to fish from up here."

"I don't want fishing off the terrace," she decreed before pointing to a corner close to the front window. "My mother's harpsichord would be perfect here. And there is a lovely rug among her things that would look beautiful in this room.

I couldn't believe Stella when she wanted to throw it out."

Brenn came up to his wife and put his arms around her waist. "This will be a grand house."

"When do we start work?" she asked eagerly.

"As soon as possible," he said. "Of course, I must wait until I receive certain lines of credit but it shouldn't take long."

"Lines of credit?" A frown appeared between her eyes. "I hope it won't take too long. I don't know if I will like living in that cottage."

"You will. It's very cozy," he promised. Now that he had confessed his secret, his hunger for her was stronger than ever. Her arms came around his neck. He pressed close, his arousal thick and strong between them.

"Once your funds are available," he said huskily, "we can start work on the house."

Tess jerked away slightly. "My funds?" Her voice rose on a touch of panic. "What of your money?"

He hated this question, but steeled himself to give the honest answer. "I used what I had to make the cottage livable and to pay for my trip to London."

She stared at him as if she'd been frozen in time. He could see himself in the pupils of her eyes. "Tess, is something wrong?"

"You're a fortune hunter."

He frowned. "No, I have prospects, and all this land." He tried to cuddle her close. "Tess, I have such plans for this place and dreams for our future. I'm already experimenting with a new breed of sheep. I want the wool from Erwynn Keep to be the best in the world." He nuzzled her neck. "With my land and your capital, we will create our own haven."

She pushed against his chest, breaking his hold.

"Tess, what's wrong?"

"You need my money."

He spread his arms out. "It's important, but it isn't everything."

"But you can't rebuild the house without my money."

He wished she wasn't making an issue of it. But he wouldn't lie. "That's right."

She shook her head. "Brenn, I have no money."

Chapter Fifteen

Brenn stared at Tess. "You're joking." He even forced a half-laugh.

"I wish I was."

His brows came together in uncertainty. "But you have a fortune. Fifty thousand pounds."

Tess nodded. "Yes, it *was* a fortune when my father was alive."

"Was?"

"Neil lost it all."

Brenn's hands dropped to his side. "All of it?"

Tess shook her head, the lump forming in her throat making speech difficult.

Almost in a daze, her husband walked toward the windows. He swung around abruptly. "It can't be true! I was with Mr. Christopher. He's your brother's man of business. He would have told me if something had been amiss in the marriage contract."

"I imagine Neil was very careful to ensure everything *looked* right and proper."

"He *deceived* me—?" Brenn leaned back against the wall. He stared out over the lake in silence.

Tess shifted uneasily. "Brenn?" She hated disappointing him this way.

He didn't answer.

She stood waiting, her hands clasped in front of her.

Slowly, he faced her. "It was fifty thousand pounds."

"Yes, there about."

"How could he lose fifty thousand pounds?"

"He invested it."

"Invested it?" Brenn pushed away from the wall. "In those Italian documents. There should still be some money there."

Tess shook her head. "He told me he'd lost it all. He gave it to a man who was a scientist. He'd invented a battery."

"A battery?"

"Yes, it's these plates and wires—"

"I know what a battery is," he said, interrupting her ruthlessly. "It's a ruse, a charlatan's trick. They touch a dead chicken with a set of wires and the electric current makes the animal's muscles twitch. It's no great discovery."

He started prowling the perimeter of the room, moving with the angry grace of a caged panther.

"Then Neil was the one that was deceived," she said stiffly.

He came to a halt. "Do you believe that?"

"It's what he told me."

Brenn's eyes narrowed as if he focused on something only he could see. "No. Hamlin is a fool but not that much of a fool." He switched his gaze to her. "Why didn't he use his own money to finance this foolishness?"

"He couldn't. Father felt that Neil didn't have

a good head for business. His will made it such that the only way Neil could spend his own fortune is with Mr. Christopher's approval and he never approved anything. I've heard Neil and Stella complain about him often."

"I imagine they did," Brenn said dryly. "Tell me, Tess, did Mr. Christopher think it a good idea that Stella buy a houseful of furniture?"

"No. He refused to let them do it. Stella had a terrible tantrum over it."

"But they went ahead and made the purchases?"

"Yes, but I don't see what it has...to...do..." Her voice trailed off, a horrid suspicion rising. She rejected it with a shake of her head. "Neil wouldn't have taken my money to purchase the furniture that Stella wanted."

Brenn crossed his arms. "The money came from somewhere, didn't it? Where else could he have gotten money? Gambling?"

Tess went very still. Deep inside her, a coldness began building. "Neil is a terrible player."

"Stella gambled too. Sir Charles mentioned that she had a fondness for gambling and expensive baubles."

Crossing her arms, Tess admitted, "Stella loves jewelry but that doesn't mean—" She stopped, unwilling to speak her suspicions aloud.

Brenn didn't share that reluctance. "They were spending your money." He gave a mirthless laugh. He ticked off on his fingers. "The furniture, the gambling, and how about that horse? I hear he paid a fortune for it and it turned out to be a nag. Would Mr. Christopher have authorized that expenditure?"

Tess gave him her back, unwilling to answer. The wind had picked up. The ominous gray clouds hung heavy in the sky. "If Neil did what we—*you* think he did, then I'm sure it is because Stella drove him to it. That woman is impossible."

"I agree," Brenn said bitterly. "Neil isn't the only man to have been ruined by a woman."

Something in his tone of voice made her turn. "What do you mean by that?" she asked levelly.

Their gazes met and she read all too clearly the recriminations. He blamed her for her brother's actions.

"I didn't know."

"Yes, you did, Tess. You were the one who told me the investments were worthless."

"I didn't know about his *taking* my money." She drew shaky breath. "I thought he'd lost the money on those investments. I never dreamed he might be borrowing it to pay for Stella's extravagances. You must believe that."

"Oh, I do." He crossed to the front door and placed his hands on his hips. "If I had Neil Hamlin here right now, I'd throttle him with my bare hands."

"He's my brother," Tess protested weakly.

"Your brother is a thief."

"It was Stella. It *had* to be Stella. Besides, you are making too much of this. The way you are carrying on, one would think you *only* married me for my money."

"I did."

Tess reeled back from his answer.

"I didn't have a choice, Tess. You can't have thought we were a love match. We were contracted to be married in less than twenty-four hours after meeting."

"But you . . . *wanted* me." Her voice didn't sound like her own.

His expression took on the hardness of disappointment. "But I had come to London for a *rich* wife. I would not have married you if I had known your coffers were empty. Nor would I have subjected a wife to this if I had not thought we could begin to rebuild the house immediately. We're ruined, Tess. Between the two of us, we have two hundred pounds."

Tess felt as if the walls of the house were crumbling around her. She staggered to one of the empty windows. Her knees practically buckling beneath her, she sank down to sit on the window edge. The lake was growing choppy. Its waters lapped against the crag of land.

For long moments, neither spoke.

She was the first to break the silence. "Do you remember telling me that if I fell you would pick me up? You also mentioned several times that together we could do anything." She looked up at him. "*Together*."

He made an impatient noise.

She stood. "Brenn, it couldn't have been an accident that the two of us met that night. No, we were meant to meet and to marry and to build this house," she said, a wave of her hand encompassing the empty shell around them.

"Tess, there are no fairies. If no one has told you that, let me be the first. Worse, I believe Maria Edgeworth has gone to your head." He paused a moment, his hands on his hips. "We were a business arrangement, Tess. And we fit well together in bed and we managed to be companionable—"

"Oh, no! We are much more than just companionable!"

"What would you know?" he said. "You were so afraid of letting a man close, you didn't have any idea."

"*Afraid?*" Tess's pride welled up. "I was never afraid. I told you I loved you and I meant it. I have never met a man who wanted to know what I thought or what I felt. I believed you were different." Suddenly, she saw the truth. It was like blinders coming off her eyes. "You *wanted* me to believe you were different, didn't you? It was all part of your plan to snare a rich wife."

He took a step toward her. "That wasn't it. Not even that first night. Not out on the terrace—"

"Don't say another word." She backed away, raising a warning hand. And then suddenly it was too much. The hurt, the betrayal, the sadness. She turned on her heel and ran.

"Tess!" he called, as if ordering her back. Well, she wouldn't listen. She didn't have to listen. Not anymore. Not since he didn't love her.

Her kid slippers made no sound as she raced across the stone floor. She almost tripped over a clump of grass. Miles was back from his chase. He made a purring noise for attention as she stumbled down the front steps but she ignored him.

Brenn came out on the step behind her. "What are you going to do, Tess?" he called. "Return to London? Return to your faithless brother?"

She didn't answer but she did slow her step, walking toward the coaches waiting by the barn.

What was she going to do?

He was wrong about her returning to London. She couldn't. Then everyone would know the truth and she would be laughed at. The high-and-mighty Miss Hamlin had fallen. There would be many a match-making mama and her daughter who would dance to hear that news!

She wouldn't give them the satisfaction.

But how could she stay here?

Not only did Brenn not love her, he was nothing more than a common fortune hunter. She curled her lip at the thought. Her father had been right. They were the worst breed of male.

Willa came out to meet her, complaining about needing to unload the coaches. "Where's the house, my lady?"

Tess stopped. She glanced back over her shoulder at the great ruin of Erwynn Keep. Brenn still stood there, hands on hips, his dark head silhouetted against the sky. He looked every inch the blackguard he was.

She walked past Willa. The maid followed practically on her heels, repeating her questions. *Think*, Tess told herself. *What do you want to do?*

She opened the cottage door. She took a tentative step in.

The cottage interior was more pleasant than she had anticipated. The floor was of polished wood. A table, several chairs, and a rocker sitting in front of the hearth made up the meager furnishings. There were no rugs to add warmth.

She supposed that this was adequate for a man, but her woman's eye saw many improvements that could be made. Willa watched from the door as Tess walked from room to room.

There was only one furnished bedroom. The main room served as sitting room, dining area, and kitchen. Two of the other rooms off to the side of the main room were empty now.

Tess returned to Willa. "Not all of my trunks will fit in the bedroom. Put the extra trunks in one of the side rooms." She began pulling off her gloves.

"You can't mean to live *here* . . . my lady?" Willa added almost as an afterthought.

"I do," Tess said simply. "Now please unpack."

Willa didn't move.

Tess raised an eyebrow. "Did you not hear me, Willa?"

"I did, my lady. But this can't be the grand house?"

"Unpack us, Willa. I've asked *once* already." Few servants dared to cross Tess when she used that tone of voice but Willa did.

"I don't think you should live here," she said. "No countess should live in such a hovel."

At that moment, Brenn appeared in the doorway. Willa had the good grace to blush. There was no doubt that he had heard her words.

"I wanted to bring this in," he said stiffly, indicating the money chest in his hands. He placed it on the table. "I'm going riding." He walked out of the cottage without looking back. Through a window, Tess saw him saddle Ace and set off in the direction of the mountains.

Willa stood wide-eyed and silent.

"Please do as I ask."

Straightening her shoulders, Willa said, "I will,

my lady. But *I'll* not be staying here. I am the finest lady's maid in all London—"

"Thanks to my patronage," Tess reminded her.

"Yes, my lady, and I appreciate all you've done. But I expected civilization. I can't stay here."

"What do you propose to do?"

"I'll return with the coaches to London."

For a moment, Tess was tempted to go with her. But her pride would not bear it. "Very well. I shall pay your wages until the end of the year."

Willa curtseyed. "That is very generous of you, my lady. I will also need a reference."

"I will provide a reference. And we won't be in this cottage forever," Tess added, wanting to make the point clear. "We are going to rebuild Erwynn Keep. It will be the finest house in all Wales," she finished, conscious that she echoed her husband's words.

"Yes, my lady," the maid answered dutifully.

It took less than an hour for Willa, Tim, and Clarence to unload the coaches. Tess had them put the silver chest, the money chest, and other valuables in the bedroom. The other trunks she had stored in one of the empty rooms. After short good-byes, they were gone and Tess was alone.

She sat in the rocker by the cold hearth. How strange it was to be here. She couldn't remember any time in her life when she had been so completely alone. There'd always been servants about.

As if sensing her thoughts, Miles jumped up into her lap and nudged her hand. She got up from the rocker, nuzzling the cat against her chest and crossed to a food hamper Brenn had ordered from the last inn. Pulling a cold roasted duck from it, she tore off a piece of skin and offered it to Miles. The cat batted it playfully with one paw before sticking out his pink tongue and taking a lick.

A second later, he snatched it by his teeth, jumped from her lap, and headed out the still-open front door with his bounty. Tess rose and shut the door after him. She rubbed her arms. She felt cold. If only there was a fire in the hearth.

If only she knew how to build a fire.

Spying a bucket by the door, she went out in search of water. She found it in the form of a pump on the back side of the house. Daylight was fading. The low clouds continued to threaten rain.

Priming the pump, Tess stared at the shell of Erwynn Keep. She blurred her gaze and tried to superimpose Brenn's drawing over the real version of the house. For a moment, she could imagine it in brick, with rosebushes climbing alongside the front door. She even imagined the dragon weathervane proudly measuring the wind on top of the cupola.

Water splashed out of the pump. Its force knocked over the bucket and wet her shoes.

With a soft cry, she righted the bucket and managed to fill it. She might not be able to build a fire, but she could pump water.

Of course, the full bucket was too heavy for her to carry. Sighing, she poured some of it out. Now she'd learned something else, she told herself. Don't ever fill the bucket too full. She carried it into the cottage and came to a halt.

Brenn stood in the middle of the room.

He turned to her. "I thought you would have left with the others."

Sitting the bucket down on the table, she straightened. "I have nothing to return to."

"I didn't mean to be so harsh earlier."

"No, you were being honest." She danced her fingers along the tabletop. "I don't think we should keep any secrets any longer."

"Sounds fair." His voice betrayed no emotion. He barely looked at her.

Tess struggled with the sting of tears. She blinked them back. If he showed no emotion, well then, she wouldn't. "I can't make a fire. Show me how."

"Where's Willa?"

"She went back with the coaches. She's a London girl."

He didn't acknowledge her poor joke. "I'll get wood."

They were strangers, she realized. Intimate strangers. She knew his body almost as well as her own. If she closed her eyes, she could imagine him inside her, feel his strength moving against her.

Many women had marriages in name only. As an heiress, she had been expected to make one. Of course, proud, proud Tess had wanted something more. Brenn had taught her that there was.

He'd also, just as easily, destroyed her trust.

He returned with his arms loaded with wood. He set it in the hearth and began building a fire.

"I don't think I want to sleep with you anymore," Tess said softly.

His hands stopped moving. But he didn't look at her. "I'll sleep in the barn. You can have the cottage."

The agreement didn't make her happy. It only made matters worse.

For a stark moment, she wished they were back on the road, that they didn't know each other's secrets.

Dinner was quiet. Neither one of them had an appetite. Brenn counted the money in the chest. "Two hundred and thirty-seven pounds and a fistful of change."

"That's a goodly amount."

"I spent a portion on the seed and supplies that will arrive in the next week or so." He put the money back into the chest, the coins jangling together. "However, if we are frugal we shall be able to make the best of it. Rents are due, so there will be income."

Sitting across the table from him, Tess picked at her skirt nervously. "How much would it cost to rebuild the manor?"

"That's out of the question. We may be able to think about rebuilding, but not at any time soon."

"How much would it cost?" She'd never considered the cost of anything in her life. This, too, was a new experience.

"I'd estimated twenty-five thousand pounds should be enough."

"Twenty-five thousand pounds?"

His lip curled. "I suppose it doesn't sound like

a great deal to a woman whose petticoats cost three hundred."

She stood, her chin lifting. "That wasn't fair. My father was alive then. It was a different time and a different place." She almost added that she was a different person now but stopped herself, surprised by the thought.

Instead, she marched over to the hearth, attempting to sort out her confusion.

His chair scraped wood as he pushed it back. "Good night, Tess."

She didn't answer but listened to his boots walk across the floor. The door opened, and then closed. He was gone.

Tess sank to the floor, buried her head in her arms, and cried.

Once Tess was able to pull herself together, she almost had to crawl to the bed. Tears were exhausting.

She climbed under the sheets, certain she would be fast asleep in no time.

But sleep was long in coming and when it did, it was fitful. She dreamed that everything in the world was gray. She was standing on the crag jutting out into *Llyn Mynyndd* but there was no house.

Slowly, walls materialized out of air and before she realized it, a house was being built around her.

Her father stood beside her and Neil was there, too. She reached for them but they turned their backs. Hurt rushed through her. She shouted at Neil, blaming him for her disgrace as she left the room and went in search of Brenn.

Wandering from room to room, she called to him. He didn't answer.

She entered the dining room. Her mother's furniture was there but not Brenn. She went to leave but the door had no handle. Frowning, she turned and discovered she wasn't at Erwynn Keep any longer but back in her house in London. Someone told her to set the table.

She had to set the table.

And she kept trying to but there were no plates, forks, or knives. Only spoons. Hundreds and hundreds of spoons. They seemed to fly out of nowhere toward her . . .

Tess bolted upright from the dream. "I know what to do," she said to the empty room. "I know how to rebuild Erwynn Keep."

Brenn lay in the dark, staring up into the barn rafters, listening to the rain.

He felt ashamed of himself. He should not have lost his temper but Tess's news had been almost more than he could stand. How could she have deceived him?

Still, he wasn't ready to forgive her yet, even if his conscience bothered him. She'd helped her brother play him for a fool.

He would rebuild Erwynn Keep even if it took most of his life. Over and over in his head, he worked the numbers from the rents. But the land needed so many improvements.

Neil Hamlin was a bloody bastard.

Brenn considered riding back to London and confronting the man.

Bundling his jacket up under his head, Brenn closed his eyes. He needed sleep. Tomorrow the good people of the village would want to know the status of the building. They had been more excited about the restoring the manor than he'd been. It meant jobs, wages, and prosperity for these people.

Purring interrupted his thoughts. Miles. The cat curled up next to his head, swishing his tail under Brenn's nose.

He pushed Miles away, but his rejection only served as a challenge to the animal. He crawled back toward Brenn.

A man shouldn't have to cuddle a cat. Especially when he had a wife like Tess. She had turned into the kind of bedmate that kept a man warm at night. And he hadn't minded her whispered words of love. In fact, they'd meant a good deal to him.

Miles settled down to loud purring and soon Brenn found himself dreaming.

At first, he didn't realize he was dreaming. Everything was vividly real. He was in the cottage. The main room was lit only by a cheery fire. All else was dark.

And then Tess walked into the room. She was naked. Her firm breasts, flat stomach, and long, lean legs shimmered in the firelight. She turned to him and he saw that her eyes had been replaced by diamonds.

In fact, she was covered with diamonds, thousands and thousands of diamonds. They coated her skin, winked at him from her hair, tipped her eyelashes.

She placed a finger against her lips, warning him to silence. Bending, she began to softly blow air over his skin.

He was nude, too. Nude and aroused. He reached for her, wanting to be inside her, to feel her pulsing around him. She resisted at first, backing away.

Brenn grabbed her and pulled her to the floor with himself on the bottom.

Slowly, she sank down on top of him.

This was heaven.

He placed his hands on her breasts, thrusting up—

But there was no welcoming warmth.

This phantom of light and diamonds was not his Tess. He could tell now. She moved against him but there was no feeling, no joy.

He ordered her to get off, to leave him alone but the words did not leave his mouth. Instead, she stared at him with her blank diamond eyes. They held no emotion, no feeling.

He struggled to free himself. He wanted his Tess! Not this she-devil. He wanted the real woman! *He didn't want the money in place of her.*

"Brenn! Wake up!"

Her voice came to him as if from a great distance. He heard her call his name again.

The dream demon faded and he was again in the dark barn. "Tess?" It had seemed so real.

Tess knelt down beside him. She was still dressed and her clothes were wet. Her damp hair hung loose over one shoulder. "I know how to raise the money."

He came up on his elbows, still groggy—or else he would have told her that it didn't matter. But his mouth only formed one word. "How?"

"This." Tess stood. A moment later, he was pelted with hard objects. He sat up and pushed them off. One was a fork. Another was a spoon.

"What is this?" he asked.

"The contents of my mother's silver chest. Even Neil agreed that they don't fashion silver like this any longer."

"Silver?"

"The finest. Brenn, we can sell them."

Now Brenn woke up. He picked up a spoon, feeling its ornate pattern and heavy weight.

"There is drawer after drawer," she told him, excitement in her voice. "Forks, knives, serving pieces!"

"There must be a bloody fortune here." Hope rose inside him. He leaned back and laughed. "Yes! Yes, this will do!"

She stood, a silhouette in the darkness. "It is enough then?"

"Aye. I imagine it will be more than enough."

"Good. Good night."

Before he could blink, she turned and started walking toward the open barn door.

He rolled to his feet, pieces of silverware dropping off of him. "Tess?"

She kept walking.

The image in his dream flashed into his mind. His body hardened and he wanted her just as he'd dreamed her, gloriously naked and sitting on top of him. He trailed after her.

"I've been thinking, Tess," he started. She didn't slow her pace or answer. He lengthened his stride. "I should never have blamed you for Neil's actions. He robbed both of us."

The night was dark. The rain came down steadily. He splashed through a puddle. She seemed to skirt them without having to watch her step.

He hurried to catch up. Rain plastered his hair to his head. "Ah, Tess. I was a bastard. I don't lose my temper often but when I do, I'm not the better for it."

"Ummm," she answered. The door to the cottage opened and for a second, the still burning fire in the hearth filled the opening with light.

"Tess!"

She turned, one hand on the door, the other against the door frame. "What is it?"

Brenn hobbled to a stop in front of her and tried his most charming smile. "I forgive you, Tess. Your brother tricked us both, but, ah, I won't hold it against you."

With her back to the light, he couldn't see her face. He leaned closer. "So listen, love, let's be off to bed now and put our argument aside."

His answer was to get the door slammed in his face.

A heartbeat later, the bar scraped the door as it fell into place. She had locked him out.

Chapter Sixteen

Brenn debated breaking down the door. Especially when Miles hopped up on the window and looked outside at him standing in the rain. The cat pressed a paw against the glass.

"No, that's fine," Brenn told him. "I don't want to sleep with her if she's going to be that way." It was lie, but it made him feel better to say it.

The next morning, he woke to the sound of someone talking. Ill-tempered, he rolled over, pulling a horse blanket over his head in an attempt to shut out the noise.

"Hold still," Tess's voice said.

Brenn poked his head out from under the blanket. "Tess?"

"Now, stop that," her voice said. "You almost stepped on my toe."

He sat up. Every muscle in his body ached. He rose stiffly and followed the sound of her voice. It came from the direction of Ace's box.

Sure enough, there she stood, dressed for riding in a military-styled habit cut of gold velvet cloth. On her head was a smartly designed cap modeled after a Tarleton helmet, the military headgear of the artillery. Of course, the artillery's helmets were not fashioned out of leopard skin and trimmed with a ruff of matching gold feathers.

She would have looked bang up to the mark in Hyde Park ... but was a bit overdressed for the wilds of Wales.

Brenn rubbed a hand over the rough beard of his face and wondered what she was up to.

Ace whinnied, a distinct plea for deliverance.

Brenn propped his arm on the stall wall. "Having problems?"

Tess flashed him an irritated look from under her lashes. She'd known he was there. "No, I'm doing fine." She finished buckling Ace's bridle. "Don't you have a side saddle?"

"No. Never had a call to use one."

"All right then," she said, more to herself than to him. "I'll just have to use this."

She picked up Brenn's saddle, the weight of it almost too heavy for her, and struggled to get it up on top of the horse.

Ace sent Brenn a desperate look.

Tess picked up the girth and studied the buckles.

"I doubt if you've ever saddled your own horse," he said.

"There can't be that much to it," she said briskly, lifting up the saddle skirt. She started buckling the girth in place.

"No," Brenn said agreeably. "But usually you put a saddle pad on before the saddle. Protects the horse's back."

Tess hit herself in the forehead with two fingers. "Yes, a saddle pad."

She looked around. Brenn's arm had been resting on it. He lifted it off the stall's half-wall and offered it to her.

"Thank you," she said in that preoccupied voice. She pulled off the saddle, put on the pad, and then heaved the saddle back up again.

Brenn couldn't help but admire her tenacity. "Do you want me to adjust the girth?"

She glared at him. "No, I will do it."

"Make sure you get it tight. I'd hate for you to fall off on the other side."

"Well, maybe you *should* check it," she said.

He did so. "Where are you off to?" he asked.

"I'm going to the village to hire help. I have a list of chores that need to be done." She showed him a page from her copybook.

He took the paper from her. *Hire a cook. Hire one maid. Search for chair fabric.*

He handed it back to her. "You won't find fabric in the village. It's too small for such a thing."

"We'll see," she said, folding her list into quarters and tucking it in the pocket of her riding habit. She led Ace out of the barn.

Brenn threw an arm over the saddle, blocking her way. "I thought you were going to use your copybook to write."

"I am, but I use the copybook for other things. My list. Willa's letter of reference." Resentment flashed in her eyes. "My writing is the one thing I've found of value in this marriage."

"Ouch."

She made an impatient sound. "Yes, I'm certain you are hurt. Now if you'll excuse me, I must be on my way."

He didn't move. "And what am I to do while Lady Tess rides into the village to visit the *little* people?"

."Your sarcasm is unbecoming." She tilted her Tarleton cap to a jaunty level and said, "But while I'm gone, you should be making plans to sell the silver. We have a house to build."

Brenn didn't like being dismissed . . . until he realized there was one problem she had not anticipated. He smiled. "Well then, I will set to work. Enjoy your ride." He started toward the cottage, knowing it was just a matter of time before she asked for a leg up. There was no other way she could get up on Ace, since they didn't have a mounting block.

When he'd walked a quarter of the way toward the cottage and she hadn't called him back, he couldn't resist a peek over his shoulder. He stopped dead in his tracks.

Tess was trying to raise her foot high enough to get her boot in the stirrup. When that didn't work, she led Ace next to a small boulder. Cooing for the horse to hold steady, she tried to get her foothold with the aid of the extra height.

Ace would have none of it. He sidled away. Tess tried again, and again.

Brenn had to say this for her: she was a stubborn woman.

"Can I give you a leg up?" he called.

"No, I'm fine." She got her boot in the stirrup as she said it and climbed into the saddle. It wasn't graceful, but she did it . . . except that she tried to sit sidesaddle.

"What nonsense," Brenn said, just as she started to topple off the other side of the horse.

He went running up to help her.

She grabbed the saddle and caught herself in time but her venture had all been for naught. She was down on the ground again, her ridiculous hat sliding over her nose.

She shoved it back and glared at him.

"What did *I* do?" Brenn asked. "I was coming to help you."

"I don't need help."

"Ah, Tess. It's only a leg up—or mayhap you think you are going to sprout wings and fly?"

Her brows came together. She pressed her lips tightly, biting back a sharp retort no doubt. When she spoke, her words were clipped. "I need a leg up."

"I beg your pardon?" he couldn't resist saying.

"I need a leg up," she repeated, louder, terser.

Brenn was tempted to make her repeat her request again but decided it wasn't wise to tweak the tigress's whiskers too much. He laced his fingers together and leaned down.

She put her foot in his hand and he put her into the saddle. Again, she insisted on attempting to sit sidesaddle.

"Fork the horse, Tess."

"That's not proper."

"Who's to see if you are proper or not? Do you want to stay on the animal or fall off?"

Tess had obviously never forked a horse before. The expression on her face was comical. He placed his hand on her waist to keep her balanced. "I look into your angry blue eyes and your mouth that's frowning at me . . . and have the damnedest urge to kiss you," he confessed.

She swung her leg over to straddle the horse. "You can let go now."

But he didn't. "Tess, stop this nonsense. We are both at fault. You can stop making me wear a hair shirt."

"I'm not doing anything of the sort. You are the one who said our marriage was a business arrangement. I am just being businesslike."

It was uncomfortable to have one's words thrown in one's face. "Tess, I was angry. I said some things I shouldn't."

She stared at a point beyond his head. It frustrated him to be ignored—but then she spoke. "I feel like I don't know myself anymore. Now I am not certain about anything. But I do know this. I will never be as trusting as I was before."

"But you love me," he reminded her.

"Do I?" She smiled, the expression sad. "The girl who said those words is changing. I have to build a life. Hand me the reins."

He did as she asked, uncertain how to take her words.

Her head high, back straight, she set off for the village.

Brenn couldn't help but admire her. And she did love him—no matter what she claimed now.

He shouted, "You are far too proud for your own good, Tess Owen!"

She acknowledged him with a wave of her hand.

Tess was glad the village was as close as it was. Ace had a gait so jarring, her teeth were rattling in her head. Worse, it was uncomfortable to ride like a man.

She rode the horse right up to Cedric Pughe's smithy. Since he was the only man in the village she knew spoke English, then she would have to talk to him first.

Pughe was a barrel-chested man about the same height as herself. His face was already wearing the grime and sweat of his trade. Three boys helped him in the open-air shop. They were obviously his sons since each had the same sad brown eyes and coarse thatch of black hair as their father.

Fortunately, Pughe had a mounting block, although her descent from Ace's back was still less than graceful. She was glad Brenn wasn't here to see it.

Straightening her hat, which had been jogged to an odd angle by Ace's movement, Tess introduced herself. "Mr. Pughe, I am Lady Merton."

Mr. Pughe lowered the hammer he'd held raised over his head. He stared at her as if he didn't believe her.

Tess took a step closer to the fire where he worked. "Lady Merton?" she prompted. "Wife of Lord Merton?"

Recognition did not appear in his eyes. Maybe Brenn was wrong and Pughe didn't speak English. Not knowing what else to do, Tess continued, "I am here because I need to hire help to work at Erwynn Keep." She took her list from her pocket.

If the man understood her, he gave no sign. His sons also watched with the same slack-jawed look.

Perhaps they were not right in the head?

She didn't know what to do. "I need a cook," she said, talking loudly and distinctly. "Cook?"

The man frowned.

Tess wanted to grind her teeth in irritation. "Lord Merton said you spoke English. Do you understand me?"

Suddenly, he seemed to snap out of his lethargic state. "Good morning, my lord," he called in a lilting accent.

Tess turned. Brenn was walking down the road toward them. He looked exactly as he had when she'd left him. He wore the same clothes, his neckcloth was tied in a devil-may-care manner, and he was hatless. He hadn't even bothered to shave.

"Good morning, Mr. Pughe," Brenn said. "You have met my wife."

"I have, my lord."

"You are seeing to her wishes?"

Mr. Pughe turned to Tess, his expression matching that of the most toad-eating courtier. "What is it poor Pughe can do for my lady today?"

Tess was about to tell him exactly what he could do with his silly acquiescence but she had a household to manage and no time for nonsense. "I wish to hire a cook and a maid. Are there girls in this village who are suitable?"

"Aye, my lady, my daughter. She can do both."

Tess hadn't considered having one person doing both jobs but it made sense, especially while she was living in the cottage. "Very well. Please send her up to the cottage."

"Yes, my lady."

"Also," she said, consulting her list, "I need a length of fabric. Something with a floral print. Where might I find such a thing?"

"Floral what?" Pughe asked.

Too late Tess realized the silliness of talking to a blacksmith about fabric. "I'll discuss it with your daughter."

"Very wise, my lady."

Tess gave Pughe a sharp glance, fearing she was being made fun of. His expression was completely innocent—as was Brenn's.

She frowned. She would not be deterred from her new goal. She turned and took a step. While she had been talking, it seemed as if the whole village had turned out. A dozen or so women, children, and a few men now stared at her with unabashed curiosity.

Brenn stepped forward. "This is my wife, Lady Merton," he said by way of general introduction and then repeated it in Welsh. "*Mae hi, Lady Merton.*"

Some of the villagers gave her a shy smile. The children stared.

"How do you say 'hello' in Welsh?" she asked Brenn in a low voice.

"Hello."

She made a sound of exasperation, her gaze still on the villagers. "In *Welsh.*"

"Tess, there isn't a person in the world who doesn't understand the word 'hello.' "

"But I want to say something to them that they understand."

"Try *Bore da.*"

"What does that mean?"

"Good morning."

Tess smiled. *"Bore da."*

The villagers looked at each other before a few repeated the greeting back to her. Several frowned. Their silent criticism only served to make her determined to win them over. After all, hadn't she once ruled London Society?

She decided that she'd been brave enough about taking charge of her life for one day. "Please send your daughter to the cottage at the first opportunity," she said to Mr. Pughe and then began walking toward Ace. She decided that attempting to mount him again held too much potential for making her look foolish—not to mention hurting her backside. Instead, she untied his reins and started leading him to the bridge.

Brenn fell into step beside her. "Aren't you going to get on the horse?"

"No."

"I'd help you mount."

Tess stiffened. Something hard and relentless built up inside of her. She hurried her step.

He quickened his pace, his long legs easily able to keep up with her. "Tess, let's go back to the way we were."

She whirled on him then. They stood on the fairy bridge; the happy sound of the water on the rocks below mocked her. "I won't go back. You make it sound simple, but it isn't."

"It is simple."

"No, Brenn. I loved you. And although you never said so, I foolishly thought you loved me." The words sounded naked in their honesty.

"I do," he declared.

For a second, she stood in indecision. A part of her wanted to grasp his words close and believe. But another part, the part that had lived in the center of Society, that had seen how jaded men and women could become, knew his declaration was empty.

"Ours is a business arrangement," she said. "Nothing more, nothing less." With a strength she didn't know she possessed, Tess jumped up and hooked her foot in the stirrup. Swinging onto Ace's back, she kicked the horse into a canter for home.

Brenn watched her ride away.

Something had happened to Tess.

She'd changed. Almost overnight. Gone was the girlishness. The blind trust. The naïveté.

In its place was cynicism, but not defeat. Doubt, but not hopelessness.

In its place was a woman.

Even physically she seemed to have changed. Her eyes had lost their starriness. The set of her mouth had become firmer.

This morning she had been still confused but she was growing stronger. She would in time become self-sufficient.

He no longer considered theirs a minor quarrel. Something valuable might have been irrevocably lost to him forever. Something he had not recognized until he no longer had it.

He'd wasted her love. Budding, untried, innocent . . . regardless, it was no longer his.

He leaned over the railing of the fairy bridge. The water winding and bubbling over the stones below laughed up at him.

* * *

Over the next three days Brenn banked the silver.

He rode to Swansea carrying bags of eating implements and returned a wealthy man. He was even glib enough to establish a line of credit with the bankers using the Italian documents as collateral.

He also found a length of floral fabric for Tess. She thanked him politely enough. The color added warmth to the cottage.

But it did nothing to warm her heart toward him.

When her mother's furniture arrived, Tess stored most of it in the barn but moved a bed into the house and fixed up one of the empty rooms for his use.

Brenn didn't appreciate her thoughtfulness. He wanted to sleep with her. He missed her. He missed her warmth, the little sighs she made when she slept, even the feeling of her cold feet against his skin!

Once before he'd insisted she sleep with him and the ruse had worked . . . but Brenn wanted something different now. He wanted Tess to come of her free will.

As the days turned into weeks, he began to wonder if that would ever happen.

Work began on Erwynn Keep. He and Tess made a good team. She was in the process of learning Welsh. She had started before he'd returned home from Swansea. Banon Pughe, Cedric's oldest daughter and their cook, was her teacher.

Brenn hired more villagers to till fields and

prepare for a fall harvest. He was a month late planting crops, but the villagers assured him he didn't need to worry. As the first green sprouts appeared, he began to believe they were right. It gave him great satisfaction to walk along his fields watching things grow.

Meanwhile, Erwynn Keep's pitted walls were quickly repaired. A team of roofers was hired and in two weeks' time, a new slate roof reflected the morning sun.

Tess continued to change. She blossomed with self-confidence and self-reliance. The darling of fashionable Society soon overcame her first impression and made herself the favorite of the village. She used skills honed on the dance floors of Almack's to win over everyone, even the laundry woman. A people known to be reticent around strangers quickly accepted her as their own.

She'd started the habit of wearing her flaming hair down and tied back with a simple piece of muslin. It was not unusual to hear her laughing at some joke a shepherd had made or even a comment from the sweaty Pughe. But she had no smiles for her husband.

Every day, first thing in the morning, she wrote in her copybook. Brenn peeked in it once. She'd written about him only during those euphoric first days of their marriage, before they'd truly known each other. After their sharing of secrets, she had started writing about the land, the pronunciation of Welsh words, making observations about daily life. He leafed through several pages and found the following passage:

At one time, I'd thought Brenn had everything I needed in the world to be happy. Now I know I must find happiness in myself.

It was dated only a week earlier.

He sat quiet for a long time, thinking.

In the first weeks, he'd selfishly hoped that his seed had taken root inside her, that she would bear his child . . . but that was not to be. It made him angry that she could be so indifferent to him—but she hadn't always been so.

He reread the words in her copybook.

If at one time he'd made her happy, he could do it again. But his present plan of waiting for her to come to her senses was not working.

He wanted his wife back. He knew how to fight in battle, but how did one fight for his wife's affections?

And then the answer came to him. It was so simple, he couldn't believe he hadn't thought of it before. Action. He would mount an attack on her heart with the same tenacity he'd shown against the French.

His spirits restored, Brenn began to plot tactics to woo his wife.

Chapter Seventeen

Six-year-old Vala Brice, the oldest daughter of Joseph the shepherd, was one of Tess's constant companions.

So Tess wasn't surprised to see the child standing on the cottage doorstep one sunny morning. What was surprising was the huge bouquet of fresh-picked wildflowers in her little hands.

"*Bore da*, Lady Merton," Vala said.

"Good morning," Tess replied, as anxious for the children to speak English as she was to speak Welsh.

"Yes, good morning," Vala answered, the dimples at each corner of her mouth appearing. "For you."

"Oh, Vala, these are lovely," Tess said, taking the flowers from her. She repeated the words in Welsh.

Vala giggled with delight and whispered, "From Lord Merton." She turned and took off running in the direction of Erwynn Keep.

Tess stepped out on the front step. Sure enough, Vala ran straight to Brenn, who was busy overseeing the workmen on the house. He patted the child on the head, gave her a penny, and waved at Tess.

She didn't wave back. Instead, she went inside and firmly shut the door. Of course *he* would use Vala to plead his case. But it wasn't going to work. Yes, it was hard to live this close to Brenn and ignore him, but she must. She had to shut away the feelings she'd once had—the hopes, the dreams, the need for someone to love.

"Those are lovely," Banon Pughe said in Welsh, giving a final stir of the cheese and beer soup she was preparing for luncheon.

Tess dared not complain. Banon was a bit enamored of Brenn, as was almost every woman in the village. They would interpret the flowers as some wild romantic gesture, which Tess did not.

No, he wanted something—and she knew what! But he wouldn't be returning to her bed.

Since the day on the fairy bridge when he'd asked to return to the way they'd been and she'd refused, she'd walked around with a hollow feeling inside. But she couldn't let him know. Her pride wouldn't let her.

Brenn had used her. She had thought he loved her and he hadn't. She would never give him her heart again.

She intended to throw the flowers out the back bedroom window where Banon wouldn't see her actions. However, as she entered the bedroom, another knock sounded on the door.

Banon opened it and then called to Tess.

Madoc Carne stood there, a bouquet of wildflowers in his hand. Madoc was only four and lisped. "Lady Merton," he said. "These are for you."

He shoved the flowers toward her and then went running off toward Erwynn Keep. "That must have cost Brenn another penny," she said to herself.

"Isn't this precious?" Banon asked. "That man is mad for you. Everyone in the village knows it." She brushed her finger across the feathery Queen Anne's lace.

"I'm surprised he has time for the roofers with all his flower picking."

"Lord Merton wouldn't pick the flowers," Banon assured her and Tess knew she was right. Another crime to place beside his name! She'd throw both bouquets out.

Another knock sounded on the door. This time it was Madoc's older sister Enid. She, too, had a bouquet.

"Isn't this sweet?" Banon asked, misty-eyed.

Tess thanked Enid. Stepping outside, she stood, her arms full of flowers, and looked to Brenn. He waved at her, his teeth flashing white in the sun.

"He's pleased with himself," Tess murmured. "He probably thinks of this as another one of his games."

"What did you say, my lady?" Banon asked.

"Nothing," Tess answered. She went about her work, even though she was interrupted almost every hour with a child carrying a bouquet.

That evening when Brenn came in for dinner, he looked very pleased with himself although he didn't comment on not seeing flowers on every table and in every corner. They ate in their customary silence. After the meal, Tess retired to her room, as had become her habit. Brenn was all-male, and his presence was too uncomfortable considering her self-imposed celibacy.

He took his nightly walk to check on the property and the growing number of livestock. Besides Ace, there were now oxen, milk cows, three squealing pigs, countless chickens, and one honking goose residing in the barn.

Usually, Tess was asleep before he returned. Dancing until dawn was a thing of the past. She'd embraced country hours and felt better for it.

But this night, after she had shut her door, she leaned against it and listened. Brenn was managing the estate himself and with crops, sheep, livestock, and carpenters to mind, he was exhausted. He usually went straight to bed after making his rounds. But occasionally, he would pause in front of her door . . . and he did this night.

Tess held her breath. She could almost see him standing on the other side of her door. She leaned against it, flattening her hand against the old wood. *Go to bed, Brenn.*

He must have heard her silent command because a beat later, his footsteps crossed the floor to his room.

She covered her mouth, straining to hear even the slightest nuance of sound.

His bedroom door closed. Tess waited.

Suddenly, there was a deep masculine swear. Tess turned, her back to the door, sliding down it with silent laughter. He'd found the flowers. She stuffed them into his mattress.

Served him right! She wondered if the

lavender would scent the sheets. Plus some of the flowers were prickly.

She was still chuckling when she finally fell asleep.

But the next morning, when the children again delivered flowers, Tess placed them in water . . . and she couldn't help but notice Brenn was pleased.

Two days later, while Brenn was in Swansea to hire a fine carpenter, a horse trader drove his wagon up the drive and announced that the pretty gray filly following him on the lead rope was for the countess of Merton.

"That horse couldn't be for me," Tess said to the horse trader. "My husband didn't say anything."

The man removed his top hat and scratched his grisly-haired head. "Don't matter if he says anything or not," he said in a Yorkshire accent. "He bought this horse and sent me on the way with it. Said it was for his wife."

She walked around the fine-boned dapple gray and couldn't resist giving it a pat. In response, the doe-eyed animal pushed her hand with its nose, begging for a bit more affection.

"Your husband gave me a message," the horse trader said.

"What is it?" Tess asked.

"He said—" The trader lifted his eyes upward as if wanting to make sure he had the words exactly right. "He said the filly's name is Flower."

Banon, standing on the cottage step, giggled. She'd been the one to clean the floor of Brenn's room of flower petals, stems, and leaves. It had

to have been the first time the girl had realized
Brenn and Tess didn't sleep together. It didn't
matter that everyone in Tess's social circle had
their own bedrooms; in Banon's small society,
husbands and wives shared a bed. She had been
dumbstruck at the knowledge Brenn and Tess
didn't. Living this close to the servants, Tess was
beginning to understand how many personal
matters they knew about their employers.

"And," the trader said, "he said to tell you
that if you and he weren't going to do any breeding then maybe the horses would and that he
was—" He pulled out a piece of paper and
consulted it before reading, "—getting bloody
tired of sleeping alone."

Tess prayed the ground would open up and
swallow her whole. She hoped Banon's English
wasn't good enough to know what had been
said.

Taking Flower's halter rope, she said tartly,
"Thank you. You may go on your way."

"Aye, that I will, my lady, but I almost forgot."
The horse trader went around to the back of his
wagon and returned carrying a handsome saddle, a *side*saddle. It was fashioned of tooled
leather and had a bridle to match. "This is a gift
from Lord Merton, too. Just the thing for a dainty
lady such as yourself."

"Did he tell you to say that?"

"No, I added that myself." With that, the horse
trader tipped his hat and went on his way.

Tess waited until he was out of sight before
saying to Banon, "You will mention this to no
one." She even repeated her words in Welsh, all
the while knowing it was a lost cause. The tale

of Brenn's gift would be on the lips of everyone in the village before dark tonight.

"Yes, my lady," the girl replied dutifully, but there was laughter in her voice.

Brenn should have known better than to have sent such a message with that man. For a second, Tess was angry enough to kick something but then Flower nudged her again for a pet.

She really was a pretty filly . . .

The second visitor Tess had while Brenn was gone was the new vicar he'd hired.

Erwynn Keep's church had sat empty since Brenn's grandfather's time, when the money for maintaining the benefice had been gambled away. It pleased Tess that Brenn was willing to take some of the money they had to fund the position. It was what an earl should do.

Vicar Rackham was new to his calling, fresh out of the seminary and ready to convert the lambs to God. He also had a slight stutter.

"I'd been w-worried about ever f-finding a position," he confessed. "My f-family has f-few connections. P-plus, I have th-this." Tess could well imagine it put people off. "B-but as I t-told L-Lord M-Merton, I have the calling."

"How did Lord Merton find you?" Tess asked, offering him a glass of wine. They sat in the chairs before the fire. Banon busied herself off in Brenn's bedroom, but Tess knew she eavesdropped.

"Th-the Most R-Reverend Dobson in Swansea was aware of my situation. I'm originally from Swansea and had been l-living with my m-mother."

"And you speak Welsh?" They'd been speaking in English.

Vicar Rackham slipped easily into his native language. "I don't stutter in Welsh. Of course, that didn't help me at the university." Suddenly, Miles jumped up into his lap.

"Here now," Tess said, wishing her cat wasn't so spoiled and yet unable to stop spoiling him.

"Oh, he's f-fine." The young man ran his hand down the cat's glossy back. "L-lovely animal. All God's creatures."

"Yes, we are," Tess agreed proudly. No one would have recognized the Miles of today from the scrawny animal she and Brenn had rescued. Between field mice and scraps from Banon's meals, he was almost fat and very satisfied.

That Vicar Rackham echoed her own sentiments toward animals pleased her greatly. "Have you seen the church?"

He hadn't, so the two of them walked over to St. David's. As they left the house, Tess caught Banon sliding a glance of interest at the young vicar from beneath her lashes.

"Would you like to come with us, Banon?" she asked.

"May I, my lady?"

Tess couldn't help but smile at the girl's eagerness. "Of course. Fetch your bonnet."

As they walked to the village, Tess noticed what a handsome couple the two of them made. Cedric Pughe would be pleased to have a vicar for a son-in-law.

Crossing the bridge, Tess shared with him her growing collection of fairy stories. Being a

Welshman, he didn't laugh at her and even told her one she hadn't heard before.

He was going to be the perfect vicar for Erwynn Keep.

The church itself was a disappointment. "Nothing is sadder than an empty church," Tess said, brushing aside cobwebs.

"It isn't bad," he assured her enthusiastically in Welsh. "I'll recruit some of the village women and we'll have it cleaned in no time."

Banon quickly volunteered to organize the women.

In the back room, they found a wooden chest containing pewter candlesticks, altar cloths, and the like. The yellowed linens were hopelessly ruined by age and insects.

"These would have dressed the altar up a bit," Vicar Rackham said. "But we can sew more."

Tess had a flash of an idea. "Wait." She sent Banon back to the cottage with instructions to fetch the petticoat and dress she had worn for her presentation at Court.

While waiting for Banon, she and Vicar Rackham investigated the cottage that served as the vicarage. It had been let over the years but was empty now. Its condition was worse than the church's. However, John Carne and his wife, who ran the alehouse at the other end of the village, came by. After introducing themselves to the vicar, they pledged the help of the village in repairing the cottage. ". . . With the earl's help, of course."

"Of course," Tess agreed with a small smile. But in truth, it made her feel good to see the renewed life in the village.

Banon returned with the clothing. "Here," Tess said. "This should make a lovely altar cloth."

Mrs. Carne exclaimed over the silver lace that sparkled in the afternoon sun. "I've a good hand with a needle." She began measuring the petticoat skirt off her nose.

"But this dress must have cost a fortune," Vicar Rackham protested.

"All the more reason it should go to a good cause," Tess answered. Her days in London seemed almost a lifetime ago. But she did not miss her former life. It lacked substance compared to how she lived now.

Tess was ready to go. Banon looked as if she could spend the afternoon helping with the plans to repair the vicarage and Tess let her.

She had started for home, when Vicar Rackham came running after her.

"One m-moment p-please, m-my l-lady."

Tess stopped. They stood in the middle of the road, not far from Pughe's smithy.

"M-my l-lady, th-there is one t-topic I m-must b-bring up in m-my role as s-spiritual l-leader."

"What is that?" she asked him in Welsh.

He answered in his tortured English. "Your husband b-begged me to b-bring th-this to your attention."

Tess felt a tingle of warning on the short hairs of her neck. "What topic is that, sir?"

"A wife's m-marital duties to her husband—"

"Say no more," Tess replied, but she was smiling. *Touché, Brenn, touché!*

"Tell my husband if he should ask that I've taken the matter to heart."

She turned and made her way back to the cottage. The emptiness she'd been nursing was starting to fade.

Brenn came home in the middle of the next day unsure of his reception.

He expected her to like the horse and the vicar, but he wasn't certain she would appreciate his pointed messages.

He found Tess by the house playing with a rope on the ground. She was so involved, he walked up to her without her being aware of his presence.

"What are you doing?"

She jumped, startled by his question. "You're home."

He made a short bow to fill the awkward moment when they would have greeted each other with more warmth. His high hopes plummeted a bit. He repeated his question.

"I'm laying on a line for the stone wall. Gerald—" She referred to one of the men working on the repairing of the stone floor inside. "—said he would build one for my rose garden if I decided what I want. Did you find the carpenter?"

"He'll take the commission. He should be here in a day or two."

For a second, there was silence between them. He wondered what she was thinking—and if she wanted to kiss him as much as he did her.

"I like the new vicar," she said abruptly. "He's young but full of good intentions."

"Like ourselves?"

Tess didn't answer but brushed the dirt from her hands. What was going through her mind?

"Vicar Rackham and I are going to open a school for the children."

He didn't want to talk about schools. He wanted to talk about them. But instead, he said, "It would be worthwhile."

"We'll be able to teach the children to read in English and Welsh. He really is a find, Brenn."

Brenn didn't want to talk about the virtues of another man either. He changed the subject. "Did you like the filly?"

"She's perfect. Absolutely one of the sweetest horses I've ever ridden."

"And the saddle?"

"I thank you for the saddle," she replied dutifully.

Again silence.

"Is there any possibility I could receive a kiss for my generosity?" he asked.

He'd caught her off guard but then she laughed. "No," she said candidly, "because I also received your *messages*."

But there was no heat in her words and the terrible sadness that had lingered around her no longer seemed to be present.

Perhaps . . . ?

"I'm not the best man in the world, Tess. I've made mistakes and, perhaps by wanting too much, I've hurt you—but that was never my intent. Do you think you could forgive me?"

She crossed her arms, hugging her middle. "I already have."

Brenn almost couldn't believe his ears. "You have—!"

"But it's not enough, Brenn. I want something more. Something I'm not sure you can give me."

"I'd give you anything," he declared. "I'd hang the moon for you."

Her expression saddened. "I don't know if it would be enough."

What did the woman want? For the life of him, he would never understand her.

"You don't understand, do you?" she said, echoing his thoughts.

"No, I don't. Tell me what I must do and I'll do it!"

She came down to him so that they stood inches from each other. "If I must tell you, then it isn't worth having."

With that riddle she walked on to the cottage.

Brenn ripped his hat off his head. He could have thrown it on the ground and stomped on it out of frustration. Was there any man alive that understood women?

"Tess!"

She turned to him.

"I want you." He felt silly making such a declaration. One of the workmen stuck his head out the door at the noise, only adding to his sense of foolishness. Brenn waved him back in.

But his words didn't soften Tess. With a shake of her head, she continued on her way.

At that moment, Cedric Pughe came up the drive in a wagon. Four able-bodied men rode with him. They were followed on foot by what appeared to be the whole village—including the vicar.

Pughe pulled the horse to a stop between the house and the cottage. "I've got something for you, my lord," he told Brenn.

Jumping down, he gave a quiet order to the

other men and together they lifted something off the bottom of the wagon.

Tess gave a small cry and Brenn couldn't help but feel pride.

It was his dragon weathervane.

Pughe had hammered it out of the copper Brenn had purchased during his first trip to Swansea. Metal flames of fire breathed from its mouth. Pughe had even managed to hammer scales into its coiled body.

"It's beautiful," Tess said.

"Aye." Brenn hopped up in the wagon with it. It was a good three feet in length. "You've done a fine job, Pughe."

"I'm pleased," the blacksmith said.

"Do you think we can put it up now?" Brenn asked.

"It's why I brought the lads," Pughe answered.

The air was festive as they marched to the house with the weathervane. The wooden scaffolding used during the wall repairs on the back of the house was carried to the front. The timbers were lashed together with rawhide strips.

Pughe wouldn't climb it—he claimed he was just too old—but Brenn and Carne did. One of the workmen also climbed onto the roof to help secure the weathervane to the cupola.

When at last the dragon was in place, Brenn stood, balancing himself on the line of the roof. He batted the dragon and it swung free on its pole. The crowd below him cheered.

And this should have been enough—but it wasn't.

Standing where he was, he could see the whole

valley—the lake, the mountains, the people. But he realized that none of it meant anything, not even the house, if he could not set things right with Tess.

With her red-gold hair, she stood out from all the others. Little Vala held her hand while she shaded her eyes with the other to look up at him.

He ached with wanting her.

A wind came up. The dragon turned on its own and Brenn almost lost his balance. Laughing, he climbed down with the others.

Pughe slyly announced that after all that work, a man could use a drink. Brenn agreed and led the men, including the vicar and the workmen, back to the village and the local alehouse for a "wee pint or two."

With a heavy heart, Tess watched her husband march off. He was a natural leader and there wasn't anything the villagers wouldn't do for him, especially after having lived under the old earl. He'd brought prosperity back. Their lives were now full of hope.

Vala tugged at her skirt.

Tess knelt down. "What is it, sweetie?"

"Mum says it's a fairy moon tonight."

"A fairy moon?" Tess stood and, taking Vala's hand, walked over to Mrs. Brice. "Vala says you think it's a fairy moon tonight."

The woman didn't even blink. Tess's interest in Welsh lore was now accepted. "Aye. It's a full moon and I can tell by the air that it will have a ring around it. The summer is passing. The time has come."

"But will there be fairies?" Tess asked.

Mrs. Brice looked to Mrs. Pughe and the other women gathered around her. Tess didn't always know if they were teasing her or not.

"One can never tell," Mrs. Brice said.

"But you have a fairy ring," Vala said.

"That's right, I do," Tess agreed. Vala had been the first to point out the pattern of weeds growing through the stones in the main entry of Erwynn Keep. It had almost formed a circle and all the children were convinced fairies must dance there. Tess was determined to find out for herself and had ordered Gerald and the other workmen to not touch the ring until she gave them permission to do so.

"So are you going to keep a watch for fairies, my lady?" Banon asked. She stood next to her mother, bouncing her latest brother, eighteen month old Clyde, on one hip.

"I think I will," Tess said, and knew they all thought her a bit odd.

The truth was, she'd always be an outsider, a Saxon, and yet the villagers admired her. She knew she'd found something special here, something that had been missing from her life in London. She'd found her place in the world.

Now, if only Brenn loved her.

He wanted her. He would like to sleep with her. He was happy to give her things . . . but that wasn't enough. Not anymore.

She wanted love. Not just any love, *his* love.

And if she couldn't have it?

She didn't know what she'd do.

Brenn stayed longer than he should have at the alehouse. John Carne knew how to brew ale.

Plus, after years in the military, Brenn enjoyed male camaraderie. It helped him somewhat—though not entirely—to take his mind off of his wife.

He turned to Cedric Pughe. "Mr. Pughe, do you understand women?"

The man broke out into a great hearty laugh. The others wanted to know what Brenn had said. Pughe repeated it in Welsh and they all joined in the laughter.

"Not one of you knows?" Brenn questioned with a grin. "Are we all baffled?"

One of the sheepherders responded. Pughe translated for Brenn. "He says that men are not meant to understand women or women men because if they did there would be no adventure. And it is the adventure that gives marriage spice." He added, as if to himself, "Aye, it was a bit of that spice that led to my last young one." He grinned. "And Rufus is right, it was an adventure. May even have another adventure tonight!" He smacked the table, laughing heartily.

The conversation turned very bawdy after that. Even knowing little Welsh, Brenn could tell. He rose from the table, signaling to Carne to keep the ale flowing and that he would pay the tab. They started drinking to his health then, and his wife's health, and the health of the house.

Brenn said good night when they started to drink to the health of the new weathervane.

It was a bit past eleven. The moon was silvery full. Its light gave the village an ethereal quality. As he crossed over Tess's fairy bridge, he could almost imagine he heard the sound of fey laughter.

The walk up the drive leading to Erwynn Keep cleared his senses of the potent ale. When he came around the bend not far from the cottage, he had to stop and look at the manor.

Moonlight shimmered off the lake and gleamed on the tiles of the new slate roof. If Brenn moved a foot or two off the path, he could see the dragon weathervane silhouetted against the lake.

It made him proud just to look at it.

The door to the cottage opened. To his surprise, Tess walked out dressed in her gold riding habit. Her hair was pulled back into a simple braid and her feet were bare.

He was about to call out to her when he noticed that she held her copybook in one hand and an ink pot and pen in the other.

What the devil was she up to?

Throwing the long train of the habit over one arm, Tess started walking toward the house.

Brenn followed her. He wasn't really quiet about his movements but she was so intent on her mission she seemed completely unaware of him. And that, he realized, was the crux of the matter. She had the ability to ignore him while he was completely, almost painfully, aware of her.

She picked her way along the drive toward the house, cautious of her bare feet. There was a rustling in the bushes off to the side. She froze, listening.

Jealousy raised its ugly head inside Brenn. Could it be that she was sneaking off to meet a lover? He thought about his jealousy over Draycutt and refuted the idea. Tess would not do that.

She believed in honor. She'd made a mistake agreeing to keep Neil's secret but she had an honorable reason to do so.

Miles pounced out of the bushes. Tess gave a start and then laughed. "I should have known it was you."

The cat turned and gave a welcoming purr to Brenn but Tess was so fixed on her purpose she didn't notice, even though he was no more than ten feet behind her. She continued on her way.

She started up the front steps of the house. The hastily erected scaffolding rested to one side of the door, listing a bit. The workmen had started to take it down but hadn't finished once tonight's opportunity to drink ale arose.

"Tess," he said, meaning to end the game.

She turned, startled by the sound of her name, just as she'd been earlier. But before she saw him, her foot stepped on the edge of her train. It pulled and she almost upset the ink pot. Trying to save it, Tess lost her balance and started to fall. She reached out to break her fall and grabbed the scaffolding by mistake.

To Brenn's horror, the scaffolding began to fall on top of her.

Chapter Eighteen

With a strength Brenn didn't know he possessed, he leaped for Tess, tackling her just as the heavy timber came down.

She fell forward, the ink pot and copybook flying, and landed on the hard uneven rocks of the front hall. One of the timbers whacked against his booted calves and then bounced off the wall and down the front steps. Brenn landed heavily on top of Tess.

The wood scaffolding finished crashing to the ground with a splintering sound.

Brenn yanked Tess up by both shoulders. "Are you all right? I didn't hurt you, did I?"

She stared past his shoulders to the scaffolding lying outside the door. Closing her mouth, she swallowed.

"Brenn?"

"Yes?"

"Did you have to be so dramatic?"

He couldn't help laughing. "I wanted your attention."

She shook her head, her eyes still dazed. "You have it."

He sat down beside her. Moonlight poured through the gaping holes of windows and pooled all around them. It turned her red hair black and her eyes shiny. Just like the diamond goddess of his dreams.

He brushed a lock of her hair, which had come loose from her braid, out of her face. The moment of danger was over and he felt a rush of relieved anger. "What were you doing stalking around in the dark?"

"I wasn't stalking. It's a fairy moon. I'd come out to record what would happen in the fairy ring."

"You and your fairies! What's this about a fairy moon?"

"Mrs. Brice told me that when the moon has a ring around it, portentous things are about to happen. She's heard people can see fairies on a night like this. Since we have a fairy ring here, the children wanted me to watch and see if the fairies came out to meet this night."

"The fairy ring?" His wife babbled about things he'd never heard of.

"Yes," Tess said with conviction. "We're sitting in the middle of it."

"The middle of *what*?" He could see nothing prophetic about where they sat.

She leaned across him. "Look. See that dandelion and the one next to it? And the one after that? There's enough of them to form a ring, or, well, an oval."

Brenn studied the stones around them. They had shifted and moved so that a rather lopsided ring had been formed. The cursed dandelions had stuck their impudent stems and leaves up through those cracks. Some even had yellow flowers that would turn to seed.

"Is this why you wanted to delay the repairs on this floor?"

"For the children. They want to know if fairies can do magic. Of course, you and I have probably frightened them off."

"Tess, you don't honestly believe in this nonsense?" He raised a hand in exasperation. "When I saw the scaffolding start to fall, I thought I was going to lose you. Why, I'd rather have my heart torn out of my chest than go through that again!"

She blinked. "What did you say?"

He frowned. "I said I don't want you traipsing around in the dark anymore."

Her hand grabbed his arm. "No, not that. About the other."

"What other?"

"Oh, Brenn!" Now it was her turn to sound frustrated. "About your heart in your chest," she said, enunciating each word.

"I said I'd rather have my heart torn out of my chest than see anything happen to you."

She searched his face. "And why is that?"

"What do you mean 'Why is that'? Because I love you!"

If he'd punched her in the nose, she could not have looked more startled. She came up on her knees. "Say it again."

"Say what?"

She rolled her eyes heavenward. "Why are you so exasperating? You know what you said. Repeat it!"

"Repeat what? That I love you?"

She rocked back on her heels. "You do?"

"Of course I do."

"But you never said it."

"Tess, you had to know. I mean . . ." His voice trailed off. "Is that why you've been so angry with me? Why you haven't told me you loved me anymore?"

"I didn't think you'd even noticed! And you were so angry over the money—"

"Disappointed, Tess," he corrected, knowing in his heart that she was right and he was wrong. He hadn't loved her then—not in the way he felt about her now.

"But you never said anything," she finished softly.

"I sent all those children to the door with flowers. I spent hours picking those posies."

"I thought you had the children do it."

He frowned. "Is that why you put the flowers into my bed?"

"No, I did it because I thought you were trying to warm me up to get me into your bed."

"I was," he admitted freely. He ran the flat of his hand up and down her arm. "I've missed you, Tess."

"I've missed you, too."

"Then when I came home, why weren't you more welcoming?" he demanded. "There was the horse, the sidesaddle. Of course, I'd thought having the vicar talk to you would tickle your funny bone . . . and I knew you would be pleased with his presence."

"Brenn."

"Yes."

"Kiss me."

He reached for her. She let him put his arms around him but before his lips came down, she held up her hand. "Say the words again. Say them for me, please."

He smiled slowly. "I love you."

Tears filled her eyes. She opened her arms wide and embraced him. The force of her hug pushed them back onto the stones but Brenn didn't mind. She lay on top of his body and it was she who did the kissing. She showered kisses all over his face.

Laughing, he rolled her over, settling himself between her legs, the skirt of her riding habit spread out on the stones around them. They stopped laughing.

"I love you, Tess Owen," he said.

"I love you, Brenn Owen."

And in that moment, something magic did happen.

Brenn hadn't realized it was needed. He hadn't even known . . .

Deep inside of him, he realized he'd changed. "The house, Erwynn Keep—none of it means anything without you," he said.

"I'll always be here."

"Try and escape," he whispered before bringing his head down to kiss her. "Dear God, Tess, I love you."

They made love then, right there in the center of the fairy ring, bathed in the light of a full moon. He took his time undressing her. She was the one who was anxious and eager.

He laughed at her impatience, using each fastening, each fold, each article of clothing as an opportunity to say he loved her. He unbraided her hair and combed his fingers through it until it hung down around her like a shining curtain around her breasts.

This was his mate, his beloved, his wife.

She'd accepted him scarred and worn from the battles of life and gave him hope. More importantly, she gave him herself.

This night, the union that had such a tenuous start a month earlier was now forged in a mettle stronger than iron—love. The words Brenn had taken so long in saying, he repeated over and over.

And she answered him. Kiss for kiss, touch for touch, passion for passion.

His wife was fierce this night. She pleased him in ways he hadn't thought possible. He sat her on top of him so that he could see the expression of love on her beautiful face in the moonlight. His hands covered her breasts.

Together, they strove for that moment when lovers become one.

As Brenn released himself inside her, he knew he'd been changed forever.

She came down to rest her head against his chest. He wrapped his arms around her. "Tess?"

"*That* was magic," she whispered.

He grinned. "No, that was love."

"Did you see fairies?" Enid asked the next morning. She and Vala stood on the front step of the cottage. Vala's brown eyes were full of hope. She held Tess's copybook in her hand.

"We found this on the floor of the house," Enid said, taking the copybook from Vala. "There were ink stains on the stones, right inside the fairy ring. Did they scare you off?"

Tess glanced over her head at Brenn who had walked up behind the children. He'd gone to the house to inspect the damage to the scaffolding before the workmen came.

"You two are up early, aren't you?" he asked, kneeling down to their level.

"We want to know about fairies," Vala told him.

He tilted his head up to Tess. "Yes, Lady Merton," he said. "Did you find fairies?"

There was something infectious about his grin, especially since the two of them had spent the night making love.

"Oh, I found a lot more than just fairies," she teased Brenn back, but she immediately regretted her words. The two girls started jumping up and down with excitement.

"We want to know about it!"

"Tell us about it!"

Tess found herself trapped. She had no choice but to weave a quick tale of fairies who came out when the ring was around the moon. It was a story based upon others she'd heard and the depth of her love for Brenn.

It must have been a good story because a short time later after Enid and Vala left, they were back with more children who wanted to hear the story.

Tess sat in a chair before the hearth. The village children sat all around her. They were insatiable in their quest for information about the fairies. Even the doubting Madoc listened closely to her words.

At last, she sent them all home. But after they

left, the stories she had told whirled in her head.

Banon was baking bread. The heat in the house was too much for Tess. She slipped outdoors with her copybook and a fresh bottle of ink. Finding a shady spot under a tree, she sat on the grass and began writing.

Brenn came by for some cheese and bread for his midday meal.

"How is the house going?" she asked.

"I have them working on the floor in the front hall."

"Have they destroyed the fairy ring?" Tess didn't know how she felt about it.

He smiled as if he had a secret. "You'll see when we are done." He went into the house and returned holding his portfolio of drawings. "Mind if I borrow pen and paper, Tess? I have a new idea for the front hall."

"No, I should get back anyway."

She watched him walk to the house, his shoulders back, his head uncovered. He was supposed to supervise but he couldn't stop himself from actually doing the work.

This house was more than just a labor of love—this was his legacy.

She pressed her hands against her stomach. Someday, probably very soon, they would have children. She would not be like Stella and hide her condition. She would be proud of it. Like Sarah, she would share the work by his side. A wonderful contentment seeped through her all the way to the bone at the thought of carrying his baby. *Their* baby.

The child would grow up in the shelter of these mighty mountains and would know his place in the world. The house would be his someday as would the title.

She wanted to leave a legacy too.

Flipping through the pages of her copybook, she realized this was her legacy. Something she would leave her child, just as Minnie had left one to her. She went in search of more writing supplies.

Several hours later, Banon had left and Brenn came in for a light dinner to find Tess bent over her copybook. She was so intent on her work she didn't register his presence.

"You are still writing?" he asked.

For a second, she was tempted to cover the book, to pretend her writing was of no importance. But she caught herself. "I've been working on some of the stories I told the children this morning."

"The fairy stories?"

"I know you think I'm silly."

His arms came around her. He nuzzled her neck. "After last night, I'm a believer in stories and legends."

Before she realized what he was about, he lifted her up in his arms and carried her into the bedroom.

And that night was legendary . . . !

Every day over the next weeks, Tess fell more in love. She couldn't believe that life was so full, so precious.

Brenn divided his time between tending the land and building the house. The crops and sheep claimed his attention first, but his real love was the house.

The carpenter arrived from Swansea. He was a young man with soulful brown eyes and steady hands. Tess could watch him work for hours as he laid the pieces of wood together that would become the huge windows leading out onto the now-non-existent terrace. Both Brenn and Tess were anxious to see how they looked. They were perfect.

But they disagreed on the design of the terrace. Tess wanted a more conservative design whereas Brenn, having seen the wonders of Greece and Italy and the glories of Egypt, wanted a huge terrace built out over the water.

"But there is no land there," she protested. "What will hold it up?"

"We'll build columns. They'll rest on the lake floor. I'll even design a little dock for boating."

"It's so impractical."

"It will be spectacular."

Brenn seemed to have changed. He was more relaxed. The demons that had plagued him the day he'd shot the highwaymen were finally put to rest. He told her it was because of her love.

"No, it's Erwynn Keep," she said confidently.

Brenn shook his head. "If I lost Erwynn Keep tomorrow, I would still consider myself blessed to have you."

The sentiment touched her so deeply, she cried.

The only dark spot in Tess's life was the resistance she met to her idea of a school, especially one that would teach the Saxon language.

But Vicar Rackham proved to be a useful ally. As a young, eligible bachelor, no mother of a daughter of marriageable age wanted to gainsay him. After a bit of reluctance, it was decided that a school would open come the winter. It would be held in the village church. Vicar Rackham would tutor the boys; Banon would teach the girls.

Tess would have been surprised if there wasn't a marriage between the vicar and Banon before the next spring.

Yes, life was good. And every day, she sat down and worked an hour or two on her book. Miles, who really was starting to grow fat, sat on the table as she worked. She fancied him a guardian of her thoughts and wrote him into the stories as a cat who loved to chase fairies.

This book was like nothing she had ever read herself. A sense of freedom and excitement came to her from molding the words to fit the imaginary world inside her head.

The village children came by once a week for a reading. It was her test to see if she'd gotten the words just right. Brenn, too, was a critic although he still didn't quite understand her fascination with the imaginary world.

"Why not write about real people?" he asked one night after she had read him the latest installment.

They lay in bed. Summer was coming to an end. The plasterers from Cardiff had finished with the walls and ceilings in the manor. Soon workmen would lay the wood floor. Brenn hoped they would be moved in before All Saints' Day, but Tess wondered if she wouldn't miss the closeness of the cottage.

"These *are* real people," she told him.

"Tess, they are fairies. They are little. They run

around making mischief. They aren't real..."
Suddenly, his eyes widened. "These are people
we know."

He'd caught her. "Some traits," Tess admitted.

"Like those of the fairy that brews nectar? He
must be Carne, the brewer. Good choice. There
is no finer ale in all England than Carne's."

She smiled.

He snuggled closer to her. "And the fairy
whose children trail after him wherever he goes
is Pughe, no?"

"Traits," she reminded him. "I didn't put the
people in literally. But I did have Erwynn Keep
in mind when I created the fairy village."

Under the covers, Brenn ran the bottom of his
foot against her leg. "So which fairy am I?"

"You can't guess?"

"You don't have a Lord of Lust," he murmured, pulling her close.

"Fairies don't lust."

"How do they make little fairies then?"

She giggled at his foolishness, a sound which
turned more serious when his head dipped under the covers and his mouth closed over her
breast.

"Tell me," he commanded softly, pausing to
take a breath.

Tess twirled a lock of his hair around her finger. "You're the Dragon King."

He poked his head out from under the covers,
his smile lazily seductive. "I expected to be nothing but."

He then showed how pleased he was.

* * *

The next morning, just as Tess began work on her stories, there was a knock on the door. Banon had gone to the village for supplies and Brenn was off seeing to the needs of one of the tenants.

She rose from her chair and crossed to the door. Life would be simpler once they moved into the house. She'd hire more servants and have a room of her own in which to work without interruption.

Opening the door, she was about to greet her caller when the words stuck in her throat. She took a step back. There on her front stoop, his hat in his hand, stood Deland Godwin.

Chapter Nineteen

"Why, Mr. Godwin, I wasn't expecting you." Tess wondered at the calmness of her understatement. His presence was so startling she could barely register any other emotion except shock.

"I should have written but I didn't have the opportunity," Godwin apologized with a complete lack of regret.

"Yes," she murmured.

"May I step in?" he prompted, hesitating before adding, "My lady? You are obviously at home."

She was tempted to refuse him. She would have been within her rights to do so, but her curiosity overrode her good sense. "Yes, please come in."

Godwin moved to the center of the room, his keen eyes taking in everything.

"I was just down to the main house," Godwin said. "The workman said you and the earl lived up here. Charming, utterly charming," he observed in a flat voice that contradicted his words. The Londoner looked completely out of place in her homey cottage.

Tess wondered when Brenn would return from his visit to his tenant.

"What do you want?" she asked.

He raised his eyebrows. "Why, Lady Merton, such a direct question."

"I've discovered an appreciation for plain speaking, Mr. Godwin."

"Must be the Welsh influence," he countered with a mock shiver.

"It must be," she echoed without humor.

Godwin placed his hat on the table and reached for her copybook. "What have we here?"

Tess felt her heart drop. She reached for the book. "It's mine. Just some notes I've been taking."

"No, no," he said, holding the book out of her range. He thumbed the pages. "Why, this looks like a manuscript. What a surprise, Lady Merton. I didn't know you were literary."

It was on the tip of Tess's tongue to tell Godwin that even if he was a publisher, he wouldn't know a literary work if he saw one, but she swallowed the insult. Instead, she admitted bravely, "I have been writing stories."

"Really?" He pulled a pair of gold-rimmed spectacles from his coat pocket and perched them on the end of his long nose. He perused the page. "What sort of story is this?"

Tess pressed her hands together. "A story about how fairies live."

That gained her Godwin's attention. His forehead wrinkled as he stared at her from over his glasses. "Fairies?"

"Yes."

"Oh." He closed the copybook with a clap.

His one-word opinion was deflating. Lately, Tess had been toying with the idea of submitting her work to a publisher, but if it was going to be rejected completely out of hand—

"Well, I admit I am confused," he said, interrupting her thoughts. He sat in the rocking chair and made a great show of tilting it back and forth. The smile on his face was as false as that of a cat playing with a mouse.

"I had thought your husband a man of means. And I had most certainly been sure that you were an heiress. Probably the richest heiress in the *ton*."

The muscles in Tess's shoulders tightened. Beneath his pleasant words was a very strong threat. And it made her angry.

Three months earlier, she would have panicked. But she was no longer the same woman she'd been then. Furthermore, the dangers of insulting this gossipmonger no longer frightened her. "Do you always call on people in the wilds of Wales, Mr. Godwin? I had been lead to believe you hadn't left London in years."

He bristled at her challenge. "That isn't true, Lady Merton. I have often visited friends in the country."

"Well, hopefully you don't bully your way into their homes they way you have just done so here."

She knew the moment the words left her lips she'd hit the man's pride. Everyone avoided Deland Godwin if they could help it. Bullying was the only method he had to force himself to be included.

He pushed up from the rocker, towering a good half a head over her. "You are right, Lady Merton," he replied with chilly civility. "My visit is not just a pleasant coincidence. I am in Wales at the behest of Lady Garland. She needed a companion to escort her while she visited her brother, Lord Faller. I'd be remiss if I was so close and didn't pay you even a short visit."

"Lord Faller's seat is fifty miles to the north of us. You are far out of your way."

At that moment, Banon came in, opening the door without a knock. She lugged two baskets, one in each hand, which were full of vegetables.

"Lady Merton, I talked to the miller—" She broke off the moment she saw Godwin. "I'm sorry, my lady, I didn't realize there was a guest."

"It's fine, Banon. Mr. Godwin was about to leave." She was being rude, but she didn't care. Godwin came from a different place and a different time in her life. Seeing him here in the same room as the sweet, unspoiled Banon gave her a terrible sense of foreboding. She wanted him gone.

"No, Banon, you be on your way," Godwin replied presumptuously. The mask of manners was gone. "I have something to say to Lady Merton and I'm certain she would wish it to be kept private. Especially since it involves her brother."

Tess pulled back slightly. "What are you talking about?"

He didn't answer her. Instead, he flicked his finger at Banon. "Go, go. Scurry away."

Banon quickly set the baskets down on the table, dropped a curtsey—something she rarely did—and left the cottage.

"What is this about?" Tess demanded. "What do you wish to say to me?"

"Shouldn't we sit down?" Godwin asked, in control of the situation. "Where are the pleasantries?"

"Oh, Mr. Godwin, what a pleasure to see you again," she mimicked. "I'm sorry but the butler is ill and you've just sent the cook hurrying out the door. What is it you want?"

"You are rusticating in the country, Lady Merton," Godwin said without humor. "You'd best return to London—but then, you can't, can you? If you did, people would start wondering, as I do, about the fabulous fortune you were supposed to possess."

"We are using it to build the house."

"I know differently, my lady."

Tess stared at him in silence a moment. "Perhaps you should sit down."

"Thank you," he said in that infuriatingly cynical manner of his.

She sat in the chair across from him. "What do you think you know?"

"I know that your brother squandered your fortune. He has just joined several gentlemen investing in ships to ply the spice trade. It seems to be a good opportunity and, with a wife like his who has markers all over London, he may need the blunt. Mr. Christopher is remarkably tightfisted. I've heard something about his wanting to preserve the estate for future generations of Hamlins."

Tess had heard enough. He'd convinced her he

knew it all. "What do *you* want? Money?"

Godwin wrinkled his nose in distaste. "Absolutely not. If it had been that then I would have gone to your brother. Believe it or not, Lady Merton, it is not you I wish to see humbled. You have always been kind. But your husband? That is a different matter."

"Brenn? I didn't even think he knew you."

"He knew me enough to humiliate me in front of my friends. He has damaged my reputation. I wish to return the favor."

"How did he do that?"

"He forced me to issue an apology."

Tess wanted to laugh. "That's all?"

"All?" Godwin came to his feet and paced in front of the fire. "Do you not realize that is *everything*? I don't apologize to anyone. Even Prinny had the good sense to listen to me when I speak. However, since my confrontation with your husband, I have been spoken to with nothing but disrespect. Me! The editor of *The Ear*. Not even my colleagues respect me."

"But Mr. Godwin, I'm certain that was not my husband's intention."

"His intention doesn't matter, and as fond as I am of you, your wishes don't matter, either. Because of our contretemps, word of my humiliation has spread. I have enemies, you know."

"Oh, yes," Tess agreed quietly.

"Someone did a cartoon of your husband with his fist around my neck. It was very embarrassing."

"My husband is not someone who overreacts . . . unless he is provoked. What did you say to him?"

Godwin straightened his neckcloth. "It is a matter between men. But let me tell you that even as we speak, my paper is printing the story of your brother's perfidy."

"You'll ruin him!"

"And your husband," Godwin agreed. "He will be the laughingstock of all England."

"No one would dare laugh at Brenn," Tess said proudly.

"Perhaps not, but there will be those who will enjoy learning of your fall from grace."

There it was. Her greatest fear.

But the realization came over her. It no longer mattered. This was her life and her home. Let the match-making mamas snicker and the Society debutantes laugh. They meant nothing. Brenn, and what they had created together, was everything.

"Tell them," Tess said calmly, "I have nothing to hide."

"Nor do I," came Brenn's deep voice from the doorway.

Both Tess and Godwin turned in surprise. They'd been so involved in their argument they had not perceived his presence. Nor was he alone. Banon hovered not far from the doorway, flanked by her muscular father and a goodly number of the villagers. As Brenn walked into the room, they crowded in around him.

"What is this?" Godwin said with irritation. "Have your created your own army? Do you still miss the call to arms, Merton?"

"They are worried about my wife, Godwin," Brenn said almost pleasantly. "Is there any reason they should be?"

Godwin smiled, his expression almost benign. "I was merely having a visit and waiting for your arrival."

"Then here I am," Brenn said. He opened his arms like a magician showing he hid no tricks.

"What I have to say, I think should be said privately," Godwin answered smugly.

Tess would have none of it. She was done with secrets. "He knows about Neil stealing my inheritance, Brenn. He says he has already printed it. I imagine the only reason he is here is to gloat."

Brenn's expression didn't change. "He won't expose anyone."

"That's where you are wrong," Godwin said. "It's done."

"Tess," Brenn said. "Fetch my dueling pistols. They are under the bed."

Tess didn't even question the order but did as he asked.

"What are you going to do with pistols?" Godwin asked, the overconfidence in his voice starting to waver.

"Put a hole in you," Brenn answered calmly.

Tess found the velvet case where he said it was. She hurried back into the main room.

"You must be kidding," Godwin was saying as she walked back into the room. Pughe and the others all waited in silence.

"No, I'm not." Brenn took the case from Tess and, setting it on the table, opened it. He lifted the finely crafted weapon and held it to the light.

"I'm not a duelist," Godwin said briskly. "I will not fight with you."

"I didn't ask you to duel," Brenn said. He began loading the weapon.

"If you don't want to duel, what were you planning to do?" Godwin asked.

Brenn replied almost cheerfully, "I thought I'd fire the ball through one ear and let it come out the other." He grinned. "Sort of an homage to your scandal sheet *The Ear*." He chuckled at his own small joke.

"You can't be serious!" Godwin complained.

"I am."

"But there are witnesses. You can't shoot me in front of them."

Brenn turned to Mr. Pughe. "What do you say, Pughe? May I shoot him?"

"Of course, my lord," Pughe said heartily. "You're our earl and we'd go to our deaths for you." He repeated what he'd said in Welsh and there was a chorus of "Aye's" to support his claim.

Brenn aimed the pistol. "Oh well, Godwin. It doesn't seem as if anyone will miss you."

Godwin turned the rocker around so that it shielded him. "You can't do this! There are laws!"

"But I'm the law here," Brenn said. "And once it is discovered that you threatened black-mail—"

"Not blackmail. I never asked for money. Lady Merton can attest to that!"

"That's true, my lord," Tess said, fairly certain that Brenn was teasing the man. "However, he does want to ruin all of us. He claims he has already."

"Well, there you have it." Brenn looked down

the sight of his pistol. "That's enough reason for me to kill you."

"But it would be murder!" Godwin shouted.

"Some call it murder; others call it justice." Brenn sighed. "Don't worry, Godwin. You won't be around to participate in the debate."

Pughe laughed, repeated Brenn's words in Welsh, and the villagers all made a big show of waving good-bye to Godwin.

Godwin fell to his knees. "You . . . can't!"

The pistol fired.

Tess reeled back in shock. She hadn't seriously thought Brenn would do it. The smell of sulfur burned the air.

She was almost afraid to look and when she did, her knees wanted to buckle she was so relieved. Brenn hadn't shot Godwin.

Although he'd come close.

The man raised his hand to the top of his hair and gingerly felt the ends.

"I parted it for you," Brenn said. "Now, shall I reload or will you return to London without a word of this to anyone?"

Godwin slowly rose to his feet. "A word about what?" he asked in a shaky voice.

Brenn lowered the pistol. "Tess, should we worry that he has printed a story exposing your brother?"

"I can print a retraction," Godwin offered.

"That would be so kind," Tess said. "Neil is guilty of doing as you charged, but he is still my brother."

"I'm certain I made a mistake in writing the story," Godwin agreed, one watchful eye on the pistol Brenn still held.

"Nor will you ever mention my wife in one of your papers."

"Of course not," Godwin said.

"I'm glad we understand each other," Brenn said reasonably. "I'll clean this and put it away." He started to move back to the pistol case when he noticed Tess's copybook.

He paused. "You are a publisher of books, are you not, Godwin?"

"Yes," Godwin replied, still shaken.

"Perhaps you can do another favor for us."

"Oh, anything." Godwin sat in the rocker.

Brenn picked up the copybook. "Lady Merton has written a book, a fine book about Welsh customs and tales. You should publish it."

Tess spoke up. "No, Brenn. I will not allow a man like Deland Godwin to publish my work." Especially since he had disparaged it earlier.

"Very well." Brenn set the book back on the table. "Now, if you will excuse me, I must return to the stables. It was a pleasure to see you again, Godwin."

"Likewise," the man answered faintly.

Brenn left the room, tucking the pistols in their case under his arm. The villagers followed.

Banon lingered by the door. "Should I not have gone running for him, my lady?"

Tess looked at the pale-faced publisher holding his head in his hand and the hole in the cottage wall where the bullet had embedded itself. "You did exactly the right thing."

Godwin looked up. "I thought you said your husband would not overreact."

"He didn't," Tess answered. She then asked in

her best London hostess voice, "May I offer you a cup of tea?"

Godwin refused. He left shortly after that, mumbling to himself about bloodthirsty Welshmen and arrogant aristocrats. Tess watched him mount and until he rode around the bend and out of sight.

Brenn came out of the barn to stand beside her.

"I was a bit heavy-handed," he admitted.

"A touch." She shrugged. "You know that he may not honor his promises."

"Then I'll have to shoot him for real," Brenn said lightly, and they both laughed because they realized that nothing Godwin could say would hurt them.

For them, their world was right here, created out of hard work, clever planning, and love.

"I have something to show you," Brenn said. He took her hand and pulled her toward the house.

"I have something to tell you," Tess said.

"No, mine first," Brenn said. "I've been keeping this secret for almost too long. They've finished and I can't contain myself a moment more."

He led her up the steps of the house. "Close your eyes."

She did as he asked.

Taking her by both arms, he guided her up the front step and into the hall. "Open them," he whispered in her ear.

Tess did and then drew back with a gasp of wonder. There, inlaid into the unfinished wooden floor, was a pattern of dandelion leaves stained a darker color. The leaves connected into a huge circle in the middle of the room.

"It's the fairy ring!" Tess tilted back her head and laughed. "It is the most marvelous thing about the house."

"I knew you would like it. I've been working on it for weeks. You've been too busy writing to notice."

She stepped into the center of the ring. "It's the best gift I've ever received, especially after you hear my news."

"What is it?"

"We're having a baby."

Brenn almost fell over. "Tess? Did you say what I thought you did?"

"Ummm hmmm."

"A baby?" he repeated incredulously, as if he still couldn't believe the good news.

Tess turned in a circle inside the ring. "I think he may have been conceived the night we made love right here."

"He?" Brenn's face broke out into a huge grin. "A boy, Tess?"

"Or a she. It will be one or the other, won't it?" she teased.

He moved then. With a big whoop of joy, he swooped her up in his arms and twirled her around until they were both giddy with happiness.

"We'll name him John, after my father," Brenn announced, his arm proudly draped around her shoulders.

"Why not Harold after my father?"

"It'll be a girl," Brenn continued, as if she hadn't spoken.

"Then we will name her Ariana."

"Why Ariana?"

"Because it means silver," she said with a sly smile.

Brenn laughed. "I like it, too." Then he turned serious. "I love you, Tess."

"I love you, Brenn."

They kissed, right there in the middle of the fairy ring . . . and it was wonderful.

Epilogue

The baby was born healthy and strong a week before Easter. It was a boy, just as Tess had anticipated.

She and Brenn did not name him after either of their fathers. Instead, they chose a name that would be uniquely his own, and indicative of their great love. They called him Drake, the Old English word for dragon.

Erwynn Keep thrived, and Tess sold her first book to a modest Liverpool publisher sometime after their third child was born. Brenn did the illustrations and nothing much had been expected to come of it. Nothing would have, if someone hadn't given the book to the daughter of the duke of Kent. The young Victoria adored Tess's stories of fairies and dragons and they became a resounding success.

When Victoria herself was crowned queen of England and became a mother, she insisted on copies of the books for each of her children. Fashionable mothers followed suit and Tess's books became classics.

Years later, when a reporter asked Queen Victoria about her favorite reading material, she included Tess's fairy books.

Asked why, she answered, "They are love stories. And each has a happy ending."

And so they did.

Welsh Magic

Erwynn Keep.   On the pristine shores of Mountain Lake and surrounded by the beauty of the Black Mountains, Tess Owen, the countess of Merton, penned her stories of fairies, magic, and dragons known to generations of children as the *Welsh Chronicles*. Fans of children's literature annually trek to this picturesque village to see where Lady Merton imagined her tales of adventure and love.

The house itself was redesigned and renovated in 1815 by the countess's husband, Brenn Owen, the 7th earl of Merton. The illustrator of many of her books, the earl was renowned for the innovative architectural design he used on the house including the terrace built on a series of columns going out over the lake.

The earl and countess's marriage and collaboration is almost a storybook tale in itself. It was for her that he designed the famous dandelion ring that graces the front hall of the house. The ring is supposed to be the inspiration for the magic fairy ring in Lady Merton's tales. Her husband immortalized it in his coat of arms, dandelion leaves encircling a fire-breathing dragon over the Welsh word for "Together," the family motto.

In truth, more than one visitor has felt the power of magic in this house. Legend has it that whoever kisses inside the fairy ring will enjoy happiness, prosperity, and fertility. We don't know if the legend holds true for today, but Lady

Merton herself was the mother of nine healthy children, unusual for her day and age.

Finish your visit with a stop at the Erwynn Keep alehouse and its award-winning ale brewed from a recipe dating back to the early 1800s. But beware! Many a tourist has seen a fairy or two after an afternoon pint.

Great Britain Magazine
August 1999, volume 36

Have you ever wondered why opposites attract?

Why is it so easy to fall in love when your friends, your family . . . even your own good sense tells you to run the other way? Perhaps it's because a long, slow kiss from a sensuous rake is much more irresistible than a chaste embrace from a gentleman with a steady income. After all, falling in love means taking a risk . . . and isn't it oh, so much more enjoyable to take a risk on someone just a little dangerous?

Christina Dodd, Cathy Maxwell, Samantha James, Christina Skye, Constance O'Day-Flannery and Judith Ivory . . . these are the authors of the Avon Romance Superleaders, and each has created a man and a woman who seemed completely unsuitable in all ways but one . . . the love they discover in the other.

Christina Dodd certainly knows how to cause a scandal—in her books, that is! Her dashing heroes, like the one in her latest Superleader, SOMEDAY MY PRINCE, simply can't resist putting her heroines in compromising positions of all sorts...

Beautiful Princess Laurentia has promised to fulfill her royal duty and marry, but as she looks over her stuttering, swaggering, timid sea of potential suitors she thinks to herself that she's never seen such an unsuitable group in her life. Then she's swept off her feet by a handsome prince of dubious reputation. Laurentia had always dreamed her prince would come, but never one quite like this...

SOMEDAY MY PRINCE
by Christina Dodd

*Astonished, indignant and in pain, the princess stammered, "Who . . . what . . . how dare you?"

"Was he a suitor scorned?"

"I never saw him before!"

"Then next time a stranger grabs you and slams you over his shoulder, you squeal like a stuck pig."

Clutching her elbow, she staggered to her feet. "I yelled!"

"I barely heard you." He stood directly in front of her, taller than he had at first appeared, beetle-browed, his eyes dark hollows, his face marked with a deep-shadowed scar that ran from chin to temple. Yet despite all that, he was handsome. Stunningly so. "And I was just behind those pots."

Tall and luxuriant, the potted plants clustered against the wall, and she looked at them, then looked back at him. He spoke with an accent. He walked with a limp. He was a stranger. Suspicion stirred in her. "What were you doing there?"

"Smoking."

She smelled it on him, that faint scent of tobacco so like that which clung to her father. Although she knew it foolish, the odor lessened her misgivings. "I'll call the guard and send them after that scoundrel."

"Scoundrel." The stranger laughed softly. "You *are* a lady. But don't bother sending anyone after him. He's long gone."

She knew it was true. The scoundrel—and what was wrong with that word, anyway?—had leaped into the wildest part of the garden, just where the cultured plants gave way to natural scrub. The guard would do her no good.

So rather than doing what she knew very well she should, she let the stranger place his hand on the small of her back and turn her toward the light.

He clasped her wrist and slowly stretched out her injured arm. "It's not broken."

"I don't suppose so."

He grinned, a slash of white teeth against a half-glimpsed face. "You'd recognize if it was. A broken elbow lets you know it's there." Efficiently, he unfastened the buttons on her elbow-length glove and stripped it away, then ran his bare fingers firmly over the bones in her lower arm, then lightly over the pit of her elbow.

Goosebumps rose on her skin at the touch. He didn't wear gloves, she noted absently. His naked skin touched hers. "What kind of injury are you looking for?"

"Not an injury. I just thought I would enjoy caressing that silk-soft skin."

She jerked her wrist away.

What could be more exciting than making your debut ... wearing a gorgeous gown, sparkling jewels, and enticing all the ton's most eligible bachelors?

In Cathy Maxwell's MARRIED IN HASTE, Tess Hamlin is used to having the handsomest of London's eligible men vie for her attention. But Tess is in no hurry to make her choice—until she meets the virile war hero Brenn Owen, the new Earl of Merton. But Tess must marry a man of wealth, and although the earl has a title and land, he's in need of funds. But she can't resist this compelling nobleman ...

MARRIED IN HASTE
by Cathy Maxwell

"I envy you. I will never be free. Someday I will have a husband and my freedom will be curtailed even more," Tess said.

"I had the impression that you set the rules."

Tess shot him a sharp glance. "No, I play the game well, but—" She broke off, then admitted, "But it's not really me."

"What is you?"

A wary look came into her eyes. "You don't really want to know."

"Yes, I do." Brenn leaned forward. "After all, moments ago you were begging me to make a declaration."

358

"I never beg!" she declared with mock seriousness and they both laughed. Then she said, "Sometimes I wonder if there isn't something more to life. Or why am I here."

The statement caught his attention. There wasn't one man who had ever faced battle without asking that question.

"I want to feel a sense of purpose," she continued, "of being, here deep inside. Instead I feel . . ." She shrugged, her voice trailing off.

"As if you are only going through the motions?" he suggested quietly.

The light came on in her vivid eyes. "Yes! That's it." She dropped her arms to her side. "Do you feel that way too?"

"At one time I have. Especially after a battle when men were dying all around me and yet I had escaped harm. I wanted to have a reason. To know why."

She came closer to him until they stood practically toe to toe. "And have you found out?"

"I think so," he replied honestly. "It has to do with having a sense of purpose, of peace. I believe I have found that purpose at Erwynn Keep. It's the first place I've been where I feel I really belong."

"Yes," she agreed in understanding. "Feeling like you belong. That's what I sense is missing even when I'm surrounded by people who do nothing more than toady up to me and hang on my every word." She smiled. "But you haven't done that. You wouldn't, would you? Even if I asked you to."

"Toadying has never been my strong suit . . . although I would do many things for a beautiful woman." He touched her then, drawing a line down the velvet curve of her cheek.

Miss Hamlin caught his hand before it could stray further, her gaze holding his. "Most men don't go beyond the shell of the woman ... or look past the fortune. Are you a fortune hunter, Lord Merton?"

Her direct question almost bowled him off over the stone rail. He recovered quickly. "If I was, would I admit it?"

"No."

"Then you shall have to form your own opinion."

Her lips curved into a smile. She did not move away.

"I think I'm going to kiss you."

She blushed, the sudden high color charming.

"Don't tell me," he said. "Gentlemen rarely ask before they kiss."

"Oh, they always ask, but I've never let them."

"Then I won't ask." He lowered his lips to hers. Her eyelashes swept down as she closed her eyes. She was so beautiful in the moonlight. So innocently beautiful.

Across the Scottish Highlands strides Cameron MacKay. Cameron is a man of honor, a man who would do anything to protect his clan . . . and he wouldn't hesitate to seek revenge against those who have wronged him.

Meredith is one of the clan Monroe, sworn enemies of Cameron and his men. So Cameron takes this woman as his wife, never dreaming that what began as an act of vengeance becomes instead a quest for love in Samantha James's HIS WICKED WAYS.

HIS WICKED WAYS
by Samantha James

Cameron faced her, his head propped on an elbow. His smile was gone, his expression unreadable. He stared at her as if he would pluck her very thoughts from her mind.

"It occurs to me that you have been sheltered," he said slowly, "that mayhap you know naught of men . . . and life." He seemed to hesitate. "What happens between a man and a woman is not something to be feared, Meredith. It's where children come from—"

"I know how children are made!" Meredith's face burned with shame.

"Then why are you so afraid?" he asked quietly.

It was in her mind to pretend she misunderstood—but it would have been a lie. Clutching the sheet to her chin, she gave a tiny shake of her head. "Please," she said, her voice very low. "I cannot tell you."

Reaching out, he picked up a strand of hair that lay on her breast. Meredith froze. Her heart surely stopped in that instant. Now it comes, she thought despairingly. He claimed he would give her time to accept him, to accept what would happen, but it was naught but a lie! Her heart twisted. Ah, but she should have known!

"Your hair is beautiful—like living flame."

His murmur washed over her, soft as finely spun silk. She searched his features, stunned when she detected no hint of either mockery or derision.

She stared at the wispy strands that lay across his palm, the way he tested the texture between thumb and forefinger, the way he wound the lock of hair around and around his hand.

Meredith froze. But he stopped before the pressure tugged hurtfully on her scalp . . . and trespassed no further. Instead he turned his back.

His eyes closed.

They touched nowhere. Indeed, the width of two hands separated them; those silken red strands were the only link between them. Meredith dared not move. She listened and waited, her heart pounding in her breast . . .

. . . Slumber overtook him. He slept, her lock of hair still clutched tight in his fist.

Only then did she move. Her hand lifted. She touched her lips, there at the very spot he'd possessed so thoroughly. Her pulse quickened as the memory of his kiss flamed all through her . . . She'd thought it was disdain. Distaste.

But she was wrong. In the depths of her being, Meredith was well aware it was something far different.

Her breath came fast, then slow. Something was happening. Something far beyond her experience . . .

What could be more beautiful than a holiday trip to the English countryside? Snow falling on the gentle hills and thatched roofs . . . villagers singing carols, then dropping by the pub for hot cider with rum.

In Christina Skye's THE PERFECT GIFT, Maggie Kincaid earns a chance to exhibit her beautiful jewelry designs at sumptuous Draycott Abbey, where she dreams of peacefully spending Christmas. But when she arrives, she learns she is in danger and discovers that her every step will be followed by disturbingly sensuous Jared MacInness. He will protect her from those who would harm her, but who'll protect Maggie from Jared?

THE PERFECT GIFT
by Christina Skye

Jared had worked his way over the ridge and down through the trees when he found Maggie Kincaid sitting on the edge of the stone bridge.

Just sitting, her legs dangling as she traced invisible patterns over the old stone.

Jared stared in amazement. She looked for all the world like a child waiting for a long lost friend to appear.

Jared shook off his sense of strangeness and plunged down the hillside, cursing her for the ache in his ribs and the exhaustion eating at his muscles.

He scowled as he drew close enough to see her face. Young. Excited. Not beautiful in the classic sense. Her mouth was too wide and her nose too thin. But the eyes lit up her whole face and made a man want to know all her secrets.

Her mouth swept into a quick smile as he approached. Her head tilted as laughter rippled like morning sunlight.

The sound chilled him. It was too quick, too innocent. She ought to be frightened. Defensive. Running.

He stared, feeling the ground turn to foam beneath him.

Moonlight touched the long sleeves of her simple white dress with silver as she rose to her feet.

He spoke first, compelled to break the spell of her presence, furious that she should touch him so. "You know I could have you arrested for this." His jaw clenched.

Her head cocked. Poised at the top of the bridge, she was a study in innocent concentration.

"Don't even bother to think about running. I want to know who you are and why in hell you're here."

A frown marred the pale beauty of her face. She might have been a child—except that the full curves of her body spoke a richly developed maturity at complete odds with her voice and manner.

"Answer me. You're on private property and in ten seconds I'm going to call the police." Exhaustion made his voice harsh. "Don't try it," Jared hissed, realizing she meant to fall and let him catch her. But it was too late. She stepped

off the stone bridge, her body angling down toward him.

He caught her with an oath and a jolt of pain,
and then they toppled as one onto the damp
earth beyond the moat. Cursing, Jared rolled
sideways and pinned her beneath him.

It was no child's face that stared up at him and
no child's body that cushioned him. She was
strong for a woman, her muscles trim but de-
fined. The softness at hip and breast tightened
his throat and left his body all too aware of their
intimate contact. He did not move, fighting an
urge to open his hands and measure her softness.

What was wrong with him?

Imagine for a moment that you're a modern woman; one minute, you're living a fast-paced, hectic lifestyle . . . the next minute, you've somehow been transported to another time and you're living a life of a very different sort.

No one does time-travel like Constance O'Day-Flannery. In ONCE AND FOREVER Maggie enters a maze while at an Elizabethan fair, and when she comes out she magically finds she's truly in Elizabethan times! And to make matters more confusing, the sweep-her-off-her-feet hero she's been searching for all her life turns out to be the handsomest man in 1600's England!

ONCE AND FOREVER
by Constance O'Day-Flannery

Maggie looked up to the sky and wished a breeze would find its way into the thick hedges; she couldn't believe she was in this maze, sweating her life away in a gorgeous costume and starving. Thinking of all the calories she was burning she wondered, who needs a gym work out? Maggie stopped to listen for anyone, but only an eerie silence hovered.

Suddenly, she felt terribly alone.

Spinning around, she vainly searched for anyone, but saw and heard nothing. "Hello? Hello?" Her calls went unanswered. She stopped abruptly in the path. She felt weak. Her heart was pounding and her head felt light. Grabbing at the starched collar, she released the top few buttons and gasped in confusion. Okay, maybe she could use that shining knight right about now. She didn't care how or where he appeared, as long as he led her out, for the air was heavy and still, and Maggie found it hard to breathe.

"Help me . . . please."

Silence.

Her heart pounded harder, her stomach clenched in fear, her breath shortened, her limbs trembled and the weight of the costume felt like it was pulling her down to the ground.

Spinning around and around, Maggie experienced a sudden lightness, as if she no longer had to struggle against gravity and push herself away from the earth. Whatever was happening was controlling her, and she was so weary of struggling . . . flashes of her ex-husband and the alimony, her failed job interviews, the bills, the aloneness swirled together. It was bigger, more powerful than she, and she felt herself weakening, surrendering to it. The hedges appeared to fade away and Maggie instinctively knew she had to get out. Gathering her last essence of strength, she started running.

Miraculously, she was out. She was gasping for breath, inhaling the dust and dirt from under her mouth when she heard the angry yell that reverberated through the ground and rattled her already scrambled brain.

She dare not move, not even breathe. If this were a nightmare, and surely it couldn't be anything else, she wasn't about to add to the terror.

She would wake up any moment, her mind screamed. She *had to!*

Drawing upon more courage than she thought she had left, Maggie slowly lifted her head. She was staring into the big brown eyes of a horse.

A horse!

She heard moans and looked beyond the animal to see a body. A man, rolled on the side of a dirt path, was clutching his knee as colorful curses flowed back to her.

"Spleeny, lousey-cockered jolt head! Aww ... heavens above deliver me from this vile, impertinent, ill-natured lout!"

Pushing herself to her feet, Maggie brushed dirt, twigs and leaves from her hands and backside, then made her way to the man. "How badly are you hurt?" she called out over her shoulder.

The man didn't answer and she glanced in his direction. He was still staring at her, as though he'd lost his senses.

Shoulder-length streaked blond hair framed a finely chiseled face. Eyes, large and of the lightest blue Maggie had ever seen stared back at her, as though the man had seen a ghost. He was definitely an attractive, more than average, handsome man ... okay, he was downright gorgeous and she'd have to be dead not to acknowledge it.

Wow ... that was her first thought.

Everyone knows that ladies of quality can only marry gentlemen, and that suitable gentlemen are born — not made. Because being a gentleman has nothing to do with money, and everything to do with upbringing.

But in Judith Ivory's THE PROPOSITION Edwina vows that she can turn anyone into a gentleman . . . even the infuriating Mr. Mick Tremore. Not only that, she'd be able to pass him off as the heir to a dukedom, and no one in society would be any wiser. And since Edwina is every inch a lady, there isn't a chance that she'd find the exasperating Mick Tremore irresistible. Is there?

THE PROPOSITION
by Judith Ivory

"Speak for yourself," she said. *"I couldn't do anything"*— she paused, then used his word for it—"unpredictable."

"Yes, you could."

"Well, I could, but I won't."

He laughed. "Well, you might surprise yourself one day."

His sureness of himself irked her. Like the mustache that he twitched slightly. He knew she didn't like it; he used it to tease her.

Fine. What a pointless conversation. She picked up her pen, going back to the task of writ-

Timeless Tales of Love from
Award-winning Author

KATHLEEN EAGLE

THIS TIME FOREVER
76688-4/$4.99 US/$5.99 Can

"Ms. Eagle's writing is a delight!"
Rendezvous

SUNRISE SONG
77634-0/$5.99 US/$7.99 Can

THE NIGHT REMEMBERS
78491-2/$5.99 US/$7.99 Can

THE LAST TRUE COWBOY
78492-0/$6.50 US/$8.50 Can

Buy these books at your local bookstore or use this coupon for ordering:

Mail to: Avon Books, Dept BP, Box 767, Rte 2, Dresden, TN 38225   G
Please send me the book(s) I have checked above.
□ My check or money order—no cash or CODs please—for $_____ is enclosed (please add $1.50 per order to cover postage and handling—Canadian residents add 7% GST). U.S. residents make checks payable to Avon Books; Canada residents make checks payable to Hearst Book Group of Canada.
□ Charge my VISA/MC Acct#_____ Exp Date_____
Minimum credit card order is two books or $7.50 (please add postage and handling charge of $1.50 per order—Canadian residents add 7% GST). For faster service, call 1-800-762-0779. Prices and numbers are subject to change without notice. Please allow six to eight weeks for delivery.
Name_____
Address_____
City_____State/Zip_____
Telephone No._____   KE 0499

America Loves Lindsey!
The Timeless Romances
of #1 Bestselling Author

Johanna Lindsey

KEEPER OF THE HEART	77493-3/$6.99 US/$8.99 Can
THE MAGIC OF YOU	75629-3/$6.99 US/$8.99 Can
ANGEL	75628-5/$6.99 US/$8.99 Can
PRISONER OF MY DESIRE	75627-7/$6.99 US/$8.99 Can
ONCE A PRINCESS	75625-0/$6.99 US/$8.99 Can
WARRIOR'S WOMAN	75301-4/$6.99 US/$8.99 Can
MAN OF MY DREAMS	75626-9/$6.99 US/$8.99 Can
SURRENDER MY LOVE	76256-0/$6.50 US/$7.50 Can
YOU BELONG TO ME	76258-7/$6.99 US/$8.99 Can
UNTIL FOREVER	76259-5/$6.50 US/$8.50 Can
LOVE ME FOREVER	72570-3/$6.99 US/$8.99 Can
SAY YOU LOVE ME	72571-1/$6.99 US/$8.99 Can
ALL I NEED IS YOU	76260-9/$6.99 US/$8.99 Can

And Now in Hardcover
THE PRESENT: A MALORY HOLIDAY NOVEL
97725-7/$16.00 US/$21.00 CAN

His Wicked Ways
SAMANTHA JAMES

"Samantha James writes exactly the book I love to read,"
says *New York Times* bestselling author Linda Lael Miller.

Avon Books is sure you'll love this exciting tale of unexpected
romance between a handsome member of a powerful Clan
and the daughter of his sworn enemy, by award-winning author
Samantha James, whose books regularly appear on the *New
York Times* bestseller list. And to add to your enjoyment,
we're offering a $2.00 rebate toward HIS WICKED WAYS.
Simply send your proof-of-purchase (cash register receipt)
along with the coupon below by December 31, 1999, and
we'll rush you a check for $2.00.

Void where prohibited by law.

- - - - - - - - - - - - - - - - - - - -

Mail receipt and coupon for HIS WICKED WAYS (0-380-80586-3)
to: Avon Books, Dept. BP, P.O. Box 767,
Dresden, TN 38225

Name _____

Address _____

City _____

State/Zip _____

ing out his progress for the morning. Out of the corner of her eye, though, she could see him.

He'd leaned back on the rear legs of his chair, lifting the front ones off the floor. He rocked there beside her as he bent his head sideways, tilting it, looking under the table. He'd been doing this all week, making her nervous with it. As if there were a mouse—or worse—something under there that she should be aware of.

"What *are* you doing?"

Illogically, he came back with, "I bet you have the longest, prettiest legs."

"*Limbs,*" she corrected. "A gentleman refers to that part of a lady as her limbs, her lower limbs, though it is rather poor form to speak of them at all. You shouldn't."

He laughed. "Limbs? Like a bloody tree?" His pencil continued to tap lightly, an annoying tattoo of ticks. "No, you got legs under there. Long ones. And I'd give just about anything to see 'em."

Goodness. He knew that was impertinent. He was tormenting her. He liked to torture her for amusement.

Then she caught the word: *anything?*

To see her legs? Her legs were nothing. Two sticks that bent so she could walk on them. He wanted to see these?

For anything?

She wouldn't let him see them, of course. But she wasn't past provoking him in return. "Well, there is a solution here then, Mr. Tremore. You can see my legs, when you shave your mustache."

She meant it as a kind of joke. A taunt to get back at him.

Joke or not, though, his pencil not only stopped, it dropped. There was a tiny clatter on the floor, a faint sound of rolling, then silence— as, along with the pencil, Mr. Tremore's entire body came to a motionless standstill.

"Pardon?" he said finally. He spoke it perfectly, exactly as she'd asked him to. Only now it unsettled her.

"You heard me," she said. A little thrill shot through her as she pushed her way into the dare that—fascinatingly, genuinely—rattled him.

She spoke now in earnest what seemed suddenly a wonderful exchange: "If you shave off your mustache, I'll hike my skirt and you can watch—how far? To my knees?" The hair on the back of her neck stood up.

"Above your knees," he said immediately. His amazed face scowled in a way that said they weren't even talking unless they got well past her knees in the debate.

"How far?"

"All the way up."

The WONDER of WOODIWISS

continues with the publication of
her newest novel in paperback—

THE ELUSIVE FLAME

☐ #76655-8
$14.00 U.S. ($19.50 Canada)

PETALS ON THE RIVER

☐ #79828-X
$6.99 U.S. ($8.99 Canada)

THE FLAME AND THE FLOWER

☐ #00525-5
$3.99 U.S. ($4.99 Canada)

THE WOLF AND THE DOVE

☐ #00778-9
$6.99 U.S. ($8.99 Canada)

SHANNA

☐ #38588-0
$6.99 U.S. ($8.99 Canada)

SO WORTHY MY LOVE

☐ #76148-3
$6.99 U.S. ($8.99 Canada)

ASHES IN THE WIND

☐ #76984-0
$6.99 U.S. ($8.99 Canada)

A ROSE IN WINTER

☐ #84400-1
$6.99 U.S. ($8.99 Canada)

COME LOVE A STRANGER

☐ #89936-1
$6.99 U.S. ($8.99 Canada)

FOREVER IN YOUR EMBRACE

☐ #77246-9
$6.99 U.S. ($8.99 Canada)